The Connors' Crisis

THE CONNORS' CRISIS

G.K. Sutton

Copyright © 2010 by G.K. Sutton.

Library of Congress Control Number: 2010905496
ISBN: Hardcover   978-1-4500-8681-3
                   Softcover   978-1-4500-8680-6

All rights reserved. No part of this book may be reproduced or transmitted
in any form or by any means, electronic or mechanical, including photocopying,
recording, or by any information storage and retrieval system,
without permission in writing from the copyright owner.

This is a work of fiction. Names, characters, places and incidents either are the
product of the author's imagination or are used fictitiously, and any resemblance
to any actual persons, living or dead, events, or locales is entirely coincidental.

The cover photograph depicts the Church of St. Ignatius Loyola (Roman
Catholic), New York City, home of a Mander IV/91 (1991) instrument.
Photograph is by Steven E. Lawson and is used with permission.

The author's photograph depicts the console of the Mander chancel organ at
Peachtree Road United Methodist Church, Atlanta, Georgia. Photograph is by
J. O. Love and is used with permission.

This book was printed in the United States of America.

To order additional copies of this book, contact:
Xlibris Corporation
1-888-795-4274
www.Xlibris.com
Orders@Xlibris.com
70081

I sought the Lord, and afterward I knew
he moved my soul to seek him, seeking me.
It was not I that found, O Savior true;
no, I was found of thee.

Thou didst reach forth thy hand and mine enfold;
I walked and sank not on the storm-vexed sea.
'Twas not so much that I on thee took hold,
as thou, dear Lord, on me.

I find, I walk, I love, but oh, the whole
of love is but my answer, Lord, to thee!
For thou wert long beforehand with my soul;
always thou lovedst me.

Anonymous, ca. 1890
(preferably to my own setting for SATB)

FOREWORD

If you've made it this far reading my books, and if you are actually reading this foreword, then I guess I could just say 'ditto'. If you haven't, then I'm going to have to stop you right now. Yeah, yeah, how am I to do this if you aren't reading this?

This is a sequel to my third book, *The Childs Conundrum*, which is in turn a sequel to my first book, *The Witherspoon Legacy*. I am rabid to make more book sales. Actually, no, I say this to provide a caveat. Unlike other writers of serial fiction, I have not spent a lot of time bringing the reader up to speed on what has happened before. There are several reasons for this. Firstly, I am an impatient person (no, not inpatient, at least not yet), and just can't find the time or figure out what the uninitiated reader needs to know. Relevance can be a relative thing. Secondly, I don't do this for a living; as in most things I do (except for the law - I have some pretty degrees and a bar certificate for that, and some days I still feel like I haven't a clue), I am an amateur. Thirdly, I have been destined for mediocrity, and I must be true to myself. Wait a minute: I heard that comment you made that a lawyer can't be 'true' to anything. Take that back: that's not nice. Anyway, the point is that there's a chance you might not 'get it', at least some of it, if you haven't read the previous tomes.

All the characters and events, and most of the venues, are truly imaginary. I know I say that every time. But in this book, as in past ones, I always dread when persons suspect the characters resemble people they know. And I cannot stress enough that I craft these personages to accomplish specific functions or purposes in the book, or to lay the groundwork for a possible future set of events. Yes, many times I know someone a little bit like a particular character, but then so do you, or you might not identify with the plot.

I really agonized over the character of Esme, and to a lesser extent Janine, worrying that I would catch grief over them (i.e., "I know who you were really writing about") more than any of the other characters I've introduced.

Almost every Southern town possesses at least one Esme, and almost every church, Southern or not, has at least one Janine (at least every one I have ever attended). I am constantly told tales by my friends about people matching the descriptions of these characters, and I knew sooner or later I was going to need a villain like them. While my novels lack that best-selling Southern homespun local color so popular with other writers, I too like to flesh out some of the resulting stereotypes to use as foils in the drama. So these characters worked really well for my purposes, while at the same time not 'being' any particular real person. Organists love to sit around drinking and swapping stories, so it was not hard to construct an amalgem from some of those nights of 'research' at organ conventions.

I actually based Esme on several legends in this geographical area, men who peddled their influence from dark smoky rooms, deciding the political fates of others for years and years. I met a couple of these larger-than-life fellows (they have historically always been male, particularly in the deep South) by sheer accident in my early career (generally by being contacted by them while incidentally representing their hired minions charged with crimes), but because I was from the other side of the tracks and devoid of politics there was no need for me, and no desire for them, to cultivate any friendship there. I was unaware of the connection to my clients until those encounters, and was merely instructed that I must win the cases or I was no good as a lawyer. I share a trait with Amanda in that I am not one to bite my tongue around such, I was thoroughly unimpressed, and I won no friends and influenced no one positively in my response.

I decided for this novel I wanted to come up with such a character, but instead of a tobacco-spitting dog-hunting male king of the good ole boys I wanted a rich, beautiful, matriarchal Southern belle, who of course despite all her political success met her match in her own son and in Amanda. Everyone knows women rule behind the scenes anyway, and the world might be a better place if we were in total charge. (Of course, then I look at Sarah Palin and shudder—oh, we won't go there.)

And I mean no indictment of the judicial selection process in Florida, but I envisioned Ralph's dream to be a judge, not some other appointed official, which would have been much less complicated to map out. He wasn't interested in running for a slot as a county commissioner, a member of the school board or a state representative. I am apparently unable to come up with simple plots, and the result is a long novel.

This novel is a bit heavy on the law side, because Amanda is recovering from injuries and unable to play organ, at least in the beginning. And there is some sex (I did expurgate some graphic scenes), because I'm a firm believer that a couple in the first stage of marriage should have lots of it, preferably with each other. But the new organ is in the planning stages, and the lives of Amanda and those around her are changing, evolving. The new generation of Mainville is bursting on the scene imminently.

A friend complained about the unimaginative name for the town. I don't like 'Mainville' either, but honey, I struggled to come up with an innocuous sobriquet. My creativity kept hitting a block wall there, and I had to give up so that I could get on with the plot. I have tried to save my hometown and all the small surrounding cities from as much unfavorable comparison as possible, while identifying some of the larger metropoli of Northwest Florida (Pensacola, Panama City, and Tallahassee; oh yeah, I did mention Appalachicola and St. George Island in the last book).

I think I spared you sermons in this book; at least I can't remember them offhand while writing this. I've been more of a reprobate lately, and I really only have one good sermon in me. A judge friend asked me the other day if I was still an Episcopalian. I told him I was a converted reprobate, and I didn't attend unless they paid me, an ideal situation. It really was a joke.

I have so many people to thank, including all my readers. I still get a thrill when someone informs me he or she enjoyed one of my books. That happens still on a regular basis; out of the blue I get an e-mail, and it's always quite a high when I do. I hope I can keep you diverted and coming back for more.

Again Fred Swann tops the list of those to whom I must provide a heartfelt thanks. As busy as he has been in 'semi-retirement' (and in my opinion the terms "Fred Swann" and "retirement" should never be found in the same sentence), and Fred is never still, he has been so encouraging, reading my stuff and making comments, assisting with the process for the new organ. A fabulous organist and consummate gentleman, he is an idol of mine, and I can never thank him enough or say enough nice things about him.

My friend Peter Storandt consented to more pain and suffering by proofing this volume as well as the last. He deserves much more than just my nine-egg super-duper cream cheese pound cake from hell for his efforts. I am grateful for his continued friendship and acerbic wit over the last twelve to fourteen years (I told you once before lawyers can't count).

My cover photograph this time comes from another uptown friend, Steve Lawson, associate organist of the Church of the Heavenly Rest, New York City (one huge honking organ; it scared me just to sit at the console—I might as well have tried to fly a 747 solo). Steve is also responsible for the work that has gone into the project launched by the New York City Chapter of the American Guild of Organists, an attempt to catalogue all the organs of the boroughs. The web site provides listings, photos and historical information concerning the extant and extinct organs of that area. The site is a treasure trove of information, thoughtfully laid out and beautifully studded with photos. Steve has been a friend for about fourteen years as well, and takes great pains to ensure I develop no egotistical tendencies.

No, the cover picture is not of the future gallery organ at St. Catherine's, Mainville (hmmm, Fred, what do you think?); it is instead a depiction of one of my favorite churches, St. Ignatius Loyola, New York City, such an awe-inspiring, warm and lovely room with the impressive Mander organ case gracing the gallery. I still think back fondly to the day when I sat at that console in the summer of 2001, at the invitation of Malcolm Wechsler, a friend who has exited this world and who I miss very much. When I saw Steve's photos I knew I wanted one for the cover of one of my books, and he agreed. I may be mediocre, but I surround myself with incredibly phenomenally talented friends: musicians, photographers, producers, historians, poets, authors, composers, and even a lawyer, judge, doctor and Indian chief here and there. And surprisingly they don't mind and are generous and kind.

There are so many who provide encouragement and support, and some of them I have mentioned before and will avoid redundancy here. But you will just have to suffer the repetition for a few. Sue Goddard in Atlanta has been so wonderful to tell the world about my books. I am always so humbled by her glowing compliments. Sheri Hundley is always encouraging, and tells everyone about the fact I am a writer. One day I'll have to hire these women as publicity agents.

There are so many people who have been an inspiration in my life, and I doubt I will write enough books to dedicate to all of them. However, I want to mention someone who is still alive and well, if no longer physically able to regularly terrorize the staid self-satisfied conservatism and social Darwinism of some corners of Christendom.

John Clinton Fowler came to little St. Agatha's after his retirement from an Episcopal church in New Mexico, his native land. Intelligent, erudite, crusty, self-confident and Anglican to the core, he visited this little corner of the South for a short time, intending to leave and navigate all the intracoastal waterways in the United States for the rest of his life. Thankfully, Divine Providence brought a nasty winter to the Chesapeake during the winter he had to dock there, and that was enough to change his mind. He sold the very lovely vessel and settled in DeFuniak Springs to be our priest-in-charge for several years, until forced into mandatory retirement because of age. Then he decided he liked snow and moved to Pennsylvania.

The little congregation here was literally dying when he appeared, with about eleven regular tithes-paying parishioners and the median age approaching seventy. I played a tiny horrid spinet organ and a dry-rotting old grand piano for the services (but even then, they heard the classics, or a sad parody of them, depending upon your viewpoint). Father infused the 100-year old church with a taste of high-church leanings, sang the Eucharist, introduced chant to the weekly service, helped with necessary renovations to both the church and parish house, and by golly managed to procure a new hand-built mahogany pipe organ for the church. He even converted some Southern Baptists into Anglicans, no mean feat. The church is alive and well today largely due to his efforts.

The man forced me, a pianist who gave up music to be a lawyer, into learning organ at the age of thirty. He talked me into being confirmed, and into serving on the vestry, and into working on the recital series for the church. He had me play so much Handel that I would have gladly personally killed Handel had he still been alive. There was little of the organ concertos that survived the onslaught. (George Frideric and I quit drinking together because we had a disagreement: I wanted the aria to be changed to "The oboe will sound", because I hate trumpets. Things slid from bad to worse a bottle or two later, and I don't remember what I called him, but he called me an 'impudent strumpet'. It got bloody and muddy after that. I just remember he had to buy a new wig.) However, that was a blessing, because I might never have developed a taste for the French romantic literature had I not overdosed on the baroque. And because of all those nightly hours practicing the organ after practicing law all day, I fell in love with J.S. Bach, a devotion that continues to this day.

Father Fowler's picture should be found in Webster's dictionary beside the term 'liberal' (I consider that a compliment), and he has been a champion of the civil rights of the common man all his life. He instilled in his congregation that the way one manifests love for God is to actively love his neighbor as himself. Himself a lover of music, theology and literature, he is always a delight, except on those rare occasions when he is a holy terror (I assume always with justification). I would that we all could accomplish as much as he has for the betterment of individuals and community, and am grateful that our paths crossed some twenty-plus years ago. I might never have developed the bravery (or is it defensiveness? Effrontery? Foolhardiness?) to write books and music and actually play in recital for a few years. So it's all (or mostly) his fault. Besides, it's kind of cruel to blame my first- and second-grade teachers: how could they know the monster I'd become?

PROLOGUE

The beautiful woman sauntered into the hotel room, her stiletto heels sinking into the lush carpet of the suite. Her dark full shoulder-length hair fanned out over a fitted black leather biker jacket and matching short skirt, reverse zipper down the front open partly to form a slit, framing her curvaceous figure.

"OK, so I'm here," she pursed her crimson-painted lips and announced peremptorily to the shadowy figure standing by the window overlooking the overcast day. "What was so important that we had to break silence and meet?"

The man did not move, but continued his study of the vista outside the window. "This is your final warning. You're not moving fast enough. I want to know your plan. I've paid you enough. Now I want everything in place, to see some results, and soon."

She laughed throatily, her luxurious thick hair cascading around her face. "You just leave the details to me, sweetie. I have several birds I intend to kill with the same stone."

"You forget to whom you are speaking," he reprimanded her, his eyes coldly appraising her. "I am not one of your conquests. I am easily annoyed, and you are treading close to the edge."

She gazed at him, her eyes narrowing. "Don't worry. I have things well in hand."

She summarized the strategy, and he nodded, his mind calculating.

"How soon?" he asked.

"I have to make it convincing. But if all falls into place, two, three weeks," she replied, her face betraying the hint of a smile. "Certainly within the month, and before a decision is handed down."

The man continued, his manner brisk. "A meeting has been arranged. I am assuming you will employ your 'skills'," he emphasized the term derisively, "to set the stage and to become chummy with my employer and her current entourage."

"Yes, I have made the initial contacts," the woman tossed her hair. "The introduction will be made in D.C. at a state dinner. She's already been invited and has RSVPed. She will be suitably impressed. Once she's in the bag, the delegation will fall like dominoes. And the deal will be done. And I have another contact to make which will start the ball rolling on your other objective." Her face softened momentarily. "Nothing like renewing old acquaintances. That part will be fun."

The man turned and faced her, his voice biting. "I'm not interested in your secondary agendas. Our time is running out, and you must begin execution immediately. I assume there will be no complications? No little personal problems will interfere? No sudden unexplained disappearances like the last job?"

"No, there will be no complications," her jaw jutted, making her face pout.

"And," he continued, his voice impassive, "no mistakes. I am watching you. If you fail, there will be consequences."

"I won't fail," she whispered, trying to control her anger. "The subject will be eliminated. I'll see to it myself."

The briefest of smiles crossed his face. "I was just going to suggest that."

PART 1

Chapter 1

"What, did you take out the trash like a good husband?" Amanda teased Jon as he reentered the kitchen. Her remark ended in a paroxysm of coughing.

Jonathan Connor, dressed in cotton jersey running shorts, t-shirt and athletic shoes, stopped at the kitchen sink and washed his hands, then dried them. The early morning sun preened itself, casting long patches over the tops of the trees and onto the expanse of rolling lawn visible outside the window. He turned to his wife Amanda sitting at the kitchen table, still in her robe. Her hypnotic gaze made him forget the clever retort on the tip of his tongue.

"Are you staring at my butt?" he accused instead, feigning sternness.

"I have a license to do so," she asserted laughingly, but coughed again.

"Why are you out of bed?" He sat down at the chair by her side and took her hand, kneading it lovingly. "You need some rest."

"I've overslept as it is," she responded, but he noted that she looked tired.

"You have coughed most of the night and ended up sitting up on the sofa for what little rest you've had," he rejoined tenderly. "You're overdoing it again, Mandy."

"It's just some bug," she protested weakly, breaking into more coughing. "I'm sorry." She was shamefaced. "I need to exercise and hit the shower and pack for our trip. I'm looking forward to it. And I need to pick out my outfit for the dinner tonight with your folks."

"Are you sure you're up to this?" Jon was concerned.

"Of course," she smiled brightly. "I just don't want to sound yucky when I'm meeting your sister and having dinner with your family and their friends."

"How did you like my parents after the first meeting?" Jon asked her, his eyes not leaving hers.

Her smile became pensive as she glanced away. "They're nice."

Jon was attuned to her tone, his gaze piercing. "I've heard when a Southerner says something is 'nice', that is not a good sign."

"They're your parents. I love them, no matter what, for your sake," she replied, her voice hoarse. She frowned. "I hope I sound better by this evening."

"I really think you should get a bit more sleep," Jon prodded.

"I'm fine," she insisted, patting his hand. "I see from your attire you've already beaten me to the treadmill this morning."

"Actually, I ran the trail. It's nice and hilly, and one can glimpse a deer or other wildlife at times, at least if Bozo doesn't decide to run with me," Jon grinned. "But I think this morning he was worried about you and stayed behind." He brought her hand to his lips. "So am I."

"I'm thinking about installing a lap pool on the back." She closed her eyes, stifling another cough. "I love the lake, but I also know once it gets hot it won't be long before water moccasin season begins in earnest. They're aggressive buggers, and don't like to share."

"I saw a snake of some kind yesterday," Jon acknowledged. "It was solid black. I would have killed it, but didn't have the means at the time."

"No, don't kill the black snakes," Amanda spoke up, opening her eyes and turning them on Jon sharply. "They are benign and eat the rats and other snakes. Any other snake you may kill with my blessing."

She mused, "But really, the pool needs to be enclosed or the snakes will invite themselves to swim there as well. And perhaps we'll make it big enough for an exercise room. Don't you want a gym? Perhaps a billiard room? A man cave?"

"The place is wonderful as it is. I'm happy just being with you," Jon told her.

"Are you really happy here?" Amanda asked, suddenly apprehensive, swallowing a cough. "I mean, it is away from civilization and not all that large. And it was where I lived with Andy." She coughed again. "Damn," she muttered under her breath, irritated. "I'm not sure your parents would like the place. It's a bit rustic."

"Why not? And besides, we're not asking them to live here anyway," Jon teased. He reassured her, "Dear, I love the farm. You don't have to do one more thing to it to please me. It is your space to do with as you like."

"No," Amanda objected, but started coughing again. It took her a minute for the coughing to subside. "This is your home too, and I want it to be perfect for you," she wheezed.

He stood and leaned over her, kissing her forehead, noting it was warm. "I'm worried, Amanda. What say we take you to be checked out by Dr. Howells?"

"No," Amanda protested. "I'll be OK by this evening. Are you really happy here, Jon?" Her eyes were round as she repeated her question.

"I love it. It's gorgeous out here, and so peaceful. Wherever you are is home to me." He turned and moved to the counter to help himself to a cup of coffee. "I have been thinking, however, that maybe it's time I invested in a piece of real estate." He looked at her. "Perhaps a place in the mountains, or a beach place for us. You apparently don't like the house you've leased down there; you never want to go there. Otherwise, maybe I could buy something like that. I just have never bought a place of my own, because I was always on the move."

"The Barnes' beach house holds memories that I find painful. I'm not going to break my lease, but I'm not sure whether I want to buy it now. But you own real estate with me now anyway," Amanda laughed, the laugh ending up in another paroxysm.

"No, dear." Jon was firm. "What's yours is yours."

She stood suddenly, her eyes flashing. "No, you are already on the deeds."

His eyes widened in surprise at the announcement, but she pushed on, undeterred. "And my idea of marriage is a sharing of everything. No divisions, no secrets." She broke off, coughing again so hard it took her breath away. Jon reached out for her, but she shook him off, suddenly the cold, distant Amanda.

"Baby, don't shut me out," he began, but she turned on him.

"Don't call me baby," she shot back, her eyes angry as she choked back another series of coughs.

He stepped back, startled at her vehemence. As she started past him, he caught her in his arms. She struggled against him, but he refused to let her go.

"Our first marital fight," he murmured as he lifted her chin and kissed her.

"I'm sorry. I don't want to fight with you," she whispered, wrapping her arms around his neck. He could feel her trembling, trying to stifle a cough.

"I think you do," he smiled as his fingers traced the outline of her lips. "But it wouldn't be fair, in your condition. I might actually win. So I intend to re-channel that energy elsewhere." He picked her up, protesting half-heartedly, and carried her through the house and up the stairs.

Jon and Amanda were enjoying their first weeks of married life alone at the farm. Jon found living with Amanda even more entrancing than the courtship. He had never envisioned being so happy with someone, nor had he imagined loving her more. But every day brought them closer, and he found himself wishing he had met her much earlier in his life.

Jon soon discovered that keeping Amanda in a resting state was harder than he initially conceived. Because she was released from the hospital the day of their wedding, they had to defer taking a honeymoon until she was medically cleared. Amanda had immediately wanted to jump in and make the farm into a home for Jon, and he found himself constantly having to curb her enthusiasm and reminding her that she was recovering from grave injuries. However, they both enjoyed their time of enforced togetherness without the intervening distractions of work and outside life.

They had met his parents for dinner at a posh restaurant on the beach the first week of their marriage. Jon's mother Gloria Connor had invited several friends, all politically influential people in the area. While Jon's father James had taken to Amanda immediately, his mother seemed cool and distant. Amanda was surprised, because she had looked forward to cultivating a relationship with her new mother-in-law.

They were scheduled to meet again this evening at an exclusive club in Panama City for dinner with Jon's family, for her to meet Jon's sister Kelly and some family friends from the area. Kelly had flown in for a couple of days to join her parents at their vacation townhouse at Panama City Beach. When Amanda had inquired as to how many residences her in-laws owned, Jon was vague, saying only that there were a few places scattered around convenient for business and their varied interests. Amanda had been surprised, not realizing the extent of Jon's family's affluence, but Jon had redirected all her questions, changing the subject.

During their time off together Jon had obtained the permission of Dr. Joseph Rand, her treating physician, and Malcolm Howells, her lifelong doctor and surrogate father, to take Amanda for several days to St. George Island to revisit the scene of their first tryst. Jon had wooed her assiduously, and they had basked in the warmth of being with each other. He kept her activities sedate, and they walked the beach, chartered a boat ride to the smaller islands shell hunting, and sat on the porch of the inn in rocking chairs soaking in the summer sun.

So far their wedded life together had been idyllic. He started sounding her out about possible venues for a real honeymoon trip, not wanting their time of close togetherness to end.

However, even though Ralph assured them that all was fine at the office, Jon had caught her several times on the telephone, dictating to Sheila, giving

The Connors' Crisis

instructions, and discussing disposition of cases with Ralph. She had insisted on going by there several times to sign documents. The discussion had gotten fairly heated over Ralph's efforts to hire another secretary to assist Sheila, with Amanda's insisting on being present for the interviews, debating the benefits package, involving herself in the final selection. And Jon had seen her on more than one occasion seemingly preoccupied, with a faraway look in her eyes, looking as though she was rehearsing some argument, and sending e-mails to Sheila with drafted pleadings attached.

At her follow-up appointment with Dr. Rand, Jon had tattled on her, and she had received some severe reprimands from Joey, who had treated her after the automobile accident. She had countered contentiously, "I'm not out running marathons or doing pushups; I'm only sitting still and keeping an eye on my law practice."

But Amanda was swimming the lake several laps per day and doing wrist exercises against Rand's advice, trying religiously to build back her strength and stamina in the affected areas. She spent time at the piano doing fingering exercises and scales. There were times Jon had noticed that her breathing seemed more labored, and Joey had again lectured her to take things easy. Rand had finally vetoed her playing any keyboard instrument for several more weeks, and had extracted a promise from her to cut down on her exercise regime. She had argued with him and chafed under Jon's continued strictures on the matter.

Amanda would still from time to time wake up at nights crying or screaming from nightmares about Billy Barnes or Eve Brown. Jon would hold her close and comfort her, and she was always embarrassed by the nocturnal outbursts. However, the occurrences seemed to be lessening, and Jon was hoping that her subconscious was slowly relinquishing those terrors.

They had otherwise remained free from argument, and their lovemaking had been emotionally and physically demanding and satisfying, as they explored the newness of each other with excitement and without restraint. Again Jon found it hard to restrict Amanda; it was as though once she had made the commitment to take Jon as her husband, she was insatiable in wanting him and in wanting to please him. "I want to make up for all that lost time," she would whisper as she pulled him to her eagerly. And he shared that eagerness, his hunger for her not slackening.

Jon had been asked to start his new job at the Destin law firm early, but he demurred, knowing that he already held but slender control over Amanda's movements, and being constantly concerned about her doing something to slow or halt her medical progress. Amanda was ambivalent about sharing her true feelings about Jon's new job, at times seemingly clinging to him and craving that their solitude continue, and at other times enthusiastically pushing him to go ahead and start his new career early.

She had also demurred regarding where she would like to honeymoon. So he decided that they should take a cabin in the mountains of Utah for a week, to get away and discuss the issue. But before the trip she developed a chronic cough and asthmatic symptoms, and Rand and Dr. Howells had advised against her flying and the change in altitude. Therefore, the newlyweds had contented themselves with planning a short driving trip to St. Augustine and the Atlantic coast on the morrow.

But by that evening, Amanda's cough had worsened, and she was wheezing from the exertion of packing. Jon had finally convinced her she was in no condition to attend dinner with his family, and had called his mother and explained the situation. Amanda, upset, would not hear of going to the hospital, and promised that she would see Dr. Howells the next morning if she were no better. She took some over-the-counter cough medicine, but it did not seem to relieve the symptoms. She fell into a fitful sleep in Jon's arms.

Around midnight Jon was awakened by Amanda's rasping cough. She had worsened, and was shivering, in a delirium. "No," she screamed hoarsely, jerking, moaning and clutching her shoulder, the cough wracking her.

Jon was immediately beside her, enfolding her to him. "I'm right here," he crooned.

She was burning with fever and looked at him without recognition. "Don't let him kill me," she gasped, clutching at him desperately. "Watch out—he has a needle."

He was suddenly apprehensive for her. "Come on, baby," he whispered. "I'll protect you."

She pummeled him weakly. "No," she repeated. "Don't call me baby," she whimpered.

Jon laid her back against the pillows, murmuring to her soothingly. He reached for his cell phone and rang Dr. Howells.

"Amanda is not well," he told the sleepy voice that answered.

Howells, immediately alert, asked her symptoms, and Jon related her behaviors.

"Can you get her to the hospital?" Howells had queried.

"She would not agree earlier, but I will try again," Jon promised.

"I'll meet you there."

Jon rose, threw on some sweats, grabbed his phone and keys, then attempted to get an incoherent Amanda into her robe. He wrapped her in a cotton blanket and carried her downstairs to the car.

"Where are we going?" she asked, her voice muffled against his shoulder.

The Connors' Crisis

"Doc Howells asked that we drop by for a minute," he told her, praying that in her state she would accept the story and not fight him.

"Stay out of the creek," she mumbled deliriously.

He made it to his car, gingerly placed her in the passenger seat, then sprang around and let himself in. He drove as quickly as he dared down the trail, jumping out and opening the gate. He drove through, and as he stepped out to close the gate, their neighbor Fred Vaughan appeared out of nowhere.

"What's up?" he peered at Amanda.

"Amanda's really ill. I'm meeting Doc at the hospital with her."

"Anything I can do?" Vaughan was gruff, pursing his lips and staring over at Amanda, whose eyes were closed, but she was still coughing and shivering.

"No, thanks. I'll let you know what Doc finds out," Jon promised.

He finally made it to the road, racing to town and the hospital.

Jon pulled up to the emergency room entrance, and Howells was already there waiting. Jon bundled Amanda up in the blanket and carried her inside, where Howells bustled them into a cubicle. Jon laid her gingerly down on the bed.

"How long as she been like this?" Howells' voice was accusing, as he took her pulse, felt her head, and took a thermometer from a nurse, sticking in her mouth.

"She had a cough last night and all day today. She seemed tired, but insisted she was OK. She would not let me bring her to see you or to the ER, and promised to see you in the morning. Then tonight she was on fire and delirious."

Howells listened to her chest with a stethoscope. "She's developed pneumonia. Her lungs are still weak." He grimaced at Jon. "She's pushing herself too hard."

"I know," Jon stared down at her, taking her hand in his. "Damn it, Doc, I've tried everything. I don't know how to slow her down."

"It's a job too big for most of us," Howells countered sympathetically, placing his hand on Jon's shoulder. "You have at least been brave enough to try."

Howells became all business, ordering X-rays, antibiotics and IV fluids, sending the nurses scurrying to do his bidding. He then turned back to Jon, still standing and gazing at Amanda apprehensively.

"I'm admitting her," Howells informed him. "I'll put her up in a room with two beds, so that you can get a little rest too."

Jon nodded mutely, his eyes not leaving her face.

Howells gave terse orders to the staff, and Amanda was quickly ensconced in a hospital room. Jon sat with Amanda, watching her gravely as a nurse

23

started an IV and hooked her up to a monitor. She was largely unresponsive, passive, coughing intermittently, a dry, shallow cough, her breathing labored, her face devoid of color.

He touched her forehead, and it was hot. She stirred. "So cold," she muttered.

He pulled a blanket up and tucked it around her, took her hand and held it between his two.

The nurse left them. Howells stood outside and gave instructions, then entered the room. He spoke to Amanda, but she didn't respond. He lifted her eyelids and examined her.

"Has she seemed lethargic lately?"

Jon replied, his eyes not leaving her, "She has remained busy since I brought her home from the hospital, driving herself, exercising the shoulder and wrist, wanting to renovate the entire house. I put on the brakes as much as I can. But she tires easily, and sometimes I know she is experiencing pain in her shoulder. She's not resting well at night. She never complains. But this cough has been with her, and it has worsened. This morning she coughed constantly. She ate very little, was shivering, and would not hear of coming to see you. I forced some chicken broth and Gatorade into her. She wrapped up in a blanket on the couch, not wanting to sit outside on the porch."

"Her fever is high. I'm worried," Howells murmured.

Jon looked up and saw the weariness in Howells' face, his features gray. "Doc, what is wrong? You're not well."

"Just not feeling my usual self," Howells smiled tightly. "I'll be fine. But I want Amanda well and able to enjoy her new life with you. I know it won't be easy even when she's in perfect health," he added. "Right now you are not getting a realistic picture of life with her."

"That's OK. I'm keeping some strength in reserve. I hope to be able to handle her," Jon rejoined amicably. "Although I must admit she's quite a handful."

"When she gets back up to speed, it'll take every ounce you have and then some," Howells grinned. He squeezed Jon's shoulder. "I'll be back to check on her. You might want to stretch out a bit. It may be a long night."

Howells walked out and Jon remained in a chair beside Amanda's bed. He dozed fitfully.

His phone buzzed. He answered it.

"How is she?" He recognized the voice of his brother, Dr. David Connor.

"She has been admitted to the hospital." Jon guessed that his mother had informed the family after they didn't appear for dinner. "She has pneumonia, a bad cough and a high fever. She's delirious. Dr. Howells is here." Jon paused. "I'm worried about her, David. I can see that he's worried, too."

"Anything I can do?" David asked.

"Just run interference with Mom," Jon tried to joke. "I'm sure Mom thinks it was some sort of conspiracy for us to no show at her dinner party. And Kelly will sulk because I stood her up."

"I'd say you have your priorities straight," David retorted. "I'll handle the family."

"Thanks, David," Jon sighed as he hung up. He stared at Amanda, who was restless, her breathing shallow, her eyes closed. He dozed again.

At some point he awoke to her voice. "Pete?" she whispered dazedly.

"Pete?" Jon started. He stood up, gazing down at her. "Who's Pete?" he asked, smiling at her.

Amanda stared up at him, not recognizing him. "Where's Pete?" she persisted, coughing and holding her shoulder.

"Petrino?" Jon asked, surprised, taking her hand.

"Don't tell Jon about us, that we kissed," she stared up at him, her eyes unfocused, glassy.

He smoothed her hair from her face, feeling her hot clammy skin. "Why not?" he asked softly. "Don't you like Jon?"

"I love him," she said simply. "But he won't love me back if he knows."

He played along. "I'll bet he already knows, and won't be mad."

"Mmm." She closed her eyes, drifting.

The nurse brought in a basin of cool water and a washcloth, soaked the cloth and squeezed it out, placing it on Amanda's forehead. "Dr. Howells said for us to try anything that might work. If you can get her to drink anything, that can only help. I'll get her some ice."

Jon mopped her forehead with the cloth, dipping it again in the cool water and squeezing it out before replacing it on her head. She reached up with her good hand. "It's so cold," she complained softly.

Jon bent over her. "Mandy, we've got to get the fever down somehow."

He turned gratefully to the nurse as she reappeared with a pitcher of ice. He took a small piece and brought it to her lips. "Come on, dear," he pleaded gently.

She took the piece of ice in her mouth. Jon poured a little water in a cup and brought it to her lips. "Sip a little water for me," he prodded, and she complied, trembling violently as she swallowed the liquid.

Howells returned to the room. Jon spoke without looking around, "She has quit coughing."

"That is not a good thing in her case," Howells replied.

The nurse took her temperature, then shook her head at Howells. "It's over 105."

"Damn!" Jon heard him mutter. He turned to the nurse and gave more instructions, then faced Jon.

"The fever is dangerously high. I'm ordering a cool water and alcohol bath. I don't really want to do that with the pneumonia, but bringing the fever down is my number one priority right now."

"I'll help," Jon asserted fervently. "Just tell me what to do."

The nurse disengaged the IV. Gingerly Jon and Howells himself undressed Amanda, who seemed unconscious of their presence. Jon pulled the sheet around her and picked her up like a rag doll, following Howells out of the room and down the hall to a large room where a tub was already half-full of cool water. Howells pulled the sheet off and Jon placed her gently in the tub.

Amanda started, her cry weak. "No." She grasped Jon by his sweatshirt, clutching him fearfully. "Car's filling up. Don't let me drown," she gasped pitifully.

Jon held her under her arms, careful not to grasp her injured wrist or shoulder. "No, Mandy, no. It's just a bath, just to cool you down." As she continued to struggle, he put his cheek to her own burning cheek. "Dear, we have to do this. I won't let anything happen to you. I promise."

She clung to him, and Jon kept his arm below her shoulder and grasped her good hand as the nurse added cold water and put a cold compress on her forehead. She slowly relaxed her grip and lay inert, shivering. Jon murmured to her soothingly and bathed her forehead with the cold cloth, oblivious to getting wet himself.

Desperately he looked up to Howells, whose eyes were closed, his lips moving silently. Jon was suddenly afraid.

Amanda was muttering under her breath. He put his ear close to her mouth. "I need to sign my new will first," she was saying, her eyes closed, her body trembling. He felt apprehension for her.

"Come on, love," he crooned, his eyes shining with unshed tears. "Fight for me. Don't give in."

She was unresponsive, quivering, her eyes closed, her breathing shallow.

"Oh, God, pull her through," Jon prayed. "Don't let me lose her now. I love her so much."

Howells put his hand on Jon's shoulder. Jon had not realized he had prayed out loud. Howells placed his other hand on Amanda's head.

Howells intoned, "Heavenly Father, we raise up to you our daughter, our wife. She has tried to serve you faithfully. She has suffered fiery trials, and only you can help her. Please look with compassion on her and heal her of her infirmities, and bring her to a state of joy in this life and the next. We ask all through Christ our Advocate, who with you and the Holy Spirit reign forever and ever."

Jon joined him in the amen. Then they both heard a weak 'amen' and looked down in surprise. Amanda's eyes were open.

Howells felt her forehead. "She is cooler," he announced.

"Does that mean I can get out of the freezing water?" she whispered, her teeth chattering.

Howells nodded smilingly, and Jon was handed a towel. He asked her, "Can you stand?"

She nodded. "I think so."

He helped her up and dried her off, and the nurse handed him a gown. Then he picked her up and returned her to her room, where the nurse scurried around stripping and re-making the bed with fresh linens. Amanda clung to him as he let her down on the bed, her breathing labored from the simple exertion.

"I love you," she murmured.

"I adore you, Mandy. I had really hoped when I married you I could keep you out of the hospital," he rejoined, grinning, as he brushed his lips over her forehead.

"OK, break it up, you two." Howells, gruff, intervened with a thermometer, which he plopped in her mouth as Jon moved back.

"Her temperature has dropped dramatically, thanks be to God," he announced a moment later triumphantly, tears in his eyes.

"Can I go home?" Amanda asked, closing her eyes, her voice tired.

"You're not out of the woods yet, my dear," Howells responded. "I want you sucking plenty of liquids, and we need to reattach the IV and get as much antibiotics in you as we can to combat the temperature and pneumonia. I want you to have a breathing treatment right away, but will let you rest a bit first."

He bent over her and kissed her cheek. "God is good," he murmured. "Get some rest. You too," he told Jon, pointing to the other bed. "One of you has to remain well."

The door opened, and Dr. Alan Young walked in. He looked at Howells with alarm. "I thought you were going home," he said, then his eyes widened as he saw Jon, then Amanda.

"I did. But we have had a bit of a crisis here." Howells explained the situation. Alan nodded, his eyes moving from Amanda to Jon to Howells.

"I'll be glad to take over," Alan offered. "Go home, Malcolm. Doctor's orders."

Malcolm nodded, then turned to Amanda. "I'll be back to check on you in a while."

Alan walked him out, then returned several minutes later. Amanda was drifting off to sleep. He watched the monitor and read the lab results in the chart.

He faced Jon. "I'm so happy for you and Amanda," Alan smiled. "She's a wonderful girl, but a hellion too. You have your work cut out for you."

"So everyone keeps warning me," Jon nodded good-naturedly. "We are both glad to see that you are doing well."

"The boys and I owe you and Amanda a debt of gratitude for solving the case and clearing me," Alan laughed quietly. "I still shudder when I think how close I came to ruin and death." He sobered.

He looked at the sleeping woman. "Is she following doctor's orders?"

Jon's eyes followed his. "What do you think? She is in the hospital again, isn't she? But I do my best."

"You are a man in love," Alan shook his head.

"That I am," Jon agreed. "And she is so bewitching I hope to never dig myself out."

Alan hovered a minute over Amanda, then checked the IV. "Doc said she had a high fever until just a little while ago." He felt her forehead. "You need to stretch out there and get a few Zs yourself."

"But first tell me." Jon moved closer, his tone low, confidential. "What's up with Dr. Howells? He is not himself."

Alan stared a Jon a minute, as if unsure whether to reply. Jon prodded, "I know he and Amanda are extremely close. I don't want anything to happen to him."

Alan nodded solemnly. "He has had some palpitations lately. His color isn't good. Bob Cardet checked him out and scheduled a stress test for him. You are right: he has not been his usual energetic self. But he refuses to take off any time, get away. This hospital is his baby."

"I'm sorry I called and woke him," Jon murmured.

"No, you'd have had hell to pay if Amanda was sick and you didn't call Doc." Alan was sympathetic. "But I am trying to convince him to take some time off, get away for a little bit, have a vacation."

He slapped Jon on the shoulder. "You worry about Amanda here, and I'll worry about Doc. It will all work out."

CHAPTER 2

Amanda stirred, then opened her eyes. Slowly she took in her surroundings. She was in a hospital bed. Light was streaming through the blinds on the window.

Suddenly Jon was standing beside her. "How do you feel?" he smiled at her sleepily, taking her hand.

"Tired," she replied, still groggy. "What am I doing here?"

"You have pneumonia, dear. You don't remember being brought to the hospital last night? The cold water bath?"

She grimaced. Some vague wisps of memory floated around. "God was there," she murmured.

"I was afraid for a minute you were going to leave the party with him," Jon admitted. "I'm glad you stayed. Now that I have finally lassoed you, I'm jealous of even God. I asked him to let me keep you a while longer."

"Hold me," she whispered.

Jon sat down on the bed beside her and gathered her in his arms. "I love it when you are lying helpless in my arms," he whispered in her ear. "I intend to experience that for a long time yet, God willing. Although I'm afraid once you get completely well, I'll have to work harder at it. It's my impression you aren't helpless very often."

"I could make an exception for you," she mumbled as she found his mouth with hers.

The door opened and in strode Alan Young and Charlie Petrino. She extricated herself from Jon, embarrassed, as he winked at her and lowered her to the pillows, before standing up and facing the two men.

"Did we interrupt anything?" Charlie barely concealed a grin.

Amanda blushed. Dr. Young walked around to the other side of the bed. "I was afraid of that. You cannot trust newlyweds alone in the same room at any time," he lamented jokingly.

He gazed down at Amanda. "How do you feel this morning?"

"Tired," she confessed, as he pulled his stethoscope over his ears and listened to her chest.

"Breathe deeply," he ordered. She attempted, but could only cough weakly.

While Alan had her occupied, Petrino took Jon's arm and steered him a few steps away. "You know one of my officers found Dr. Howells slumped over the steering wheel of his car this morning only blocks from his house?" he announced, his voice low.

Jon was alarmed. "He hasn't been gone from here more than about three hours. He met me with Amanda up here and admitted her last night." He glanced over at Amanda, who looked back at him and smiled, thermometer in mouth, as Alan wrote in her chart and talked to her.

"Where is he now? How is he?" Jon asked anxiously.

"Joe called me and brought him here, and Alan called Dr. Cardet immediately. Doc apparently had a heart attack. He is conscious, but Cardet is talking about surgery."

"We're going to have to tell Amanda." Jon was grave. "He has made her his health care surrogate, and she has power of attorney if anything should happen to him."

He turned back to the doctor and Amanda. "What's the verdict, Dr. Young?" Jon smiled at them, but his heart was heavy.

"Alan to you," Young rejoined pleasantly. "The fever has broken, and is within manageable limits, we hope. But the pneumonia is going to take longer to combat." He looked pointedly, accusingly, at Amanda. "You have been doing more than you should."

"No," Amanda objected, but Jon quelled her with a look.

"She's been swimming laps at the lake several times a day, exercising the wrist, playing scales on the piano, and doing manual labor at the farm, all against my admonition and Joey's recommendation. And she's been doing work from home, and moving furniture, and everything her doctors have ordered her not to do."

"Geez, man, can't you exercise more authority over her?" Charlie remonstrated, winking at Amanda.

"Shut up, Charlie," Jon gritted out testily. Amanda looked at Jon in surprise.

Alan took her hand tenderly. "Mandy, I've got some bad news. Dr. Howells has had a heart attack."

Amanda's eyes grew wide. She gasped and sat up. "Doc? How is he? He's not -?" She coughed, doubling over, then trying to get out of bed.

Jon moved toward her concernedly. Alan reached across her and placed his hand on her good shoulder, blocking her forward movement. "He's in the hospital here, and is conscious, alert. Cardet thinks there are three blockages, and he's advising surgery stat. He's in with Malcolm right now."

"But he has to do it. There's no other choice." Amanda was agitated, her breath coming out in short wheezes. Jon placed his hand on her forehead. "Mandy, calm yourself. It will all be OK."

Alan took Jon's lead. "Yes, it will. Malcolm may be hard-headed like you, but he's a smart, yea, brilliant doctor, with loads of common sense. He'll weather this fine. We have to concentrate on getting you well for now."

"Can I see him?" Amanda pulled the covers back and leaned forward again as if to get up.

"No!" Jon and Alan exclaimed in unison, as they both prevented her from leaving the bed.

Charlie stepped forward. "Mandy, Alan and I will keep an eye out on Doc and report back. He is more concerned about you than himself right now. You both can do the other much more good just by taking care of yourselves right now."

"And I promised him I would take extremely good care of you," Alan smiled as he tucked the covers back around Amanda.

"How much longer am I to be in here?" she demanded, as Alan adjusted the oxygen mask over her face.

"Until you are well," Young retorted firmly. "You need to wear this. It's not an optional accessory. Recovery is partly up to you. So you need to learn to behave and be patient. We'll see how the antibiotics work in breaking this stuff up in your chest. But Mandy, the thing about pneumonia is you're not getting enough oxygen. That makes you tired, and it's so much harder for your body to work. It's imperative that you lie back and just rest. Fluids and rest. That's the quickest way to get well."

"Is there anything I can do for Doc?" Jon asked quietly.

"Just take good care of her and keep her in line. Doc said he would send Charlie to buy you a bullwhip if necessary." Alan and Charlie both grinned.

Charlie looked Jon over critically. "I can tell you've had no sleep. I can always spell you while you get some rest."

"No." Jon was defensive. "I can handle matters, thanks."

Alan straightened up and moved toward the door. He pointed toward the other bed. "Doctor's orders—both you and Amanda need a nice long nap, or I'll have two patients. You know pneumonia can be contagious, and you've been all over her." The two men grinned, and Jon smiled tentatively in return. "I'll check back in, and hope to have some more news about Doc."

The two left as quickly as they came. As the hospital door closed behind them, Alan observed quietly to Charlie, "What did you do to him?"

31

Charlie shrugged. "I can't think of anything. Maybe he's just exhausted."

"I think he's jealous," Alan smirked. "Some of that caveman mentality—this is my woman; hands off. And he probably feels he has to prove to everyone that he can take care of her."

"I just hope she lets him," Charlie muttered.

"Do you think he knows you had a thing for her all those years?" Alan prodded, his eyes on his friend.

"He knows," Charlie looked away.

"Do you still?" Alan persisted softly.

"What kind of fool question is that?" Charlie bristled. "That is deep-sixed, my friend. We've both moved on." He turned away, his tone gruff. "Let me know if I can do anything for the invalids. I gotta get back to work."

Later that day David and his mother arrived at the hospital. Jon, haggard and solemn, rose from the chair by Amanda's bed as they entered. Gloria Connor looked at her son in alarm.

"Are you OK?" she came forward.

"I'm OK." He could barely muster a smile. He motioned them to follow him to a corner of the room away from the sleeping Amanda. "This is the first real rest she's had in several days," he explained, whispering. "I wasn't sure she'd make it last night." He gazed on her sleeping form. "I've been afraid to go to sleep," he added, his voice low.

"You should have told us," his mother's voice was quiet, accusing.

"She was insistent it was just a bug and she'd get over it. She was adamant she was not going to miss the dinner, and was anxious to meet Kelly. But her fever was dangerously high last night."

He turned to David. "Dr. Howells had a heart attack after leaving here this morning. He is in the hospital as well."

"No!" David exclaimed.

Amanda stirred. "Jon?" she called hoarsely, her voice frightened as she pulled the oxygen mask off.

Jon moved back to her. "I'm here," he took her hand and squeezed it. "You have a couple of visitors," he informed her. "Mom and David are here."

She turned her eyes on them groggily. "I was just thinking about what to wear tonight. I'm looking forward to meeting Kelly," she asserted breathlessly.

David guffawed. "The dinner was last night, Sis. You apparently decided on this four-star accommodation instead."

"Last night?" She was confused, looking at Jon.

"You were here in the hospital last night," Jon reminded her.

Agitated, she sat up. "I'm so sorry." She was shamefaced. "I missed the dinner? Oh, how terrible." She started wheezing. Jon pulled the mask back over her face.

Jon explained, "She was delirious last night, and still out of it a bit today."

Jon looked at his mother, his eyes beseeching. Gloria Connor stepped forward and took Amanda's hand, as David and Jon exchanged alarmed looks.

"My dear, it is perfectly all right," she crooned. "We'll do it again once you are well."

Jon sighed with relief, and Amanda looked at her and tried to smile.

"Now, that's enough for now." Jon put his hand on Amanda's shoulder. "Close your eyes."

He accompanied them out of the room and stood just outside the door with them. His mother put her hand on his arm, concerned. "Jon, you're all in. You know you'll catch this if you are not careful."

"I'll be fine," he muttered, trying to smile.

"You're not doing her any good like this. Go home and get some sleep," David offered. "I'll stay with her until you get back."

Jon looked at him gratefully, but hesitated. "I don't want to leave her." He looked from one to the other. "It was so hard to win her. I didn't think I'd get her to the altar. She was coughing the last two nights, and refused to let me take her to the doctor or ER. I could see yesterday she was steadily getting worse. And then last night . . . I mean, she scared me. I don't know what I would have done . . . ."

He shook his head, overcome. David put his arm around Jon. "Amanda's going to be all right. Tell you what - take Mom to see the farm. Let her tut over you and get a couple hours shut-eye and a shower. I'll stay here."

"That's a capital suggestion," Gloria spoke up brightly.

Jon looked at David with trepidation as David smiled mischievously. David turned to his mother, squeezing her arm. "Leave everything in Amanda's home as it is. Don't rearrange the furniture or the kitchen drawers. Remember it's their home."

"Why, David," she flamed, as Jon shot his brother a grin before swallowing it.

As they walked out, Jon threatened, his voice low, a glint in his eye, "And keep your hands off her. She's my wife, and I will kick your ass if you mess with her."

David shook his head, smiling. Jon turned away. "And don't think I won't this time," Jon warned.

David sat quietly with Amanda as she slept. He noted that her breathing was shallow, and that it was punctuated by wheezing.

She stirred. "Jon?" she whispered, coughing.

David stood over her and felt her forehead. "It's David," he crooned. "I sent Jon home to take a nap and a shower. You still have a fever, Sis."

She closed her eyes. David poured some water in a cup and tried to entice her to sip some through a straw.

Alan Young walked into the room. He stopped and stared at David.

"Hello," he said uncertainly.

David smiled. "Hi, I'm David, Jon's brother."

"The resemblance is strong," Alan smiled back. "I'm Alan Young, Amanda's doctor." Walking up to the other side of the bed, he grinned down at Amanda. "Actually, Mandy and I go way back, to elementary school and Sunday School days. She stole my heart in first grade when she beat up some guy who pushed me down in the lunchroom."

"Sounds like something she'd do," David laughed.

"You're a doctor, aren't you?" Alan inquired.

"Yes," David acknowledged.

"He saved my life," Amanda chimed in, her voice hoarse.

The men grinned as she opened her eyes and stared up at Young. "It's about time you joined this conversation."

Alan bent down over Amanda. "Dear, you need to take another breathing treatment." As she frowned, he added, "We've got to break up this congestion in the lungs. It will strangle you." He smoothed her hair away from her forehead and smiled. "It's better than the old remedy of beating your chest."

"We could always do that as well," David joked, his eyes dancing wickedly.

"You seem to be making a lot of hospital calls," she complained weakly.

"I have a couple of very special patients." Alan's eyes twinkled as he examined the IV bags. "They're both hard-headed and as difficult to herd as cats."

"I'll make sure she takes the treatments," David promised. They discussed the dosage and frequency.

Alan added gravely, "You did right in sending Jon home a while. Jon really needs to rest and keep his strength up. Mandy here is a handful. She was a very sick girl last night, and I'm going to do all I can to get her well, or Doc Howells will have my head on a platter."

Jon drove home, his mother chattering all the while about the previous night's dinner party and the old family friends who had been there. He was unable to concentrate on her words, the picture of Amanda's distress the previous night still fresh in his mind. The exhaustion is taking over, he decided.

"You haven't listened to a word I said," his mother accused.

"I'm sorry." Jon was rueful, as he dragged himself back to the present. "I'm just so worried about Amanda. I should be there with her."

"You aren't going to do her any favors if you get sick," Gloria protested. "I wish you had told us about her, and that we'd have had a chance to meet her before the wedding." His mother was reproachful.

"I'm sorry," he repeated himself. "But Amanda had said yes twice before, only for something to happen to botch it. When the opportunity presented itself, I took it."

"But why the big hurry?" Gloria Connor was insistent.

"Because I love her," Jon replied patiently. "I didn't want to wait another minute."

"Not even long enough for us to make it to the wedding?"

"No," Jon was direct. He glanced at his mother. "I'm sorry if I hurt you, but I love her more than anything. She really is wonderful, Mom. I know you will love her too once you get to know her. Give her a chance."

"Jon, I am not averse to her. She seems to be a lovely girl. But if she is so wonderful, why did she stand you up twice before?"

"It's a long story," Jon responded, as he turned off the highway onto a dirt road.

His mother started. "Where are we going?"

"Home is off the beaten path," Jon smiled tightly.

"You live out here in the middle of nowhere?"

"Actually, it's a little more isolated than this," Jon warned.

Gloria was so surprised she fell silent, and Jon negotiated the road until he made it to the gate at Fred's farm.

She looked around her confusedly. "Is this it? Why didn't you stop at the house instead of at the gate here?"

"Because we are not there yet," Jon quipped, as he stepped out of the car and waved at a man in work clothes, who stopped a tractor and jumped off, walking toward them.

As Jon opened the gate, Fred made it to him, peering into the car.

"Amanda is still in the hospital," Jon explained, as his mother nodded at Fred. "Fred, this is my mother Gloria Connor. Mom, this is Fred Vaughan, our neighbor."

He nodded politely to the woman. "Nice to meet you," he smiled briefly. Turning to Jon, he queried, "How is she?"

"It was a rough night for her," Jon's voice was tired. "She has pneumonia. Her fever was high, but miraculously dropped this morning."

"Joanna just left the house," Fred volunteered. "She came to clean my house this morning, and I sent her on up there, let her in to do yours. Figured it was the least I could do, being Amanda's sick and you look all in."

"Thanks, Fred," Jon smiled gratefully. "I'm going to get a shower and a couple hours' sleep. David is with her, and Mom wanted to see the place."

"I'll check in later to see if you need anything," Fred promised, nodding at Mrs. Connor.

Jon regained the car and drove through the gate. A few minutes later Jon rounded a corner, and Gloria caught her breath. The home, yard, barn and lake lay before her, pristine and inviting. In the yard were a couple of deer grazing. They looked up interestedly and loped off as Jon pulled up in front of the farmhouse.

"This is it?" she asked, awe in her voice.

"Yes." Jon looked at her quickly to note her reaction.

"It's so—so picturesque," she managed. "Did you buy this together?"

"No," Jon replied. "This was Amanda's before we met."

"So this is where Amanda lived with her former husband?" Gloria asked sharply.

"Yes. They bought the property from Fred and built this house." Jon paused. "Actually, with the demands of the Bureau being what they were, Andy did not have the opportunity to be here very much, and Amanda shunned the place after his death. She only moved back here and renovated the place about seven months ago."

Jon glanced at his mother and added defensively, "It wasn't much of a marital home, sadly, even as much as they loved each other. The interior is very different now from the time they lived here together."

Gloria looked at her son curiously. "Are you happy living out here in—" she paused, "in their home?"

"Actually, I am," Jon smiled at her. "I am amazed anew every day at the beauty and isolation of this place. The sights and sounds of nature, being away from the grind of daily existence, and living every day with Amanda, are indescribable." He paused. "I'm happier than I've ever been. I can understand Andy's fascination with the place now."

"It is lovely," she conceded, as they both climbed out of the car.

"Amanda told me the other day she was concerned about your reaction to the farm, whether you would consider it good enough for your son," he spoke as they walked up the steps and he punched in the security code.

"She did?" Gloria was intrigued as Jon opened the door and beckoned for her to precede him.

She stepped inside and looked around her at the neat and cheerful interior. Jon placed his keys on the console beside the door and watched her as she walked around surveying the room, looking out the French doors to the porch, deck and yard beyond, with the wooden dock stretching over the lake.

Jon yawned. "Make yourself at home," he stated. "On second thought, leave everything as it is," he grinned. "Amanda has rearranged the place several times trying to please me, despite my assurances that I like everything like it is."

"Shall I cook you something?" his mother asked.

"No," Jon smiled, his voice tired. "I know you want to be motherly, but I really don't want anything right now. I'll make a meatloaf sandwich when I wake up."

"Meatloaf sandwich?" Gloria arched her eyebrows.

"It's actually delicious. Amanda is a good cook," Jon assured her. "Just enjoy yourself. And if you go outside, watch out for Bozo."

"Bozo?" she echoed.

"The dog," Jon replied, knowing his mother disliked pets. "He is obedience trained, so will respond to 'sit', 'stay', 'heel', and 'down' in a firm tone of voice."

"You have a dog?" Gloria was astounded.

"Fred's dog, but Amanda's sworn protector." Jon yawned again. "Mom, I'm beat. I'll be upstairs for just a few winks."

Jon disappeared upstairs, and Gloria was left alone to wander the room. She looked at several framed photographs on the mantel and walls, noting one of Jon and another man with a marlin, and several of Jon and Amanda with others dressed in wedding finery, and Amanda with her arms around two small twin boys.

She explored the other rooms downstairs, noting a guest room and another room, which appeared to be a bedroom remodeled to be used as their dressing room. Each of the rooms possessed its own bathroom. There was a study with daybed and treadmill.

She resisted the temptation to look through the desk drawers in the living area. However, there was opened mail in a glazed ceramic inbox, and she peeked at it.

"My heavens!" she whispered as she noted the balances listed on the bank statements. Amanda must not want for money, she thought. Jon did not tell us she was wealthy. But why would she live here and not in some huge home in town?

Gloria checked the bar, then walked into the kitchen, noting the crisp clean glow of the white cabinetry against colorful blue and yellow tiled backsplash. She examined the oven and the refrigerator/freezer, both appearing clean and in good order. Gloria also took in Amanda's collection of china and crystal, some quite old and valuable, displayed in a built-in glass-paneled breakfront in the large dining area. Charming, she thought. She has good taste.

Returning to the living room, she looked through the wall of bookcases until she discovered some photograph albums. Pulling two to review, she let herself out onto the back screened porch and seated herself on the comfortable pillow-lined large porch swing. Although it was warm outside, the overhead ceiling fan kept a refreshing breeze stirred.

Reclining, she opened the first volume and studied the pictures. She noted all the different faces, but could not figure out the relationships. There were notations to Mom, Dad, Jeff, Mandy, Miss Marjy, Mr. Jerrod, Monica, Billy, Charlie, Alan, Ralph, Andy, and later photos of some of the same persons. She resolved to ask about Amanda's family. She saw a wedding photo of Amanda with another man, the same man in the fishing picture with Jon. Ah, so that must have been Andrew.

She became drowsy in the swing and leaned back against the comfortable pillows. Staring out at the lake and a long blue heron picking its way around the bank, she fell asleep.

She didn't know how long she lay there, but she was awakened by the sound of mewing at the back screen door. She walked over and spied a black and white cat, which looked up at her demandingly.

Gloria frowned. The cat continued its litany, seemingly unconcerned at the woman's demeanor.

She went inside and found a saucer and some milk, and brought back the offering to the cat, which pranced in past her and stood impatiently waiting until she placed the saucer on the floor. The cat then calmly lapped up the milk and sat washing herself contentedly, before walking back to the screen door and requesting exit.

Gloria picked up the albums and returned inside the house. She could hear water running upstairs. It soon stopped, and several minutes later Jon reappeared, clean shaven, dressed casually and toweling his hair dry.

The Connors' Crisis

"Well?" he baited her. "Did your 'research' net any answers?" He bit back a grin.

"I didn't snoop. It's a charming place. I like it."

Jon headed toward the kitchen. Gloria followed him.

"What are you doing?" she asked, piqued.

"Time for meatloaf," he laughed. "Want some?"

She started to demur, but realized she was hungry. "Don't you want us to get something in town? I thought I saw a nice restaurant on the way in."

"Probably Jack's," he surmised. "It is, but it doesn't beat this."

He pulled out two containers. Soon he had two plates prepared and put them in the microwave, one at a time, and hurriedly set two places.

At first Gloria turned up her nose at the look of the meatloaf covered in gravy on toast with English peas on the side, but the aroma overcame her hesitancy as Jon placed the plate before her. He completed the meal by preparing her a glass of iced tea.

A moment later he joined her with a plate of his own. He bowed his head a minute silently, then looked up at her. "Dig in," Jon commanded lightly.

Gloria was at first surprised to see Jon pray, then to watch him devour the dish before him. She tentatively took a bite. It was good. She found herself eating voraciously, then looked up to see Jon watching, the beginnings of a smile on his face.

"What?" she demanded, peeved.

"So you like it?" He tried to hide his grin.

"It's very good," she admitted.

"I'll tell my wife you approve," Jon laughed out loud.

Later that evening as David drove them back to the condo, he unabashedly pried. "Well? What did you think of Amanda? The farm?"

"You didn't tell me she was rich," his mother complained.

"Well, that is pretty recent. She inherited a big chunk of money last year from her real mother. But she wasn't exactly indigent before that," David laughed at the expression on his mother's face. "Amanda is a hard worker, a successful attorney much in demand around here."

"Her real mother?" Gloria echoed. "What is that about?"

David glanced over at his mother. "Why don't you have Amanda and Jon over just for a quiet private visit and dinner? No outsiders. Quit trying to impress her or embarrass her. I'll bet she'll tell you anything you want to know."

He paused. "I guess you didn't know that Senator Thomas Whitmore is her father-in-law."

"I didn't know," she breathed sharply. "She is that Amanda Childs, the one from the papers? You mean Andy -?" her voice trailed off.

"Yeah," David nodded, his eyes on the road. "That was a recent shock. Jon says Amanda wants you to know everything about her, and to be the one to tell you about herself. The last year of her life has been exciting, to say the least. Jon says she is in fear you will hear rumors and not like her."

He reached over and took his mother's hand. "Mom, give her a chance. I think you will really like her. And she loves Jon terribly."

Gloria's features softened. "He is head over heels about her. I've never seen him like this before. I just want her to be good enough for him, and not hurt him, like the last one did."

David retorted, "I just hope he is good enough for her. Amanda's the best thing that has ever happened to Jon."

CHAPTER 3

The next day Jon had run by the farm to shave and change, and was about to leave for the hospital. Amanda's cell phone, still plugged into its charger on the desk, started ringing, and he picked it up. The number was long-distance and he didn't recognize it.

"Hello?" he spoke into the receiver.

"Um—is Amanda there?" the male voice stammered.

Jon felt a momentary pang of jealousy. "No. This is Jon. May I help you?"

"Uh—Jon, this is Jeff Andrews, Mandy's—Amanda's brother," he heard the voice reply hesitantly.

"Jeff," Jon replied warmly. "Good to talk to you. How are things in Philly?"

"Fine," the voice came back strained. "I was just calling to—to leave a message really."

"I don't know if Amanda has talked to you in the last week," Jon remarked pleasantly. "She's in the hospital."

"Hospital?" Jeff sounded surprised. "N-no, we haven't talked in a couple of weeks. Is she OK?"

"She's developed pneumonia, a complication from her injuries in the accident," Jon explained. "She's been really sick. I was really worried night before last."

"Accident?" Jeff queried anxiously. "Was she hurt badly? She hasn't said much about that. So it was pretty serious?"

Jon was stunned. "I know she has talked to you since we got married," he submitted slowly. "She didn't tell you?"

Jeff's voice was stilted. "No, but then she didn't invite us to the wedding either."

Jon took a deep breath. "Don't blame her for that. That was my fault," Jon apologized. "I didn't give her any advance warning. My parents weren't invited either. I asked her while she was in the hospital, the doctor released her, and we went straight to the church and tied the knot."

"Just like that?" Jeff asked, surprised.

"Just like that," Jon replied, smiling. "So there were only the locals here who got word that it was happening and showed up. I'm sorry, Jeff. We didn't mean to offend you by excluding you. We just didn't want to wait any longer."

"Is she OK?" Jon heard the concern in his voice.

"She's still pretty sick, but the doctor says she will recover. I'm on my way back to the hospital now. I'll tell her you called."

"I—I," Jeff was clearly uncomfortable, "I just wanted to let her know we aren't coming for Memorial Day."

"Oh," Jon was surprised. "I'm sorry. She is excited about seeing you all and introducing us. She has taken a lease on the Barnes' old summerhouse and was hoping you'd like to stay there."

"Um, ah—there's just so much going on here. We've been really busy. I think we're taking Desiree to Disney World instead." Jeff was abrupt. "Listen, I need to go. If you will let her know for me, I appreciate it."

"Sure. I'm sure she'll want to call you back," Jon declared, puzzled. Thoughtfully he pocketed her cell phone to take with him.

He mulled over the conversation, troubled. Jon knew that Amanda and Jeff spoke by phone every couple of weeks, but Jeff had not returned her call the last couple of attempts she had made. He also knew that she had been hoping to set up a get-together for Jeff and some of his old school buddies during his family's annual Memorial Day week trip to the beach, which was coming up very soon.

Jon hesitated about telling her about Jeff's call, because he knew she was still weaker than she let him know. But Jon also worried about what her reaction would be if he didn't tell her and she found out later, and he didn't know what plans she had already made that might need to be canceled.

So later that day, Jon detailed the phone call back to Amanda, and she immediately asked for her cell phone.

"Are you sure you're up to this? I mean, you're still having trouble catching your breath," Jon protested gently.

"I will worry about it until I know what's going on," she reasoned, holding her hand out.

He handed her the phone, and she placed a call to Jeff.

"Hi, Jeffie," she greeted him brightly, her voice still hoarse. "Now what's this about your going to Disney World instead of coming here? You can't do both?"

"Phyllis has decided we shouldn't—shouldn't go to the beach this year."
Jeff was clearly reluctant to talk.

"Jeffie, if it's a matter of money . . ." Amanda began.

"No!" he objected forcefully. "I don't need any of your 'inheritance money', damn it."

There was a second of silence on the line. Amanda broke it, her voice weak. "I'm sorry. I didn't know that was a sore subject."

He remained silent.

"OK, Jeff, tell me what is really going on. You know I count on seeing you, and you're already so busy we only get together twice a year. What's wrong?"

There was an uncomfortable pause on the line. "Phyllis is—she's embarrassed by the media coverage, all that you've been involved with—with down there, the criminal stuff and all that," he stammered. "She doesn't think we should subject Desiree to that. So she thinks we should—should—should distance ourselves from you, protect her from exposure," he finished miserably.

Jon noticed Amanda's features change, and watched in horror as the tears fell unheeded down her cheeks. "You mean I'm a bad influence? Jeff, you know I didn't ask for any of this. It wasn't my fault. I would give anything if it hadn't happened. I'm sorry if you are ashamed of me."

"I'm not ashamed," he countered, his voice desperate. "But—"

"But Phyllis is," Amanda completed for him, her voice almost a whisper. "Oh, my God. Please don't do this. I love you, Jeff. You're the only brother I have. Won't you reconsider? Come down for July 4." She began wheezing, and tried to swallow it, pushing to make her voice stronger as she held her chest, biting back a sob.

"I don't know," Jeff whispered. "Phyllis thinks it is better this way. Maybe I can change her mind before next summer."

"Next summer? Does this mean I'm not invited up for Thanksgiving either?" Amanda demanded shakily, the hoarseness taking over. She coughed painfully. "Are you not going to talk to me? I won't see Desiree? Jeff . . ." Her voice ended in a sob, and she started shaking, overcome.

"Mandy," he tried to soothe her, "I didn't mean to upset you. You're sick, Jon says. Forget all this. It will blow over after a while." He paused. "Are you OK? Mandy?"

"I need to—" she choked, losing her voice as her throat constricted. She gasped.

"Mandy, are you there? Are you OK?"

Amanda, her chest heaving as she fought for air, dropped the phone beside her on the bed and turned away, her body convulsing with silent sobs, unable to make sound.

"Amanda, what is it?" Jon, alarmed, asked her, grasping her hand.

She refused to face him, her back still to him, gripping the bed rail, gasping and shaking. Jon immediately pushed the call button for the nurse and quickly moved to the other side of the bed. He placed the oxygen mask over her face. "Breathe in, Amanda," he begged.

David Connor walked into the room. Right behind him a nurse scurried in, pushing past David and murmuring an apology as she strode to the bed.

"She was on the phone to her brother and became upset," Jon said anxiously, looking up and seeing David. "She can't breathe."

David strode quickly up to the bed, took one look, and grabbed the nurse's arm. He gave quick instructions.

She just gaped at him.

"I'm a doctor, dammit," he shouted. "Page Alan Young—he's in the building somewhere. But do what I told you first, or we'll lose her."

The nurse disappeared. David turned to Jon. "Let's turn her back around," he ordered. "Turn loose, Amanda." His voice was no-nonsense, brisk.

She obeyed slowly. "Now," David commanded.

Amanda's eyes were wide in fear, and she was shaking, still crying, rigid, trying to suck in air. "Amanda, listen to me," David said crisply, business-like, adjusting the oxygen level. "Focus. You've got to relax. Relax the muscles. Let's raise the bed a bit. Open your mouth. Take it in. C'mon, girl."

He could hear some sound. Reaching down, he found her cell phone and handed it to Jon. "There's someone still on there," he said tersely.

Jon cut off the phone and absently laid it on the tray table, his eyes wide and face drawn, hovering and watching David. The nurse appeared with a vial and hypodermic. David grabbed a pair of gloves and donned them, snatched up the needle, quickly measured a dose, and administered it to Amanda.

Dr. Young walked in. David didn't look up. "I know what I'm doing," he said quickly. "I have done this before."

Alan quickly walked around Jon as Jon moved out of the way. Young lifted Amanda's eyelids, checking her reactivity. "Are we going to have to intubate her?" he asked David anxiously. "Mandy? Can you hear me? Stay with me."

She was unresponsive, her eyes closed, her breathing shallow, raspy, asthmatic.

The Connors' Crisis

"Do as I say, Sis," David persisted, his voice tinged in anger. Jon looked over at his brother, who had transformed before him. David was watching her closely. "Inserting a tube without any anesthesia would be quite uncomfortable, but if this doesn't work . . . . If she will just relax, dammit," he said softly. "We'll know in just a minute. If I have to, we'll do it right here."

Alan turned to the nurse and gave orders, and she hurried off.

After a moment, Amanda's rigidity began to slacken, and as it did, her breathing gradually became less labored. Her eyes fluttered open, and David stood over her, his hand smoothing out her hair from her forehead. "That's right. Look at me."

She obeyed. David crooned. "Keep your eyes on me. Clear your mind. There's nothing more important than breathing in, breathing out right this minute. That's your mission. I order you to accept it. Nod your head if you understand me."

She nodded dazedly.

"That's good," he smiled at her. "Are you feeling better?"

She nodded again.

"Now if you don't follow orders and remain calm, keep from upsetting yourself, and throwing yourself into another high fever, we're going to have to stick one of those old nasty tubes down your throat."

Alan added, "And you're a lawyer. You know you don't want anything to interfere with your ability to talk."

"Jon?" she whispered weakly, her voice barely audible.

"He's right here," Alan assured her.

David turned to Jon, as Charlie Petrino walked into the room. "She'll probably be asleep in a bit."

Alan nodded. "We'll watch carefully. If her levels don't increase, we may still have to insert a tube."

"What happened?" Charlie demanded, looking down at her, then at Jon, his eyes wide.

Jon stepped back, and Alan joined him and Charlie a few feet from the foot of her bed. Jon's voice was low. "I made a serious mistake and told her that her brother had called, something about their not making it down here for Memorial Day weekend. She insisted on calling him back, got really upset, and couldn't breathe."

"What did he say?"

Jon relayed what he heard of Amanda's conversation.

Charlie flushed with rage. "That son of a bitch. That's his wife talking. I thought Jeff had more spine than that."

45

"Her own brother is ashamed of Amanda? Why? She can't help that the media has paraded her troubles all over the front pages," Jon mused aloud, his anger barely veiled.

"Mandy has helped Jeff through many a scrape with his wife," Alan submitted softly. "And she dotes on that little girl. They only see each other twice a year. Amanda generally foots the bill for the trip down here just so that she can spend time with them, so it's not like they're out any money. And Jeff is an engineer, has a great job, makes a nice income."

"Why only twice a year?" Jon was surprised.

"Because that's the only time Phyllis allows it," Charlie muttered angrily.

Amanda made some sound, and Jon moved over to the bed. Charlie snatched up her cell phone. "Excuse me a minute," he told Alan, striding out of the room.

He walked down the hall to an exit. He punched the last number dialed. A female voice answered.

"Phyllis, I need to talk to Jeff," he said shortly.

"But he's on another line," he heard her peevish reply.

"You tell him Charlie Petrino is on the line, and if he does not talk to me, I will have felony charges filed and have his sorry ass extradited to Florida for attempted murder. If you think you're embarrassed now, I'll be happy to oblige with more."

A minute later, he heard Jeff. "Charlie? What's happening?" His voice was anxious.

"What in the hell did you say to her?" Charlie was livid. "Did you not have any clue not to distress her, that she is seriously ill?"

"Y-yes, but she called and demanded to know why we weren't coming to Florida." Jeff was defensive. "Is she OK? I lost her. I heard noises, but no one came back on the line. I was just trying to call the hospital."

"She almost died just now. You upset her, and she hyperventilated. Her air passages closed up on her. If her brother-in-law hadn't happened to walk in, she'd be dead."

"Oh, God," he heard Jeff breathe, his voice quavering. "I'm sorry. Oh, geez. What can I do?"

"You and Desiree should get on the next plane down here to see her," Charlie ordered. "And leave that bitch of a wife at home this time."

"But—" Jeff started.

"Do you give a damn about your sister or not?" Charlie asked hotly. "As much as she's done for you? I'm sure she or Jon will reimburse you, if it's the money you're worried about."

"It's not the money," Jeff spurted angrily.

The Connors' Crisis

"Here is my number." Charlie reeled it off. "Call me when you've made the reservation. I'll pick you up. Show her you have some balls and care for her enough to come see her without her having to beg," Charlie spat. He hung up.

He walked back into the hospital. As he reached her room, Alan walked out and spied him.

"Do you think that was wise?" Alan posited quietly.

"What?" Charlie was gruff.

"I know what you did." Alan shook his head. "If Jeff has so little gumption as to upset her when she's sick, do you think it's going to be any better if you force him to come down here for a face-to-face appearance?"

"I don't care. But they don't have to keep the kid from seeing her aunt," Charlie was defensive. "And Jeff can at least pretend he cares. Amanda has saved his ass enough times. She certainly does not deserve any more fallout because of the things that have happened to her."

Alan smiled broadly. Charlie scowled at him. "What?" His jaw jutted in irritation. "Stop it. It's not what you think."

"I'm sure it's not." Alan opened the door to her room and walked back in, cutting off Charlie's chance to retort. He slunk in after Alan, unobtrusively laying the phone back on the tray table.

Amanda was falling asleep, and her breathing was regular but raspy. Jon did not turn around, but David looked up. "I apologize for stepping in," he smiled apologetically at Alan. "But I was afraid we might lose her unless something was done immediately."

"I'm glad you walked in when you did," Alan nodded gravely.

"I am, too," Jon murmured, glancing over at his brother.

David gazed at Alan Young. "If you won't be upset, I have nothing better to do than stay a while and keep an eye on her. Besides, I'm certified in Florida."

"She's in good hands, then," Alan countered.

"I need to get on back to work, but I'll be glad to spell you," Charlie said to Jon. "But," Charlie held up both hands, "it is only an offer, and you don't have to bite my head off for making it."

Jon's eyes met Charlie's, and he grinned as Alan chuckled. "I'm sorry, Charlie, and I do appreciate it. I promise if I need help, you'll be the first one I call. Please let Ralph and Claire know about Amanda, so I don't catch grief from him."

The next day Amanda had surprise visitors. Jeffrey Andrews and Desiree walked into the room.

Desiree, her eyes sparkling, bounced beside the bed. "Auntie, are you feeling better?"

"Now I am," Amanda smiled tiredly, as she removed the oxygen mask and squeezed Desiree's hand affectionately.

Jon walked in behind them. "You need to keep that on," he admonished her.

"Just a minute and I'll put it back on," Amanda demurred weakly. "How's my favorite girl?"

"Just fine. I made all As in school, and we're going to Disney World," Desiree bubbled happily.

"I'm happy for you. Tell Goofy hi for me," Amanda smiled. "Desiree, this is my husband Jon. He's been looking forward to meeting you." She paused, the exertion tiring her.

Desiree held out her hand for Jon to shake.

"In fact, why don't you and Jon go get us both a soft drink? I'm dying for one," Amanda suggested.

"Sure," Desiree looked at Jon, smiling her instant acceptance. Jon was mesmerized.

As they left, Amanda looked at Jeff. "You really shouldn't have."

His eyebrows arched. "But I wanted to."

"Bullshit," Amanda whispered. "Who called and threatened you?"

Jeff looked sheepish. "Charlie did," he admitted ruefully, briefly outlining the conversation. "But he's absolutely right. He met us at the airport and drove us here. Alan let Desiree come in."

He took her hand. "I'm so sorry, Mandy. I know none of that was your fault. But Phyllis was so—"

"Insistent?" Amanda supplied.

"That's the nice way of putting it," Jeff hung his head. "And I was mad, so I didn't fight her."

"Mad?" Amanda turned her eyes on him questioningly.

"I found out that my scholarship to Auburn was actually paid for in full by Marjorie and Jerrod Witherspoon."

He saw the stunned expression on Amanda's face. "You didn't know?" he demanded.

"No," she coughed, taking some oxygen.

"I went to a conference at the university a few weeks ago, and the Vice-President called me aside and talked about you and all the news. Then he let me in on that piece of information. I was embarrassed. I didn't call you or come down to see you while I was down."

"I'm so sorry," Amanda said softly, squeezing his hand. "I don't know why they did that."

"Mr. Witherspoon was always really nice to me and asked me questions like what did I want to do when I grew up. I guess that must have fueled their plan to do that." Jeff looked away unhappily.

Amanda pulled the mask off. "Jeffie, I can't believe if they financed your education they would be so devious about it. That is an established scholarship, and I'm sure you got it fair and square. But I'm sure whatever they did was for a very good reason. And I'm certain Mom and Dad didn't know. You know how Dad was about accepting any charity.

"Besides," she sighed, "you deserved it. You were an excellent student, just like Desiree. You have nothing to be ashamed of."

Jeff looked up at her face and noted her paleness. "Are you all right? Put your oxygen mask on. Just take your time; don't get excited."

She obeyed. Jeff smiled sheepishly. "I got really scared when Charlie called, Mandy. Charlie said you almost died. And you didn't tell me how bad this accident was." He stared at her accusingly. "It wasn't an accident, was it? I always knew that Billy Barnes was an ass."

Amanda looked at him questioningly. "Charlie told me about this Evie woman trying to kill you."

"Desiree -?" Amanda breathed in sharply, alarmed.

"No, she had her headphones on, watching her movie on the way here," Jeff read her mind and reassured her.

"Charlie needs to keep his nose out of my business," Amanda muttered.

"Charlie's always had his nose in your business," Jeff laughed at her. "Why didn't you marry him? Dad and old Sheriff Petrino always hoped that would happen."

Amanda, suddenly uncomfortable, countered, "Jeffie, just why did you marry Phyllis?"

Jeff looked away, his laughter dying. He swallowed. "You can do the math - because she was pregnant." He shut his eyes momentarily. "And I wouldn't give anything for my daughter," he replied sadly. "She is the joy of my life."

"She is wonderful," Amanda whispered through the mask, grasping his hand.

Jeff stared at her a minute, as though wanting to say something.

"What is it?" she demanded.

"You know, I always knew you weren't really my sister," Jeff muttered, his voice low.

Amanda looked at him intently. "I didn't. But even so, you have always been, and still are, my brother," she reproached him quietly. "I love you, and I still need for you to be that brother."

Jeff flushed. "I'm sorry, Mandy. I just meant that I always knew that Mom wasn't really pregnant. And I knew that Mrs. Witherspoon was hanging around, always hovering, asking about you. I just put two and two together." He paused. "I still love you, and you are still my kid sister." He was clearly embarrassed. "I admit I was envious when I heard you inherited all that money. But I would never do anything to hurt you. I'm sorry. I do love you."

He looked up and stared out the window. "I should stand up to Phyllis. Charlie is right—she is a bitch. But I do love her, although nowadays I have to remind myself of that fact. But I look at Desiree and it all comes back."

Desiree and Jon burst back into the room. Desiree announced, "Uncle Jon said you could only have a little."

"Meanie," Amanda took off the mask and smiled, as Jon poured a little soft drink into a cup and provided a straw.

"No, he's right. If you are sick, you need to do what the doctor says."

Amanda looked at her. "Did he bribe you to say that?"

"No, ma'am," Desiree replied, biting her lip and glancing over at Jon, a hint of a mischievous smile on her lips.

They all laughed.

They had a delightful visit for about an hour, until Alan came in. "I hate to break this up, but I have it on good authority that my patient is not wearing her oxygen mask, and I really want her to get well."

Jeff stood. "I wish we could stay longer. But I really have to be at work tomorrow. The boss had a minor heart attack when I told him I wasn't going to be in today." He bent over and kissed Amanda's cheek.

Desiree ran up to the bed. "Daddy says we are coming on July 4 to the beach, if it's OK with you," she announced excitedly.

Amanda's smile was winning. "I can't wait." She clasped Jeff's hand gratefully, as Charlie came to collect them.

"And Charlie, don't be abusing your authority any more," she ordered quietly.

He just grinned and winked at her as they left.

CHAPTER 4

A couple days later Amanda was much improved, and was breathing more normally. She had bribed an orderly, while Jon was gone on an errand she contrived, to help her into a robe and wheelchair, then wheeled herself down the hall to the cardiac care unit to find out about Dr. Howells, who had undergone surgery the previous day for stints to be inserted.

She managed to sneak into the CCU, and suddenly she came face-to-face with the charge nurse, a towering male who scowled at her. "Mrs. Childs, I mean, Connor, you don't need to be in here," he admonished her gently, although the set of his jaw indicated he was perturbed at her advent.

"I thought we were on a first name basis, Jimmy," Amanda purred charmingly. "Everyone has been so busy, so I took it upon myself to come check on Doc Howells." She looked past the nurse. "He's in that room, right?"

"I don't think you ought—"

"Oh, hell, let her in," Dr. Cardet spoke up behind the nurse. "She's a damned lawyer, and you're wasting perfectly good oxygen fighting with her."

Amanda smiled her sweetest. "You know you love me, Doc. Think of all the times I got you excused from court."

"You have no business being out of bed," he was stern. "I only know that when Dr. Young finds you are not in your room, he will thrash you." Cardet's eyes twinkled, despite his severe tone. He walked up and grabbed the handles of her wheelchair and pushed her forward into the room. "Only a minute," he insisted.

The sight of Howells lying in bed very still brought her up short. She closed her eyes and swallowed. But he stirred and opened his eyes.

"You have visitors," Cardet informed him gently. A woman rose from a chair in the corner and came forward. Until then Amanda had not seen her.

"Gwen?" Howells' voice was weak.

"Yes, Malcolm," she reached over and kissed his cheek, squeezing his hand affectionately. "You certainly have a way of scaring a woman," she smiled tremulously. "And look who else is here."

She helped push a button to raise the head of the bed a bit, and he caught sight of Amanda. "What are you doing out of bed?" he demanded. "Where is your keeper?"

"I sent him on an errand so that I could check on you," Amanda retorted as Cardet pushed her chair forward and she was able to touch his fingers. "You really look like hell," she added mischievously.

"Thanks, dear," he grimaced. "We can't all be as lovely as you."

"At least Gwen is here to keep an eye on you, although I doubt even her ability to keep you out of trouble." Amanda winked at Gwen, who smiled back, tears in her eyes. She really cares for him, Amanda thought happily.

"I think the problem has been averted," Cardet announced. "I know, Malcolm, you have been pretty good with diet and exercise, but the stress has finally caught up with you. When you brush with death, some adjustments need to be made. You and I will have that discussion a little later. For now, you need to rest."

His trained ear could tell that Amanda's effort had cost her in energy, even though she tried to hide the wheezing. Cardet turned to the two women. "Sorry to break up this party, but you two will have to leave for now. He'll be ready for you come visiting hours."

Gwen spoke up. "Here, let me wheel you to your room, Amanda."

Reluctantly they took their leave of Howells, and the two women left the CCU together.

As they moved down the hall, Gwen asked her suddenly, "What would you think if I stayed at Malcolm's house a little while to take care of him once he is released?"

Amanda bit back a grin. "Gwen, I think it would be a great idea, if you think you can handle him."

Gwen blushed. "I didn't want him to be the subject of little-old-lady gossip, but Dr. Cardet thinks he will need a little help at first, mainly to slow him down." She added shyly, "And my daughter Janine is in town, on the outs with her husband again."

"So you'd like an excuse to be scarce from home. Sounds as if you might be killing two birds with one stone," Amanda laughed slyly. "At least two," she added, her smile spreading across her face.

"I'm really fond of Malcolm," Gwen admitted sheepishly. "His heart attack gave me quite a scare."

"Me too," Amanda nodded fervently. "I'd like it if the two of you end up together."

"But I fear that won't happen. He cannot stand Janine, and has been really vocal about her," Gwen lamented softly. "And sometimes I can't stand her either. I don't know where I went wrong there."

"I believe her intentions are generally good," Amanda countered cautiously.

"Yes, and the road to hell is littered with good intentions," Gwen remarked drily. "But I doubt even her intentions. She just creates such havoc with her gossip and her unwelcome involvement. I always dread to see her visit."

"We'll figure out something," Amanda reached up and squeezed Gwen's hand.

Gwen smiled in response. "Which room is yours?"

"That one, where the crowd is congregating," Amanda pointed. As they approached, they could see both Jon and Alan Young standing in the hallway, Alan perturbed and Jon's anger barely masked.

Reaching the two men, Amanda started to speak, but Alan held up his hand. "I for one don't want to hear it. Mandy, there are sick people in this hospital. You are one of them. There are all sorts of contagions floating around, and in your weakened condition you are susceptible to them. And we don't know but what you could be infectious as well."

"Bull," she rebuked softly, and Jon flushed. "No one would tell me how Doc was, and I took matters into my own hands."

"I need to get back to work," Gwen excused herself, sensing the battle about to erupt.

"Later," Amanda nodded, as Jon took over the handles of the wheelchair and propelled her into her room, Alan following.

Alan sighed. "Jon, she's your wife. If you want to beat her, I'll testify the marks are self-inflicted."

"When can I go home?" Amanda ignored the gibe, although her breathing was labored.

"If you get through the night taking the breathing treatments I have prescribed and with no fever, I'll consider it tomorrow, but only after you have completed another regimen of antibiotics."

"Can I get a strait jacket for her upon discharge?" Jon scowled, his eyes softening as Amanda stared at him and licked her lips.

"I'll tie her up myself," Alan remarked, as they managed to get her back into bed.

He checked her temperature and listened to her chest. "You are better, but you are not well yet. Mandy, Doc will bust my balls if I let you go home and anything happens." Alan looked at her pleadingly. "You have got to promise to follow my orders and obey your husband."

"But of course," she gazed at the two of them guilelessly.

He shook his head and addressed Jon. "She's all yours. I'll be back."

As Alan exited, Mandy took Jon's hand and drew him to her. "Don't be mad," she whispered pleadingly. "Besides, I want you badly, Mr. Connor."

He glared at her, but she saw the beginnings of a smile playing around his lips as he sat down on the bed beside her. He gently pinned her down to the pillows and kissed her. "I want you badly, too, Mrs. Connor."

She whispered, "Go lock the door."

But he laughed. "No can do. If you make it through the night OK and are discharged tomorrow, I'll see what I can do."

She smiled at him slyly. "I'll want a homemade cheeseburger too," she coaxed.

"In what order?" he teased her.

Alan released her the next day under strict orders. Jon drove her home to the farm, and life resumed. Amanda, weakened from the episode, did take things easier, and was complaisant for the first week.

Two weeks later, Alan reluctantly released Amanda to go back to work part-time and light duty only, and Amanda prevailed upon Jon to take his new post at the law firm in Destin. As they waved goodbye to each other on the highway going in opposite directions, she felt a pang of melancholy and realized suddenly that she hadn't wanted their exile to end.

But she threw herself back into work with a vengeance, and kept a daily vigil on Dr. Howells, who was being diligently cared for by Gwen. He had also returned to work, albeit his duty was also light, because Drs. Cardet and Young forced him to take it easy.

One day she decided to swing by Dr. Howells' house to check on him at lunchtime. When she rang the doorbell, Janine, Gwen's daughter, answered the door. Janine, who was about six years Amanda's senior and a former classmate of her brother Jeff, scowled at her.

"Hello, Janine," Amanda spoke pleasantly. "I'm here to see Doc."

Janine held the door partially closed. "He's not seeing visitors right now," she said.

"I'm not a visitor." Amanda put pressure on the door with her good arm. Janine, surprised, tried to block her progress, but Amanda pushed past Janine.

"You know, Doctor Howells and my mother would be happier if you didn't barge in here all the time," Janine spoke rancorously, following Amanda.

"That's excellent advice for many people," Amanda retorted drily.

Janine was oblivious to Amanda's meaning. Warming to her subject, she opened her mouth to continue.

"Janine! What are you doing still here?" Gwen's voice was reproving as she appeared in the hallway. "I asked you to leave thirty minutes ago." She walked up to her daughter. "Have you been snooping?"

Janine grew defensive. "Well, it will be my house too once you get married."

"No, it will not," Dr. Howells had appeared behind Gwen. "You have no business going through my checkbook, and nothing of mine will ever belong to you."

Janine flushed angrily. Howells looked tenderly at Gwen. "I'm sorry, dear, but I will not tolerate her chaos in my own home. Please show her out and make sure she goes this time. And Janine, now that you are clearly aware of my feelings, you are not to grace this home again." Turning, his voice softened. "Amanda, please come on in. Gwen will join us momentarily."

Amanda smiled shamefacedly at Gwen, who was obviously embarrassed by her daughter's meddling. Amanda hesitated, but Howells beckoned to her.

She walked up to him and kissed him on the cheek, as he led her into the study. "I'm glad to see you are still improving," he smiled at her.

"How are you feeling?" Amanda inquired.

"Much better. It's amazing what improved blood flow will do for a person," he chuckled.

"I'm sorry I caused a scene back there," she apologized.

"No, my dear. You are my heir, dear. No one has any right to deny you anything of mine. This is your home when I am gone."

"Me?" Amanda gasped. "Why me?"

"Because I know you don't need it, and that you will put the estate to good use. Besides, Gwen insisted that she wanted nothing of mine if we should marry, and wants prenuptial agreements drawn up. I don't like that, but understand that she does not want her daughter's interference in our lives, and she feels that is the easiest way to dissuade Janine. But as long as her hellion of a daughter is around, it creates friction. And I'm just too old to swallow it and be nice to her."

"But doesn't it hurt Gwen?" Amanda asked softly.

"I'm embarrassed as hell by her," Gwen replied, as she glided into the room.

"I'm sorry. I didn't mean to be talking about you." Amanda gazed at her sadly.

"Don't be sorry. I made a mistake in marrying her father, then in order to keep harmony after the divorce I agreed to joint custody. She is the product of her father's manipulation and my weakness." Gwen was somber. "Now I see my own grandchildren being pulled the same way between their parents, and I am helpless to do anything but provide some respite for them. But I don't do it often enough, because I don't want to be around my own daughter."

Gwen's eyes shone with tears. Amanda crossed over to her and embraced the woman. "I'm so sorry."

"Amanda," sniffed Gwen, "you are so understanding. With all that you've gone through, your heart is still tender, loving and forgiving. How can that be?"

"Why, I don't see myself that way at all," laughed Amanda. "I'd hope that people would only see the tough mean side."

Howells and Gwen both laughed with her.

"When are you two going to tie the knot?" Amanda prodded.

"Not until we come to a resolution about Janine," Howells stated emphatically.

Surprised, she looked at Gwen, who nodded in agreement. "I'm not sure if a talk alone will do any good. We tried today. You see the result. But I may have to evict her and send Henry to come retrieve her."

"Well, if there's anything I can do to facilitate a marriage between you two, count me in," Amanda grinned.

Amanda made an appointment to meet with Arnold Freeman, leaving early from work one afternoon. She was surprised to see him waiting for her.

"My last session was completed early, and I'm a little anxious to hear how things are," he smiled as he took her hand. "Your life has certainly been full."

"It has," she agreed as he led her into the room and indicated for her to sit.

"First, I want to hear from you about what is happening in your life since I've seen you last," Freeman insisted.

"You mean, other than almost getting killed again?" she retorted.

"I'm sorry that your life has been fraught with danger." He was solemn. "But if you are happy now, then I am most certainly happy for you. How did you come to the decision that Jon was indeed right for you?"

"Everyone was advising me not to put my life on hold any longer." She stared down at her hands. "Even when I agreed to visit Stephen Marks at the prison, he advised me that deep inside I knew what was important, what would make me happy. Right then I decided I didn't want to wait any longer." She smiled, and Freeman sensed an inner glow. "I went and found Jon."

She described the events of that weekend, and Freeman nodded, not interrupting except with an occasional question.

"I thought I might lose it all there at the end," Amanda confessed. "Suddenly, just as I reached out and touched happiness, it was being snatched from me." She paused. "That scared me. I couldn't believe God would do that, and I fought to keep it."

"And you're still fighting, so I hear," Freeman murmured. "Father says you have been battling pneumonia as well."

"Yes. But God has been good, and I'm better," Amanda beamed.

"And how is married life?" Freeman studied her.

"It has been wonderful," Amanda confessed. "I had forgotten just how fulfilling having someone could feel. I really love Jon. I feel safe, whole with him."

"So why are you seeing me?" Freeman grinned.

"Because you know and I know my marriage hasn't solved all the problems, just put them aside for a while." Amanda looked down at her hands again. "There was an article in one of the syndicated papers last week about me. There are calls from time to time from reporters and solicitors. Clients and church members ask me."

She sighed. "A past that was secret from me is now fodder for public speculation. Arnold, I still cannot face that past. I don't have glib answers to give to people's questions. I don't know how I feel about Marjy, about—about Marks. I still don't know what to say about all the hype over the suspicion that—that I was involved in criminal activity. I'm still embarrassed by the questions. I am thankful Mom and Dad aren't alive. They would be mortified."

Amanda swallowed. "As it is, my own brother's family was shunning me. I'm tongue-tied when the subject is brought up. I shut down inside." She bit back tears. "I have to somehow figure it out."

"What about the matter with Senator Whitmore?" Freeman asked gently.

"I'm to have dinner with him," she replied. "Everything about Andrew has been so painful. I know the senator is anxious to hear about his son, and I want to share with him what I can. But I've just managed to escape that prison of Andy's memory. I'm stronger now, but I'm afraid to reopen the door." She whispered, "There are times I still feel guilty for being happy now."

"You mustn't hide from it," Arnold spoke quietly. "Perhaps now that you've found love with Jon, you will be secure enough to face the issues, look at them from a new perspective."

"I just know I have to try," Amanda smiled bravely. "I don't want to hold back anything. I want all my energies channeled into loving my husband

and being a good wife." She took a deep breath. "I'm hoping the occasion will present itself so that I can tell his family about me."

"That's a good place to start," Freeman agreed.

"But I want so badly for them to like me, to be good enough, for them to accept me," she blurted suddenly. "I'm so scared they won't like me, and that Jon will love me less because of it."

Freeman took her hand. "Amanda, Jon knows your past and loves you. Is there anything he doesn't know?"

Amanda shook her head warily, her eyes flickering away momentarily.

"So if he loves you, he is going to do everything in his power to make his family do so as well." Freeman met her eyes. "He has already chosen you over his family, by marrying you before they even met you."

"But will he regret that decision?" Her eyes swept away from him.

"Don't go borrowing trouble," Freeman laughed. "You're tackling too many fronts today. We need to work through the issues one at a time. As you resolve each problem, you will see solutions to the next one."

"I know. I'm just anxious not to blow this opportunity I have with Jon." Amanda was tremulous.

"Be honest with him. The best relationship you two can build must be based on trust."

Amanda nodded mutely.

"Have you told him about the sessions with me?"

She shook her head. "Not yet. There's been so much else going on."

"Perhaps you should."

"But I don't want him to think I'm crazy, or that I'm unhappy with him," Amanda objected anxiously.

"He won't if you tell him," Freeman was gentle. "But this is a small town, Amanda. If he finds out otherwise, by accident, he's going to wonder, and he's going to be hurt."

She nodded. "You're right."

"So next Tuesday?" Freeman smiled.

"I'll be here," she assented. "I really want to figure out how to deal with my feelings about Marjy and Marks, so that I can field the questions from others. And Arnold, you have been a lot of help."

As she walked out of Freeman's office to her car, a vehicle pulled up in front of hers and parked. She was at first oblivious, then was shaken out of her reverie as she recognized Jon getting out.

He smiled at her. "Hi, beautiful," he drawled, as he walked up to her.

"Hi," she smiled pensively, suddenly uncomfortable. "How did you know where to find me?"

"I didn't," he admitted. "I took off from work early, and happened to be looking for an address down this street of a property on a list of assets in one of my probate cases, and suddenly saw you standing there."

"I was just thinking about you." She looked at him guiltily.

He glanced curiously at the medical office complex building she had just exited. "Are you OK?"

"Yes. I had a session with Dr. Freeman." She was direct, gazing at him, deciding to come clean.

He nodded, concern written on his face, but he was silent.

"I had been seeing him before the—the accident about—" she floundered, "about all the confusion in my life."

"Amanda, you don't have to tell me if you don't want to." Jon's eyes searched hers.

"I want to," she smiled, taking his hand. "Jon, there's so much I still don't know how to deal with, such as my feelings about Marjy and—and Marks, and how to answer people's questions, deal with the media. And until I came to you I was full of doubt, and despaired about finding my way out of the maze."

She squeezed his hand. "When you married me, you inherited a lot of my baggage. I love you so much, and don't want to burden you with that." She looked down at their entwined hands. "I don't want to scare you away. But neither do I want to keep any of it from you. No secrets."

He wrapped an arm around her. She smiled self-deprecatingly. "This is not the ideal place to talk about it, on the sidewalk in front of the doctor's office. But I want you to know."

"I want to know everything about you," he whispered, as he leaned forward and kissed her hair. "There's nothing you have to face alone, Amanda."

He cupped her chin in his hand. "You would tell me, wouldn't you, if I can help?"

She nodded, her eyes locked on his. "You are helping me, and I'm very happy, Jon."

He hugged her. "Why don't we go home? That way we will be undisturbed, and you can tell me all you want." He laughed slyly. "I had thought about beating you home and having steaks on the grill when you walked in the door, with wine and candles. But now that I've told you, I've spoiled the surprise."

"It still sounds like a great idea," she laughed. "I'll drag race you home."

CHAPTER 5

Amanda was hard at work, with a huge stack of files piled on her office conference table, along with a laptop computer. A dictating machine was behind her on a small console. She was poring over one file, typing a memorandum of law to accompany a motion to suppress, clicking to another document and typing a praecipe for subpoenas, making notes of motions she needed to file, and periodically turning and dictating into the microphone instructions for Sheila.

Dinah Patterson, the new office assistant, a young woman dressed in business suit, walked in with a diet cola and two aspirin.

"Thanks." Amanda did not look up, but reached for the aspirin, swallowed them and swigged some of the cola. "Do not tell Ralph I asked for any pain reliever," she ordered sternly. "It's none of his damned business, and he's a tattle-tail."

"Ralph demanded that I tell you to drink an entire soft drink," Dinah spoke timidly. "He called a minute ago, and said he wanted some caffeine in your system before he gets here from the courthouse."

"You inform him he is not invited in here," Amanda replied as she resumed typing furiously, her teeth clenched.

Dinah started to leave, but Amanda stopped her. "Dinah."

Dinah turned nervously. Amanda looked at her and tried to smile. "I know Ralph has infused in you the fear of God where I am concerned. But Sheila will tell you my bark is worse than my bite. At least," she laughed, "some of the time."

Dinah blushed. "I didn't mean—"

Amanda interrupted, shaking her head. "When Ralph and I fight, we're like two siblings. We're not going to actually maim and kill each other; it only sounds like it. So there's no reason to be frightened or have 9-1-1 on your speed dial. Just duck if we start throwing things."

"Yes, Mrs. Connor," Dinah spoke, before fleeing. Amanda looked after her a moment, then went back to work. She rubbed her wrist distractedly, then reached for and downed the soda.

A few minutes later Sheila brought in some papers, and Amanda stopped to review and sign them. Sheila looked hesitantly at Amanda.

"Out with it," Amanda sighed, sitting back in her chair, unconsciously rubbing her shoulder. "Is Dinah posing a problem?"

"No," Sheila smiled reassuringly. "She's going to work out. She's just nervous, and wants badly to impress you two."

Amanda's voice held a tinge of weariness. "It's been just the three of us for a while now, and we know each other so well. It's hard to adjust to another person on staff, and I'm sure it's hard for her to get used to us as well. Ralph and I are accustomed to just giving you something without dictating exactly what needs to be done. And I just don't have the time right now to deal with one more problem, with all these trials scheduled."

"I will whip her into shape. You don't worry about it," Sheila promised. Amanda smiled her thanks.

"At least Ralph has been on his best behavior the last few days," Amanda quipped, her hand moving unconsciously back to her shoulder. "That's one good thing."

Sheila peered at her, her concern apparent. "Amanda, you're in pain. You really don't need to be working this hard."

"I'm fine," Amanda protested. "If I was at home, I'd be just sitting doing nothing. At least here I can sit and dictate and type, get something accomplished. It's really no different."

"But Jon said you should be taking it easy, and I don't think you are." Sheila gestured toward the pile of case files. "Dr. Rand called and left a message for you to check in with him. Not many doctors would do that. I'll bet you haven't returned his call. And Dr. Howells has called this morning. He sounded worried, and said that Father Anselm informed him you had been at the church practicing."

"I'm fine." A note of irritation crept into Amanda's voice. She flexed her left hand, grimacing. "I've got to find some practice time somewhere. Ken can't cover for me at church forever."

Sheila sighed and turned to leave, but Amanda spoke up. "Sheila."

Sheila looked back. Amanda was gazing at her, her expression worried. "If Ralph makes judge and asks you to be his judicial assistant, will you take the job?"

Sheila smiled. "You sure don't mind putting people on the spot, do you?"

61

Amanda was pensive. "We've been together going way back. The reason I was insistent on being involved with hiring Dinah is that I am so afraid I'm going to lose you. I don't want to."

Sheila was surprised. Amanda went on, looking down at her computer screen. "I know state benefits aren't bad, and the work would not be as hard. I'm sure it would be easier working for just Ralph. I've always been a bear. But," she paused, her voice suddenly softer, "you know I would match anything they offer you, benefits included."

Sheila chuckled. "He already can't afford me," she quipped, as she walked out.

Sheila felt good. She knew that Amanda had just given her one of the highest encomiums of which Amanda was capable. Amanda was not one to flatter; she generally said what she meant, sometimes to her own detriment. But the judiciary and the bar thought highly of her for her honesty and integrity. And Amanda demanded the very best. If she was worried about losing Sheila, it was a high compliment indeed to Sheila's work. And Amanda already paid Sheila more than the judicial assistant job would provide. Although Amanda's work standards were high, she amply rewarded Sheila's excellence.

Looking at the other desk, Sheila didn't see Dinah, so she made her way to the kitchen. Dinah stood there pouring herself a cup of coffee. She turned, saw Sheila and stiffened, intimidated.

"I didn't mean to bother Mrs. Connor," she started, suddenly defensive. "But Mr. Carmichael—"

Sheila held up her hand. "It's OK, Dinah. I'm not looking for you to chew you out. You're doing just fine. Just a few pointers. Firstly, formal address is required when others are around, but when it's just you and them, they want you to call them by their first name. Ralph is more into the 'Mr.' thing, but Amanda bristles when you call her 'Mrs.'"

"I noticed that, but didn't realize what I was doing wrong," Dinah stuttered, embarrassed.

"It's OK. A lot of people don't know that," Sheila reassured her pleasantly. "When Amanda is really angry, she leaves no doubt."

Dinah smiled nervously. "I'm just afraid of not being satisfactory. They have a reputation of being really good, perfectionists."

"They are," Sheila nodded. "This is not an easy job. But you came with excellent references, and so far Ralph has had nothing but praise for you."

"Really?" Dinah looked doubtful. "I don't get the impression he is happy with me." They drifted back into the office to their desks.

Sheila nodded. "I think Ralph is a little self-conscious with you here, which is a measure of his consideration for you. He is pretty irreverent here on the home turf when clients aren't around. But he doesn't want to offend or embarrass you while you are new. He thought he scared you the first day of work."

"I was really nervous, but I like him and Mrs.—Amanda," Dinah replied shyly. "Do you really think they are worried about my reaction?"

Sheila nodded. "You are still a stranger, and they don't want to scare you. They also want to be sure they can trust you. When things start hopping around here, you'll get a taste of what they are really like. And they are a lot of fun, and try not to take themselves too seriously. Amanda is playing catch-up right now after being out for over a month." Sheila frowned. "And she apparently has a mission against Clarence Banks at the moment, hence all these trials. So you are likely to see them both in action very soon."

Sheila confided, "Amanda has only recently loosened up. She is generally very business-like, brusque sometimes, but it doesn't mean she is mad. Once you get to know her, her moods are actually easier to read than Ralph's. Ralph is so full of wisecracks, but his delivery is sometimes so dead-pan you think he is serious. And he masks his irritation, then he'll explode without warning.

"I was unsure of Ralph when he first came into the firm with Amanda. And they go at each other sometimes pretty fierce, but it's all an act. When the volume goes up in the office, just stay out of the way and let them have at it. Amanda taught me to know when to stroke him, and when to give him as good as he sends. He expects that now. Just follow my lead."

Dinah looked dubious, but Sheila laughed. "We'll come up with a set of hand signals or something. Dealing with the two of them is like an advanced course in human behavioral analysis. They're not hard to deal with, once you get used to them. And they're actually a great source of entertainment, better than any TV show. You'll do just fine."

Dinah smiled. "Thanks, Sheila. I really am happy to be working here, and want to do my best."

Ralph strode into the office with Clarence Banks, the chief assistant state attorney. "In there," he ordered the attorney in a no-nonsense tone, peremptorily pointing to his office. Clarence nodded unsmilingly and disappeared. Ralph kept moving across the room, not acknowledging the two women as he made his way to Amanda's office and entered, shutting the door behind him emphatically.

"This will not be good," Sheila remarked quietly. "When he doesn't speak, the fireworks are about to start."

"OK, we need to talk," Ralph announced to Amanda, who was holding the microphone to the dictating machine.

She clicked the microphone off and looked up at him, asperity in her voice. "Can't it wait? As you see, I have a mountain of work."

"That's what we need to talk about." Ralph stood at the table, towering over her. "It's important. Amanda, you are already back at work before you should be. You haven't fully recovered. Jon told me Dr. Rand did not release you to come back full-time yet, but you promised to sit here and take it easy. Jon is calling me several times a day just to make sure you are not overdoing it. But you have now decided to ride hell for leather on the criminal trial docket."

"Ralph—" she began imperiously, but he raised his hand.

"Enough, Mandy. This vendetta against Clarence Banks has got to stop. We cannot try four major criminal trials in one week. And you and Alex are in cahoots. He has scheduled three more himself. You know that dog is not going to hunt."

"What's this 'we'?" She raised her voice. "I'm not asking for your help."

"This Burnham case is a plea, pure and simple," Ralph argued, picking up a file from the top of the stack. "There is no reason to be teeing it up, and you know it."

"Clarence can't try his way out of a paper bag," Amanda retorted, her eyes flashing. "The week will be nothing but an exercise in humiliation for him."

"Yes, Clarence is an administrator, not a litigator," Ralph conceded. "And with his being short a prosecutor and having to take the division himself, you have him at a distinct disadvantage. But you're not doing your client any favors here. There's no way that even Clarence can lose this one. And you know Judge Latimer will stroke our client at sentencing."

Ralph crossed over, took the microphone out of Amanda's clenched fist and laid it on the console. He sat down beside her. "I know you and Alex always liked to gang up on the prosecutors and load their wagon for them in your public defender days. But this thing against Clarence has gotten out of hand." He looked at her reproachfully. "And I thought you and I had an agreement that I would take the lead in the criminal cases."

She looked at him stonily. He continued fearlessly, "I'm sure that if you were completely well you could handle these all by yourself without batting an eyelash. But you are breaking your promises to the doctor and Jon. I'm not going to let you do this."

She started to retort, but he interrupted, taking her hand. "Enough. Judge Latimer called me in and ordered me to negotiate a truce between you two, or he's going to throw you both in the same jail cell and let you settle it in a death match."

"What? Is it all over town? Is the local bar gossiping about little wicked witch Amanda? That's sexist. He wouldn't intervene if it were two men," she sputtered angrily, withdrawing her hand.

"Bullshit," Ralph refuted softly. "He's done it before, many times. And he's worried about you, too."

Ralph shook his head at her. "Judge Latimer has always had a soft spot for you. He's let you go down the rabbit trail in cross-examination longer than the rest of us, because he knows you aren't beating the bushes. You always have a reason, a set strategy, and he wants to see where you are heading." Ralph grinned. "He's already bet twenty dollars on your winning the death match, even with your current handicap, because he figures I can't bring you two hardheads to the table."

He pleaded with her. "I really want to prove him wrong, Mandy."

She flared, "All you are trying to do is score brownie points with the judiciary. I know your scheme."

"Is it so bad to aspire to judicial office?" Ralph demanded testily. He stared at her exasperatedly. "Don't you think I'd make a good judge?"

She clenched her jaw.

He held up his hand. "Forget that. We don't have time to fight that battle. You are forcing my hand here, Mandy. I don't want our clients to get wind of any rumor that you and I can't agree on how to handle our cases. The wheels of justice are about to grind to a complete halt due to your anger at Clarence."

She looked down at the table. "What Clarence did to Alan was unforgiveable. If the boys had been in the room when the deputy handcuffed their father and dragged him out—"

"But they weren't," Ralph submitted softly.

"But only by the grace of God," her voice rose ominously.

"But Clarence has apologized to Alan, in a public place. At the Kiwanis meeting, no less. If you attended the meetings, you would have been there to see it. If Alan can forgive, you need to also."

She was silent. Ralph did not press her, because he knew she was considering what he said.

"I'll think about it." She was grudging.

"Great, because Clarence is in my office right now," Ralph countered.

She rose quickly, her rage to the fore. "Damn you, Ralph," she shouted. "I am not into your fun and games."

"Just promise me to hear him out," Ralph rose and grabbed her by the shoulders, shaking her gently.

She winced, sucking in air, trying to swallow her gasp of pain.

"I'm sorry. I forgot about the shoulder." He looked at her penetratingly. "It's hurting you, isn't it? Damn it, Mandy, you shouldn't be here."

"I'm fine," she coughed.

"Come on," he took her arm and gently pulled her after him toward the door. "I'll take advantage of your momentary weakness. Don't hit him. And keep your mouth shut. I know how hard that will be."

"For how long?" Her eyes met his, the beginnings of a smile playing around her lips.

He propelled her in front of him through the door. "As long as it takes."

He marched her down the hall and across the assistant's work area to his office door. She tensed as he opened the door.

Clarence Banks, sitting in one of the client chairs, stood suddenly, facing her, his face impassive. He and Amanda stared at each other unsmilingly as Ralph gently pushed her toward his executive chair across the desk from Clarence, and took a seat in a chair between them and beside the door, blocking their exit.

"Sit down, both of you." His tone brooked no opposition.

They both did so reluctantly. Amanda started to say something, but Ralph pointed a finger at her. "You, shut up." He turned to Clarence. "You, start talking."

Clarence turned his eyes from Ralph to Amanda, licking his lips nervously. "Amanda, I—" he stammered, looking again at Ralph, who nodded encouragingly, "I—I'm sorry for the pain I caused Alan Young and—and you. I was following orders at the time, but that's no excuse."

"Yeah, since when—" Amanda began.

Ralph turned to her and hissed, "I told you to shut up."

Clarence continued haltingly. "You're absolutely right. The state attorney is supposed to be an independent arm of the executive branch, and not taking marching orders from the judiciary. And I knew better than what I did. Gerald was clear that he wasn't going to sign off on the autopsy until he had reviewed everything. And he was absolutely right."

His eyes became beseeching. "But you have to realize that Larry—I mean, Judge Kilmer, was convinced that Alan Young had killed his wife to be with Evie—Eve Brown. She had made sure Judge Kilmer thought that, and he was anxious to see that such an act did not go unpunished."

"I'll bet," Amanda said under her breath. Ralph stared her down, trying to will her to silence. She ignored Ralph. "But you also have known the Young family for years. What would make you believe her and throw that knowledge of Alan's history away? I can understand Kilmer's motivation," she sneered, "but you're a staunch Methodist. Have they thrown out the Golden Rule at your church? What would possess you to inflict such emotional distress on Alan and his boys the day after Shelby's funeral?"

Clarence was ashen. "Amanda, I'm so sorry," he mumbled.

"Are you?" she persisted. "Or were you just wrong, and caught at it?"

He flushed. Ralph turned to her. "Damn it, woman, the man is trying to make it right."

The door opened, and in walked Alan Young. They all rose, Amanda bewildered. "Alan, what—"

"Amanda, I just found out what you are doing," he spoke, slightly breathless. "This has got to stop. We have to pick up the pieces and move on."

"What? How?" she gasped.

"I just made it back to town from Lawrence Kilmer's probable cause hearing before the judicial qualifications commission," Alan responded.

"What?" she was astounded. "What were you doing there?"

"I was a witness, and I spoke out on his behalf." Alan excused himself as he pushed past Ralph, standing beside her and taking her hand.

"Why would you do that?" she asked shakily.

"Because I guess the man is now my brother," Alan declared, his voice low. "Shelby is gone, and he didn't kill her." He looked at her sadly. "We can't bring her back, Mandy. What Larry Kilmer did was wrong, but at least some of his motives were justifiable in his mind, based on the information he had.

"So you need to turn loose of this anger on my behalf. I have accepted Clarence's apology, and now it's time you did."

She looked over at Ralph accusingly. "Did you put Alan up to this?"

Before Ralph could answer, Alan replied quietly, "No. I heard the scuttlebutt just this morning from the JQC prosecuting attorney. Apparently when you are on the warpath, the other lawyers take note. I had no idea, Mandy." He looked at her reproachfully. "I made it back here as fast as I could."

His voice dropped to a whisper. "I will not allow you to continue the suit against Clarence. I want the matter dropped. Now."

Clarence stepped forward. "I am sorry, Amanda, truly I am." He attempted a feeble joke. "And I know you are preparing to wipe the floor with me in court. You have every right to, and if you persist, I'll take my punishment. But I don't think this is a lesson I will soon forget. I know I could easily be up on grievance charges as well."

Amanda looked at them all and sighed. She was silent several minutes, while they waited on tenterhooks.

"OK, I admit maybe I was being vindictive."

"No shit," Ralph swore under his breath.

Amanda reached over the desk and extended her hand to Clarence. "OK, I will agree to a truce, and accept the apology." She smiled shamefacedly. "I guess my client has pulled the rug out from under my feet."

Clarence took her hand and shook it gravely.

Ralph intervened smoothly. "Now we need to work out these trials. Then we'll all do lunch. My treat."

Alan demurred. "Sorry, guys, but I really have patients waiting for me. I promise a raincheck." He kissed Amanda's cheek. "I want you to go home," he whispered. "You have no business being back at work so soon."

"Neither do you," she pointed out.

"Touché," he smiled then. "But unlike you I'm only doing half days." He turned to Ralph. "Make sure she takes the afternoon off." He shook hands with Clarence and Ralph, and made his way out.

Ralph turned back to the two of them. "Sit," he ordered. "You're not going anywhere without us discussing these cases."

He turned to Amanda. "What about Burnham?"

Clarence intervened, "I will reduce it to a third degree felony. That will knock the sentencing guidelines' points down, and I will recommend credit for time served and probation."

Amanda stared at him, surprised. "OK. I think my client will go for that."

Ralph nodded. But Amanda continued, "But I have to try the Roberts case."

"No, you don't," Clarence smiled slightly. "I *nolle prosequied* it on the way over here."

Amanda was stunned. He continued, "You had me dead to rights there. I knew it, and I was going to dismiss it before trial anyway," he admitted shamefacedly. "But you had my back to the wall when you announced ready for trial on all four cases, and I had to have some holdout position."

Amanda just gaped at him. Ralph noted it, and persisted gently. "The Johnson case?"

"It's a first offense," Amanda countered quickly, her eyes still on Clarence.

"I'll withhold adjudication and recommend a fine only."

"But—" she began.

"But nothing," Clarence cut her off. "I know no fine is assessed on a withhold, but your guy didn't want probation. So he'll have to agree to it, and pay it at sentencing. I don't want you coming back later and arguing it was an illegal sentence. That way we both get what we want, and it's not like he doesn't have plenty of cash."

"That's generous," she muttered grudgingly. "And Philips?"

"That's my strongest case," Clarence asserted. "I can't do much there. I could file notice that your client qualifies for habitual felony offender status. I haven't yet," he offered meaningfully. "Recommendation of guidelines sentence versus habitual felon treatment."

As she opened her mouth, Clarence shook his head. "No conditional plea. That's as good as you will get from me. I'm not tying the judge's hands, but I'll make the recommendation and stand silent while you argue."

Ralph interjected, "That sounds like a possible plea. I'll talk to the client and his father today." He stood. "Now we're all going to Jake's."

Both Amanda and Clarence started to object, but he snapped his fingers, silencing them. "I happen to know that the judges are having lunch there today, some pow-wow. My fee as mediator is that you both sit at the same table and eat lunch amicably in a public display of mutual friendship."

"Friendship?" echoed Amanda in mock disbelief. "Let's not get crazy here."

Clarence and Ralph grinned.

Clarence turned to Amanda. "Call Alex and tell him that I'm in a dealing mood today, and today only." He smiled at her. "I know what you were doing, the old tag team trick." He grinned. "I can't believe the two of you would do that to me again after all these years. But some things never change. I won't be as nice to him if he persists."

Ralph opened the door to the office and ushered them out. "I might even spring for drinks at lunch." He looked at Amanda sharply. "Then Mrs. Connor, Esquire, is going home for the rest of the day."

CHAPTER 6

Jon had seen several clients and dictated some initial probate pleadings. Looking at his watch, he noticed that it was almost noon.

Don Lattimore, one of the senior partners of the firm, stuck his head in the door. "Got a minute?" he asked.

"Sure," Jon smiled, as Don let himself in.

"I just wanted to ask how you're liking things so far."

"It's great," Jon replied pleasantly. "Everyone has treated me well, and so far I have no complaints. And you all are keeping me busy. I like that."

"We're glad to have you, with all your credentials. And you have some big guns for references." Don strolled to the window by Jon's desk and peered out over the harbor, dazzling in the sunlight. "Would you like to do lunch?"

"I'd love to, but I'm booked with a client over the lunch hour," Jon apologized.

"You really don't have to work that hard," Don laughed.

"Well, the client happens to be an acquaintance of mine. I'm not sure what he wants to discuss, but this one might be *pro bono*," Jon replied, suddenly serious. "I hope that is OK?"

"Fine by me," Don nodded. "I was just curious."

Jon turned in his seat and looked straight at Don. "About what?"

"Why you left a glamorous job to work here, and why you even have to work." He flushed, suddenly chagrined. "What I mean is Amanda Childs was a catch even before she became an heiress. I'd think with her money both of you could take it easy, sail around the world, live high on the hog."

Jon laughed heartily. "You apparently don't know Amanda that well. And, well, I like to make my own way."

"But then why would you leave the FBI, man? Your job sounded pretty exciting."

"I admit I enjoyed it, but it came at a price. Once I fell for Amanda, I knew I wanted to spend my nights with her, and not God-knows-where."

"Well, the Bureau's loss is our gain," Don grinned.

"Let's hope I keep you thinking that way," Jon agreed good-naturedly.

"Just let me know if you need anything. We want to keep you happy. Bobby told me he's afraid you won't stay long."

"Why?" Jon laughed. "A position with this firm is nothing to sneeze at."

"He told me you were too good to be true," Don smiled. "I hope he's wrong, and that you'll stick around." He waved as he walked out.

After Don left, Jon stood and stared out the window unseeingly. Although the newness of his job had been bustling and he remained busy with the meticulous detail of the work, he did miss the constant buzz and unpredictability of the former job. But he also knew he no longer missed the long hours and the loneliness. And his new life with Amanda was more than ample compensation. He found himself for the first time reluctant to go to work in the mornings, hating to be apart from her.

His thoughts turned to Amanda. I ought to call Ralph to check on her, he thought. He and Ralph had become constant confidants on Amanda's welfare, because Jon had become acutely aware of her reticence to discuss her work and her tendency to minimize her pain and discomfort. Just earlier that morning, during their morning telephone ritual on Jon's drive to work that Ralph jokingly called 'the morning report', Ralph had confided about Amanda's scheduling several criminal trials behind his back, and that he was going to have to confront her. Jon couldn't help but worry about her. Although she tried to hide it, he was aware that she was still not fully recovered, and that she was pushing herself hard.

The intercom buzzed. "Mr. Connor, your 12:00 is here."

He shook off his reverie. "Thanks, Susan. I'll be right there. Go on to lunch. I will take care of them."

He strode out of his office to the well-appointed waiting area. There were two men waiting for him. He stuck out his hand. "Hello, Stephen, Adam," he smiled, shaking the hands of both men. "Why don't you two follow me?"

He led the way, and motioned for Stephen Marks and Adam Brownlee to be seated on the sofa, and took a seat in a wing chair across from them.

Marks, formerly a bishop of the Episcopal Church, was dressed in a dark suit which hung on his spare frame, sans collar and the trappings of his former office. He still carried some of his old arrogant bearing, but Jon sensed a hesitancy about him. And Jon noted that Adam, still a priest and dressed in clerical collar and blazer, seemed subdued as well.

"I'm happy that you were able to obtain parole," he smiled, trying to put Marks at ease.

"Yes, thanks to you and Greg Boyer," Stephen responded, gratefulness in his voice.

"I've not seen a lot of either of you lately," Jon added. "I do apologize."

"Yes, your life has been busy," Stephen smiled, his golden green eyes so much like Amanda's. "I hope that your marriage to Amanda has been a happy one for both of you."

Adam tried to smile, but was obviously preoccupied. "I'm glad that you have found each other. Are you happy?"

"Incredibly," Jon admitted. "More than I thought possible."

He surmised from their faces that they had serious business to discuss. "But that's not why you're here."

Stephen leaned forward, his face earnest. "Jon, I think we need your help. I really didn't feel comfortable going to Amanda with this." He paused uncomfortably. "Despite our breakthrough just before—" he cleared his throat, stumbling over his sentence, "at our last encounter, I'm not sure how she feels about me now. I'm afraid she thinks I was trying to frame her for Bill Barnes'—death," he finished uneasily.

"I don't think so," Jon spoke carefully. "I have tried to convince her of your insistence on trying to take the blame in your efforts to protect Adam and—and Evie."

"That's partly why I am here." Stephen paused, clearly distressed. "As you know, no probate has been done on either Billy's or his dad's estate. I'm certain that much of the assets were confiscated by the federal government as 'fruits of a criminal enterprise'."

"I am aware of that." Jon's mind was whirring. Was Stephen seeking probate of those estates for himself?

As if reading his mind, Stephen shook his head. "This inquiry isn't for me. It's very probable that I would have been the next of kin for inheritance purposes. But some information has just come to light which has changed everything, and it is because of that I'm pursuing this."

He pulled a picture out of his jacket pocket and laid it on the table before Jon. Jon picked it up and stared at the face. He immediately noted a resemblance. He looked up questioningly.

Adam spoke up. "You are looking at the heir of the Barnes estate, whatever there is of it."

Jon frowned. "I don't understand."

Adam leaned forward, his face grave. "We discovered this just before Stephen was released from prison. We've examined the evidence. This little girl is the offspring of—" he took a deep breath, "Billy Barnes and—and my sister Evie Brown."

Jon was transfixed. "How—how could that be proved?"

The Connors' Crisis

Adam coughed. "Apparently there was a paternity action filed in Alabama, and Billy had the court records sealed sometime before his death. However, Mary Bascom, an old family friend, contacted me just last week. She had not been aware of Evie's—Evie's death until just recently. Evie had left the child Donna in Mary's care, and provided her copies of the pleadings, the DNA paperwork and judgment of paternity.

"Mary had not heard from Evie in a while. She finally found my cell number written on the papers and called me." Adam paused, clearly battling being overcome. "It was a shock, to say the least."

He pulled out a manila envelope. "These are all the papers that Mary had. You will see the DNA confirmation, and a secret agreement that Billy and Evie entered into for the support of the child. He apparently promised the child would want for nothing, as long as the matter remained secret until they both agreed to divulge it."

Stephen took over. "Evie said nothing, even after Billy's death. But obviously Donna has lost both her parents, and her only remaining family consists of myself and Adam."

"So she was living in Alabama?" Jon inquired.

"No," Adam shook his head. "Mary lives in the north end of this county, and the baby has been with her for all her life, almost four years."

Jon was silent, digesting the information as the two men sat there, both anxiously awaiting his reaction.

"There's the possibility of two probates. We'll have to do an ancillary probate for any property or assets in Alabama, that is, if we find any," Jon mused aloud. "I'll need to ask a member of the bar up there to handle that portion. I can handle the accountings."

He looked at them. "Have either of you told Amanda about this?"

"No," Stephen looked sad. "I have not seen Amanda since the—the accident, and this is something I felt needed to be told her face-to-face. I just don't know how she might react."

Jon nodded. Neither did he. "You know I cannot keep this from her."

Adam spoke up. "As much as I want to protect Donna from adverse publicity, I'm not willing to lie about this. It will probably come out anyway. Amanda should know, preferably from one of us." He looked pleadingly at Jon. "Hopefully from you."

Stephen reached out and laid his hand on Jon's arm. "You don't think she'll be upset if you handle this? I mean, she can't harbor fond feelings for the two people who almost—who caused her so much grief," Stephen stammered.

"I'll deal with that," Jon promised. "The child will require a guardianship over her person and property. Who is going to act as that? Are either or

73

both of you willing to serve as personal representative and/or guardian?" Jon was direct.

They both nodded soberly.

Stephen cleared his throat. "I will do anything for this child, but I just don't know if the court will appoint me, given—given my history."

"You're right, Stephen. Being convicted of a felony disqualifies one as both guardian and personal representative. But that doesn't mean your help will not be needed. It may require some research and digging to determine what estate there is. You're going to be the best available source of that information."

Stephen's face flooded with pain. "I will lend my support to Adam, and am willing to provide what assistance I can."

Jon questioned him, and Stephen answered readily, with Adam chiming in with additional information. After several minutes Jon sat back.

"OK, let me see what I can find out regarding the estate," Jon promised.

The men rose. Stephen clasped Jon's hand. "Thank you so much, Jon. This is such a shock, and we must take care of her. She has no one else to look out after her interests."

Jon stared at him. "What are your plans now, Stephen?"

"I was going to visit my aunt in Ocala, try to make a new start away from here. But," he looked over at Brownlee, "Adam has convinced me that I need to remain and help with this new situation. I feel unequal to caring for a small child. And you would agree I'm not much of a role model."

"God works in mysterious ways," Jon suppressed a grin.

"And in this case his call to redemption shows a great deal of irony, or perhaps a healthy dose of his humor," Stephen smiled sadly.

Adam interjected. "Stephen will be staying with me for the time being. My congregation and vestry have agreed," he frowned pensively.

"I'll contact you as soon as the paperwork is ready," Jon promised.

He saw the men out, then returned to his office. He did not know how Amanda would react to the news that Billy was a father, or to Jon's agreeing to take on the case.

He heard a knock at his door. "Come in," he called.

Susan walked in with a styrofoam plate and a soft drink. "Don sent some lunch over, and said to make sure you kept your strength up," she grinned.

"Thanks," he smiled gratefully.

"Oh, and Ralph Carmichael called. He said to call back if you want the 'noon report'."

Jon nodded. "Thanks."

He opened the plate, looking at the offering, and stood, taking it over to his conference table. Taking a swig from his drink, he pulled out his cell phone and pushed a button, dialing Ralph.

"Well, did you beat my wife, or did she beat you?" he asked genially.

"We called a truce. We got some good offers. I think all the trials will settle. I had another 'come to Jesus' meeting with her, as if that accomplishes anything," Ralph sighed. "Alan ordered her home this afternoon, so after lunch I sent her on her way."

"Alan?" Jon echoed.

Ralph relayed the morning's events. Jon laughed, picturing Ralph mediating between Amanda and the prosecutor.

"But are you sure she is on her way home?" Jon queried.

"Hell, man, your guess is as good as mine where she is," Ralph retorted. "But between you and me we have spies all over town. My guess is that one of us will hear something if she doesn't take herself to the house."

Jon's call-waiting beeped. He looked at the number. "I'll lay odds I know where she is right now. Father Anselm is calling. Later."

He answered. "Father Anselm? How are you?"

"My dear boy, I don't mean to bother you, but—"

"But my wife has shown up at the church and is practicing the organ," Jon guessed aloud.

"Yes." He could hear the anxiety in the priest's voice. "Malcolm has been adamant that she doesn't need to be exerting herself. But, Jon—"

"It's OK, Father," Jon assured him. "You know we have little authority over her. But I will have a talk with her tonight, again."

"I'm just so worried—"

"Father, Dr. Rand told me that he thinks it is OK for her to start playing again, but he opined that if he imparted that to her she would be doing marathon practice. As long as she thinks it is still *verboten*, she will sneak around and do it, but in moderation. So let's keep that our secret for now, OK?"

"My lips are sealed." Father's voice held a sigh of relief.

"And if she does it for more than an hour, march in there and threaten her that you're calling me," Jon laughed. "I doubt that will have much effect, but it'll make me feel better."

Jon hung up. Next he called Kimball at the FBI.

"How's the private sector? Want your job back?" Kimball greeted him.

"I'm OK," Jon laughed. "But I could use some assistance from you."

He explained the situation about the newly found heir to the Barnes' estate. "Kimball, can you find out what of Barnes' and Billy's property was impounded by the feds? And Marks' property as well? It may be too late to make any kind of homestead or other claim of exemption, but no one knew about the child until just recently."

"I'll see what I can do," Kimball replied. "So Billy Barnes and Evie Brown had a kid together? What are the odds? What does Amanda say to that?"

"She doesn't know yet. I'll tell her tonight."

After working up some accountings for some active probate files and leaving some dictation for Susan, Jon looked at his watch. It was 4:05 p.m. Well, no calls from anyone, so maybe the little woman is actually home, he smiled to himself.

He tried her cell phone. She answered after the fourth ring. "Yes?" her voice was breathless.

"I know you're not that excited to hear from me," he reproached her gently. "What are you doing?"

"I'm sitting on the porch with Bozo," she replied, her tone defensive. "I had to run for the phone. Why wouldn't I be excited to hear from you?"

"How many laps have you swam?" Jon used his best interrogation voice.

"None." She was petulant. "There was a moccasin on the bank when I went down there," she confessed. "He was gone by the time I found my gun. I called a pool contractor. He just left."

He bit back laughter at her exasperated tone. "I was actually calling to see if you would like me to take you out to dinner tonight."

"No need," she countered. "I have meatloaf in the oven."

"Meatloaf?" he purred. "Your very own home-made meatloaf?"

"Yes." He knew she was smiling. "What other kind is there?"

"I love your meatloaf," he murmured.

"I know you do," Amanda laughed. "I can cook other things, you know."

"But I love your meatloaf," he repeated.

"What's for dessert?" she inquired impishly.

"The same thing as last night. Is that OK?" he teased her.

"That was awfully good," she sighed.

"I'll be there in an hour," he told her.

"So soon?" Amanda was surprised. "Will the boss approve your leaving work early?"

"I think so. Just tell your other boyfriends to clear out before I get there," Jon joked.

"Bozo might not appreciate that," Amanda laughed.

Jon hung up and grabbed his jacket. On the way out, he ran into Don.

"Susan is glad you're leaving early," Don smirked. "She says you work her too hard."

Jon smiled, shame-faced. "Sorry. I'm a fast worker. Comes from having more work than time at the Bureau."

He said his goodbyes and headed out to his car. Soon he was threading his way through traffic, intent on reaching home and wondering how he was going to break the news about Barnes' little girl to Amanda.

Finally he pulled up outside the farmhouse, thankful for the break in the already relentless summer heat. He felt the momentary thrill that he always did when he pulled up to his new home, about to see Amanda again.

He bounded up the steps to the house and let himself in. He quietly made his way to the kitchen, from where some wonderful aromas emanated. He walked in to see Amanda lifting a frying pan with both hands.

He stood in the doorway and watched her silently. She set the frying pan down, then winced.

"So it still hurts?" he asked.

She jumped, surprised. "Why are you sneaking up on me?" she demanded shakily.

"No 'Hello, darling, how was your day?'" he gazed at her flushed features, before walking up to her and not so gently hauling her against him.

"I'm angry at you," he whispered as he ran his fingers up her neck and through her hair, dragging her mouth to his insistently.

"Why?" she asked against his lips as she returned his kiss hungrily.

"Because you are breaking all the rules," he murmured against her mouth. "My spies all over town have confirmed it. I cannot trust you to take care of yourself. You need punishing." He picked her up and started toward the door.

"But the meatloaf," she cried.

He turned around and walked to the stove with her still in his arms, turning off the oven and the stove, then striding back through the door with her, depositing her on the sofa.

She gazed at him as he jerked his tie off, then joined her. "The meatloaf will wait. You won't." As he claimed her he swore under his breath, "Damned clothes. You are not to wear any when I get home from work."

She laughed softly.

He whispered, "This is going to hurt me more than it does you."

"If you're really good," she whispered back.

Later, he walked into the kitchen, where she was dressed in a robe, ruefully examining the supper.

"Looks good enough to eat," he quipped, as he nuzzled her neck and she rolled her eyes.

"Guess you'll have meatloaf sandwiches now," she grinned.

"My favorite way of having them."

A few minutes later, she had completed the gravy, sliced the meatloaf and provided condiments on the table. He helped by setting the table, then they sat down together, and she said grace.

"I had some visitors today," he started casually.

"Clients?" she asked, pouring iced tea.

"Yes," he replied. "Stephen Marks and Adam Brownlee."

She looked up, surprised. "Why?"

"Stephen is now out of prison on parole. But they had a matter they requested my assistance on—a probate matter."

"What?" she frowned. "Wait a minute. Don't tell me Marks is going after the Barnes' estate?" Her eyes flashed.

"Not exactly," Jon hesitated. "It's not what you think. They were seeking it on behalf of someone else."

Amanda stared at Jon uncomprehendingly. "Who else is there?"

Jon took her hand and squeezed it. "Dear, they had some surprising news. It was quite a shock to them as well."

She just looked at him dumbly.

"Mandy, there is a child, an heir."

Her eyes widened. "A child? Who is this child?" she asked, her voice small.

"The child of Billy Barnes and Evie Brown."

She was silent a moment, looking down at her plate. "That cannot be," she whispered. "Billy has a child? But he's been dead almost a year."

"The little girl is almost four."

The news had the effect of shattering glass. Amanda abruptly pulled back from the table and stood, stalking over to the kitchen sink.

"Billy has a kid, four years old, with Evie Brown, and he kept this a secret?" she spat.

Jon stood and moved toward her, but she raised her hand, stopping him. "And you are doing the probate for them, and I guess a guardianship as well? Why?"

"Because little Donna is going to need someone to care for her, and the wherewithal to make it happen," Jon answered quietly. "If there's an estate, she's entitled to it."

"Donna?" Amanda echoed. "That was Billy's mother's name." She swallowed convulsively. "Did Mr. Barnes know about this?"

"We don't know," Jon was truthful. "The records were sealed, but paternity was established and a secret agreement entered into between Billy and Evie. Evie had copies and provided them to the child's caregiver."

"Sounds like something the elder Barnes son of a bitch would have done." Amanda was white-hot with anger.

Jon was taken aback by her swearing. "Does it matter now?" His manner was tender. "Despite what the Barnes have done, they are both gone, and there is yet another innocent life left hanging in the balance."

She was silent. "Stephen wanted you to know, but was afraid of your reaction," Jon added as he watched her sympathetically.

"It's no business of mine," she turned cold. "I'm just sorry you have been pulled into it."

Jon was surprised, but sensed the struggle going on inside her. "Someone needs to step up to the plate for this little girl. I'm simply going to file for Brownlee to be the guardian, and determine whether there's any estate left so that it can be claimed for her."

Jon walked over to Amanda and enfolded her to him. She did not respond.

"Don't you think it's the right thing to do?" he importuned her gently. "Aren't you the least bit curious about her?"

"Why should I want to know anything about the offspring of two people who tried to kill me?" she mumbled. "One of them was supposed to be my childhood friend, and every word out of his mouth to me was a lie."

"But this child can't help that," Jon argued, his mouth against her ear.

"Do what you must; just don't involve me." She pulled away roughly.

He caught her hand and drew her back to the table. "Eat something," he begged.

"No." She shook him off and exited the room quickly.

Jon stood there a moment, sighed, then turned and looked at the table. That meatloaf didn't stand a chance tonight, he thought. But damn it, I'm hungry, he suddenly realized.

So he sat down and helped himself to a slice of meatloaf. He remembered her comment to someone at church one day that meatloaf covered with ketchup was anathema. Smiling at the memory, he ladled some of Amanda's gravy on top. Tasting it, he thought, Now, that is good stuff. He wolfed it down hungrily. He indulged himself with another slice. She is good at so many things, he concluded to himself, savoring the meal.

He washed dishes and put away the food, stopping first to make her a plate, with meat loaf on top of toast, and gravy covering it. He microwaved the dish, then took it with a glass of iced tea, a fork and napkin and went in search of her.

He found her dressed in a silky coral-colored nightgown and robe, sitting up in bed, a book in hand, staring off into the distance. He went up to her and sat on the bed beside her, placing the glass of tea on the bedside table.

"I told you I don't want anything." She was cross.

"But this is so good." He cut a bite with the fork. "I'll bet you can't say no to it."

He held it to her lips. She stared at him, then took the bite.

He watched her face intently as she tried not to react. He bit back his own smile as he realized that she enjoyed it but didn't want to give him the satisfaction of knowing that. He cut another bite and held it on the fork. "No one can eat just one bite," he coaxed, holding it to her.

She took the bite, chewing it and regarding him, saying nothing.

He kept feeding her one bite at a time, until the corners of her mouth curved into a hint of a smile.

"There, there, all gone," he said as though talking to a small child. He placed the plate on the bedside table and pulled her to him, kissing her.

Satisfied, he released her.

"I need to brush my teeth now," she muttered with annoyance, but he knew she was only pretending that she was still angry.

"That's fine, but you'd better lose that gown and robe before you come back to bed," he warned her. "You know the rule."

"Or you'll do what?" She threw out the challenge as she rose and walked toward the bathroom.

"Or that expensive sexy lingerie will be shredded and thrown in the wastebasket," he announced, his eyes on her retreating form.

He took the plate and returned it to the kitchen and turned out the lights, stopping in the guest bathroom to brush his own teeth before returning to the bedroom, where it was already dark.

He slipped into the bed and found her there, waiting for him. She reached for him.

"I love your meatloaf, Mrs. Connor," he whispered, drawing her roughly to him.

"New rule," she intoned as she kissed him. "No unpleasant news during dinner."

"Deal." He gripped her hips and smiled.

CHAPTER 7

Amanda Connor, dressed in a fitted suit in a becoming shade of blue, walked into the plush lobby of the Carlyle Hotel and crossed the marble floor of the expansive foyer to the doorway of the restaurant. The *maitre d'hotel* nodded pleasantly at her and soon had her seated at a table by the glassed wall looking out on an English-style garden. She was handed a menu, and sat quietly studying it.

"Hello, Amanda." A female voice cut through her reverie.

She looked up into the cold blue eyes of a woman, older than she but still beautiful, with carefully coiffed light brown hair which curled around her ears and neck, dressed in a perfectly tailored cream suit with peach-colored blouse and white pearls adorning her throat and ears.

"Hello, Esme," Amanda spoke politely. "How are you?" She tried to exude warmth.

The woman walked around and sat down next to her at the table. "Never better. And you, my dear?"

Amanda smiled warmly. "Never better," she echoed. "I notice you've done a lot of renovation to the place. It looks nice."

Esme Townsend laughed, a silvery sound. "Probably a little too ostentatious for Mainville, don't you think? Toby thought it 'eau de gaudy', as he put it, silly boy, but I told him the hotel is my toy, and I will dress it up as I wish."

"Whatever pleases you," Amanda chuckled pleasantly.

"I hope you don't mind my joining you for lunch," Esme continued, smiling sweetly.

"Normally not, but I'm meeting Bradley Warren—some business he wanted to discuss."

"Bradley has been otherwise detained. He sends his regrets. His closing on the Palmetto Ridge properties will have to wait, a complication

81

of my making, I fear. But I hated for you to lunch alone," Esme simpered sanguinely.

Amanda gazed at the woman, suddenly understanding. "So this was just some ruse by you? Why do you wish to see me? Why didn't you just call and ask?"

"Why must you find some intrigue behind everything I do?" Esme pouted slightly. "But yes, it was planned. I figured otherwise you would find some excuse to say no," Esme rejoined lightly. "And I really wanted to catch up with you on what is going on in your life. We've not talked in a while."

Esme Townsend was one of the South's wealthiest women, from one of the old established families that settled Mainville. She owned various real property holdings across the state as well as the hotel in which they were sitting and a couple of resorts elsewhere. The wife of a state senator who had ended up on the appellate bench in Tallahassee before his death, and the daughter of a renowned former U.S. Representative, she was a powerful force in local and state politics, dabbled with national races, and wielded her influence liberally.

A waiter walked up to the table. "Mrs. Townsend, Mrs. Connor. May I get you anything to drink?" he asked pleasantly.

"A couple of mimosas," Esme ordered before Amanda could speak.

Amanda shook her head. "Water for me," she countermanded.

"No, I insist we toast your marvelous if precipitous marriage," Esme smirked. "Do as I say, Mark," she commanded the waiter, who scurried off. "And what better than the drink that I plied the little old ladies with at the altar guild luncheon, what was it, three years ago?"

Amanda shook her head. "Marjy was not terribly pleased with your spiking the punch," she countered, smiling.

"But those dears had the best time of their lives, and oh, the stories," Esme laughed. "You have to admit it was fun. And to see Vera Stewart and Sally Summerlin, as much as they've plotted and schemed against each other for decades, arm in arm singing together, was worth it all."

"I never understood why you hosted that." Amanda looked at her questioningly.

"Miss Mary Kate and I go back a long time, and it was announced she was retiring from St. Catherine's altar guild. I wanted her to go out in style," Esme smiled slyly.

The waiter returned with their drinks. Esme picked up one of the glasses. "Join me," she ordered lightly.

Amanda picked up the other glass and clinked it with hers. They both sipped.

"I had the chef squeeze the oranges himself this morning," Esme murmured.

"You would," Amanda retorted, grinning.

Esme looked over at her and laughed. "Let's order."

After their order was given and the waiter retired, Esme leaned back and looked at Amanda. "Marriage agrees with you. You radiate wellbeing. You look happier, younger."

"Thank you," Amanda murmured, a mild suspicion lurking in her eyes.

"Amanda, you are so much fun. We could have a good time together if you would just allow yourself to like me. You are certainly fond of my son."

"Why would you think I don't like you? And how is Toby these days?" Amanda asked, ignoring the gibe.

"He just turned down an invitation to design a huge multi-storied resort in Hawaii." Esme studied Amanda over her glass as she sipped some more of the champagne. "Why would he do that?"

"Perhaps because he knew you were behind the deal," Amanda offered quietly.

"I only have his best interests at heart." Esme's face was suddenly stern.

"Toby has always had a mind of his own," Amanda spoke sympathetically. "And he's doing quite well for himself, making a name as a premier architect in the Southeast. That seems to be what he wants."

"He could have been judge," Esme whispered, a tremor of anger betraying her smile. "He could have followed in his father's footsteps. He could have married Cynthia Caswell and sired some grandchildren for me to carry on the family line, while keeping his 'leanings' respectably discreet."

Amanda shook her head. "But, Esme, he fought the path you wanted for him. It wasn't his path. I think you can be proud of him, of who he is." Amanda momentarily touched Esme's hand. "He is a lot like you, proud and stubborn and determined to make his mark."

"You stole him away from the Presbyterians," Esme accused quietly.

Amanda laughed heartily. "I did no such thing. You allowed him to attend the college choir events at St. Catherine's. He was already a fixture when I returned home. You sponsored some of the trips, if I recall correctly. You and he even chaperoned one a few years back, the ski trip."

"Yes," Esme said slowly, her features softening. "I remember—right after my James' death. It was—it was good for me."

Amanda nodded. "And I think he talked you into hosting the reception after the inaugural recital of the organ, didn't he?"

Esme laughed. "Yes, and I did so, just because I knew it would perturb Marjy."

Amanda smirked. "What was it with the rivalry between you two?"

"Rivalry?" Esme echoed, her eyes resting on Amanda.

"Yes, rivalry," Amanda nodded, their eyes meeting.

"It was all in fun," Esme murmured. "Marjy, like you, disdained my dabbling in political matters. And I thought her a bit too prim and proper, so I liked to ruffle her feathers."

"But all this reminiscing isn't the reason you set up this lunch, is it?" Amanda changed tack, her gaze quizzical.

Esme's smile was coy. "I'm getting to that. Why are you in such a hurry?"

"Because I'm a working woman, and I told Bradley I only had an hour to meet with him today," Amanda replied. "So I'm a paragon for the direct approach."

"A very rich woman," Esme supplied. "But a working woman, nonetheless, who has crossed the tracks." She smiled as the snub hit home.

"That was at best unkind, and you know it," Amanda flushed. "If you really thought that, you would not deign to have lunch with me in a public place. Furthermore, I am not, and shall not ever be, defined by the money left me by Marjorie." Amanda gazed at her lunch companion, her eyes flashing. "I am who I am." Amanda stopped herself, biting back the rest of the sharp retort on her tongue.

"I meant no disrespect, Amanda," Esme murmured, staring at Amanda, aware she had crossed a line.

"Indeed, you did." Amanda's return gaze held no smile.

"I apologize, Amanda." Esme broke off her own gaze, looking at her glass, and spoke with a sudden and uncharacteristic show of humility. "You're absolutely right, and it was uncalled for."

Esme downed the rest of her mimosa. "I admit I enjoy sparring with you. You aren't afraid of me, are you?"

"Why should I be?" Amanda sipped her water, steadying herself. "I have nothing you want. I am no threat to you, just a nobody from the other side of the tracks, as you put it. And I don't intend to treat you any differently than I do anyone else, no matter the extent of your influence."

"Even after all my help with the recital series, and my occasional business thrown your way?"

Amanda leaned forward intently. "And why did you do that? Am I now required to show gratitude in some way other than what I've already done? What exactly do you want?" Amanda was trying to control her rising irritation.

Esme nodded at some people across the room. Her voice lowered. "There are several upcoming vacancies in political office in Mainville. I merely wondered who you might be backing."

Amanda looked at her, bewildered. "You know for whom I'm cheering. It's no secret that two of my best friends are considering a run. Charlie Petrino has already qualified for the sheriff's race. Ralph Carmichael only hesitates about throwing his name in the hat for the judgeship because he worries about my reaction."

"Are you going to use your newfound wealth and influence to lobby for them?" Esme sipped her drink, eyeing Amanda.

"You know I have no talents in the lobbying business," Amanda retorted cautiously. "I leave that to the more experienced." She looked pointedly at Esme.

"Like me, you mean?" Esme smirked. "You know, you should be putting your own name in for the judgeship."

"Why? I'm surely not your choice, am I?" Amanda laughed shortly.

"You might be surprised," Esme smiled back.

Amanda frowned. "That is not something I aspire to. I am happy with my little law practice, my work at St. Catherine's and my new life with Jon. In fact, as much as I love him and want Ralph to be happy, I will be hard pressed to find a law partner nearly as good."

Amanda paused. "Surely you don't think there are any candidates out there more qualified than Charlie and Ralph?"

"Let's just say I'm not yet persuaded that having either will be in the best interests of Mainville," Esme purred.

"Is it Mainville's best interests you are concerned about?" Amanda countered sharply, her ire coming to the fore despite her effort to keep her tone light.

The waiter appeared with their food, and they were silent until he left. Then Esme leaned forward. "Sheath your claws, Mrs. Connor. This is a friendly little conversation, that's all."

"I'm sorry, but these two men's abilities and integrity I can vouch for, and I feel very strongly about defending them both."

"Still carrying a torch for Charlie?" Esme asked quietly, her voice so low that only Amanda could hear her. "And Ralph has always been sweet on you as well. It's all very touching."

"I have never carried a torch for Charlie," Amanda controlled herself with difficulty. "Ralph, Charlie and I are lifelong friends, nothing more. You know that. Are you trying to goad me?" Amanda clutched her napkin in her lap, her jaw set, trying to rein in her anger.

"No, I am as convinced as everyone else in town that the three of you are only the best of friends," Esme responded drily. "Although I have always speculated on whether there was more than meets the eye between you and Chief Petrino."

Amanda's hand at the edge of the table visibly clenched into a fist. "You would ruin a man's lifelong dream by spreading rumors about him and me?" she whispered, her eyes dilated.

"I never said that." Esme's eyes bored into Amanda's. "But I can't help but wonder. As I wonder why you would take Ralph Carmichael in and make him a partner."

Amanda shook her head. "Apparently your ideas and mine about frienship differ, Esme," she maintained quietly. "People act from motivations other than money and power. These are guys who are excellent at everything they do. I can't think of anyone better suited for the positions. Furthermore, they have risked their lives for me, and I would do the same for them. They are like family to me."

"That's very touching," Esme smiled saccharinely.

"You'd do the same for Toby, would you not?" Amanda whispered.

Esme's eyes flashed, and Amanda knew she had touched a nerve.

Amanda quickly changed the subject and took the offensive. "So, since your protégé Judge Kilmer has been escorted off the bench, just who are you eyeing to replace him?"

Esme leaned back, sipping her water and looking out over the deck outside. "Ouch, Amanda," she remarked, a tight smile plastered on her face, and Amanda knew she had just made another hit. "You had to remind me that Larry was my pick. Hell, if we were men of the last century, I'd be compelled to slap you in the face with my gauntlet."

"I'd have popped you first for the remarks about Charlie, Ralph and me," Amanda retorted, "and we'd already be facing off in the street wild-west style."

Esme turned her eyes on Amanda. She began laughing, and Amanda did too. "You can smile after the nasty barbs I planted?"

"The image of the two of us dueling in the street did me in," Amanda nodded, giggling. "I can take you in a face-off. I'm just worried about those bullets in my back."

Esme shook her head, still laughing. "You know, Amanda, I need to groom someone to replace me as the unofficial matriarch trustee of Mainville and environs. I'm thinking of retiring from the lobbying business soon, and I like your style," Esme remarked lightly. "You make a great fire-breathing dragon, but your schmoozing needs some work."

Amanda hooted, and Esme joined her, both of them laughing merrily. Several people looked their way.

"I'm so sorry to disappoint you, Esme, but I'm afraid I can't change my stripes," Amanda rejoined, clearing her throat.

Esme was silent a few minutes as they ate, then spoke up. "I'd really like to see you apply for the judgeship, Amanda. Toby thinks so highly of you."

Amanda was surprised. "I'm flattered, but you know I won't. I'm not cut out for it. And as I said I have nothing to offer you. I'd much rather you considered backing Ralph, although he is not for sale, and for that reason, because he is not for sale. The same goes for Charlie. You've known both of them all their lives, and know they are of the highest calibre. That is the reason they should have the positions."

"You amaze me with your naïveté," Esme murmured.

"I'm not naïve, but I have to continue hoping that the most qualified have a chance to make it into positions where they can help change the world for the better," Amanda retorted quietly, staring at Townsend.

Esme reached over and touched her hand momentarily. "You wouldn't reconsider, for Toby's sake?" her voice was almost pleading, her face suddenly pale.

Amanda was suddenly concerned. She leaned forward, gripping Esme's hand. "What is wrong, Esme?"

"Just a touch of heartburn. I'm fine." Esme pulled away with a touch of asperity. Esme looked at her a moment, a mask pulled over her features. "Dessert?" she asked.

Amanda looked at her watch. "Heavens, no," she remarked. "I really must be getting back. I have an appointment at one."

"See? You're running away," Esme accused lightly.

"I really am telling the truth." Amanda stood. "One of my kids at church is about to be expelled from school. His mother asked if I could go with her to meet with the principal." Amanda laughed shortly. "He isn't terribly accommodating schedule-wise, and she had to take precious time off work without pay for this. So I can't be late."

Amanda rummaged through her purse. "Forgive me for running out on you," she remarked, looking at her hostess.

"Think nothing of it. My treat," Esme smiled benignly.

"Oh, no, you don't." Amanda smoothly pulled out a one-hundred dollar bill from her wallet and laid it on the table. "My treat. Now you're beholden to someone else for a change."

She saw Esme flush, and grinned. "It's only fair. I have just lobbied you on behalf of my best friends. I hope you will consider backing them. I enjoyed our lunch and talk very much, Esme. We need to do it again soon, so that you can rid yourself of the impression that I don't like you. But next time just call me and we'll schedule more than an hour to chat. I promise."

Amanda walked out briskly, the *maitre d'* bustling behind her to notify the valet of her exit. Esme looked after her thoughtfully, then over to the corner of the room where a man in tailored suit was lounging. He smiled languidly as he raised his wine glass to her.

CHAPTER 8

Amanda had completed her rehearsal of her prelude. Ken had protested at her playing on Sunday, but she was matter-of-fact. "I've chosen something extremely easy that doesn't tax the left hand. I know I still can't play the whole service just yet, but I've got to get back on the organ bench some time."

He shook his head. "Amanda, I just don't want Doc and your husband coming after me when they discover you're playing the prelude for church this Sunday. And when they see 'Bach' on the bulletin, they will assume it is difficult."

"But you are my witness that this E-minor prelude and fugue is easy as pie," she argued. "In fact, I only play it this time of year because Emma for some reason likes it. And she's home to visit this week."

He looked at her dubiously. Amanda added, "I'm not wearing my robes. I'll just slip in, play it, and slip back out. I doubt anyone will notice."

"Yeah, right," Ken snickered.

So Amanda completed her run-through of the prelude and fugue, satisfied. I feel like I'm starting back at the beginning, she thought. Maybe next week I can handle all or at least some of the hymns. I've got to get back to some serious work on my repertoire.

As Amanda slid off the bench, Ken walked up. "There's something you've gotta see." He took her arm.

"What is it?" she spoke, surprised.

"Come with me to the choir room," he beckoned. "Hurry."

Curious, she followed him through the ambulatory to the choir room, where a very small girl was sitting at the piano, oblivious that she was the center of attention for the three or four people standing there silently regarding her.

Amanda caught her breath in shock when she saw the tiny creature. "My God," she breathed.

"Listen," Ken whispered, as the child sat and unerringly plunked out the beginning notes of the prelude Amanda had just rehearsed.

"There you are," a male voice cried with relief. Turning, she saw Adam Brownlee moving quickly toward the little girl, who looked up and saw all the eyes upon her. She acted as though she would cry, but Adam picked her up and comforted her, and she clung to him. "These are friendly folks," he told her solemnly. "They don't bite." As he turned and saw Amanda's eyes on them, he added, "At least most of them."

Amanda was frozen, unable to reply.

A voice behind her spoke. "Amanda, I'd like you to meet little Miss Donna Barnes."

She turned and looked into the eyes of Stephen Marks, who regarded her gravely. Jon walked in behind him and took her hand reassuringly.

"She looks just like Bill, only with red hair," Amanda blurted, then crimsoned. She swallowed convulsively.

"Where did she learn to pick out music like that?" she asked Brownlee, trying to cover her embarrassment.

"She just does it," Brownlee turned the little girl to face the adults, her eyes regarding them solemnly. "She listens to anything and can just remember it and immediately locate the notes on a piano. It's uncanny."

Amanda stared at the child, transfixed.

The little girl squirmed. "Down," she whined.

"OK, but you've got to hold my hand," Adam replied seriously to the child. He set her down, but she ran off.

"Excuse me," he apologized, moving off quickly after her.

"She is a willful child," Marks smiled indulgently. "But she is going to need music lessons and quick. I was hoping you could suggest a teacher."

Amanda found her voice. "How are you, Stephen?" she found herself asking.

"I'm well, thank you. And are you OK?" he looked at her, his golden-green eyes mirrors of her own.

"Yes," she smiled stiffly. "I'm happy to hear you are released on parole," she asserted aloud, floundering for something to say, wanting to hurt him, but ashamed of her feelings. The sight of the child so closely resembling Billy Barnes had unnerved her.

"It's OK, Amanda." Stephen held her gaze with his own, his voice quiet. "I don't expect anything from you," he added. "I only desire your happiness. I want to see this little one provided for, then I intend to disappear, no longer a reminder to you of our past."

He took her hand briefly. "But I must let this congregation know of my repentance. I wronged them as well as you, and I cannot relegate that sin to silence. So I apologize now for any additional pain I may cause you. That's why I am here today."

Amanda stared at Marks, her eyes wide and luminous. She finally tore herself away. "I must get ready for church," she murmured, panic in her voice.

Jon looked at her, dismayed. "What do you mean?"

"Please excuse me." She shook free and strode out of the room, quickly making it to a nearby restroom, where she ensconced herself in a handicapped-accessible stall away from prying eyes. She ran the cold water of the faucet over her wrists, taking deep breaths.

She heard the choir warming up, and was suddenly thankful to Ken all over again for taking care of the music program in her absence.

She slipped out of the bathroom, and turned, running right into Jon, who had been waiting for her. He caught her in his arms.

"Are you OK?" He was concerned, his arm resting on her waist, his hand running down her cheek to cup her chin.

"Yes," she smiled, covering her agitation.

"You are going to sit with me today, aren't you?" he asked, a twinkle in his eye. "I mean, it is a rare Sunday treat for me to sit with you in church."

"Yes, of course," she remarked briskly. "But I have to check on something for Ken, so go ahead without me, and I'll be right there."

He looked at her suspiciously. She kissed him quickly. "I promise," she whispered.

He left her and she waited a moment before following behind him through the ambulatory to the steps leading to the organ. She silently ascended and seated herself at the organ console. She adjusted the music and checked her registrations, satisfying herself that all was in readiness. She looked down at her hands, flexing the left one. No pain except for some tenderness running down the thumb. The numbness in the fingers was almost completely gone. Piece of cake, she thought.

She shut out everything else from her mind as she began the music, weaving the simple melody around until it culminated in chromatic chords, building to an equally simple fugue. For some reason this facile piece had always reminded her of Gerard Manley Hopkins' *The Windhover*, one of her favorite poems. She could almost fit the words to the notes, and could feel the lifting of her spirit like wings above a cloudless horizon.

All too soon she completed the piece, hit the cancel button, and slipped silently past Ken, who winked at her as he took her place. Applause erupted in the room. "See the fan club," he whispered, gesturing toward the back of the room. She was stunned to see the entire choir, acolytes and clergy standing lining the back of the church, as the congregation stood and gave voice to their joy at her return to the organ.

She quietly slipped into the congregation, past all the well-wishing parishioners, and found Jon, who regarded her solemnly as he stepped out to let her in the pew beside him.

"You could have told me you were playing today," he whispered in her ear.

"I'm sorry. I was sure you would not approve," she murmured nervously.

He took her hand during the opening strains of the processional hymn. "I'm not your enemy, my dear," he whispered. "I'm just looking out for you."

She gave him a heart-stopping smile as they sang together the first hymn.

Father Anselm gave a homily about forgiveness, tying in the Gospel of the day. Then at the end he paused. "There is someone here today that has requested special permission to address you, the congregation of St. Catherine's, this morning. I think that there has been much pain and confusion in our family this past year, and I feel God is leading this person to help open the doors to heal some of that. I ask that you give him your prayerful attention."

The congregation stirred, and Amanda tensed, as Stephen Marks made his way up the aisle to the steps of the chancel. Thanking Anselm, the tall spare man turned to the congregation. Jon sensed Amanda's apprehension and put his arm around her comfortingly.

"You all know me, and our pasts have been intertwined throughout the years. Many of you who read the papers are aware of my transgressions. I stand before you this morning, not as a man of God, but as the worst of sinners in need of forgiveness. As your bishop I should have been the shepherd of this flock, but instead I gave in to greed and selfishness. I willfully neglected this congregation in particular, used the church for my own ends, and helped to steal from you. And in that process I hurt many people."

He paused, clearing his throat, before looking up at the congregation, who to a person was hanging on his every word. "During my time in prison I have had time to reflect on the enormity of what I've done to so many." He looked over to where Amanda was sitting, and she shrank. Jon squeezed her hand in his.

"Mrs. Childs, Connor now, had nothing to do with the misappropriation of funds. She was entirely unaware of the crimes committed in her name. She and Marjorie Witherspoon have always placed St. Catherine's wellbeing as one of their highest priorities, and have given much to this congregation and community. I'm thankful that her name was cleared and that she has survived the ordeal for which I am to blame.

"I have learned to pray, and have prayed for God's forgiveness, and that you all might be willing and able to forgive me as well. I wanted one of my first visits to church after my release from prison to be to this community of believers.

"I know what I ask is not easy. And I don't ask it for me, but for the sake of others who must still bear the consequences of my sins. I don't want to take much of your time, but thank you for hearing me this morning."

He returned to his seat. Anselm looked out at his congregation a moment, then turned toward the altar and intoned: "I believe in one God, the Father, the Almighty, maker of heaven and earth, ..."

Jon looked at Amanda, whose face was ashen. He whispered to her, "Would you like us to slip out?"

She shook her head, and struggled to stand. With Jon's arm supporting her, she haltingly joined in reciting the Nicene Creed.

During the Prayers of the People, Anselm specifically offered up prayers for forgiveness and healing based on Marks' statements, and for thanksgiving for Amanda's recovery and ability to play that morning. Amanda was surprised by the number of audible murmurs in concurrence at that point.

During the Eucharist, she and Jon went up together past the choir to receive communion. When they arrived, there was an open space at the railing. Amanda started forward with Jon, then momentarily froze. There was Marks already kneeling next to the vacant place.

Jon looked askance at her. She closed her eyes, swallowed, and nodded, allowing herself to be led to kneel beside Marks.

She took communion, and stood to leave quickly. Marks whispered, "Thank you, Amanda. I know that was hard for you."

She nodded mutely, not trusting herself to make a sound, and left the altar area.

———

After the service Claire found Jon loitering in the parlor at the coffee hour, hands in his pockets.

"Where's Amanda?" she demanded.

"She is in emergency conference with Father Anselm and the vestry, something about this new parishioner that is charging around like a bull in a china shop, wreaking havoc with the recital series and the altar guild."

"Oh, Janine," Claire nodded.

"You know her?"

"Yes, Gwen's daughter." At his blank look, Claire added, "Gwen is the one seeing Dr. Howells."

"I didn't know Dr. Howells was seeing anyone." Jon was nonplussed.

"Gee, Jon, how do you miss all this stuff? Anyway, Janine blows into town ever so often, and it is crash and burn time when she is here. Apparently she has taken as her mission an anti-Amanda smear campaign during this visit."

"Why? Amanda does not need any more stress," Jon remonstrated.

"Because Janine sees Amanda as some sort of threat to a match between Gwen and Doc. Janine has no clue that she is the problem there. Amanda would like nothing better than to see Doc Howells happy with someone. But Doc himself is quite vociferous that he will not abide Janine's interference in his life, and Gwen herself is quite embarrassed about the constant turmoil Janine seems to stir up."

"I had no idea," Jon breathed. "So that's why the special meeting?"

"Yes. Now Janine has somehow obtained the recital series mailing list and sent out form letters asking whether they'd like a change in the format." Claire's eyes flashed angrily. "And Marjorie and Amanda footed the bill for this series in the beginning and made it what it was. Donors and supporters are calling and writing in droves, wanting to know who this woman is and angry at the thought of a change in quality."

"Damn," he exclaimed under his breath. "Amanda is already stretched thin. I didn't realize this was going on."

"Don't worry," Claire laughed softly. "Since the last year, the old guard and most of the newer members have rallied around Amanda, particularly after the disclosures about her innocence in the embezzling scheme. There are still some gossip pockets in the church and community, but they don't get far. And Toby Townsend is the senior warden this year, and he's one of her biggest fans. I have a feeling that Amanda will be pleasantly surprised after the meeting today. It is my understanding that the vestry wants to send out a letter disclaiming Janine's involvement."

Claire looked around, clutched Jon's arm and pulled him to a corner.

"Jon, you have got to talk to Amanda," she spoke confidentially.

"What about?" Jon asked, surprised.

"She's given Ralph the brush-off ever since Thursday afternoon, when he told her he had made his decision to apply for county judge. He's hurt. They're not talking. I don't understand it."

Jon whistled under his breath. "So that's why she's avoided the subject all weekend when I asked her what's going on with Ralph."

"Doesn't she think he would make a good judge? Why would she act this way?" Claire's voice dropped to a whisper. "Maybe she doesn't think he's good enough."

Jon quelled her with a look. "Claire, you know better than that. Amanda thinks Ralph is one of the finest attorneys anywhere, or she wouldn't be partners with him. But I think I know what's going on."

"What?" Claire frowned.

"Amanda believes that many judges get a taste of power and become egotistical prima donnas. She's afraid of losing Ralph, but more than that, she's probably apprehensive that he will become just like them."

"But it's Ralph we're talking about!" Claire replied indignantly.

"So?" Jon shrugged his shoulders. "It can happen to the best of them. Amanda knew many of the judges before they became judges. The position does change them."

Looking at her stricken face, he added gently, "Don't take it personally, Claire - it will all work out. Amanda and Ralph are extremely fond of each other, and she enjoys the good-cop, bad-cop team they've set up. She will be hard pressed to find another partner so thoroughly competent that complements her mind-set, and she knows it. But she'll come around."

"What about you? Why don't you two go into practice together?" Claire demanded.

"What was it Shakespeare said? 'Let me not to the marriage of true minds admit impediments'? I'm quite fond of being married to Amanda so far. Being in a business partnership with her would probably sound the death knell to the Connor happy Christmas marriage. Besides, we haven't had that honeymoon yet."

Claire looked at him hard, then burst out laughing. Jon joined her. "She's not known as 'the Good Witch of the South' for nothing, and she'll be the first to tell you that. And I am careful not to step on her ruby slippers. We're both headstrong. Marriage is challenge enough. And I've not even experienced her at full strength yet."

Ralph entered the room, a hang-dog expression on his face. Seeing the two of them, he moved across the room to join them.

"Where's Amanda?" Jon asked.

"The meeting is over," Ralph shrugged. "Father cornered her right afterward on some matter."

Toby Townsend walked up. "Good to see you, man," he spoke to Ralph, slapping him on the shoulder. "Haven't had time to just talk and find out how married life is treating you." He reached over and kissed Claire's cheek.

"Best thing I ever did," Ralph beamed.

Toby shook Jon's hand. "And you?" he grinned.

"Ditto," Jon laughed.

"I'm amazed at how Amanda has mellowed," Toby teased. "Being a warden has opened my eyes to the business of the church. But I shook my head in amazement all during that meeting. Before she met you, she'd have been on that situation like white on rice. But she sat back today and let the vestry take charge. Just what have you done with the real Amanda?"

Jon was nonplussed.

Toby smiled. "It's all good, man." Spying a young man standing in the doorway of the parlor, he continued, "Gotta go. See you all next Sunday. Ralph, call me for lunch this week."

As Toby moved off, Jon turned to Claire. "Do you two have lunch plans?"

Toby walked out of the parlor, running into Amanda. "Oops," she laughed, as he grabbed her by the arm. "Hi, Chris," she addressed the other man standing there, who nodded smilingly at her.

"Thanks so much, Toby, for supporting me," Amanda said warmly. "For years I was never sure where I stood in the congregation's eyes. It means a lot to me to see people sticking up for me. And I have you to thank."

Toby laughed. "No, you should be thanked. I always thought you were paid for all you do here. I never realized, Amanda, the extent of your contribution, both in time and money. After reviewing the books, I am flabbergasted at how much of yourself you have given to this church. We can't afford to lose you, and it's time we showed you."

Amanda reached over and kissed his cheek. "You do, Toby. I am so proud of you. As young as you are, you have accomplished so much, and still find time to serve at St. Catherine's."

"Yeah, tell that to my mom," Toby shook his head, frowning.

"I have and will continue every chance I get," Amanda promised, surprising him. She waved goodbye as they parted.

Back in the parlor, Ralph's expression changed. "Darn it," he sighed. "You'd think I ran over Amanda's dog or something. She will barely speak to me, even in the meeting just now. Would it be so bad if I actually made judge?"

He did not see that Amanda had entered the room and was walking up behind him. Before Claire or Jon could warn him, Amanda had grabbed his arm. Ralph, surprised, turned, and he looked chagrined as he realized that she had overheard him.

Amanda reached up and kissed him on the cheek. "I'm really sorry, Ralph," she spoke contritely. "My feelings have nothing to do with you and everything to do with me."

Ralph's face softened. "Then you're not mad at me?"

"Hell, yes, I'm mad at you," Amanda returned. "Why would you want to be a judge? They are all such - well, you know," she finished lamely, realizing she was still at church. "If you get it, you'll take a cut in pay and lose a fabulous partner."

Her eyes misted, and Ralph gazed at her soulfully, then engulfed her in a bear hug.

"If you get it, you are not taking Sheila with you," Amanda muttered, feigning severity. "I will kill you myself."

"We'll see," Ralph grinned mischievously.

"Like hell we will," Amanda retorted. "You will have the shortest term of office in history."

Jon intervened. "Please, kids, no scenes. Let's get out of here and grab a bite."

A smile played at the corners of Ralph's mouth as he asked playfully, "What, is Amanda cooking?"

"Sounds just like a lazy good-for-nothing judge. No, you and Jon are," she rejoined. "Steaks on the grill, while Claire and I take a dip in the lake. Bring your suits and some beer on ice. We'll make it a ground-breaking for the new pool. We'll celebrate Ralph's announcement and the fact we have no services or rehearsals tonight. See you around three."

And as they started out the door, Amanda called, "And call Jill and Charlie and ask them to join us. She needs to get out a little. The morning sickness has been really bad for her."

"I feel her pain." Ralph grinned at Claire, as Claire pinched his arm.

As Jon and Amanda entered his car and Jon pulled away from the curb, he asked, "How did the meeting go?"

"I don't really know," Amanda admitted. "I think well. The vestry assured me that they would ensure Janine ceased and desisted from further interference. I think they're ambitious at thinking they can easily stop her, but I'm grateful for their support. Toby was leading the charge, and I am so grateful that he is senior warden."

She mused aloud, "I wish I could figure out something to help Gwen with her daughter. Janine aggravates me, but I see that she is dying to do something important, be someone important. She craves attention, and she thrashes around wreaking havoc and embarrassing Gwen. More importantly, Janine is jeopardizing Gwen's happiness with Doc."

Jon was surprised. "You feel sorry for this Janine, when she is causing you trouble?"

Amanda smiled. "I guess so. She is so unhappy. I am ecstatic with you, and wish that others could find happiness like I have. I really want to see Doc find someone. He lived all those years with unrequited feelings for Marjorie. I know Gwen loves him, and I'm pretty sure he returns that feeling. I want

Janine to find some fulfillment so that she'll leave her mother alone and let her be happy too."

"You're strange," Jon smirked.

"I guess so," she giggled. "And before Marjy's death I would have been up in arms about Janine's mucking with the recital series. I guess my priorities have changed."

Jon, changing the subject, remarked, "You made Ralph feel better back there. I think he really wants this judgeship, but he values your approval."

"Don't I know it?" Amanda responded, a tinge of bitterness in her voice.

Jon, surprised, pressed, "And you don't want it for him?"

Amanda, embarrassed, looked away. "I guess I always knew that our business association was too good to last. Ralph has always had a political bent. Yes, I'm proud of him and he'd make a fine judge. I'm just selfish. I don't want to start over. I like having a partner, and I don't think there's another one like Ralph out there."

"Claire asked why we didn't go in together," Jon remarked casually.

She laughed, then grew serious. "The thought had crossed my mind. But Jon, I love you so much. I'm not sure I could concentrate on work if I were around you all day. And there's always the danger that we might become too competitive or too possessive."

Jon took her hand in his as he stopped at a red light. "Would you be jealous of all my women clients?" he inquired smilingly.

"Insanely," she answered, smiling back.

"Probably not as much as I would be of your men clients," he rejoined, kissing her fingertips as the light turned green and he accelerated forward. "Guess we know how the division of labor would have to fall."

She sighed happily. "We'll talk about it. I just don't want anything to spoil what we have."

"Neither do I, Mrs. Connor," he breathed.

Soon they were on the private lane leading toward their home. Pulling up outside, Jon ran around and got her door. They went arm in arm up the front steps. He pulled her in after him, then shut the front door and backed her up against it. He pinned her body against the door. He kissed her long and hard, as she returned the kiss fervently, both of them breathing quicker.

He said huskily, "You're probably right about our not practicing together."

She murmured breathlessly, "I am?" as he ran his hands up under her dress to stroke her thighs, and nuzzled her neck.

The Connors' Crisis

"Yeah. We might not accomplish many billable hours," he whispered. "We'd always be late getting to work. Then there would be the long lunch hours. No working late. And of course tea time."

"Tea time," she echoed, aware of nothing but his nearness.

Taking her hand, he bodily dragged her up the stairs after him and through the bedroom door. "We don't have much time," he whispered urgently in her ear as he lowered her to the bed, one hand unzipping her skirt as the other pushed it away, claiming her skin. His eyes bored into hers as he continued undressing her. He traced her lips with his fingers. "You drive me mad, woman," he said huskily. "You are indeed a witch."

"Then my spell must be working," she whispered as she grabbed his tie and dragged him to her.

Afterward, they lay in each other's arms, spent and satisfied. He wiped the tears coursing down her cheek as he kissed her. "Are you OK?" he asked her concernedly.

"Wow," she replied with a weak smile. "I'm glad you're cooking, because I am not sure I have the strength to move."

He laughed, running his fingers down her side as she shivered.

She told him, "I could stay right here forever with you."

"No need, because we have forever together," he murmured in her ear. "There's still tea time to come."

It was her turn to laugh, as he raised himself up and held out his hand to her, lifting her to him.

CHAPTER 9

Amanda walked into the kitchen, a gauzy cover-up over her one-piece bathing suit. Jon, dressed in swim trunks and a light unbuttoned shirt, gazed at her as he marinated the steaks. She began washing the vegetables for a salad, unmindful of his eyes upon her. As he came up behind her at the kitchen sink, molding himself to her to kiss her neck, they heard a knock at the door and Ralph calling.

"Saved by the knock," she said lightly, as Jon released her and went to help Ralph carry in a cooler.

Claire, dressed similarly to Amanda with the addition of a large-brimmed straw hat, breezed into the kitchen. "I stopped for some dessert at the deli. That salad is looking good." She looked intently at Amanda's flushed cheeks, before accusing her. "Been busy?"

Amanda blushed as she asked, "Am I that obvious?"

Claire laughed. "You're in love, and you show it. It looks good on you."

"I am in love," Amanda confirmed.

Ralph walked in, bristling with excitement. "Did you hear the news?" he demanded seriously.

"No, what is it?" Amanda turned to him.

"Sheriff Watson had a massive heart attack. He died this morning," Ralph was somber.

"No!" Amanda exclaimed. "That is so sad. Of course, it's been a long hard battle for him with the cancer, and he was already weak."

She swallowed. "Poor Mary. How horrible for her. I didn't always agree with the sheriff's politics, but still he was a good man, and hired competent people who knew their job."

"I know," Ralph rejoined soberly. "But I'm wondering who will be appointed interim pending election."

100

"I hope the governor will appoint Charlie. Charlie has already qualified to run in the upcoming election, and I think he has the experience to do a great job. And the Department could use some organization," Amanda mused aloud.

"We'll see. That is an appointment fraught with politics," Ralph reminded her. "Speaking of which, did you call Charlie too?"

"Jon called, but Jill is still suffering terrible morning sickness, and Charlie is being the loving husband and waiting on her today. He sends their regrets."

"He seems ecstatic at the thought of being a father." Ralph watched her carefully for her reaction.

"I think so. They're both beaming," Amanda laughed, turning away as he left to join Jon on the deck.

The women chattered as Amanda finished the salad and whipped up a dressing. Jon walked past her, pecking her on the cheek. "The grill is ready, and the corn and bread are on. The steaks are about to join them. If you girls are going to swim before the meal, do it now and make it quick."

He whispered in Amanda's ear, "I personally chased off the water moccasins and put out a 'do not disturb' sign. But don't tell Claire that—Ralph says she's deathly afraid of snakes."

The two women placed their wares on the table on the screened porch, then raced down to the dock, pulling off their wraps and diving in. Coming up for air, Amanda started breast stroking her way across the lake. Her shoulder was still tender, but Dr. Rand had told her that swimming was good exercise for strengthening the area after her injury, although he was less than happy that she was doing so much. So she completed two laps, meeting Claire bobbing at the dock.

Laughing, Claire pulled her close. "I have a secret."

Amanda looked at her radiant face expectantly. Claire stared at her and whispered, "Can you guess?"

"No," Amanda said slowly, then the news dawned on her. "You're expecting?"

Claire nodded. Amanda hugged her. "That's great news, Claire," Amanda replied fervently. "Does Ralph know?"

"Yes. You have to act surprised, because he is dying to make the announcement at dinner. I couldn't wait. We want you and Jon to be godparents."

"I'm so happy for you," Amanda sighed happily. Her face clouded over.

Claire noticed it. "What is it?" she queried concernedly.

"You two are such good friends, and I don't want anything to spoil that."

"What would interfere? Oh, you mean if Ralph makes judge? Amanda, don't worry. The process is filled with uncertainty - it may never come to pass. Nevertheless, nothing will change the way Ralph and I feel about you and Jon."

Amanda smiled distractedly, as Claire started up the steps to the dock. "Come on, let's eat."

Amanda floated in the water a moment, reluctant to leave it, before following Claire.

They quickly set the table, and Amanda brought Claire a large glass of iced water. Ralph, coming up behind them, had a platter of corn on the cob and bread, as Jon followed him with the steaks.

Ralph saw the glass of water and turned to Claire. "You already told her?" he accused.

Amanda looked at him, feigning wide-eyed innocence. "Told me what?"

Ralph shrugged in mock disgust. "Women can't keep a secret," he grumbled.

"Wait a minute!" Amanda's eyes flashed. "Who was it that couldn't for the life of him keep the secret of his own Christmas gift to his fiancée?"

"OK, OK," Ralph conceded, laughing.

Jon looked at them all in consternation. "I'm still in the dark - what's up?"

Ralph beamed as he set the food on the table and slipped his arm around Claire. "You're going to be a godfather."

Jon looked quickly at Amanda, then at Claire. "A baby?" he breathed, incredulous. "Wow, this is great news. Congratulations, you two." He walked up to the two of them and put his arms around them, kissing Claire's cheek, as Amanda looked on smiling.

"We have a lot to be thankful for," Amanda remarked, as they took their places at the table. Jon's fingers lingered around hers as they said grace and everyone began eating and talking at once. He could tell that while she was delighted at their news, she seemed dazed. No wonder, he thought. What a day, a week, a month and a year.

As she excused herself to go inside and turn on some background music, he followed her. "Are you all right?" he whispered to her.

"Fine. Why?" she asked, startled.

"I don't know. You don't seem to be all here. A part of you is somewhere else. Is it the news of the baby?"

"I don't know," she confessed. "Ralph's seeking the judgeship, and the advent of a baby - these are big life-changing decisions."

"Does it change your mind about our putting off having a child?"

"No, not right now at least. Does it for you?"

"Raising a child is a huge responsibility, although something I wouldn't mind, if you wanted it too," he replied tenderly. "But I really want you all to myself for a while. I'm willing to wait and see how we feel, leave it in God's hands. Either way I can be happy."

"Good," she breathed a sigh, visibly relieved at his answer. "I was worried at your reaction to their news."

"Oh, milady," he murmured, kissing her. "I love you so much."

Ralph called, "There's food getting cold out here."

Jon smiled at her. "Tea time will have to wait." He returned to the porch, as Amanda turned on the radio and tuned it to the local jazz station.

As she returned to her seat, Ralph announced, "It's very rude to be making out in the next room when you're entertaining guests."

Claire slapped his arm. "Speak for yourself - what were you doing while they were in there?"

Ralph wrinkled his forehead. "Woman, I thought you were on my side."

They all laughed as they lazily enjoyed their repast under the whirring ceiling fans, making the summer heat cooler. After dinner and clean-up, the men flipped a coin to see which one would score the opportunity to lie down in the long porch swing, and the women went down to the dock to sit on the dock and watch the sun lowering in the sky.

Claire, settling herself into the deck chair Amanda offered, sighed happily and looked over to Amanda, who draped herself at the end of the dock. "How about you and Jon? Have you discussed starting a family?"

"Yes, we have, but we have decided to hold off and see," Amanda smiled. "Besides, let's focus on you and Jill; that will be enough babies at one time. Let's spoil yours before crowding the horizon. You don't know how happy I am for you."

She paused, then steered the conversation away from herself. "How about Ralph? He seems so proud."

"He couldn't wait to let all the family know. He's good with children," Claire replied. "I think he'll make a good father. "

"I know he will," Amanda agreed.

They sat quietly, listening to the sounds of the birds, crickets and frogs as the lake became a chorus of wildlife noises. Amanda looked over to see Claire with her eyes closed, lightly slumbering. Smiling, she turned and dangled her feet just above the water line as she silently watched a blue heron pick his way around the edge of the opposite shore.

Suddenly she was grabbed from behind. Feeling herself falling over the edge of the dock, she felt a moment of panic, and instinctively latched on to her attacker. They both splashed noisily into the water. Coming up sputtering, she found herself face to face with Ralph, who was paddling and laughing at her. Before he could dodge, she placed her right hand on his head and quickly and forcefully dunked him into the lake, quickly pushing away out of his reach.

It was his turn to bob back to the surface coughing as she regarded him from arm's length. Then he dived under the surface, grabbing her by the feet and pulling her under.

As they both resurfaced and Amanda reached out in retaliation, he called out, choking, "Time out! Truce."

"No fair," she cried, wiping the water from her face.

Jon and Claire sat on the dock watching them. "Play fair, children," Claire called, as Ralph and Amanda started splashing each other. Suddenly Amanda turned and started splashing water toward Jon and Claire, as Ralph followed her lead. Jon took a running leap and landed in the water just behind them, and Claire laughed as the three kept splashing and dodging each other.

As Ralph swam to and climbed up the ladder to join Claire on the dock, Jon grabbed Amanda and turned her to face him. "Deep breath," he whispered. As she inhaled, his mouth covered hers and he drew her down with him under the water, holding her to him and caressing her. She wrapped one arm around his neck and held on, returning his kiss until they slowly emerged from the water.

Breathless, she turned and swam to the dock, with him in close pursuit.

Later, they all sat on the screened porch to watch the sun losing its battle with the sky. Ralph, his voice slurred, turned to Claire. "Woman, take me home."

Claire laughed, as they said their goodbyes. Jon and Amanda watched them drive away, then walked back in the house arm in arm.

"What is this about you and Ralph manipulating my schedule at work?" she demanded suddenly.

Jon squeezed her tighter. "That was supposed to be a secret. I am trying to plan our post-wedding reception and honeymoon. I hoped to make it a surprise. But Ralph tells me that you have always been resistant to taking time off, and he is having a devil of a time doing it behind your back."

She shook her head at him. "That's why you should not keep secrets from me. Sure, we can plan that."

He looked at her in surprise. She continued, "But you don't understand my strategy. Since Andy's death until now, I really have had little reason to take off for any long period of time. Marjy would drag me away for short getaways, but my practice, church and community work were my life, my reason for continuing." She looked shamefaced. "It was all I had. That, and the prison I made for myself with Andy's memory."

They arrived indoors. She rested her head on his shoulder. "But now I want to spend time, lots of time, with you, Jon." She smirked. "But I don't want Ralph to know how badly I want that."

Jon was amazed. "Why not?"

"Our practice is very busy, and we do extremely well. But when there is down time, Ralph becomes a procrastinator, putting things off, becoming lazy. And it's worse now that he's married to Claire." She paused. "And I know I am subject to that same danger now. There is life now outside our careers, and instead of our work being the reason for our existence, it is a means to making our living so that we can enjoy our lives."

"It makes sense, but what has that to do with your taking off for a honeymoon?" Jon asked, playing with her hair and fondling the back of her neck.

"I just have to plan it and make it so that it falls at a time that is moderately busy, not heavily so, and certainly not too slow. That way Ralph will not be burdened with too much to do, but be busy enough to combat that restlessness."

Jon looked skeptically at her, but she laughed. "There is this unwritten rule that when one of us is gone, the other is under the gun to make it so that the office is running smooth as glass and everything in great shape when the partner gets back. When one of us is gone, we're secretly hoping that we're missed, and that the office won't run without us. However, we are also reluctant to return to a huge mess of work."

"And Ralph goes along with your strategy?" Jon asked.

"Well, as a woman, I have learned to make it his idea," she laughed. "You men can't survive without the manipulations of us women."

"He and I would both agree with that," Jon pulled her to him and kissed her.

She wrapped her arms around him. "But if he becomes judge, all that will change, and I will be alone again," she lamented. "So if I'm to ever have a honeymoon, we need to plan it soon."

"Maybe we need to practice a little," Jon murmured. "Besides, it is tea time."

The phone rang, shattering their repartee. He reached over, Amanda still in his arms, and answered it.

"Hello? Oh, hi, Mom. No, we weren't doing anything," he grinned as Amanda disentangled herself.

He listened a moment, as Amanda started to walk away. He then thrust the phone at her.

"Mom said she wants to talk to you."

Amanda was surprised, but took the phone. "Hello, Mrs. Connor, how are you?"

"You make me sound so old. Call me Gloria, dear. How are you?"

"I'm feeling much better, thank you."

"I enjoyed our dinner together back—it must be over a month ago now," Gloria Connor spoke, a hint of reproach in her voice. "We really would like to spend more time with Jon—and with you," she added.

"That would be nice," Amanda replied, as Jon regarded her with a question in his eyes. "Are you down this week?"

As a matter of fact, we are, to get our week of hot weather. I'd like to plan for us to get together while we're here."

"That would be great," Amanda said brightly. "When would be a good time?"

"Well, I'm trying to adjust the itinerary. I'll just call Jon in the morning and try to set up something, OK?"

"Sure," Amanda conceded.

"Now may I speak to my son again?"

Amanda handed the phone back to Jon, and walked into the kitchen. Jon's eyes followed her as he answered his mother's questions.

After he hung up, he went off searching for Amanda. She was staring out the kitchen window into the dusk.

"So Gloria wants us to get together?" he asked.

"Yes," she nodded.

"She castigated me for your calling her Mrs. Connor," Jon chuckled.

"I'm sorry," Amanda turned away. "It's hard for me after just one meeting to feel right calling her by her first name."

"You're still not comfortable with them, are you?" Jon queried.

"Your dad seemed to try to make me feel at ease. But I still feel like an outsider," Amanda confessed. "I know it will get better. But your mother asked such pointed questions. I admit I don't think I was well prepared."

"You are a lawyer," Jon reminded her smilingly. "Give her as good as she sends, dear."

"I really want them to like me," Amanda muttered.

"Don't try so hard," Jon pulled her to face him. "It will come all in good time. Be yourself. I love you as yourself, whether they do or not." He checked himself, as Amanda gazed at him, the sudden question in her eyes. "What I mean is that they are going to love you as much as I do. Give it time."

Gloria hung up the phone and turned to her husband. "I'm having lunch with Samuels tomorrow."

"Samuels?" Her husband James laid down his book and stared at his wife. "Why?"

"I engaged him to do some checking on Jon's new wife," Gloria replied, not looking at James.

"Dammit, Gloria, can you not leave matters alone?" James remonstrated.

"I just want to know the calibre of woman my son has married," she was defensive. "And Jon hasn't been forthcoming with information."

James stood and paced in front of the glass doors leading out to the deck facing the gulf. "Jon is an FBI agent, and this woman started out as a suspect in a case. He was a close friend and colleague with her husband. Don't you think there's little about her he doesn't already know? He didn't blindly fall in love with her."

"There's just a lot going on in her life, and I think we should know," Gloria replied stubbornly. "Did you know that Senator Whitmore is her father-in-law?"

"So?" James hissed angrily. "If you had invited the two of them for a private visit, there's probably a lot she would have told us herself. Instead, you have these little soirees, and cross-examine her in front of strangers. I could look at her and tell how uncomfortable she was."

"I didn't think I asked anything that shouldn't be publicly known. Her life should be an open book," Gloria sputtered angrily.

"Do you want me to announce to everyone the last time you had sex with me?" James rejoined pointedly.

Gloria flushed. He continued, "Look at our three children. Jon and David are in their thirties, and Kelly is thirty this year. Jon's first marriage didn't take. David hasn't even tried. Kelly eloped, and look how that turned out. Kelly's long-time boyfriend booked and moved here to Florida. Joey is a fine young man, grew up with the boys, is like one of our family, and he won't even come to the family gatherings. Kelly does nothing but mope around. Are you going to keep telling me none of that is your fault?"

Gloria stood, enraged. But he held up his hand.

"I don't have to listen to this, James," she hissed.

107

"Please." He walked up and took her arm, his voice pleading. "Don't you want grandchildren? I do. I want to see our children happily paired up. I want little ones to enjoy. I didn't get to be around much for my children when they were growing up, because I was working so hard to make the business a success. I want to make up for that with their children."

He held both her arms and stared into her eyes. "Gloria, please don't mess this up for Jon. Didn't you see how he couldn't take his eyes off Amanda that night? And she was just the same with him. They are in love. She's beautiful, intelligent, obviously doesn't want him for his money, and doesn't seem to care one whit about our status. Give her a chance."

"What if he's made some terrible mistake?" Gloria cried.

"It's his life and his mistake. He's an adult and can handle it without your meddling." James released her and walked away. "But if you interfere, you will either ruin it for him or alienate him from us." He turned and looked at her coldly. "As much as I love you, I don't want that for our son."

He strode out of the room.

CHAPTER 10

It was Saturday. The weather was warm, and the lush greens of early summer were preening on the farm. The sky was scattered with hazy clouds periodically punctuating the otherwise brilliant vista of blue.

Jon jogged down the stairs, dressed in khakis and polo shirt. Not seeing Amanda, he strode into the kitchen, where he found her, her hair pulled back in a ponytail, dressed in an oversized man's shirt and khaki shorts, poring over designs, a proposal and a stoplist scattered over the kitchen table, looking at several blueprint sketches critically.

She smiled at him. "Steve is coming to meet with the vestry next week about plans for the new organ. He sent all this for my review. I've sent copies to Fred Swann, and we are going to talk by phone tomorrow afternoon if his schedule permits."

"I've got to run to town on a few errands. Want to come along?" Jon proposed.

"I think I'll stay here." Amanda didn't look up from the plans.

Jon was surprised. It wasn't like Amanda to beg off from accompanying him.

Amanda looked up and noted the expression on his face. "I don't want you to feel you have to drag the ball and chain with you wherever you go," she answered his unspoken question. "And I know what's up. Ralph is wanting you to stop by Betty's for lunch. He has big plans of an all-guy deep-sea fishing trip he wants to discuss."

Jon swallowed a grin. "How did you know about that?"

"I have my ways," she purred. "And he's afraid I am going to make a fuss because I won't be invited."

"I'm not going without you," Jon murmured, pulling her into his arms.

"No," she demurred. "I think it is a good idea for you guys to do a little male bonding. Besides, I think we girls can find our own trouble with you all gone. You might point out to Ralph the trip may cost him and Charlie more than they bargained for, when they get the price tag for the new nurseries and maternity clothes and the like when we go shopping without you all."

Jon kissed her and murmured, "And what sort of baubles is Mrs. Connor going to purchase?"

"Well, I hope to purchase the baby furniture for Jill and Claire as a surprise gift. For myself I haven't decided yet, but I'm leaning toward the lingerie department." She kissed him back.

"Ah, such a glorious waste," he laughed. "You look so good in them for the few nanoseconds you get to wear them." His kiss deepened.

"You know," he whispered, "we need to decide on you a new set of wheels. I mean, I got a brand new Land Rover, but you're the one who needs a new car. It doesn't seem fair that you are driving my Mercedes. With your luck running as it has been, you need four-wheel drive more than I do."

"I think I'm happy trying out a different brand of vehicle," she smiled at him. "My luck with the Beemers has been pretty shaky lately, with one side-swiped and the other submerged in a creek. I think we can hold off a bit longer until I decide what I want. Besides," her eyes twinkled, "if you make it a habit of going off with the guys, I may need to invest in a real hottie convertible, with matching lingerie and lipstick."

"There's no danger of my neglecting you, dear," Jon assured her. "In fact, I can think of several things better than having lunch with the guys today."

She pushed him away playfully. "Get out of here before I change my mind and decide you can't go."

"What are you going to do?" he demanded.

"As little as possible," she replied.

"Now why do I not believe that?" Jon looked at her skeptically.

"I'm serious," she laughed. "I'm going to be lazy, enjoy the sunshine and wait for you to come home. In fact, why don't you bring dinner with you?"

"I'll do that," he kissed her hand. "Anything in particular?"

"Make it light. I have some definite ideas about dessert," she smiled slyly.

She walked him out to the driveway and waved goodbye as he left.

She turned and looked down the trail toward the stream. She could make out Fred's pickup truck just in sight at the end of the path. Speaking of fishing, that's just the ticket, she thought.

Several minutes later she was decked out in waders, with fly fishing gear in hand and an old battered straw panama hat on her head. She set off down the trail, happily taking in the lovely day and the slight welcome breeze wafting through the leaves of the oaks and poplars and maples.

A few minutes later the large brown dog came wagging up to her as she reached the bank. "Dear Bozo," she smiled and scratched his ears affectionately. "Are you having any luck?" she crooned.

"They're biting slow," a voice replied. She looked up at Fred Vaughan, dressed similarly to her except for a cloth bucket hat with flies attached to the outer band, as he surveyed her critically.

"Have you caught any?"

"A few." He pointed to his basket. "You feeling lucky?"

"Hope springs eternal," she quipped. "One day I will land a fish in this stream. Maybe today."

"There's one out there with your name on it," Fred nodded. "Jon gone to the planning meeting?"

"You knew about that?" Amanda laughed. "Why aren't you there?"

"This is my type of fishing," Fred retorted. "More skill, less talk."

"OK, so let's get to it," Amanda smiled. "I'm starting back at Fly Fishing 101, back to the spot Andy first planted me. We'll see what happens."

"Cast to the left, in that shady spot next to the other shore between the two patches of sunlight," Fred advised, pointing.

Amanda nodded as she gingerly stepped into the clear creek and slowly waded to her destination, trying to stir the water as little as possible. Arriving, she took her time tying a fly onto the line, concentrating on the task at hand.

She then tried a few test casts, trying to get a sense of the forgotten rhythm and determining the wind direction. She kept at it until she started relaxing into a pattern, hitting her mark with some regularity, letting out a little line.

Amanda looked out across the water to the point just visible where she knew Andy had regularly fished, and smiled. I can finally think of you without gut-wrenching pain, she told Andy silently. Although I will always miss you, now there is someone who fills the emptiness, who makes me whole again. Thank God I have a second chance at love.

Time seemed to stand still, and there was no sound but the breeze in the trees and an occasional frog or cicada. The sun was warm and the slight wind caressing as she doggedly continued casting, doing a little false-casting to periodically dry out her fly. She finally paused, deciding to try another fly.

Tying it on, she cast, missing her mark. But before she could mend the lie, there was a sharp tug on the line. Caught totally off guard, she stumbled and stepped into a hole, but had the presence of mind to hold her rod up and tighten up her line as she hauled herself back up.

Hell, she thought, I'm not sure what to do now that I've actually hooked one. She started laughing as she went about trying to set the hook and bringing the catch in.

"Don't tangle the line," Fred called, noting her activity, turning and laying his rod on the bank where he was fishing, and heading in her direction.

"Don't let me lose him now that I've finally hooked one," she gasped, still laughing with delight.

Fred watched critically as she tightened the line and struggled with the catch. "Keep the rod tip up. Steady - you got him," Fred assured her as he moved in front of her to retrieve the trout. Reaching down, he grasped the line with one hand and the fish by the mouth with the other, hauling him up for her to see.

"Fine specimen," he noted. "Good eating."

She grinned, admiring the fish gazing back at her, a rainbow stripe down his torso. "He's so beautiful. I'm suddenly like Caleb—I wish I could keep him. But you're right—he'll taste good out of the pan."

Fred smiled one of his rare smiles, but said nothing. He released the hook from the fish and handed her the fly. "Better put on a dry fly and get another to go with him," he advised. "I'll take care of this one. Good going, Amanda."

She grinned broadly, reaching into the breast pocket of her shirt for a small tin container of flies, retrieving one to tie on as Fred slowly moved away, reviving the trout in the water. Amanda was oblivious to all else around her as she prepared to cast again, hitting the same spot. Almost immediately she had a strike.

"Dang, Fred, I think I have another," she gulped. Fred swallowed a smile as she concentrated her effort on landing the second fish.

But this one had different ideas, and started a run. She played out a little line, then knew she had a challenge. Stepping off her ledge, she moved forward, keeping the rod high and tensing up on the line. The rod bent as the trout fought back, pulling her forward. She clamped down on the line with her left hand in a panic to prevent more line from running out. She winced as the line caught between her thumb and forefinger and tugged. She bit back an epithet.

Fred turned back to see her. "Watch out for that—" but it was too late, as she stepped headlong into a trench. She came up sputtering, her rod still held high, her hat floating off with the current.

"Damn," she muttered, jerking back on the rod, feeling the fish still on the line, again trying to tauten the line and close the distance between her and the pesky cold-blooded creature she was suddenly determined to best.

The Connors' Crisis

"If I have to strong-arm wrestle your ass underwater, you are mine," she swore. The rod again bent.

"Take your time," Fred called, noting her struggle and again heading in her direction. "Don't let him tangle you up in the grass. Pull up and head to your right with him."

"If he breaks my rod, I'm going to chase him down and smash his head in with a rock," she retorted.

"There's another hole at your two o'clock. Move back behind it," Fred instructed.

She did as he stated and pulled the rod higher, doggedly dragging in line. "Smooth," Fred said calmly. "Don't jerk too hard—he is tiring now."

"So am I," she remarked.

After a couple more minutes' fighting, which seemed much longer, Fred helped her retrieve the culprit. "Ooh, this one is too nice to eat," Fred murmured as he reached down and gently snagged the large trout by the mouth. "He belongs on the wall, even if he ain't your first."

Amanda beamed as Fred gently disentangled the hook from the mouth of the trout and moved him back and forth in the water. "I'm putting him on a stringer so we can keep him in the water until I can bring the cooler for him," Fred explained.

He looked up at Amanda and laughed at her bedraggled appearance, her hair and shirt wet, her hat missing. "Wanna try for three?"

"No," she held up her hands in a gesture of surrender, the rod gripped in the right hand as she looked ruefully at the darkening burn on her left palm. "I'm done today. I have to play tomorrow."

"I think this one may beat Andy's best for size from this creek," Fred remarked. "We'll get some ice on your hand. Andy would be so proud."

"Yes, he would," Amanda nodded, smiling.

"We're going to have to eat some fish, what with your catch and mine today," Fred continued.

"You're right, but I'm too lazy to cook them this evening," Amanda giggled.

"We might make it a Sunday evening meal tomorrow," Fred suggested. "I'll even clean and cook them with the fixings. You do the dessert and wine."

"Sounds good," she assented happily.

She sat on the bank, held the end of the stringer and admired the trout while Fred went to get the cooler. When he made it back, he had brought a camera and took her picture with her catch.

Later that afternoon Jon returned home. "Amanda?" he called, several shopping bags in hand. Not finding her, he dumped his cargo on the kitchen counter and went in search for her.

Jogging up the stairs, he looked out the window and spied her lying on the grass in the back yard. Grinning, he retraced his steps to the kitchen, retrieving a bottle of chardonnay, opening it and recorking it, and grabbing 2 wine glasses. He found an empty basket and placed his offerings in it, along with some cheese, a cutting board, grapes, a knife, some napkins, and some French bread. As he walked through the living room he grabbed up a throw.

He walked out and joined her, sitting down on the grass beside her. She was dressed in a sunny halter top and some khaki shorts, her hair curling around her face. She opened her eyes.

"Oh, hi," she smiled.

"Shouldn't you sun in a bathing suit?" Jon reached over and pecked her on the cheek, then pulled her to him, framing her face in his hands as he kissed her.

"Oh, I am just admiring the blue sky," she mumbled as she kissed him back. "Join me."

"But there's something much more beautiful to admire sitting right beside me," he murmured. "And I brought you a treat."

He stood and spread out the throw, then pulled her to sit beside him, opening the basket. As she reached for the wine glass, he noticed a large discoloration between the thumb and forefinger of her left hand.

He took her hand gently. "What happened here?" he asked, his voice suddenly stern.

"Just a small skirmish earlier today." She winced as he touched the bruised area. "Which I won."

"What have you been doing?" he looked at her questioningly.

"Oh, nothing much," she answered brightly. "By the way, we are invited to Fred's tomorrow afternoon for dinner. We're to bring dessert and wine." She withdrew her hand and held it out for the wine glass.

He poured her some wine, then set out his cheeses on the little marble cutting board he had brought. "If I recall correctly, you are not averse to a little smoked gouda and brie," he smiled, cutting a small piece and proffering it.

"I am not," she murmured, as he placed the sliver in her mouth, and his fingers lingered on her lips.

"And we sweeten it a bit with the grape," he followed up with the fruit.

"So how did the meeting go?" she smiled as she chewed and sipped her wine.

"Ralph took my message from you as a threat, and wanted us to invite the wives to come along, to keep you all out of trouble. But Charlie and I decided you girls should have the option."

She giggled. "I know the answer to that one. Jill will not want to spend the day on a rocking boat smelling fish in her current state. And Claire's idea of roughing it is a salon that doesn't carry her shade of nail polish."

"You could still come out with the guys." Jon leaned forward, stroking her hair.

"No, 'twould cramp your style if you have a girl tagging along," she teased. "So when is this 'men meet fish' adventure to take place?"

"Actually Ralph had a suggestion, which might make for a nice compromise. He suggested we all spend the weekend at the Barnes' beach house, since you still hold a lease on the place. It's big enough for all of us. The guys could rent a charter and go out during the day, and the girls could shop, sun, do whatever. Then we could all hang out together at night. Inasmuch as the Fourth of July is already upon us, we discussed doing it then, but both Ralph and Charlie have family gatherings that holiday, and I know you are expecting Jeff and Desiree. Ralph suggested the weekend after that."

Amanda sat up. Jon watched her reaction closely. She was expressionless for a moment, then swallowed and nodded. "That might work," she smiled unconvincingly.

"Not if it resurrects bad memories." Jon reached out and took her hand.

"Perhaps we can replace the old memories with some new ones," she countered softly, but he could feel her body tense. "That's a great idea," she assented.

Jon downed his wine, then moved toward her. "Are you sure?" He drew her to him, enfolding her to him and kissing her hair, her ear, her cheek.

"Yes," she replied, as she wrapped her arms around his neck and pulled him down with her on the blanket.

CHAPTER 11

Amanda alighted from her car and accepted the valet ticket from the attendant. She made her way inside the tall imposing beachside hotel, a slim attaché case in her hand, and walked to the desk of the hotel concierge.

"Hello." He smiled at the pretty woman. "May I help you?"

"I was told to check in here when I arrived. I am Amanda Connor."

"Ah," the concierge nodded knowingly. He beckoned to a young man dressed in dark suit. "Paul, please escort Mrs. Connor to Penthouse 1B. She is expected."

"Thank you," Amanda told the concierge.

"Enjoy your dinner," he replied as he watched her slim form elegantly dressed in an expensive ensemble following the young man to the bank of elevators. The senator's son must have had good taste, he thought admiringly.

Another man sat in one of the comfortable club chairs and watched the young woman breeze by. She didn't notice the sudden interest of the man, a tabloid reporter who also did private investigation on the side. So strait-laced Senator Whitmore was meeting with his erstwhile daughter-in-law discreetly, the man mused. Wonder what that's about. Maybe she's playing a little politics, or maybe he's taking a more than a fatherly interest in her. Although Amanda Childs, now Connor, was newly remarried and probably not ripe for hanky-panky. Still, one never knew.

Amanda was unaware she was being watched, and entered the elevator with the young man. He smiled sunnily at her as the doors closed. "Know the Senator well?" he asked innocently, oblivious to his social *faux pas*.

"Actually the Senator is my father-in-law," Amanda cast her eyes on the precocious young man.

"Oh," the young man flushed. "You must be—"

"Amanda Connor." She blushed also.

"I read about you in the papers. What a terrible thing, to lose your husband and then be accused of all those crimes," he continued, uncouth.

Caught off guard, she swallowed convulsively. "Yes, it was," she murmured, shrinking back to the wall of the elevator.

Seeing her expression, the young man exclaimed. "I'm sorry. I didn't mean—"

"It's all right," Amanda murmured, desperately looking at the control panel. Please let's get to the top quickly, she prayed.

The youth fell into an embarrassed silence. Finally the doors opened, and, flustered, he led her to a set of double doors, the entrance to the suite, where another man in suit stood. "This is Mrs. Connor," the young man stammered.

The man nodded and opened the door for her, allowing her to enter and shutting the door behind her.

She took a deep breath. She was standing in a large open airy suite that overlooked the Gulf of Mexico, bathed in the setting sun. The walls were painted a pale green, with a rich carpet, gold colored furnishings, and tastefully arranged lighting.

A distinguished looking white-haired man dressed smartly in dress shirt and slacks was standing looking out the window at the scene, and turned as she came forward.

"Amanda," he spoke warmly, and came up to her, taking her hand in both of his. "Thank you so much for agreeing to meet with me. I have looked forward to this."

"It's good to see you again, Senator Whitmore," Amanda smiled tightly, still uneasy about being alone with the famous, powerful man now known to her as Andrew's father.

"Please call me Tom," he replied warmly. "I hope you had no problems getting here."

"No," she was polite, looking around the room.

"May I mix you a drink?" Whitmore indicated the bar.

"A whiskey, please, with some cola," she responded.

As he mixed two drinks and handed one to her, he inquired, "Did Jon not come with you?" He gestured for her to sit, and he seated himself across from her.

"Jon thought we might speak more freely about Andy if he wasn't present," Amanda swallowed. "It is still a painful subject for me sometimes. And he is having dinner with my new in-laws tonight."

"Ah, the Connors," the Senator murmured.

"You know them?" Amanda was surprised.

"Oh, yes," the Senator nodded. "Inasmuch as they are quite active in Colorado politics, and very influential people on the national scene as well, I have met them on several occasions." He looked away.

"I was not aware," Amanda's voice was small. "And?"

"And what?" Whitmore smiled uncomprehendingly.

"And what did you think of them?" Amanda was direct.

He was taken aback by her forthrightness. "Politically speaking, or personally?" he hedged.

"Both," she remarked. "You obviously know more about them than I do. And I have the feeling I need as much information as I can get," she laughed lightly.

He looked at her in amazement. "Amanda, you're not telling me you don't know the family into which you've married?"

She colored. "Apparently I don't," she whispered, sipping her drink anxiously.

"But you knew about Jon's family's connections with the President and the previous administration, that Jon had distinguished himself in the service, and had been at the beck and call of several Presidents? He had been tapped for several important assignments. He volunteered for the investigation that ended up involving you." Whitmore watched her reaction carefully.

She paled. "Jon has not revealed—I mean, he is modest and doesn't talk about himself much. I knew that he had earned several citations and was decorated for service." Her voice trailed off. "Perhaps you can tell me about his family."

Whitmore shook his head, laughing softly. "I can see what my son found so irresistible about you. He was highly intelligent and good at everything he did. But I was so aggravated at the time, because he seemed more averse than naïve to the political bartering that vaults one into fame, fortune or other forms of success. He was oblivious to manipulating his opportunities and making his way to the top. It seemed the more I tried to secretly push him, the more he sensed something political was afoot and resisted it. And here you are, also successful and an heiress, and just like Andrew, so seemingly impervious to politics."

"I think Andy and I were willfully blind," Amanda admitted. "We believed fervently in civil rights and liberties, and wanted so much to believe in the American dream for everyone that our exposure to the political machinery was sometimes soul-crushing." She gazed at the drink in her hand. Suddenly embarrassed, she flushed and looked at Whitmore. "I'm sorry—I didn't mean to offend."

"No offense taken." He was amused.

"I knew Andy had been given several opportunities for advancement, but each time he ended up in a situation that he said he knew he could not tolerate long-term, and backed away."

Whitmore nodded. "I would get frustrated when Burton would tell me that Andrew had turned down some promotion." He paused. "I always thought perhaps you were the reason."

Amanda looked up, her eyes shining. "I'm sorry," she whispered.

"No, my dear," Whitmore reached over and took her hand. "It wasn't you, at least directly. I believe you and Andrew were a matched pair in temperament and very high scruples. You both seemed to believe deeply in your commitments."

"I loved him so much," she murmured.

He squeezed her hand. "But you are finding new happiness with Jon, aren't you?" Whitmore asked her.

"Yes, I am." Amanda turned her gaze on him, and he was startled at her loveliness as she smiled. "I never thought I could feel that way again. I refused to allow myself to try for so very long."

Suddenly embarrassed again, she changed the subject briskly. "I brought you some things." Amanda gently pulled her hand away. She reached into the attaché and brought forth a portfolio. "I decided that you should have some of these photos and mementos of Andy. I think he would have wanted me to give these to you."

She handed the package to Whitmore, who took it and opened it reverently. He pulled out the contents, and swallowed as he saw the photograph of himself holding Andrew as an infant and the photo of Emily. There were also the framed photograph of Andrew and Amanda on their wedding day, and several other small items, small carved figures Amanda had found in the wooden chest.

He looked up at her, his eyes blinded by tears. "Oh, my God," he whispered. "I was so busy trying to be someone important that I missed out on the most important thing of all: having a relationship with my son," he cried piteously. "And he spent a lifetime not knowing me but hating me. I can never undo that."

"I'm so sorry." Amanda's eyes filled with tears too. She set her glass on the table, and moved around to sit beside the senator, putting her arm around him as he cried.

"Did he ever talk about—me? Did he say anything about his father?" Whitmore mumbled.

"No," Amanda answered sadly. "I tried several times to get him to open up, but it was a private hurt, something he could never share. The revelation about you opened my eyes to the fact that there was a lot about Andrew I never knew. And that hurt terribly."

"At least Mike Knox said Andy meant to tell you." Whitmore took her hand and patted it clumsily.

"We'll never know what might have happened." Amanda squeezed his hand. "But Andy's letter to Mike was clear that he wanted you to have a 'shot at redemption'."

"I know. Mike showed me his items as well," Whitmore smiled through the tears, as he took out a handkerchief and wiped his eyes.

"I have also brought you the originals of the paperwork that Andy received from his aunt through Mike, and what he left behind for me to find," Amanda provided. "They are yours as well."

He looked at her with surprise. "Mike also thought it only appropriate that you should have the originals," she added.

He smiled his gratefulness. Amanda continued, "I have been trying for five years to let go of Andrew. I think perhaps providing all this to its rightful owner is another closure for me as well."

"It was thanks to you that he wanted Mike to give me a chance to come clean," Whitmore suggested. "I think Andrew called it something like your 'stubborn devotion'."

Amanda smiled too. There was a knock, and the door opened to a waiter rolling a tray into the room.

"That is our first course," Whitmore told her. "We'll have plenty of time to talk during dinner."

Jon started to open the front door, when it was flung open. There stood a beautiful dark-haired, dark-eyed woman. "Jon!" she cried, flinging her arms around him.

He hugged her affectionately, kissing her cheek. "It's been too long, baby sister."

"And whose fault is that?" Kelly jabbed him in the ribs. "Mother is on the warpath," she whispered conspiratorially.

"It seems she always is when there is no audience to play to," he said, his voice low, as he squeezed her arm affectionately.

She looked behind him. "Where's your bride?" She was curious.

"Amanda had an engagement she couldn't get out of," Jon explained.

"More important than meeting me?" Kelly teased good-naturedly, as Gloria appeared in the foyer, came forward and pecked a kiss on her son's cheek.

The Connors' Crisis

"Apparently we are not high on her list," Gloria remarked drily.

Jon looked at her impassively. "I've already explained to you, Mother. She had promised Senator Whitmore she would meet him for dinner before your invitation materialized."

"Oh?" Gloria raised her eyebrows. "So her ex-in-law is more important than her present ones? I thought when I told her I was making plans for us to have dinner this week she might leave that time free of other engagements."

"It's amazing. She was afraid you would say exactly that," Jon laughed, but his eyes did not. He took Kelly's arm and moved to the large living room. "She was anxious, not wanting to stand you up again. And this is actually our first evening apart.

"But I told her it was more important for her to keep this appointment. The Senator was in the area this evening only. They had some unfinished business to discuss about Andy, and she had not been able to meet with the senator before now because—well, because she's been recovering."

"What unfinished business is that?" Gloria inquired.

"None of your business, dear," her husband James quipped as he walked into the room. "Jon, come on in and ignore the bright lights in your face and your mother's interrogation. David will be a bit late."

"Why?" Gloria inquired, arching her eyebrows.

"He was doing a favor for me," James was enigmatic, looking over at his daughter fondly as he spoke. He pointed to the bar. "Drink, Jon? I bought this Glenlivet just for you."

"Well, then, I'd hate to disappoint you," Jon chuckled. He walked across the room and accepted the glass from his father, their eyes meeting, a knowing and apologetic smile on James' lips. Jon knew that look; it meant that he was in for a third-degree grilling over dinner by his mother about his new bride.

"I'm here," David announced as he walked into the room. James looked at his son inquiringly, but David just shook his head. James frowned.

Jon noted the exchange and moved to the sofa to sit by his sister. Kelly took Jon by the arm. "I so want to meet her," she gushed. "David says she is a looker."

"Trust David to zone in on that fact," Jon laughed quietly.

"I heard that," David retorted good-naturedly. "But she's smart as hell, as well as being easy on the eyes. How is she feeling these days?"

"She is much better," Jon smiled. "Ralph says she is kicking ass and taking names at work, as much as he is trying to slow her down."

"Ralph?" Gloria echoed.

121

"Amanda's law partner," Jon explained. "They have known each other since elementary school, and they carry on like brother and sister."

"He's black, isn't he?" Gloria interjected.

"I cannot believe you just asked that," David interrupted the conversation, asperity in his voice. "Yes, Mother, he is black," David's tone turned sardonic, surprising Jon. "Surely that doesn't clash with your moderate political views? By the way, he's one of the most sought-after criminal defense attorneys in the region. He might even be up for county judge."

Jon raised his eyebrows inquiringly. David chuckled. "We've been playing racquetball whenever I'm in the area, and a little one-on-one every now and then. He's tough, hasn't lost those moves."

The butler walked to the doorway and looked askance at Gloria. She nodded. "Dinner is served," he announced.

"But I haven't had my drink yet," David protested.

"You can bring it with you," Gloria retorted. "I'm hungry."

David sidled up to Jon as he and Kelly stood. "That means she is anxious to begin cross-examination of Bro here," he whispered theatrically, as Gloria frowned.

Jon rolled his eyes and took his sister's arm. "Amanda was really sorry to miss meeting you again. She asked if you might be interested in a day of shopping on Saturday, just the two of you."

"I'd like that," Kelly smiled, as Jon handed her a card.

"Those are all her phone numbers. She said to feel free to give her a call."

"That would be enjoyable," Gloria answered.

"I don't think you were invited," James spoke then.

Her eyes flashed angrily at him as he returned her look placidly. "Let the young ones have their fun without your meddling," he rejoined quietly as he took her arm and led her into the dining room.

As the soup was served, Whitmore poured some wine into the glasses. He laughed self-consciously. "This is the first time since my wife died that I've actually had a private dinner with someone. There is generally no time for this indulgence, unless it is part of some meeting or obligatory political function." He smiled at Amanda. "And it is doubly nice that I don't have staff constantly hovering and interrupting. I'm very happy that you are here."

"I'm glad we could finally have the time to meet and talk," she concurred. "Actually, this is my first dinner without Jon since our wedding."

"I'm sorry if I took you away from your husband tonight," Whitmore was contrite.

"No, it is fine. I really wanted to honor my promise to you," she smiled. "Besides, I don't think my mother-in-law cares for me much."

"Gloria Connor is a formidable woman," Whitmore replied. "I would be surprised, and perhaps a little frightened, if she did like you."

Amanda laughed. "Surely she is not that bad?"

"She has caused great men to quake in their boots," he spoke, his eyes watching her. "But why do you get the impression she doesn't like you?"

"Our first meeting was uncomfortable. I felt like I was in a police interrogation. And it was all unfolding in a public arena, with their friends looking on."

"What did you think of James Connor?" Whitmore tasted his soup.

"He was quite pleasant, and seemed to want to put me at ease."

"He is a good man," Whitmore murmured. "I had heard rumors that the marriage was perhaps strained."

"Really?" Amanda was alert. "I would hope not, for Jon's sake."

"Perhaps it's just vicious gossip," the senator suggested. "Forget I said anything."

They talked on desultorily, and the salad course was served. As he offered her more wine, he asked, "What about the local political scene in Mainville?"

"There are about to be some changes," she remarked. "Our sheriff died from cancer just last week. And the circuit judge was forced to resign. It looks like our county judge will be selected to replace him, which of course leaves his slot vacant."

"And are you considering applying for a judgeship?"

"Heavens, no," Amanda laughed. "I have no judicial ambitions. I'm afraid I do not have the temperament."

"You might be surprised," Whitmore said gently. "If not you, do you know who is applying for those two positions?" Whitmore asked.

"Well, I do have friends vying for both," she smiled sheepishly. "One of my childhood friends, Charles Petrino, has already qualified to run for sheriff, and of course his name has been submitted for the governor's consideration as interim sheriff. And my law partner Ralph Carmichael informed me he wants to run for the county judgeship."

"Did Andrew know them?" Whitmore watched her avid features with interest.

"Yes, Charlie and Andy became close colleagues and friends. Andy didn't know Ralph as well, because Ralph was away from home at college, law school, then practicing in South Florida. Ralph didn't come home to practice with me until after Andy's death. But Andy had met him when Ralph played basketball at Duke."

"Is there any reason either wouldn't be selected?"

Amanda paused. "If you're asking whether they are qualified and would do a good job, they both are top notch. If you are asking whether there are better qualified, I think not. But we both know that is not the deciding factor."

Whitmore leaned forward. "If you were the one deciding, would you choose them?"

"In a heartbeat," Amanda proclaimed fervently, "although I don't want to lose Ralph as a partner. I can never replace him. But he wants it so badly. He was the first in his family to get a college degree, and he has gone on to distinguish himself. He would be the first black official in our county, and a fine one." She paused. "And Charlie has always dreamed of following in his father's footsteps and being sheriff. He has made the police department a law enforcement agency to be reckoned with."

Whitmore was fascinated watching Amanda as she talked about her friends. "Who pulls the political strings in your area?" he asked.

Her face clouded. "Well, there are a few party functionaries that keep their fingers on the pulse, but I guess Esme Townsend is one of the most influential people in the area."

Townsend nodded. "I've heard of her, and met her at one of Ernie's fundraising parties. She seemed quite the Southern belle."

Amanda laughed. "She's hard as nails underneath all that charm."

"Is she going to back your friends?" Whitmore gazed at her.

Amanda shrugged, but he could sense concern in her eyes. "That I cannot tell you."

They paused as the main course was served. "I hope you like fish," Whitmore gazed at her.

"I've lived here all my life. I love fish."

After the waiter had gone, Whitmore leaned forward. "Are you going to politick for them?"

Amanda laughed heartily. "I have no political clout. I don't generally care, but at times like these when I see qualified people up for the positions, I wish I had. I will call a friend of mine, chief of staff for the governor, and see what I can do. But I'm out of my league there."

The senator leaned back. "I'm unused to being in the presence of someone so unspoiled by politics."

"I wouldn't say that," Amanda laughed. "Politics are unavoidable. I just stay as far away as I can."

"You know your current husband has considerable influence?"

The Connors' Crisis

"Jon?" Amanda was surprised. "I guess I never thought about it."

Whitmore smiled at his daughter-in-law. "This grouper is quite wonderful." He changed the subject.

As they enjoyed dinner he asked her how she and Andrew met, and she relayed the story. He nodded understandingly as she weaved the tale and told him about the events leading up to Andrew's murder, and the later investigation where she met Jon.

As he drew her out, haltingly she told him about her discovery of her true parentage, and the harrowing experience and close call at the hands of the Barnes family. He could tell that she was still haunted by the memories.

"I'm very sorry if all this news about me has damaged you in any way," she finished, not looking at him.

"Dear, you had no control over your past. You mustn't worry about those things you cannot change. I have learned that lesson the last few months." Whitmore reached over and patted her hand. "And the media blitz will subside when they find another victim."

They were silent as the dinner plates were removed and dessert was served with coffee. When they were left alone he asked her, "So you have had yet another brush with death in the hospital?"

She nodded wordlessly. He continued, "And this friend of yours, Petrino, saved your life twice now?"

Actually three times, she thought but did not say. "Yes." She paused. "Thanks to Charlie and my neighbor Fred Vaughan, I have enjoyed almost as many lives as a cat. I am truly blessed."

"And what of your father?" Whitmore asked.

Amanda looked at him confusedly.

"Your real father," Whitmore whispered.

Amanda sucked in her breath. "I don't know how to answer that. It has been hard for me to deal with the fact that my mother and father weren't actually my parents. And Marks raped my—Marjy, and I was the product of that."

"That would be hard for anyone to swallow," Whitmore squeezed her hand sympathetically.

"It just seems that I've had to attempt a mountain of forgiveness lately, and it is very hard," Amanda quavered, sipping her coffee.

"And have you forgiven me?" Whitmore interjected.

"You?" Amanda was surprised. "Senator—"

"Tom," he reminded her gently.

"Tom, there's nothing for me to forgive. You have done nothing to wrong me. I think if Andy were here, he would forgive you. But again I cannot speak for him."

Whitmore nodded sadly. "Let's adjourn to the sitting area again," he suggested.

They moved over to the sofas and sat down. They engaged in small talk, as Amanda asked him about his work and future plans.

Amanda inquired, "And are you going to seek the Presidency?"

Whitmore shrugged. "There have been several discussions about that. There was a time when this decision would have been a no-brainer for me. I was ambitious, confident. But now I'm not sure whether I should, given the news about my fathering a son and my lack of responsibility. If I were a younger man, I could just wait it out another four years before making the decision. But at my age that is not an option. And I am so afraid of subjecting you to more scrutiny by the media."

Amanda bit her lip. "I'm happy that you are concerned about the effect of your decision on me, but you mustn't let that sway you. I will survive the media attention. All of us are human, including you. Your transgressions are no worse than many other great men who came before you. Furthermore, you are a good man, and have been a good statesman. If you feel the call, you must answer it."

Whitmore gazed at her. "So you think I should?"

Amanda laughed. "Senator—"

"Tom," he corrected her.

"Tom, I have no experience with politics and cannot advise you. The road to the Presidency is a hard one, I'm sure. It requires a great deal of sacrifice. However, we need good men who are willing to make that sacrifice. That is a decision only you can make. However, I will support you all that I can, no matter which path you take."

"My dear," Tom murmured, reaching out and taking her hand. "Will you come be my chief of staff?"

"Now that would sound the death knell to your run right there," Amanda laughed.

He smiled. "One never knows. Sometimes a fresh perspective is good."

Amanda blushed, looked at her watch, and noted it was late. "I have truly enjoyed this evening, but I need to get home."

"I have enjoyed this so much," Whitmore murmured.

"I feel as though all we've talked about is me." She was shamefaced.

"That was my plan," Whitmore grinned. "I wanted to know about you. You're an intriguing woman, Amanda. I'm very happy you married my son."

Amanda rose, and Whitmore followed. "I really would rather you didn't drive this late at night," Whitmore argued. "There is an extra guest room here."

"But I don't want this to also be the first night away from Jon," she smiled. "I'll be fine."

"I can have you driven home, if you insist."

"I will be fine," she repeated, smiling at his persistence.

He walked her to the door. He put his arms on her shoulders and kissed her cheek. "Thank you, my dear Amanda," he murmured. "I'm so happy to finally meet you. I hope we can be friends, and that we can do this again."

"I do, too," she reached up and kissed his cheek.

As he opened the door, a suited man turned. "Please call for Mrs. Connor's car," Whitmore ordered him. "And please have her escorted to it." He turned to her. "I will insist on making sure that you make it as far as Mainville safely. I do not want to answer to Jon that I did not protect you."

She smiled as she left with the suited man who walked up.

As she was escorted through the lobby to her car, she did not notice the man who surreptitiously took photos of her as she passed.

Jon sat next to his sister, with his mother at the end of the dining table to his left, David across from him, and his father at the other end of the table.

"Now, tell us a little more about your bride," Gloria started.

"What do you want to know?" Jon was wary.

"Well, tell us a little of her history, her parents, her family," Gloria replied, smiling brightly.

David kicked his brother under the table and grinned. Jon frowned back.

"Amanda apparently had a normal small-town childhood," Jon looked at his mother guilelessly, ignoring David. "Her dad was a small-town businessman, her mother staying at home to raise the children. She has an older brother who now lives in Philly. Ralph says she was very smart, valedictorian of her class. She went to college and law school, graduating with honors, and left a firm in Orlando to end up back home caring for her mother. She was a public defender for a time, then opened her own office."

"Where did she attend college?" James chimed in, interested.

"Florida State," Jon responded. "College and law school. Two of her best friends attended the university at the same time, Charlie Petrino and

Billy Barnes. Charlie said she graduated with high honors from college and law school."

"This Barnes fellow is the one who was killed, the one who was part of the conspiracy?" Gloria supplied.

Jon nodded, hiding his surprise. "Yes. Amanda had no idea that Billy was using her name to steal and launder funds through the church. It really wasn't until the Bureau's investigation heated up that it was discovered about Amanda's true parentage, and about the fraud perpetrated by her 'friend' Barnes."

"Her true parentage—you mean that she was the product of rape?" Gloria interjected.

Jon flushed.

James intervened smoothly. "Dear, she obviously had no control over that situation. And scandal is not unknown in our own family," he added placidly.

It was Gloria's turn to flush.

"Marjorie Witherspoon had harbored the secret all those years, and had apparently hoped Amanda would never know. She wanted Amanda to have a normal childhood. Amanda was apprised only when Billy Barnes told her, just before he and his father attempted to kill her," Jon said smoothly, although his eyes were flashing ominously.

"And then she was accused of murder of the elder Mr. Barnes, wasn't she? At the prison?" Gloria continued, after the salad plates were collected and the next entrée was served.

"Wrongly accused," Jon replied. "And again she was framed and almost killed by a deranged woman, who was guilty of murdering several others and almost took out her friend Dr. Young as well."

"Seems she has been framed a lot." Gloria's voice was snide.

Kelly's eyes grew wide, and David sucked in his breath. Jon's eyes flashed in anger. Attempting to steer the conversation to other matters, Jon abruptly turned to Kelly. "What is the latest between you and Joey?" He was direct.

Kelly blinked, looking down at her plate. "I think he's going to accept the offer here in Florida," she replied, her voice small. "He seems really happy here."

"Bullshit," David countered softly. All eyes turned to him.

Gloria remonstrated, "David, I will not countenance that language at the dinner table."

David's jaw jutted angrily. "He is miserable, and Kelly is miserable." He looked at his sister. "You are both stubborn. I can't believe you can't find a happy medium."

It was Jon's turn to kick his brother under the table warningly.

"I just think it is probably a sign that they each need to get on with their lives and find someone else," Gloria responded drily.

Jon heard Kelly's swift and painful intake of breath. "Maybe it's time our mother apologized to Joey and made him feel more like the family member we all consider him to be." Jon's voice was controlled and quiet as he bit back his anger.

"I've not done anything to hurt Joey. I cannot say the same for him," Gloria interjected haughtily.

"Please, can we talk about something else?" Kelly pleaded, biting her lip, her eyes luminous, beseeching her father desperately, silently.

James patted his daughter's hand comfortingly. "David tells me he's looking at real estate around here. Sounds like he might want to settle down, quit the jet-setting." He smiled at David, attempting to steer the conversation to a safer topic.

Gloria interrupted, ignoring James' statement and turning to Jon. "Do you think your wife's close relationship with all these high school classmates to be entirely innocent?"

David choked, as Jon looked at her woodenly.

"My God, Mother, what do you think? Perhaps Amanda has made her money running a brothel?" David retorted. "You know some people actually have lifelong friends." His voice was cutting.

Jon set down his knife and fork, and sipped his glass of wine. He turned to his mother, a steely resolve in his eyes. "I know you, and you're going somewhere with all this innuendo. Why don't you just come out with it and skip the suspense?"

Gloria smiled tightly. "It's just that I have done some checking on Amanda, and she's had such an—interesting—life."

"You mean you've had one of your spooks running around gathering dirt?" Jon demanded hotly.

Gloria stared at her son. "Jon, you are in love and oblivious. I just want to make sure that you haven't made some huge mistake, that you know all there is to know about your Amanda." She pointed to the sideboard, where a large fat manila envelope had been set. "There's what Samuels has discovered so far. I want you to have it to review."

Jon pulled back from the table and stood, his napkin in hand, towering over his mother. "If you want to find out information about Amanda, you can just ask her and me. But keep your goddamned investigators with their rumors, gossip and lies out of our lives."

A broad smile crossed James' face, and David hooted. "Good show," he crowed. He stood and faced his brother. "I want to shake your hand, for having the balls to stand up to Gloria."

"That's quite enough!" Gloria said sharply, her voice raised. "You will both refrain from using objectionable language at dinner, and sit down."

Jon stared at her. "I'm quite finished," he said, throwing his napkin on the table. He turned and bent down to kiss his sister's cheek. "I can't wait for you to meet Amanda," he asserted. "And you need to run, not walk, away from here and find your happiness with Joey, if that's what you want."

He straightened up. "Good night."

Gloria stood. "Jon, do not leave," she ordered, her eyes wide.

"Mother, you have made it quite impossible for me to stay. You have offended me, but more importantly, you have insulted my wife. I'm so happy she couldn't make it tonight to hear all this."

Jon turned, but his mother strode to him and took his arm. "Jonathan," she pleaded. "Don't leave. I'm sorry. I only had your best interests at heart." She tightened her grip and pleaded piteously. "Please."

He looked at her coldly, his jaw set. She released him quickly.

"Why your actions should surprise me I don't know," Jon said evenly. "But I guess hope does spring eternal, and I really hoped you would just be happy for me. It hurts that you can't, and that you don't respect my wife. But you're wrong if you think that I'm going to let you destroy what I have with Amanda." He turned to go.

"Jon, I really didn't mean it. Give me another chance," his mother begged softly. David and Kelly looked at each other, amazed.

James also stood at that point. "Please, Jon, don't leave. You know that's as close as your mother has ever come to an apology," he smiled deprecatingly.

Jon tried to smile back at his father. "I know, and I appreciate her effort." He was careful not to address his mother. "But I need to leave and cool off."

He stared at Gloria coolly. "I don't intend to tell Amanda about this, because it would wound her deeply. The last year of her life has been hell enough without her suffering more pain at your hand. She wants so badly to be accepted by you. But I'm telling you that you need to figure out a way to make it up to us, to make it so. For better or worse, she is your daughter-in-law now."

Jon strode out the door.

CHAPTER 12

Jon stood looking down the long dock, around which a variety of sailing vessels nestled, to where the *Lucky* was berthed. The sun was barely peeking over the horizon, but it was already steamy, portending a hot July day.

"Here, help me with this," he heard a voice behind him and turned. It was Charlie, carrying a large cooler. Jon grasped one end and helped Charlie to the boat with it.

"Some of our bait," Charlie explained with a smirk.

"So that's why you disappeared so early this morning," Jon grinned back.

Charlie nodded to a man in jeans and white t-shirt, who walked out from the wheelhouse to meet them. "Jon Connor, this is Matt Thomas, our captain and host for the day."

Jon shook hands with the captain and looked around the boat. "Nice vessel you have here."

Matt smiled broadly. "Thanks. I like it. She's brought me through a lot of hard times and helped catch a lot of pretty fish. So I try to keep her spiffed up."

Petrino nodded back at the end of the dock. "I have another cooler of drinks and snacks, if you'll help me, Jon."

Jon nodded and followed Charlie down the dock to Charlie's pickup truck.

"Where the hell is Ralph?"

"I left him in the car talking to Claire on the phone," Jon grinned.

"Geez, we just left there." Charlie shook his head. "So Amanda is letting you come, and not insisting on joining us?" Charlie asked genially.

"Looks that way," Jon quipped. "She was actually quite insistent that we have our time of 'male bonding', as she called it."

"I wanted to ask last night, but didn't in front of the others, in case it was still a secret. Did she tell you she finally caught her first trout out of the creek the other day?" Charlie smirked.

"Fred showed me the pictures," Jon smiled. "She kept it a secret at first, but Fred spilled the beans. She's made arrangements to have the trophy mounted, and was going to wait until it was done to spring the news. But the cat is out of the bag."

Charlie laughed. "Fred told me about it, too. Said she stepped right into a hole and kept on fighting."

"Yeah, she had banged her hand up apparently trying to bring in the second one. But apparently it's all right."

Charlie looked straight at Jon. "How are things since you hooked her?"

"Good. Really good." Jon turned serious. "Although I've not been without worries. At first she had nightmares about Bill Barnes and Evie Brown, but those have subsided. I was afraid she was going to re-injure the shoulder and wrist at first, because she was overdoing things. But she is feeling much better since her bout with the pneumonia."

"Putting up more fight?" Charlie grinned.

"Actually, I'm amazed at how good married life is," Jon replied, his eyes meeting Charlie's. "I wish I had found her a long time ago."

Charlie smiled. "Marriage is good, isn't it?" he concurred.

Jon cleared his throat. "I know we have you to thank for finessing that situation with Amanda's brother."

Charlie shook his head, snorting. "How was the Fourth?"

"Jeff and Desiree came down for the weekend, and we had a great time at the beach house. Kelly and David showed up and we cooked out and swam. Joey showed up for dinner. Amanda and David are trying to pair Kelly and Joey up. But it was still a little strained. Jeff's wife didn't come."

"That was a blessing," Charlie muttered. "That is a woman with ideas above her station. I think she has always been jealous of Amanda. I don't know what Jeff sees in her."

"Well, at least Jeff and Amanda have patched up their differences," Jon averred. "And Amanda apparently called Malachi Feinstein to check on the matter that angered Jeff."

"What was that?" Charlie paused, nodding for them to set down the cooler.

"Jeff had been told by some university administration official that his scholarship to engineering school was actually a gift engineered by the Witherspoons."

"Ouch," Charlie remarked. "The Andrews family has always been rather proud, and Mr. Andrews would not have allowed him to accept it had he known. And that would have been a shame, because Jeff graduated at the top of his class, both in high school and at Auburn."

Jon nodded. "Come to find out that it wasn't true. Malachi knew the real story, because he was the one who negotiated the deal. The guy back then was a Vice-President of Admissions. He was wanting to give the scholarship to a football player they were recruiting, even though Jeff had already been selected to receive it. The athlete didn't even qualify for it. The Witherspoons found out and made it possible for Jeff to have his scholarship and then some, by supplying the funds for the athlete's tuition and board. Jerrod was a major contributor to the school. This administrator was embarrassed in the process for trying to steal away the scholarship, and he apparently saw a belated chance to get a dig in at Jeff. He apparently didn't think there was anyone left alive to gainsay him."

Charlie gazed at Jon. "Now I know if Amanda has found out this information, she did not sit still with it. She has always been a bulldog when it comes to her family."

"You are right." Jon looked out over the marina. "I don't know exactly what she did, but Malachi Feinstein extracted a letter from the president telling the real story and apologizing to Jeff for the misinformation."

They grasped the cooler and resumed, arriving at the dock and handing the cooler over the side of the boat to Matt. Charlie straightened up. "I'm glad you two found each other. You both deserve some happiness."

He looked off toward the water. "I'm surprised Amanda didn't insist on coming out with us. She's a big fisherwoman. She spent many hours with Tom Andrews fresh-water fishing while growing up. Andy taught her fly-fishing. She even went out with Andy and me in the gulf once. She was disappointed she didn't land a big one, but she pulled in a respectable drum." He paused. "If Amanda ain't out here today, there's something afoot."

"I'm most definitely aware of that," Jon laughed, and Charlie joined him. "But being the investigative mind that I am, I know the plan, and am happy to say I have approved it."

"Shit," Charlie retorted. "Amanda has just let you think you're in on the plan."

"You could be right," Jon nodded, grinning. "But I know you and Ralph will be footing the bill."

Ralph sauntered up, dressed in a shirt of impossible print and some baggy knee shorts, a pair of Nikes on his feet and a rod and tackle box in hand. Charlie countered, "What, you sit in the car until we've hauled the heavy stuff to the boat?"

"I was on the phone." Ralph was defensive.

"Yeah, you just left the woman at the beach house," Jon countered. "There was something you forgot to talk about before you left?"

"Well, you know a beautiful woman like Claire has to be stroked constantly," Ralph muttered.

"Yeah. You're more afraid of what she might be doing while you're not around today," Charlie gibed. Charlie looked at Ralph critically. "What, are you trying to scare the fish away?"

Ralph grinned. "They'll be proud to know they were caught by a good-looking black man when they see me. Ain't like you're anything to look at," he turned up his nose at Charlie's khaki baggy shorts and denim shirt, worn boat shoes on his feet, a Florida State ball cap on his head. Then they both eyed Jon, who was dressed in a t-shirt under a faded blue open-front button-down collar shirt and khaki cargo shorts, with brand new boat shoes. "Of course, we can't compare to Mr. GQ here."

"Hey, don't say a word. My bride dressed me and packed my tackle box," Jon joked. "You address any criticisms directly to her."

They all guffawed. "Like hell we will," Ralph hooted. "We're just as scared of her as you are."

They walked back together, grabbed their gear and trudged back down the dock. Very shortly they had stowed everything on board and cast off.

Amanda smiled at Jill as she sat down at the table beside the pool. "How are you feeling this morning?"

"Much better than I have been," Jill smiled back. "I'm looking forward to our shopping trip today."

"Some orange juice? Toast?"

"Yes, thanks. I'm now able to hold breakfast down," Jill giggled.

Claire walked out, dressed in a casual white linen outfit. "Your color is better too," Claire remarked, grinning at Jill, who was dressed in a colorful striped cotton pant ensemble.

"But nobody glows more than Amanda here," Jill remarked, looking at her friend.

Amanda beamed. She was dressed simply in denim Bermuda shorts and a white tank top that showed off a light tan, her feet encased in a pair of pretty strappy white sandals.

"I'm happier than I think I've ever been," she confessed.

"Jon must be pretty good?" Jill's smile grew larger.

Amanda blushed prettily.

Claire nudged Jill as she placed a cup of coffee before her. "He has to be, if Amanda can still look like that after meeting her mother-in-law."

"Let's not bring up unpleasant topics." Amanda turned away.

"What? Tell me. I didn't know about this. Are there problems?" Jill's stare bored into her back.

"I'm just not sure she likes me," Amanda mumbled as she poured Jill some orange juice.

"How could she not like you?" Claire retorted. "What does Jon say?"

"Amazingly little, except to tell me not to try so hard," Amanda admitted. "Funny—I got the impression that she was this warm motherly type. But she doesn't seem that way at all."

"Jon didn't prepare you for her?" Julie was surprised.

"Jon probably sees his mother with rose-tinted glasses," Claire piped up. "She is quite a political bigwig, I've been told."

Amanda flushed. "I guess I was pretty uninformed about his family's influence. But no, he really doesn't say much at all about them," Amanda replied thoughtfully.

"That's because all the men are scared of my mother," a voice chimed in.

Amanda turned at the sound. "Kelly!" she spoke warmly as Jon's sister, dressed similarly to Amanda, walked onto the deck. Amanda's face flushed as she realized that Kelly had overheard some of the conversation.

"Hope you don't mind my dropping by," Kelly came up to Amanda and kissed her cheek. "My brother mentioned the fishing trip this morning."

"Not at all. I'm glad you did." Amanda quickly introduced Kelly to Claire and Jill. "I'm sorry—I didn't mean to speak ill of your mother."

"I don't recall hearing you say anything bad," Kelly grinned. "Mom can be rather formidable. As they say in golf, you gotta 'play on through' where she is concerned, and ignore some of that snootiness. I just wish everyone followed that maxim."

Claire hooted, and even Jill smiled. Amanda was embarrassed. Kelly squeezed her arm. "Don't for a minute let my mother get to you."

Kelly paused. "Did Joey happen to show up for the fishing trip with the guys?"

Amanda bit her lip knowingly, a smile playing around the corners of her mouth. "No, he said he couldn't get away this morning. But he's coming to dinner tonight. You really should come, too," she added, her eyes wide-eyed, feigning innocence. "It will be a real informal affair, jumbalaya and shrimp and more shrimp, lots of fun."

"Girls, you need to chop-chop, because the stores await," Claire broke in. "Kelly, if you don't mind joining a bunch of married women, two of which are pregnant, you're welcome to spend the day with us."

"I'd like that," Kelly laughed. "It's nice to get away from Mom's stuffy set. I think she may have forgotten what fun is."

Her cell phone rang. She looked at the number. "It's David," she spoke. "Excuse me." She took the call, walking out toward the pool, chattering excitedly.

A few minutes later, she reappeared at Amanda's side. "Bro wants to talk to you," she announced, shoving the phone toward Amanda.

"Hello, David," Amanda spoke into the receiver. "Where are you?"

"I'm up in D.C. for a bit, met up with a woman," his voice answered.

"A woman? Are you being untrue to me? Is this someone of whom I'd approve?" Amanda asked.

"Of course not," David laughed heartily. "She's nothing like you. There's nothing good and virtuous about her. But she is kinda hot."

Amanda purred, "Oh, I see."

"I'm coming down your way pretty soon. Are you going to have time for me?" David teased.

"Inasmuch as you are my favorite brother-in-law, I'll see what I can do," Amanda replied slyly.

"I'm your only brother-in-law at the moment, so I'm not convinced that number one slot counts highly," he joked. "You know, I'm so much better than Jon at so many things," he added wickedly.

"That is very hard to believe," Amanda recounted devilishly.

"Take care of my sister," David was suddenly serious. "You know she's in love?"

"I'm getting that impression." Amanda looked at Kelly, who was staring back at her quizzically.

"Are you two talking about me?" Kelly demanded.

"I'm hoping to advance that cause," Amanda smiled mysteriously. "Maybe even later today."

"Good. Let me talk to her again."

Amanda handed the phone back to Kelly.

"I never knew morning sickness could be that rough," Charlie was saying, as he handed out cigars to the men and they watched the shore slowly disappearing. "I've felt so badly for Jill. How she can be so ill and yet manage to be so cheerful makes one admire feminine fortitude."

"I wouldn't know," Ralph rejoined. "Claire has not been sick a minute."

They turned to Jon as though expecting him to respond. He grinned. "Don't look at me."

"Yeah, we're gonna wipe that grin off your face one day when you need some commiseration." Ralph stuck the unlit cigar into his mouth.

"What, don't you want kids?" Charlie asked, his eyes on Jon as he lit his cigar.

"I don't know if we could be happier right now. I'm willing to wait and see—either way is fine. But sometimes I get the impression Amanda doesn't want children."

"What woman doesn't want children?" Ralph retorted.

"No, I think Jon might be right," Charlie spoke up. Jon looked at him sharply. "She loves children, don't get me wrong. But have you ever noticed that she doesn't seem overly anxious to hold babies?"

He caught Jon's eyes on him, and hastened on, "I mean, I noticed this with the twins. She adores them, but when they were small, she acted, I don't know, almost afraid of them, and didn't hold them much. Shelby used to tease her about it unmercifully."

"Yeah, you may have something there," Ralph piped up. "I noticed that when Louise had little Danny, Amanda shied away. She said she was afraid of breaking him." He hooted. "We have discovered her kryptonite. She is scared of babies."

Jon replied carefully, "I think she is going to have ample opportunity soon to rid herself of that phobia, thanks to you guys."

Matt came up. "Boys, you can gawk all day, or you can be baiting some hooks, setting some lines."

"I thought the way you talked, the fish just jump in the boat with us," Ralph rejoined.

"Only when you litter the deck with Cheetos and anchovies," Matt replied drily. "Preferably not previously eaten."

"OK, that was a bad trip," Ralph was defensive, as Charlie and Matt grinned at him.

"Is that why you eschewed the tequila last night?" Jon asked slyly.

"I try not to touch the stuff," Ralph said loftily. "It is bad for your health."

"Yeah, makes you walk around naked in mixed company, doesn't it?" Charlie retorted knowingly. "But it's all that French wine that makes the babies, isn't it?"

"Don't be giving Jon the wrong idea about me," Ralph muttered good-naturedly, opening a tackle box.

"I think I've already got you pegged," Jon laughed.

"Besides, Charlie hasn't revealed his baby-making secret," Ralph raised his eyebrows at Petrino.

"I was under orders." Charlie puffed his cigar thoughtfully.

Matt slapped him on the back. "I don't picture Jill ordering you around, but then I could be wrong."

"One never knows." Charlie glanced over at Jon and smiled. "Jon, aren't you glad now you came on this little trip?"

"Ecstatic," Jon quipped, opening his box, then choking. He looked closer and started laughing, doubling over.

Charlie walked over and looked into the box, reaching down, hooking with his finger and pulling out a bright red frilly garter with note attached. It read, "I've been informed by the Cabela Company that this little beauty doused with some Catfish Charlie and hot sauce really attracts the male marlin. You should give it a try. Of course you could just wear it under your clothes and think of me. Love, AC."

He bit down on his cigar in amusement and handed it to Jon. "She's your bride. I think you should wear this the rest of the trip, for luck."

Ralph, taking a swig of bottled water, glanced over and saw the garter, and in his amazement poured the water down the front of his shirt. The others started laughing at him.

He sputtered, "You know, she is known for her research skills. She probably did read that somewhere."

"Well, the first fish caught gets his picture taken wearing this," Jon announced.

"That's definitely going to improve our chances of catching something," Charlie shook his head in mirth. "But you're right. Don't be crossing her."

"Tell him the story about the jumbalaya," Ralph urged Charlie as he threw a bottled water to Jon.

"We have a rule—no beer until the first fish has been caught. A keeper. In Ralph's case, that means we may be sober all day."

"Aw," Ralph protested.

"What story?" Jon was interested.

"Naw, he should find out for himself," Charlie demurred.

"Charlie here told Andy right after he married Amanda that she adored country music, and it was a real turn-on for her."

Charlie started baiting hooks. "You've spoiled it, Ralph. Now we can't try this with Jon."

"*You* don't want to try it again," Ralph joked.

"You're damn right there," Charlie agreed. "It was a painful lesson. Hurt me a lot more than it did Andy apparently."

Jon looked over at the two as he reached in the cooler for some bait. "Don't hold out. You've piqued my curiosity now."

Charlie looked chagrined. "I told him that she was a true red-neck at heart, liked Mad Dog 20/20 wine and Porter Wagoner music, lots of Porter Wagoner music, that it drove her mad."

Ralph hooted, "It does drive her mad. She hates country music with a passion."

Jon nodded. "I noted a complete lack of the genre in her collection."

"I thought he knew I was joking," Charlie was defensive. "Anyway, he set up some romantic evening for her using my 'suggestions'." He grinned. "I think he meant it as a joke, but hell, I'm only speculating. It obviously did not go as planned."

Jon bit his lip to keep from laughing. "Do go on," he prodded.

"It started out as almost a dare. But I was never provided the details of what really happened. Andy was surprisingly mum afterward, and I forgot about it.

"Then one day out of the blue I walked into my office and there was a small crockpot of jumbalaya with a note. Amanda thanked me for being such a good friend to Andy and her, and had made my favorite dish. She was clear with the staff that it was ALL for me, no sharing allowed."

"Yeah, he didn't know why he was being thanked at the time," Ralph supplied, chuckling.

"Anyway, I immediately sat down at my desk with a huge bowl of it. She had even provided a bottle of my favorite hot sauce, knowing that I would generously douse the dish with it. Something should have tipped me off when Bruce Williams brought me a huge glass of ice water and set it down, but I knew that Amanda's jumbalaya was spicy."

Jon murmured, "I can almost see where this is heading."

"I started eating with a vengeance, because she does a mean jumbalaya, inherited the recipe from Mrs. Andrews, and I loved the stuff. But Amanda had laced the shit with enough rooster-spur and Mrs. Andrews' bird's-eye pepper to set the house on fire." Charlie shook his head. "I'm not sure but what she threw a habanero or two in there for good measure. Now I like it hot, but geez—" he shook his head again at the memory, "it took several minutes before I realized that it was not just a little hot, and by then I was in pain. She even provided homemade cornbread, so I stuffed some of that in my mouth, thinking it might absorb some of the heat. That stuff was full of hot peppers too."

Jon bit his lip, choking back laughter.

"Bruce said I turned purple at one point. I couldn't see for the tears; they were pouring down my face. The Big Man even got worried about me, after he had a good laugh with the others over me. After about an hour I spent in attempted recovery, convinced I was going to have the big coronary, downing two or three gallons of ice water, Bruce handed me a gift-wrapped package. It was a Porter Wagoner CD and a bottle of MD 20/20."

Jon and Matt were by then guffawing, Matt doubled over. "And that night I had to cancel a hot date and spend the night close to the smallest room in the house. Bruce and some of the others have never let me forget that day."

Ralph cracked, "He hasn't touched her jumbalaya since."

"Andy never disclosed what his punishment was," Charlie continued, washing his hands over the side of the boat.

Jon suddenly nodded. "Oh, so that's—" he stopped.

"What?" Ralph asked.

"Oh, nothing. It just all makes sense now," Jon smiled.

As they arrived at the shopping center, Amanda pulled Kelly aside. Amanda whispered. "I want to get Claire and Jill to pick out the furniture they want for their babies' nurseries. It's going to be my gift to them, but they don't know that. The owner of the store is in on the plan, but I need your help too. We have to get them to tell us what they want without their buying the furnishings themselves. Let them buy all the accessories and beddings and clothes they want."

"Oh, this should be fun," Kelly murmured.

"If you get a commitment out of one of them, let the owner know," Amanda added with a wink.

So the women spent a couple of hours oohing and aahing over the items in the store and another one down the street. Amanda finally checked her watch.

"Girls, you've been on your feet long enough. We need to let you rest and have a bite of lunch," Amanda announced.

They walked next door to a new tastefully appointed bistro, scoring a table almost immediately. After ordering drinks and perusing the menu, they discussed all the baby furniture they had examined, Amanda winking over at Kelly.

After the food came, Jill asked, "What will we do after lunch?"

"You mothers-to-be need to put up your feet and rest while I make our dinner."

"Not jumbalaya?" Claire asked wickedly.

"You already know the story?" Amanda was surprised.

The Connors' Crisis

"Oh, yeah. Ralph told the family last year at the Fourth celebration. Louise had made some jumbalaya, and Ralph said Charlie had told him the story."

"I haven't heard this," Jill chimed in, looking at Kelly, who shook her head.

"I taught Charlie a little lesson right after Andy and I married," Amanda smiled. "Charlie was being a smart-ass and told Andy I liked Mad Dog and Porter Wagoner music. I came home one evening expecting a romantic night. Instead, there was a flannel nightgown on the bed, country music wailing in the background and that awful stuff in my wine glasses."

Kelly hooted, and Jill looked at Amanda amazedly. "And it wasn't true?"

Claire put her hand over her mouth, stifling a laugh at Jill's naïveté as Amanda looked earnestly at her friend. "No, Jill, it wasn't true. I hate country music, as well as the rest of the accoutrements."

Jill was wide-eyed. "What did you do?"

"Once I got over the shock, I walked to my lingerie chest and pulled out my sexiest briefs and handed them to him. I purred, 'Here, it would really excite me if you would try these on for me.' He looked at me incredulously and said, "Mandy, you know I can't get in your panties.""

Claire, unable to hold back, started laughing loudly, as Kelly joined her and other restaurant patrons looked over at them curiously. Claire whispered hoarsely, "I don't think I can handle the punch line."

Jill bit her lip, smiling. Amanda leaned forward, and the others followed suit. "I informed him he was absolutely correct, and that he would not be getting into them as long as he pulled stunts like that," she said softly.

Tears formed in Jill's eyes as she joined the others in uproarious laughter. "Oh, my," she whispered, as the others tittered merrily. "But where does the jumbalaya come in?"

"I managed to find out that Charlie was the source of Andy's little folly. A few days later I prepared Charlie's favorite dish, my mother's jumbalaya. He likes it spicy, and I accommodated him," Amanda smiled. "My mom always grew a variety of hot peppers, and I threw a few extra rooster spur peppers and everything else hot in the mix and sent it to him, along with a bottle of his favorite hot sauce, a Porter Wagoner CD and some MD 20/20. Even the cornbread was 'hotter than blue blazes', as Mom would say. He apparently imbibed it in front of most of the sheriff's department staff, and I'm told by some very reliable sources that he suffered the consequences."

"Remind me never to get on your bad side," Kelly countered as the waiter came up and they composed themselves to order dessert.

Just after sunset, the men showed back up at the beach house, tired and tanned.

Claire was lounging in the den reading a magazine. "Any luck?" Claire asked as they walked in the house.

"A few," Ralph replied as he leaned down to kiss her.

She wrinkled her nose at him. "You smell fishy."

"Can't understand that, inasmuch as he didn't come in close contact with any fish," Charlie countered wickedly.

"You didn't catch anything?" Claire was incredulous.

Ralph hung his head, downcast. "Even Jon caught a couple of nice redfish."

"But Matt and Charlie cleaned house," Jon offered, slapping Ralph on the back. "Where's Amanda?" he asked casually.

"She is in the kitchen finishing dinner and entertaining Dr. Rand and Kelly," Claire supplied. "And Jill is prettifying herself for her husband," she added slyly for Charlie's benefit.

"I invited Matt to join us, but he said he had a hot date," Charlie announced, as Jon left for the kitchen. "I'm calling dibs on the first shower," he added as he disappeared around the corner.

Jon found Amanda sitting at the counter drinking wine and entertaining Joey and Kelly while a young man was cooking shrimp. Amanda was dressed in a yellow sundress. Jon walked up to her and took her hand, kissing it.

"I'd pull you into my arms, but I'm all fishy," he murmured, as he turned and greeted his sister and Joey.

Amanda introduced him to the young man presiding over the stove. "Jon, this is Raoul, a protégé of Jake's. I asked to borrow him so he could clean and cook the shrimp for us tonight. He also whipped up the most wonderful dessert. I invited him to stay and partake of the dinner he worked so hard on."

The young man with dark hair and eyes smiled at Jon and nodded. Jon greeted him, then looked back at her. "I'm jealous he got to spend the afternoon with you. I take it he did not prepare the jumbalaya?" he asked meaningfully.

"No, that's my job," she purred, as the young man laughed.

"I'm going to get my shower," he released her hand. "Save some Mad Dog for me," he suggested playfully.

"I'm surprised Charlie confessed to that escapade," she laughed.

He just grinned as he exited. She turned to her two guests. "You know, there's supposed to be a really lovely sky tonight, if you want to follow those stairs up to the gazebo," she winked. "Dinner will be served as soon as the men become presentable."

"Don't forget the appetizers," Raoul reminded her.

"Yes, we have emptied the gulf of all shrimp tonight," Amanda smiled. "There are cocktail shrimp and some rumaki straight out of the oven, some with liver, some without. And all good."

She watched the couple drift out and take the stairs up to the widow walk, a satisfied smirk on her lips. She sat and talked with Raoul a while, discussing recipes and ingredients with him as she helped set up the food for serving.

Several minutes later she headed down the hall toward the bedroom she and Jon shared. As she came abreast of a door, it suddenly opened, and Charlie stepped out into her path. They collided. He reached out and steadied her, as he pulled the door closed behind him, moving him even closer to her. His body brushed hers, pinning her next to the wall. She could smell the scent of his soap and aftershave as his mouth came close to hers.

"Sorry," he laughed apologetically, releasing her.

"Is Jill all right?" she caught her breath, looking at him. She suddenly tensed.

"Yes, she just awoke from a nap and decided to freshen up," he smiled mischievously.

"Yeah, right," she smirked, starting to move past him. "You're incorrigible, you know."

He put his hand against the wall, halting her progress, reaching up with the other hand to smooth a lock of hair out of her face. His face moved closer. "I noticed you put Claire and Ralph up in your old room," he said softly.

"Yeah, that was thoughtful of me, don't you think, for both of us?" She stared at him, swallowing and biting her lip before pulling his arm away and moving down the hall to her room.

She opened the door and let herself in quickly, shutting the door behind her, suddenly breathless. Then she turned, and there was Jon, standing there in only his boxers, staring at her.

"What's wrong?" he came up to her. "You look flushed."

"I just wasn't expecting to see that good a sight waiting for me," she laughed shakily as she embraced him.

"Umm, that's good." He traced her lips with his fingers before cupping her face in his hand and kissing her, hard, insistently, backing her up to the bed and following her down.

She allowed a small moan to escape as he imprisoned her, his mouth trailing down her neck. "Oh, I missed you today," she whispered.

"Not nearly as much as I missed you. I want you so badly I don't care if I mess up your pretty dress," he said huskily. "Would it be rude if the hostess was late to dinner? Would they notice you had to change clothes?"

"Yes, this group would notice and make catty comments about it," she laughed softly. "I can handle it, if you could. But the shrimp will be cold, and all Raoul's work for nothing."

"Damn it, woman, you don't have to be so logical," he shook his head good-naturedly. He smothered her with another kiss, before releasing her. "We are turning in early," he warned her. "They can entertain themselves. As it is, I'm going to have an impossible task keeping my hands off you."

"Me, too, baby," she smiled as he stood up and gave her his hand, pulling her up off the bed.

"You look like a woman who has just been thoroughly kissed," he chuckled.

"Thanks. That was the look I was after," she rejoined lightly.

He quickly dressed as she repaired her makeup. Then he took her hand and led her out of the room.

As they moved down the hall together, he placed his hand on her butt.

"Behave," she whispered, swatting at him.

At the foyer she pushed him forward. "Go on in with the others," she ordered. "I need to make sure everything is ready, and call the lovebirds from upstairs."

"What lovebirds?" Jon asked.

"Your sister and her *novio*," she whispered wickedly.

"Kelly is here?" he smiled. "I hoped that little phone call might bring her."

"Yeah, she showed up this morning trying to find out whether Joey went fishing with you all. I invited her to spend the day with the girls and to join us for dinner," Amanda explained.

"You are wonderful," Jon kissed her.

"I know—all the men tell me that," she replied flippantly, pulling away.

She moved into the kitchen and smiled at Raoul. He pointed out the French doors to the deck and swimming pool. "I put the appetizers out in the den on the bar. The lovers are out there," he grinned.

She looked approvingly at all the food. "I think we're ready to chow down, except for one thing."

She moved to a place setting and took up the soup bowl. Carefully, she ladled jumbalaya into it and set it back in its place, setting a bottle of hot sauce by the bowl. "Now we are ready."

She called loudly, "Dinner is served."

Within minutes the dining area was full. She pointed to the place where the gumbo was already served. "Charlie's has been served and is cooling. He gets to taste it for us and approve the dish."

Charlie looked at her suspiciously, as she batted her eyes at him sweetly. He picked up the bowl with jumbalaya and headed toward the kitchen trash can.

She moved quickly to him and forestalled him. "I assure you it is fine," she charged, her hand on his arm.

"You're going to endanger two pregnant women?" he scowled.

She took the bowl from him, and reached over to the flatware drawer for a spoon. With everyone looking on, she took a mouthful.

"Oh, that's hot," she said excitedly, blowing and fanning her mouth. Then as a broad smile crossed her lips, she took another bite. "Just perfect," she murmured, taking another spoonful and handing it over to Charlie, who stared at her and took it.

He chewed the shrimp and swallowed, waiting. Everyone else stared at him. "OK," he pronounced grudgingly. "It is pretty damn good, if a little mild."

"That's why your favorite hot sauce is on the table." She pushed him playfully.

"Here, I'll take that." He grabbed the bowl from her.

"Raoul, please help me serve the rest of the jumbalaya," she ordered as people took their places.

PART 2

CHAPTER 13

SUNDAY

"You know, it's been a while since I've seen a few of these people," Jon remarked as he pulled up to the front of the huge antebellum structure housing the country club. Amanda shook her head at him, amused, as he straightened his tie in the rearview mirror.

"You're not seriously trying to convince me you're nervous, are you?" she asked lightly, stroking his arm.

"No," he chuckled. "It's just different. One spends all day working with these guys, in close quarters on cases, stake-outs, investigations, and there's a certain camaraderie. It's not the same now that I've moved on. You'll find out soon enough if Ralph makes judge. As Thomas Wolfe wrote, 'You can't go home again.'"

She nodded, suddenly solemn. "I know. Do you regret leaving the Bureau?"

Gazing into her eyes, he smiled and touched her nose tenderly. "No, love. I miss the constant fast pace, but I'd give it all up again for you, for what we have. Why? Do you regret having me so close at hand?"

"Never," she whispered, reaching over and kissing him quickly. "I just worry that life in the private sector will be more sedate. I don't want to be the reason you are bored."

He smiled. "It is an adjustment. There are times at work I have to pace myself, because working for the Bureau I always had more work than time. But I love being close to you, every morning, every night. I wouldn't give that up for anything."

Straightening back in her seat, Amanda murmured, "It's time we made our grand entrance for Bubba and Della's engagement party, don't you think?"

He squeezed her hand. "I think it's time we planned your own reception, my dear. I want it to be perfect for you, and I think with your health improving we don't want to wait much longer."

Jon slipped out of the car, striding around to the passenger door to open it and offer his hand to Amanda. Amanda glided out, her slim form encased in a trim flowing magenta raw silk jacket covering a matching sheath which ended just above her knee. Jon slid his arm around her waist as he escorted her up the steps of the porch, whispering in her ear, "You're beautiful."

As they entered, it was evident that the party was in full swing in the ballroom. The band was playing, and several couples were dancing. The rooms were filled with people, several of whom stopped to greet Jon and Amanda as they made their way slowly through the throng to a couple surrounded by well-wishers.

"Connor," a voice rang out as George turned and sighted him. "Come over here, man."

Connor pulled Amanda alongside him as he shook the man's hand and they slapped each other on the back vigorously. "Bubba, you remember Amanda?"

The beefy man with close-cropped hair and tuxedo embraced Amanda. "How could I ever forget the golden-eyed vixen that stole your heart? And you both remember Della, my fiancée?"

The woman beside him, dark-haired and petite, in a flowing pale pink chiffon dress, smiled. "My favorite couple in the whole world," she declared emphatically.

Amanda breathed, "I am so happy for both of you. I owe you both so much. It's wonderful that you are together."

Della squeezed her hand. "Thank Jon for that. George and I would never have hitched up if he hadn't put the bug in George's ear. And I'm happy that the case turned out as it did, exonerating you."

George put his arm around Connor's shoulder. "Zeke and his main squeeze are around here somewhere. And Petrino and Jill, Randall, Kimball, Boyer, the whole gang." His face went somber a minute. "She's made me give away my hunting dogs," he whined, hanging his head.

Jon grinned. "No woman wants competition for her man's affection, Bubba."

Della matched his look. "When George went off on his last trip, he made me take care of those critters. They howled so badly the neighbors complained, even out there at the Godforsaken lodge. When he got back, they were all adopted into good homes."

"It almost broke us up right there. The things we do for women," George lamented melodramatically.

150

Amanda laughed at him. "And I notice you have been grieving," she said, thumping his figure.

"Someone had to eat all the leftovers," he complained good-naturedly, "once the dogs were gone."

They all laughed, as Petrino and his wife came up and greeted them. Amanda hugged both, as Jon shook Petrino's hand and kissed Jill on the cheek.

"Where's Ralph?" Petrino asked Amanda during a lull in the conversation, while Jon and Jill chatted.

"He and Claire are on their way, I'm sure," Amanda replied. "How's Jill feeling?"

They drifted away as others came up to offer congratulations to the couple. Petrino steered Amanda out of the way of a waiter carrying a tray of champagne glasses. "She's doing well so far. The morning sickness is not as severe, she says, and her doctor thinks she is doing great."

"She looks blooming," Amanda stated. "I have you both in my prayers."

"When are you and Jon going to start a family?" Petrino was blunt.

"I'm not sure," Amanda was honest. "We're not in any hurry—there are going to be plenty of babies around soon enough, with Jill and Claire both pregnant."

She paused, peering at him intently. "Any word from the governor's office?" Her voice was barely audible.

"Amanda, it would be unseemly for the governor to announce a decision so soon after Vince's death," Petrino replied smoothly.

"Unseemly?" Amanda smiled. "Since when do politicians worry about being 'unseemly'?" Watching the corners of his mouth turn into the trace of a smile, she continued, "I guess then my call to an old friend on his staff was unseemly as well."

"Mandy, I can't imagine you politicking," Charlie chuckled. "For whom, might I ask?"

"I know this great guy, with fabulous experience," she looked away, trying to maintain an innocent air. "He's been wasting his time as chief of police long enough."

"Thank you, baby," Petrino leaned forward and pecked her cheek. "Did your friend disclose anything about my chances?"

"Actually, he mentioned that there was someone very influential with the governor making noises, but he could not reveal the candidate or his or her sponsor." Amanda was grave. "Although I tried very hard to pry."

"Well, I'm not entirely without references, so we shall see." Charlie pressed her hand affectionately.

"We can't afford another good ole boy like Vince, as much as I liked him and am sorry he's gone," Amanda whispered, as a familiar voice boomed through the crowd, and she recognized Ralph and Claire making their way toward them. Ralph was handsome in a navy suit, and Claire wore a white crystal-pleated dress. He quickly waylaid the waiter and whispered to him, before coming up and hugging Amanda and shaking Petrino's hand. Jill appeared, and the two expectant women hugged each other warmly as everyone chatted enthusiastically.

Momentarily the waiter appeared with a tray. Ralph handed Claire and Jill each a glass. "Sprite," he explained, as he captured champagne flutes for Amanda, Petrino and himself. Holding up his glass, he drawled, "To the future generation of Mainville and their happiness."

As all held up their glasses, clinking then drinking, Amanda's eyes wandered across the room. She saw Jon talking with Kimball. A beautiful brunette in a vivid red short strappy chemise, with matching fingernails, came up and embraced Connor intimately. Petrino followed her gaze.

"Who is that bombshell?" he asked quietly.

"Don't know that I've seen her before," Amanda replied, her voice low, as she watched the woman entwine her arms around Jon and kiss him on the mouth, and Jon attempt to disentangle himself gracefully. As she looked on, Jon was laughing at something the woman said, as she kept her hand on his arm lingeringly and apparently addressed both men.

"I'd think I'd be finding out," Petrino growled, before clearing his throat to answer a question put to him by Ralph.

"May I have this dance?" Amanda heard as she felt a hand on her arm. Turning, she saw David.

"Why, I'd be delighted, Bro," Amanda beamed, taking his hand and handing her glass to Ralph.

"I cannot believe my luck," David drawled. "I didn't have to fight my brother for you."

"So you made it back here as promised, I see," Amanda purred.

As they whirled onto the dance floor, David stated, "This is certainly a happy day for George. To think Della would say yes and make an honest man out of him."

"And all that time she was waiting for him to screw his courage up to ask her," Amanda laughed.

Changing the subject, Amanda asked him, "And just who is your date for the evening?"

As her eyes traveled over to Jon and the brunette, David asked, "Have you met Lauren Mallory?" nodding toward them.

"No, I haven't," Amanda confessed, sheepish that he had caught her looking.

"She sort of invited herself," David went on. "She used to be Secret Service. She worked with Jon for a time before she became a consultant. She was hell on wheels, moved up the ladder quickly."

"Really?" murmured Amanda casually, although she was burning to know more.

"We just happened to walk in together," David said, half-apologetically, his eyes still on the woman.

"Looks like more to it than that to me," Amanda teased. "Is this the Washington woman?"

"I'll never tell. But you see she's over there with him and not with me," David rejoined wickedly.

Amanda smiled as his eyes searched her face. "Why, David, I think you are testing me to see if I am jealous. I trust Jon."

"So she says, sheathing her claws until tonight when she gets him home," David whispered, a devilish grin on his features.

"You're such a bad boy," Amanda told him, laughing, as he twirled her. "You, however, seem to be the one smitten by her."

David laughed too. They were still laughing as Jon appeared. "May I cut in?" he inquired, smiling at their mischievous grins.

David relinquished Amanda to his brother, and Jon pulled her into his arms. "Mrs. Connor, you are making me extremely jealous, laughing with my brother over something. Can't you let me in on the secret?" he wheedled, his eyes locked on hers.

"Oh, David thought I would scratch your eyes out over the brunette hanging on your arm over there," Amanda replied guilelessly.

"I'd never let you do that," he whispered as his lips found hers, tantalizing her, before he released her mouth and twirled her, catching her again in the circle of his arm. "Besides, what or who could possibly tempt me when I am married to the most beautiful woman in the room, when I am the envy of every man here?" he told her, pulling her closer.

"Here I was thinking how lucky I was to be with the most handsome man," Amanda teased him. "Now you're telling me I'm the cat's meow."

Earnestly he looked at her. "Amanda Connor, I love you like no other."

She felt as though she was glowing. He continued holding her as the music ended and another number began. As they began moving on the floor, they were suddenly interrupted by the sultry brunette at Jon's arm. She purred, "Would the little woman mind if I cut in?" Her eyes did not leave Jon's face.

"Perhaps not, but I would. I am otherwise occupied," Jon replied, smiling, as he whisked Amanda away and left the woman standing there.

Amanda looked at him quizzically. "That was rather rude, dear," she remarked.

"That's the only way to deal with Ms. Mallory, my dear," he rejoined lightly. "When I've got the cat's meow in my arms, I'm not settling for less," he winked.

During dinner, Amanda and Jon, Ralph and Claire, and Charlie and Jill sat talking with Joey Rand and David, as they recounted stories of their childhood. Amanda asked mischievously, "Where's your date, Bro?"

"She really isn't my date," David protested. "She was down and wanted to see all her old friends, and I asked her to accompany me."

"Sounds like a date to me," Ralph murmured.

David frowned. "I just got back from doing some procedures up there with a colleague, and ran into her. We used to know each other. Now where were we?"

"You were telling us about how you and Joey got interested in medicine," Jill reminded him.

"Yes, I'm sorry I interrupted. I really want to hear this," Amanda apologized.

"Tell them about the sharks," Joey laughed.

David grinned at his friend. "Joey and I had anatomy lab together in high school, and we made a bet as to who could best 'restore' his dogfish shark after lab. So we broke into lab after hours."

Joey interrupted him, smiling. "No, you're leaving out details. We made the bet before lab, so we knew beforehand we were going to reconstruct the corpse, put everything back as it was. So I was very careful with the incisions and taking everything out, marking it carefully. I thought I was doing fabulously well. But Lancelot here, who designated the prettiest girl in class to be his 'nurse', decided to cheat."

"It wasn't cheating," David chuckled. "I just borrowed some tissue from another shark and made some neat patches. But you were trying to do laparoscopic surgery on the damned fish."

"Whatever worked," Joey guffawed.

"Who won?" Amanda asked, her eyes dancing with merriment.

"Professor Melinsky finally figured out what we were doing and called a tie. She sent us to the head of surgery at U of Colorado, and he gave us summer jobs shadowing doctors with the interns."

David added, "Yeah, when we weren't called on to help the nurses with bedpans." He stood and turned to Amanda. "Brother-in-law wants another dance." His eyes twinkled.

As Amanda took his hand and he led her off, Jon's eyes followed them. Ralph and Claire also joined them on the dance floor, and Petrino and Jill excused themselves to mingle, leaving Jon with Rand.

"Couldn't get Kelly to come?" Jon asked intuitively.

"She's gone back to Denver, something about work." Rand was suddenly glum.

"Damn it, just ask her, Joey," Jon berated him mildly. "She's crazy about you."

"But Jon, I cannot keep up this competition against your folks for her affections," Joey sighed. "My best is not good enough for Gloria, and I want off that merry-go-round. And Kelly has apparently decided your dad needs commiseration from her more than she needs me."

"I wouldn't be so swift to make that judgment," Jon shook his head, his eyes still on Amanda. "Kelly feels your absence keenly. Why do you think she is making all these little trips to Florida?"

Joey smiled self-deprecatingly. "I guess so."

Jon patted him on the back. "Don't throw in the towel yet. Everyone else in the family is rooting for you, including Dad." Jon again glanced across the dance floor.

Joey noticed Jon's attention on Amanda. "You're not worried about David's affection for Amanda, are you?"

"I guess I'm still cautious," Jon remarked. "For all our time together, Amanda and I still don't know each other that well."

"You haven't shown her the trophy room, told her of all your accomplishments?" Joey was astounded.

"No, and she hasn't asked," Jon smiled.

"A girl who loves you for you," Joey mused. "Sooner or later if you don't tell her, Gloria will." He paused. "Are you afraid she might fall for David?"

"Well, David is more the life of the party, more of a charmer. And it's not like he hasn't stolen my girlfriends before." Jon couldn't keep a trace of bitterness out of his voice.

"Like Lauren?"

"God, no," Jon laughed. "That was a huge mistake, a weak moment on my part. I was glad to have her off my scent. David came in handy there."

Joey leaned forward, his voice lower. "You do realize that David was pretty serious about Lauren?"

"No way," Jon breathed sharply, suddenly sober. "She's a man-eater, and he has never been serious about any girl." He sighed. "But I do worry about Amanda. I have trouble disguising my jealousy when he's around her."

Joey smiled broadly. "Do you not notice how Amanda is constantly seeking you out with her eyes? She may be laughing with David, but she's in love with you."

Jon was silent a minute. "And I confess I can't keep my eyes off her as well. I feel a connection with her I've never felt with anyone before. I cannot describe it. I was afraid this was only infatuation and would wear off, but the more I'm with her the more my love grows."

As if to echo his words, the band began playing *I only have eyes for you.* Jon stood. "Later, Joey—that's my cue."

Jon strode over the dance floor to Amanda, gently claiming her from David.

David watched them a minute admiringly, then waved at Joey, moving toward him. He was arrested in mid-stride by the woman in red. Shrugging at Joey, he allowed her to entwine her arms around his neck and lead him away.

As Joey continued to look on, he noticed David and Lauren engage in animated conversation. David's demeanor grew more serious as a heated discussion ensued. The music ended with them still arguing, as David took her arm and guided her manfully off the dance floor.

Jon and Amanda returned to the table, followed by Ralph and Claire. As Amanda started to sit, Claire pulled Amanda aside and whispered, "Accompany me to the powder room, will you?"

Jon forestalled them. "Where do you two think you're going?"

Claire giggled as Amanda intoned mysteriously, "The secrets of what we women discuss as we are powdering our noses cannot be revealed."

The two women walked arm in arm into the restroom. Amanda washed her hands, and stopped to review her lipstick critically in the mirror. The next thing she knew the gorgeous brunette in red was beside her, looking her up and down.

Amanda, smiling, held out her hand. "Hello, I'm Amanda Connor. You must be Lauren."

The woman was taken aback, but laughed throatily as she took Amanda's hand. "Oh, you are Jon's lovely little wife. You are just too cute."

"Thanks," replied Amanda politely. "It was good that you were able to be here for George's and Della's party."

"I wouldn't have missed it," Lauren purred. "And it is so good to see all my old friends."

"Yes," Amanda murmured as she took out her compact.

"You are so lucky," the woman gushed. "Jon is such a catch, so masculine, and so extraordinarily good in bed. I remember when—oh, excuse me," she interrupted herself, looking at a jewel-encrusted watch on her wrist as Claire walked up. "I must be getting back. It was nice meeting you, Madeline."

She glided out of the room as Claire looked at Amanda's stunned features. "Did she just say what I thought she said?" Claire demanded, her hands on her hips.

Amanda recovered, and looking at her friend's indignant face in the mirror, burst out laughing.

Claire just stared at her. "I would be calling that woman out to the back alley right now if she said that about my man."

Amanda doubled over, howling. After a moment Claire joined her. They held each other by the arms, laughing hysterically. Amanda asserted, gasping between breaths, holding her side, "What a woman after my own heart. Do you know she must have planned that whole scene? And she probably purposefully didn't get my name right. And what's so funny is that just last week you were accused of being 'the other woman' and having an affair with Jon."

Claire looked at her like she had suddenly produced a gun. "Me? Who came up with that—oh, I know. Janine at the church. Let's lock her up in the same room with the *femme fatale* that just walked out of here."

"Oh no," Amanda moaned good-naturedly. "Now I have to repair my makeup." As she pulled out her compact, she looked over at Claire through the mirror. "Not a word of this to Ralph—you know how he is. I'll never hear the end of it."

Claire nodded, still tittering. "Scout's honor."

Soon they returned to their table, and Jon stood as they approached.

Claire inquired, "Where is Ralph?"

As Jon seated Claire he remarked, "He was drafted to dance," and nodded toward the dance floor, where Ralph was looking quite uncomfortable as he tried to extricate himself from the embrace of Lauren Mallory. Claire glared at the couple on the dance floor.

Jon pulled Amanda's chair out for her. As she sat down, he whispered, "You were gone much too long. How do you feel about saying our goodbyes and getting home?"

She looked at him, and his eyes twinkled mischievously. Reading his thoughts, she murmured, "That would be nice. I did not have dessert." Watching his consternation, she smiled sweetly.

"You vixen," he said, his voice low in her ear. "You know I was thinking of you as the main course."

She laughed as Ralph made his way back to the table, looking flustered. Claire was hissing in his ear as he kept protesting, "I swear I've never seen her before in my life."

Jon winked at Amanda. "I smell the fireworks," he whispered as they rose and said their goodbyes.

Later, as they pulled up into the driveway, she purred, "I met Lauren Mallory tonight in the powder room."

Jon looked at her momentarily. "And?" he demanded.

"She told me how wonderful you are, so masculine and good in bed," Amanda replied evenly.

Jon shut off the car. Sighing, he responded, "I'm sorry, Amanda. I never thought I'd see her again, and I'd give the world if she hadn't done that to you. It's true—we had a short fling several years ago."

Amanda laid a hand on his arm. "Tell me about it," she murmured.

"There's not much to tell. Several years ago, when I was again single, there was a joint operation with Secret Service. One of us had to be liaison for protecting the President at a diplomatic function at Camp David. Andy was opted out—he was going home to you on leave for a few days. We all knew Lauren the man-eater was going to be the SS leader. We drew straws, and I was it.

"Well, she came on me, as she was wont to do when given the opportunity and a willing victim, and I hadn't been with anyone in a while. I admit I was jealous knowing what Andy was probably doing back home, and flattered that this beautiful woman wanted me.

"We had a weekend together. I came back to the office, was the butt of a lot of smutty talk, and it was over. I realized she was not what I was looking for. We were quickly bored with each other, and both went on our separate ways. I've not seen her but once since then, and I made it clear that I was not interested in picking back up where we left off."

He paused. "She holds no allure for me. I want you to know that in case she ever shows up again. Does it matter?"

Amanda placed her hand on his cheek. "I love you, Jon Connor. I didn't expect you to be a monk before you married me. It hurt momentarily to hear her talk that way, but I realized what she was doing. She wouldn't have said that if she wasn't jealous of what we had."

Connor placed his hand over hers and pulled it to his lips. "And you need never fear my feelings for you, milady," he spoke fervently.

She laughed, a silvery sound. "Jon Connor, are there other women from your past who are going to come out of the woodwork?"

He smiled slyly. "Hopefully not. There was that girl at Duke that made me turn down going to Stanford to law school."

"She did? Must have been pretty special," Amanda murmured.

"Actually, the day before classes started she dumped me. But that was OK. It was at Duke I decided to apply to the FBI."

The Connors' Crisis

"But she wasn't the only one, I'll bet," Amanda teased.

"Oh, there was one or two," Jon shrugged.

"Only one or two?" Her eyebrows arched in mock indignation.

"Well, a few," he smirked wickedly, as he pulled her toward him and kissed her. "Let's hurry inside so I can prove my marital devotion."

He made it around to her door and opened it, taking her hand and helping her out. They walked arm in arm up the steps, and he disengaged the alarm, unlocking the door and holding it for her.

Once inside, he took her hand and pulled her to him, dancing with her. She rested her head against his shoulder as they slow danced together.

"Tell me, Mrs. Connor, about the men in your past," he whispered.

She laughed softly. "Nothing to report there," she offered. "I'm afraid you already know all about that." She looked down, embarrassed. "I told you I was nerdy. My experience with men is rather lacking, Jon. I've led a boring life."

"Never," he kissed her hair. She relaxed against him as he held her close, their bodies swaying together.

"Tell me about you and Charlie."

He felt her tense and her swift intake of breath, as she pulled away and gazed at him, her eyes wide with surprise. He noted a sudden wariness, but she asked simply, "What do you want to know?"

He took her hand and led her to the sofa, pulling her down to sit by him. He placed his arm around her. "I want to know everything about you, Amanda," he said fervently, "including my competition. I want to make you happy, to outshine all the past men in your life, and to never allow you to regret your decision to be with me."

"You have no competition," she murmured, taking his hand in hers and squeezing it.

"But I already know there was something between you two. You told me."

"I what?" She was dumbfounded.

"The night you were in the hospital with pneumonia. You were delirious, thought I was Charlie, begged me not to tell Jon about you two. Tell me what?"

She looked at him, aghast. "What else did I tell you?" she demanded softly.

Jon kissed her forehead. "You stated that I wouldn't love you if I knew. I cannot imagine anything that would cause me not to love you."

She looked down, fingering the buttons on his shirtfront. "Did I also happen to give you my high school locker combination?"

"I saw his face while we were waiting at the hospital after your accident." Jon's voice was quiet. "He was in anguish over you."

She caressed his hand absently as he kept his arm around her and waited patiently.

"There's nothing between Charlie and me. We've been friends since childhood." She faltered. "Jon, you're the man I love, the one I married."

He kneaded her neck and gently lifted her chin to face him. "He made the remark once, back before we married, that at one time he thought he had a chance with you."

She froze, then shut her eyes. He kissed her cheek. "I'm sorry. I shouldn't push you. We don't have to talk about it."

She was still and silent, passive as he held her. She finally sighed and shook her head. She stared down at her hands. "Charlie and Alan and I grew up together. He and Billy and Monica and I hung together a lot. His family and mine and Alan's attended the Baptist church together. Charlie's dad and mine were friends. He was always around, and teased me unmercifully back when I had a crush on Billy.

"Charlie was quite the jock, and had his choice of girlfriends. I wasn't in his league. But from time to time we'd pal around, even in college and while I was in law school. He and Billy played football in college. We both liked football and basketball, and he had season tickets back when he was working at FDLE and I was in law school. He would drag me to the FSU games when he didn't have a date."

She fell silent. Jon stroked her arm reassuringly.

"Charlie and Andy became close friends. Charlie came home to work for the sheriff's department about the time I came home to care for my mother. "Charlie accompanied the sheriff to tell me Andy had been murdered. He would check on me from time to time after that."

He was silent, sensing her struggle. She drew a shaky breath. "I was going through a bad time. It was the one-year anniversary of Andy's death. The Bureau showed up without warning, delivered his badge and a commendation."

She swallowed. "I was barely holding things together as it was. It was the last straw. I went berserk. I ran away to the beach house. I thought I had lost everything, and I wanted to die, to walk into the sea, to end it all."

She took a deep breath, remembering that time. A tremor went through her. Jon felt it, and pulled her closer. "Oh, Mandy," he stroked her cheek, bringing her head to his shoulder.

Amanda continued, her voice a whisper. "Marjy sent Charlie to find me. I threw myself at him." She paused. "I couldn't stand to be alone any more."

She was silent, her eyes closed a moment. She bit her lip. "Charlie was at the point in his life where he was ready to settle down. Then I did—what I did," she stammered miserably. "I wasn't capable of loving anyone then, Jon. I was so overwhelmed—I could not wean myself from Andy's memory."

She looked up at him, her eyes shining. "Charlie was so good—" she broke off, her face flaming. "It was a huge mistake, and I almost lost a good friend. It took a long time to mend those fences, because we avoided each other—I was terribly embarrassed that I led him on. We are now friends again."

She looked up at Jon. "It was only that one weekend. I broke it off. A year later I introduced him to Jill. That was that."

Amanda's voice was pleading. "Jon, no one knows about this, except he apparently told Jill, and Dr. Howells guessed. It was a terrible mistake."

"Amanda, it's OK," he whispered reassuringly. "But you loved him? He still loves you." Jon stroked her hair, his eyes sympathetic.

"No, you're wrong," she looked away and stood abruptly, her voice raised in protest. She turned her back to Jon. "It wasn't love. I was lonely and desperate. It was all my fault. It's over."

She walked to the stairs. "I'm sorry if I've done anything to shake your confidence in me." She ran up the stairs.

Amanda made her way to the bedroom closet and stripped off her dress, hanging up the silk. She walked into the bathroom in her lingerie, and stared at herself in the mirror. Some things never die, she thought wearily. Oh, Charlie, someone keeps opening that door.

Amanda closed her eyes, blinking back more tears, and took a deep breath, her hands braced on the lavatory. She heard a noise behind her, and turned her back to the door, wiping her eyes. Jon walked up to her, standing behind her and gripping her arms gently.

"Love, I never meant to make you think I don't trust you," he whispered. He pulled her around to face him.

"Jon, you're the one I love, the one who makes me happy. I don't know how to convince you."

He smothered her in embrace. "That's the beauty of it. You don't. I already believe you, Mandy. And I love you like no other."

He kissed her eyelids. "Please don't cry."

Jon's mouth descended on hers and she responded. "I hope you're always happy with me, Amanda Connor," he spoke against her lips.

The kiss deepened. He murmured, "You are so tense. I think perhaps a warm shower would be the ticket, don't you?"

She stirred in his arms. "Together?" Her voice was muffled against his mouth.

"How else?" he laughed softly. "But you need to get out of all this women's artillery," he smiled, his hand moving down her back and unfastening her bra, slowly undressing her as she stood, passively enjoying his touch.

"Then afterward perhaps a good massage, then some meatloaf sandwiches," he suggested mischievously.

CHAPTER 14

MONDAY

Amanda breezed through the office at 8:15 the next morning. "Morning, Sheila," she called to the woman in the kitchen. Making her way into her office, she left the door open as her cell phone rang. She recognized Jon's number from her caller ID.

"Hello," she said breathlessly, dumping her purse onto the desk.

"Hello, yourself," Jon's voice greeted her. "Are you OK? Make it to work on time?"

"No, thanks to you," she grinned. "I'm late and all befuddled," she continued as she punched on her computer and allowed it to warm up.

"I'm so sorry. I'll try not to distract you so early in the morning," he teased.

"You'll always be a distraction, and a welcome one at that," she assured him, as she waited patiently for her calendar to appear on the monitor.

"What is on the agenda for today? Are you free for lunch?"

"I don't know yet," she informed him. "I'm waiting for the computer to tell me. I miss the old-fashioned appointment book. And not everyone has the day off like you."

"You could have called in sick. Ralph would cover for you," he laughed wickedly.

"You are bad for business, Jon—what the hell?" she muttered suddenly, irritably as she spied a name on the day's appointment log.

"What is it?" he demanded.

Amanda retorted, "Why would your old girlfriend have an appointment with Ralph this morning? When was this scheduled?"

"What old girlfriend?" Jon was adamant. "Who are you talking about?"

163

"Lauren Mallory's name is down for an appointment with Ralph at 10:00."

"Why?" he asked incredulously.

"Why indeed?" Amanda echoed. "There's no subject. Did she mention any of this to you yesterday?"

"No, but we didn't make that much conversation," Jon told her.

"So I noticed," Amanda countered slyly.

"You vixen!" he exclaimed. "If you think she holds any interest for me—"

"I believe you," Amanda soothed him. "And yes, I am free for lunch."

"Good," he relented. "I'll pick you up at 11:45, and I want a blow-by-blow account."

"You know I can't do that," she reminded him sweetly. "There's something called the attorney-client privilege."

"Woman, don't make me beat it out of you," he threatened good-naturedly.

As she hung up, she looked up to see Ralph standing in front of her desk. "Hi, partner," she smiled, but the smile dissolved as she saw his worried face. "What is it?"

"This 10:00 appointment—this woman makes me nervous," Ralph stammered.

"She seemed pretty comfortable with you yesterday on the dance floor," Amanda asserted mischievously.

"Claire almost had a cow last night when we got home. She was so angry. I don't know this woman, Amanda—have never met her before yesterday. She said she had heard that I was putting my name in for county judge, and told me she has influential friends with the governor's office and would be willing to help me."

Amanda, concern written on her face, came around to where Ralph was standing and put her hand on his arm. "Ralph, do you think you need that kind of help? Just how badly do you want this?"

Ralph gazed at her dazedly. "Amanda, I have always wanted to be a judge." He sank heavily into the chair in front of her desk. As Dinah appeared in the doorway with papers, Amanda quickly shook her head and motioned for Dinah to close the door and leave them alone as she leaned back against her desk.

Ralph continued, "You know and I know that it takes more than skill and smarts—it takes connections. And I'm a black kid from the other side of the tracks."

"I know," Amanda murmured. "But you're the best attorney I know, you've been an officer of the local bar several times, you've taken your turns on the various committees, you've handled pro bono matters and won awards, and everyone likes you. You've earned the respect of all your colleagues. The judges all respect you. You are not without connections. And you know Jon and I will do all in our power to influence as many as we can in your favor."

Ralph looked at her with shining eyes. "You will? Thanks, Amanda—you don't know what that means to me." He faltered. "But this woman Lauren—what do you think? Should I hear her out?"

Amanda took the chair beside him and took his hand. "Ralph, I don't know what to tell you. My first impression of her was certainly not favorable. I don't trust her, but I could be biased. Jon knows her. Call him."

"Jon knows her?" Ralph echoed. "But how?"

"I'll let him tell you that," Amanda frowned. "But he is at home today, and can fill you in before you meet with her." Standing, she added, "Just be careful, Ralph—don't sell your soul."

She glanced at the desk, to a cup holding pens. She pulled one out. "Where did these pens come from?" she demanded suddenly.

Ralph looked at it distractedly. "Dinah apparently had to deal with a new office supply salesman last week. He gave her several, told her to put one in each office and see if people liked them."

"They're ugly, and they look expensive," Amanda complained.

"They were apparently free to try."

"I just don't like solicitors," Amanda grumbled, dropping it back into the cup.

Amanda had just seen her last client out for the morning when she came face to face with Lauren Mallory. Smoothly she covered her surprise, saying warmly, "Miss Mallory, it's good to see you."

The beautiful woman looked at her through heavily mascaraed eyelids. "Hello, Mrs. Connor. Marilyn, isn't it?"

"Amanda," corrected Amanda politely.

"Amanda, it's so wonderful to see you. And well, your partner is just so charming. I think we shall get along very well. Ta-ta, darling."

Amanda stood staring at the door from which Lauren disappeared, not aware of a presence behind her. Turning, she gave a small cry of alarm.

"Goodness! Jon, you scared me."

He smiled as he leaned over and kissed her cheek. "Sorry."

"You just missed Ms. Mallory. I'm sure if you hurry you could catch her."

"Really?" Jon started toward the door.

Amanda grabbed his arm. "You're not serious, are you?"

"Gotcha." Jon turned, a grin on his face.

"Oh, you!" Amanda exclaimed, as he pulled her to him.

Enfolding her in embrace, he whispered, "I asked Ralph to join us. I hope you don't mind."

"No," she mumbled against his jacket. "I'm interested in knowing what the two of you talked about, and what your ex had to say to him."

"Well, if you two are ready, we can quit speculating and tell all," a voice behind them spoke. "I'm driving. And let's go to Tallulah's—I want some comfort food and could use a drink."

Later, as they were downing drinks and salad, Amanda demanded, "OK, firstly, did you and Jon talk about Lauren before the meeting?"

"Yes." Ralph turned to her. "And he told me to go ahead with the meeting—what could it hurt?"

"I just don't trust her," Amanda muttered. "So what did she say at the meeting?"

"Yeah, who was this influential person whose services she offered?" Jon asked, reaching for a roll.

"She didn't reveal any names, but said the person had a major role in both the governor's and president's elections."

"Everyone who gave over $1,000 says that, too," Jon reminded him.

"She apparently knows quite a few people in Washington and Tallahassee on a first-name basis, having been a lobbyist for the last several years," Ralph continued.

"What's her *quid pro quo?*" Amanda wanted to know.

"What do you mean?" Ralph asked, his eyes not meeting hers.

"What does she want in exchange for this help?" Amanda persisted. "She's not doing this out of some love for her country."

"Ooh, the cat is showing her claws," Ralph countered, chuckling.

"From what I know of Lauren, I think Amanda's right," Jon interjected, his tone serious. "Lauren wants something. Did she tell you what?"

"No," Ralph admitted. "And I must tell you I was not comfortable. She's very touchy-feely, and Claire is already mad at me after my dancing with her last night. But she initiated it."

"Yeah, sure," Amanda gibed, but Jon shook his head.

"I saw it," Jon affirmed quietly. "Lauren came right up to him and pulled him onto the dance floor. She's very persistent."

Suddenly the subject of their conversation appeared at their table. "Why, my two favorite men!" she exclaimed, a polished hand on a shoulder of each of the two. "And the little woman, too. You weren't discussing me, were you?"

Amanda smiled broadly, her eyes twinkling wickedly at Jon. "You were one of many topics of conversation, Miss Mallory. Won't you join us for lunch?"

Jon looked at Amanda in surprise, as Lauren shook her head sunnily. "No, I'd love to, but I have another appointment. Some other time." She leaned down and brushed her lips against Jon's cheek. "So good to see you all again." She then turned to Ralph, placing her hands on his shoulders and kneading them familiarly as she whispered in his ear.

As she straightened up, Amanda observed her glancing out a window. Lauren suddenly seemed to pale, and Amanda thought she detected fear. Amanda looked and glimpsed a blonde haired man turning away, his face in profile. She glanced back at Lauren, who had recovered her poise. Amanda for a moment wondered if she had imagined the incident.

As Lauren strode away, Jon briskly wiped his cheek with his napkin, as Amanda and Ralph regarded him with amusement. "I don't know what I ever saw in her," he muttered darkly.

"Oh, she seems utterly charming to me," Amanda retorted sarcastically, as Ralph guffawed in laughter. "Of course, if she calls me 'the little woman' one more time . . . ."

"I don't know, but I think she accomplished exactly what she set out to do, which was to discomfit the two of you," Ralph inserted mischievously.

"And now she's courting your attentions," Amanda, suddenly sober, reminded Ralph.

"Ah, I'm not worried," Ralph rejoined smoothly, smiling.

"You should be," Jon replied, surprising Amanda with his fierceness, scowling at Ralph. "Have you discussed any of this with Claire?"

"No," Ralph admitted ruefully. "She was already mad last night, so I thought better than to tell her about the appointment. I took Claire to the airport early this morning. She's on her way to Cleveland to visit her sister for the week at the family cabin, her great-aunt's birthday party. She was already unhappy with me, so I didn't want to add to the unpleasantness."

"I wonder who Lauren's meeting," Amanda pondered out loud. "Perhaps there are VIPs in town today?"

As they rose to leave, Amanda glanced toward a private dining room, and happened to see Lauren Mallory seated at a table with the local state senator, the U.S. representative for the area, and Esme Townsend. And another man sat at the table, his features dark, his eyes cat-like. She knew she had seen him before, but did not know him. He caught her eyes on him, and gazed at her intently, a sardonic smile on his face. She turned away as the door to the room closed.

When they had seated themselves in the car, she spoke. "There is a contingent of political bigwigs in the private dining room meeting with Esme Townsend. And your girlfriend is also an invitee."

"She's not my girlfriend," Ralph retorted. But his frown deepened. "But I guess I should be worried."

Jon smiled broadly. "Don't despair yet. If your meeting with her went well, perhaps she is touting your name."

"I'm not sure we have reached that stage in our relationship," Ralph joked, but Amanda could tell he was worried.

Ralph suddenly changed the subject. "What were you and Charlie scheming yesterday at the party?"

Amanda blushed as she felt Jon's eyes on her. "Oh, I was just wondering about whether he had heard anything from the governor's office. I had put in a good word for him for the sheriff appointment."

Ralph smiled. "Yeah, Buddy keeps his finger on the pulse. Did you ask him for me too?"

"But of course." Amanda patted him on the shoulder.

"Who's Buddy?" Jon wanted to know.

"One of Mandy's old boyfriends," Ralph replied devilishly.

"He is not," Amanda protested, shaking her head.

"He wanted to be," Ralph teased her. "And I recall you went to some fancy function on his arm a couple years ago, and a couple of exclusive inaugural parties prior to that."

"Oh, really?" Jon raised his eyebrows.

"Buddy is a college classmate, and we were in law school together. We've kept in touch," Amanda was defensive. "He manages to stay in good with every administration. He has some job with the governor's office presently."

"Yeah. Nothing important, just chief of staff," Ralph winked.

When they arrived, Ralph walked on into the office and left the two of them standing outside hand in hand. Amanda looked at the door where Ralph had just disappeared. "Damn it, Jon, I don't want to lose Ralph as a partner. But he wants this so badly," she remarked sadly. "I just don't trust this woman. And if she's wining and dining with Esme Townsend . . . ."

Jon squeezed her hand. "Do you want me to talk to Lauren on his behalf?" he teased her.

Amanda turned her full gaze on him. Jon was mesmerized. "I would do anything to help Ralph, but I really don't want you entangled with her either." Amanda was serious.

"With Lauren or this Townsend woman?" Jon smiled at her. But Amanda did not smile back.

"Avoid both of them. Run, don't walk, the other way," Amanda frowned. She mused aloud, "I could talk to Esme again, sound her out. But there has to be another way." She stared off thoughtfully.

"You know her?" Jon was surprised.

"Yes. She is Toby's mother," Amanda quipped diffidently.

"Really? How well do you know her?" Jon demanded.

Amanda was suddenly reticent. "One does not live in Mainville and not know Esme, and I've been here all my life."

"Would you have influence with her?"

Amanda sighed. "Esme does nothing for free, and her asking price is generally too much pound of flesh for my budget. I've never been in a position to want anything she has, so I've been fortunate. We are friendly, and we have lots of mutual friends and acquaintances. She throws a few dollars at the recital fund from time to time. Toby was in St. Catherine's youth choir growing up, and I've done some legal work for him over the last couple of years." She looked down. "Esme and I have ended up at a few receptions together, back—back when I would accompany Billy or Buddy from time to time." Amanda shook her head. "She can be rather nasty when she wishes. Our last conversation was not overly pleasant."

She withdrew her hand. "Jon, I really need to get back to work."

"I know," he smiled at her. "My parents asked if we could join them for dinner Thursday evening."

Amanda smiled, but it didn't meet her eyes. "Sure, that will be nice."

"You're a lawyer; you can do better than that to convince me." Jon bent and kissed her on the cheek. "Lighten up, girl. My mom is coming around. Seriously. This dinner invitation is an olive branch."

"Yeah, sure," Amanda muttered. Then, seeing the hurt expression on Jon's face, she added contritely, "I'm sorry, darling. I want so badly to impress your folks, but I'm just not in their league."

Jon was suddenly concerned. "Mandy, I don't understand. You don't have to impress them. You have nothing to prove. I just want you to get to know them and have an amicable relationship with them."

"I know. But I want them to think I'm worthy of their son, and to love me." She whispered, "It's important to me that they approve of your choice."

"They do and they will," he murmured. "You're just too sensitive on the issue of your background. It doesn't matter."

"It matters to your mother," Amanda said softly. "I see how she looks at me."

Jon sighed. "My mom is a little odd, no, make that more than a little, but she knows I am crazy about you."

Amanda smiled pensively, but made no reply.

Jon interjected, "We can always say no. But she did promise this event would be without an audience, just us four."

"You know I'll do anything for you." Amanda reached up and kissed him.

"Anything?" Jon returned her kiss.

"What do you have in mind?" Amanda shot back suspiciously.

"Take the afternoon off and let's run away together," he smiled mischievously. "I could arrange a little rendezvous on the beach, or maybe on a blanket in our own back yard."

"How am I to go back in to work after you do that to me?" she shook her head. "I would if I could. But I can perhaps swing getting off a little early to enjoy the sunset."

"It's a date." He embraced her.

"We ought to invite Ralph out to dinner. He's baching it tonight," Amanda whispered.

"As long as I can have you to myself before and after," Jon murmured.

CHAPTER 15

TUESDAY

Amanda wearily unlocked the door and let herself into the house, groping for a light switch. Tuesday had been unusually long, and after a morning of seeing new clients and drafting pleadings she had spent most of the afternoon waiting with her client for his hearing to be called. The judge was delayed; therefore, the hearing went late, and she was drained. Thank God I practiced at the church during lunch hour, she told herself.

She called the office to let Ralph know she had come straight home, but got the voice mail at the office. Oh, that's right, she thought. Dinah had left that morning on a cruise, Sheila was off this afternoon, and Ralph said he was going to cut the phones off to get some work done. She left a message.

Where could Jon be? she wondered. It was unlike him to be late, but then again she was usually home before now herself.

She dropped the keys onto the console table beside the front door and the mail on the desk, kicked off her heels and padded to the kitchen, pouring herself a glass of iced tea and looking around her with satisfaction at the pristine white kitchen. She stood there musing, planning the meal, trying to overcome her lethargy.

Suddenly there was a knocking. Startled, she jumped at the sound, then set down her glass before making her way to the door. Her eyes widened in surprise.

"Is this where Jonathan Connor lives?" a uniformed sheriff's deputy inquired.

"Yes, Officer," Amanda replied. "May I help you?" She smiled at the young man.

"Is Mr. Connor home?" the officer asked timidly.

"No, he hasn't made it here yet," Amanda replied. "What is it?"

171

The young man shifted uncomfortably. "I have papers to serve upon him."

Amanda frowned. "What sort of papers?"

"Civil suit." The man was clearly nervous. "I could come back later."

"Well, he does live here, and I'm his wife, so I could accept service on his behalf." Amanda reached for the documents in the man's hand, which he reluctantly surrendered. "Go ahead and fill out your return, Officer—" she paused, looking at his name tag, "Williams. It's a long drive out here. There's no need in your having to come back."

The officer hurriedly complied and fled, as Amanda returned inside with the papers in hand, cutting on lamps as she walked through. Rifling past the return and summons, she began reading. Her face registered confusion, then horror as she continued. She suddenly sat down heavily on the sofa, her face white.

"My God! Surely not—he would have told me," Amanda whispered.

She sat there in shock, not knowing how much time had elapsed, her mind whirring. Another knocking interrupted her reverie. Papers still clutched in her hand, she opened the door.

There stood Charles Petrino. He took one look at her face and at the papers in her hand.

"I had to come," he said simply.

"How did you—it doesn't matter," she muttered, as she stood aside and allowed him to enter.

"Is Jon home?" he asked concernedly.

"Not yet." She shook her head negatively, waving him to a seat in the living room. Instead he walked over to the bar and poured bourbon from a crystal decanter into two glasses, then handed one to her.

"Here, drink this," he spoke gently. "You're white as a sheet."

She took the glass and downed the drink in one gulp, then coughed as the liquid burned its way down her throat. "Why is it that every time there is a crisis, you show up and feed me liquor?"

"I think we've established that it's a helluva lot safer than taking you into my arms," he quipped as he took a swallow of his own drink.

She barely registered his reply, her mind churning in turmoil. "I can't believe this," she mumbled. "Jon the father of an eight-year-old child by Lauren Mallory? Why didn't he tell me?"

"Don't jump to conclusions," Charlie reprimanded her. "Ask him first. He loves you—he'll tell the truth."

"So that's why she's in town? A paternity action. Why now, after all this time?" Amanda demanded angrily. Turning to Charlie, she countered accusatorily, "How did you know about this?"

Charlie's eyes bored into hers. "You forget—there's little goes on in this town that gets past me. I have a friend or two at the courthouse and sheriff's department."

"God! It is probably all over town by now," she cried, as she slumped onto the sofa.

"Well, I did ask that they not spread the information, but yes, this is all a matter of public record, so it will get out," Charlie replied, as he gulped the rest of his drink, took her glass and refilled it, handing it back to her. "How soon before Jon gets home?"

"I'm here," a voice replied, as Jon's frame loomed in the doorway. "I come home to find my wife entertaining the chief of police." He smiled tightly at Charlie. "To what do we owe this pleasure?"

He stopped short as he saw no return smile on Charlie's face, then looked over at Amanda's stricken features. He made his way to her, kneeling in front of her. "It's bad news, isn't it? What is it, love?" he whispered. "What's happened?"

"I'll be getting on now," Charlie muttered. "You two need to be alone."

"What is it, Charlie?" Jon demanded as Amanda stared at him, making no response.

"I think those papers will explain everything," Charlie remarked as he exited.

Jon shook Amanda gently. "Tell me, Mandy."

She awkwardly pushed the papers into his hand, then sat passively while he sat beside her and reviewed them. His face registered first surprise, then shock, culminating in anger. "It is not true," he retorted dazedly. "It cannot be true."

"Why not?" Amanda asked, her voice sounding small in her ears. "You and she were together—you told me that."

"But only for those couple of days, Amanda," he countered, his eyes pleading with her. "And we took precautions. I couldn't be the father. And I never had anything to do with her again. I had no idea she had a child. A girl. I didn't lie to you, and I'm not lying now."

"How can you be so sure?" she whispered.

Jon turned and grasped Amanda by the shoulders, his face close to hers. "You must believe me. If I knew I had a child, I would have acknowledged the child. And I would have told you."

His face darkened. "This is one of Lauren's little games. But for what purpose? What is she up to?"

"Honey, I'm home," a voice greeted them from the doorway.

Amanda winced. "I forgot," she whispered. "David called and asked if he could spend the night in the guest room. I said yes. He has another appointment with a real estate agent early tomorrow morning."

173

Jon frowned, unhappy at his brother's appearance. He searched Amanda's eyes. "Please believe me."

She returned his gaze briefly. "I want to very much," she whispered, before pulling away to greet David.

"Did I interrupt something?" David grinned. The grin died as he glimpsed the expression on Jon's face. "What's wrong?"

"Nothing," Amanda assured him, smiling wanly, and approaching him, allowing him to kiss her on the cheek. "I'm happy to see you, Bro. Let's go see what I have in the larder for dinner." Without looking back at Jon she took David by the hand and steered him into the kitchen. Jon sighed, sat down, downed the rest of Amanda's drink and reviewed the documents again.

Hearing the easy banter between his brother and Amanda, Jon felt his irritation grow, as he walked to the bar, poured and downed a second drink, a single-malt. I know I'm not the father of Lauren's child, he told himself angrily. Yet he found himself wondering about the little girl. And there's David flirting with my wife in there, he thought crossly. That rake has never been accused of fathering a child, as many women as he's been through.

Jon shook himself mentally. I'm just letting my anger get out of control, he sighed as he rose, left the papers on the coffee table and walked to the kitchen. David was dancing around Amanda as she deftly chopped onions and peppers and threw them into a sizzling cast-iron skillet.

"I still can't find Mom's butcher knife," she muttered crossly.

David caught her up and twirled her around. She ended up in front of Jon, flushed and wary.

Jon's eyes smoldered with jealousy. David noted it and spoke to Amanda. "The old ball and chain is getting that envious look. Show him a little of that true passion."

Amanda, breathless, averted her eyes as Jon swept her into his arms. "I love you so much," Jon whispered to her, his eyes shining. "I know it's hard, but I need for you to trust me."

"I do," she replied, as her mouth found his. David disappeared as they remained locked in embrace for several minutes, he kissing her and she responding.

Laughingly, Jon finally released her. She lightly remarked, "I think we may have chased Brother David away."

There was a sudden muttered oath, and the sound of the front door slamming. Startled, they ran into the living area, but David was gone. The sheaf of papers comprising the paternity complaint was lying scattered on the floor.

"Why do you think David ran out like that?" Amanda mused as she absently cleaned the counter for the fourth time.

The room was full of the odor of smothered chicken and seasonings as Jon regarded her. "I don't know. When I called his cell phone, he just said he had forgotten something, and would see us later."

"That's unlike him," Amanda remarked.

Jon began slowly, "I'm afraid he may have seen the paternity complaint. I always suspected that he and Lauren may have had an affair at one time, but he never owned up to it. Joey alluded to it at the party, and that David may have been more serious about her than I realized." Jon looked down. "I just don't know, Amanda, what made him rush off."

"Well, I'm sorry he is missing my cooking," Amanda replied as she placed serving dishes on the table.

They ate in silence, engrossed in their own thoughts. Jon periodically sought her eyes, but she seemed preoccupied. He found his mind wandering back to the paternity action. Was he the father? No, he rejected that possibility. I know—we were both insistent on contraception.

Jon helped Amanda clear the table as she prepared a plate for David. "Just in case he comes back hungry," she quipped, as she placed the container in the microwave.

Jon took her in his arms. "I'm sorry I get so jealous of the attention you give my brother," he crooned to her. "And I'm sorry for the current mess and its effect on you."

Just then the telephone rang. Irritably, he reached for the kitchen wall phone. "Jon Connor here," he said curtly. Listening, his eyes grew wide as he replied, "What? Hang on. Yes, I'll be there right away."

He hung up, drawing away from Amanda. "What is it?" she demanded.

"It's Ralph. He's in trouble—there's been a disturbance at his house," Jon spoke as he walked out of the kitchen.

Amanda followed him toward the front door and grabbed her car keys. Jon protested, "There's no need in both of us going. You stay here."

"Oh, no," she responded petulantly. "If Ralph is in trouble, I want to be there."

Jon sighed and took her car keys out of her hand, placing them back on the console. "OK, but let me drive."

Moments later they were speeding down the dirt drive in Jon's new Land Rover. "What did he say?" Amanda asked anxiously.

"Not much, just that it's bad, and the police are there. And no, I don't know anything else, but we'll be there soon," Jon tried to soothe her.

He gripped the wheel and soon reached the highway. They were silent as he reduced the miles between them and town. As they turned onto the lane taking them to Ralph's house, they could see the street ablaze with lights, police cars, rescue vehicle and ambulance with blue and red lights flashing, and people milling around outside.

"Oh, no," Amanda breathed, terrified, as she climbed out and ran toward the house, Jon quickly parking the vehicle and following her. At the door she was stopped by a uniformed officer.

"You can't go in there, miss," he began, but she interrupted.

"I'm his attorney—you've got to let me pass."

Charles Petrino stepped up. "They're OK," he spoke briefly to the officer, nodding toward Amanda and Jon. "Please follow me."

"What has happened?" Amanda demanded, fighting panic. "Is Ralph all right?"

"Yes, but there's been a homicide," Petrino replied quietly.

"Who?" Jon's voice was low as he caught Amanda's arm and steadied her. They followed Petrino as he threaded them through the living room filled with law enforcement and steered them into the large den, pleasantly furnished. Sitting on a large sofa was Ralph, grimly facing two plain-clothed investigators. As Amanda approached, she was brought up short by the sight of another man sitting at the other end of the sofa, who stood as he saw her.

"David!" she cried. "What are you doing here?"

Ralph stood and started toward her, but was detained by one of the officers. Bruce Williams, Chief Investigator, came forward and stopped her. "Not now, Amanda," he warned, but Petrino intervened, speaking in low tones to the officer.

Ralph argued brusquely, "I told you I'm not answering any more questions until I've talked to my attorney, and I'll advise you," indicating David, "to do the same."

The officer who had detained Ralph threw up his hands in frustration. "Fine," he warned. "Neither of you is free to leave at this point."

Petrino intervened. "I'll be responsible for them, Bob. They have demanded counsel. Give them a few minutes with Amanda and Jon. Clear out and let them have some privacy."

In a few minutes the room was empty except for Ralph, David, Amanda, Jon and Petrino. Petrino turned to Amanda. "Let me give you a heads up. Dispatch received an anonymous call that there had been a murder, and sheriff and police were sent to this address. Ralph and David were both here when officers arrived. And a body in the bathtub. And blood in the bedroom, on the bedsheets, and down the hall."

"Who?" Amanda whispered, suddenly cold.

"Lauren Mallory," David answered her, his face tense.

"My God!" Jon exclaimed, his voice catching. Amanda turned to look at him woodenly.

"But why? Why was she here? Why were you here?" Amanda implored David, tearing her eyes away from Jon.

"At this point I think I shall excuse myself. I'll be just outside the door," Charles informed them.

"Is this place secure?" Amanda inquired pointedly.

"Yes, you may speak freely. My men will have more questions, and FDLE has been called and is sending field officers." He turned to Ralph. "I'm sorry, but you and David are obviously witnesses, so don't disappear."

"You mean suspects," Ralph retorted softly.

"Probably," remarked Charles as he turned and left them.

As the door closed behind him, Amanda turned to the two men, burning with questions. But Jon put his hand on her shoulder. "I think we should talk to them separately. You talk to Ralph, and I'll try David."

Amanda nodded and sat down beside Ralph as Jon motioned for David to follow him to the window. She turned to Ralph. "OK. I'm all ears."

Ralph's face was haggard. "I was at the office trying to get those special interrogatories completed in the Emerald Condo case, when a sheriff's deputy walked in and served me."

"With what?" Amanda's heart caught in her throat.

"A civil paternity complaint," Ralph finished. "I swear it is not true."

"Who's the complainant?" Amanda stammered, as Ralph buried his hands in his face. As the truth dawned, she added, "Not Lauren Mallory?"

"The same," Ralph replied, his voice muffled. "I never met her before the party for Bubba and Della, much less have sex—oh, God, what am I to do? Claire will never believe me. She'll leave me. I'm ruined. Amanda, what am I going to tell her?"

Amanda, her arm around him, wanted to cry too, but instead prodded him gently. "Were you alone at the office?"

"Yes, because Sheila had the afternoon off, and you were at court."

"Any clients? Anyone call? Appointments?"

"No appointments or clients. Sheila left the phone on voice mail so I could work. I made some calls out."

Not strong on the alibi suit, Amanda thought. "OK, so you received the summons. Then what happened? What did you do next?"

Ralph raised his head. "I was devastated, then angry. I couldn't concentrate. I worked for a little while longer, then decided to come home. I was going to get a shower, clear my head and call you, see if I could come over and talk to you. I didn't know what else to do."

"And?" Amanda prompted him.

"I arrived home. It was getting dusk, but not dark. There was David getting out of his car in front of my house. I asked what was he doing here, and he said he had received a call to meet someone here. Then he asked what was I doing here.

"Well, I laughed and said this is my house, so I had first dibs. But when we got to the front door, it was ajar. I didn't like that. David said maybe we should call the cops. I did, but then I didn't want to wait. That's when we found her."

"Was she—" Amanda choked.

"Dead? Yes, David checked. There was no pulse. Her throat had been slashed. There was blood everywhere in the bedroom and down the hall." He swallowed. "She was naked," he whispered piteously.

He regarded Amanda, his eyes pleading. "I didn't do it. And David was getting out of his car when I arrived."

"Had you talked to her today?" Amanda wanted to know.

"She had called this morning, and said she had a surprise for me later today." Ralph paused. "I really didn't like this woman. I always felt like she was toying with me. And then this complaint. But I didn't kill her, Amanda."

"I believe you, Ralph," Amanda assured him. "Where is the complaint now?"

"I left it on my desk at the office," Ralph responded distractedly.

Amanda's mind was in turmoil. What was going on? First two paternity actions from the same person were served in one day, then the complainant was found dead in Ralph's bathtub.

Jon approached them. He stated softly, "David insists on talking to you, Amanda."

CHAPTER 16

Ralph took her hand, clinging to it. "I want you representing me," he pleaded. "Don't conflict yourself out."

"They're not going to charge you with anything, Ralph," she asserted, gently disentangling her hand.

Jon countered softly, "He's right. You don't know that. If he or David should be charged, the other will be a witness, maybe a co-defendant. Do you think it's wise to talk to both?"

"I have nothing to hide," a voice spoke behind them, as David stood there looking at Amanda pleadingly. "And I'll tell you everything. Not him." He shook his head at Jon.

"But, David, that's not a good idea, for your own sake," Amanda asserted gently, stepping forward and taking his arm.

"I know, but I didn't kill her, and I want you to know that," David's voice broke.

Amanda's heart went out to him, as she steered him away out of earshot from the others. "You loved her, didn't you?" She stroked his arm sympathetically.

"I thought I did," he sniffed unhappily. "Amanda, she was such a bitch, but there was a time . . . ."

"Oh, David," Amanda breathed, her heart going out to him.

"And then I saw the papers on the coffee table in your living room, and then there she was, lying there, dead—oh, God. What has she done?"

"You know I shouldn't be talking to you. You have a right to remain silent and to an attorney."

"I know, but I need to tell you."

Amanda hesitated. "David, I owe you my life. I can't let . . ."

"Yes, you can," he interrupted her, pulling her down with him to sit on the large brick hearth seat. "Just shut up and listen."

179

He turned her to face him. "I had an affair with Lauren back years ago. I met her right after she had a go with Jon. She came around looking for him one day, and I pursued her. She let me catch her, and we had a great time. I thought I was in love.

"Then she just disappeared. I couldn't ever locate her—it was like she dropped off the face of the earth. Until I ran into her in D.C. last week." He paused, his face tense. "It was like she never left. We spent time together up there, and she came down here to the beach with me. Then the next thing I knew, she disappeared. On the day of Bubba's engagement party, she called me and wanted to go with me.

"I was in shock—here she was, out of the blue, back like nothing had changed."

He paused. Amanda prompted him gently. "David, please don't. Let me protect you from yourself. Don't tell me anything else."

"No," he exploded with a vehemence that surprised her. "I saw those papers on your coffee table. Amanda, *I* was with Lauren at the time she conceived. That could be my child.

"I was so hurt, so angry, when I read that complaint. Not only did she keep from me that she had a child, but she was accusing Jon of paternity, not me. I had to get away, be by myself, get a grip. And when Jon called, I noticed I had a voice message from her on my cell, telling me to meet her at this address."

Amanda moaned, "No, David, please," but he silenced her with his fingers on her lips.

"Amanda, I swear to you I had just pulled up to the house when Ralph showed up. I had no idea this was his house. The door was standing partly open. I told him we should call the cops, but when he started charging in, I was so anxious I went in with him.

"He struck on the lights as he headed down the hall. I was right behind him when he found her. She was—naked, lying in the bathtub. She was already dead," David's voice cracked again. "Why was she here?"

"I don't know," Amanda murmured. "David, you realize that if the cops hear any of this, they will have a motive to pin you with her murder?"

David slumped despondently. "I don't care," he mumbled. "I want a DNA test to see if I'm the father."

"That's not a good idea right now," Amanda whispered. "Let's get past this first."

David gripped her hand so tightly it made her wince. "I don't care. I didn't kill her. I've got to know the truth, Amanda. You can file something in the paternity case for me."

The door to the room opened, and Charlie strode in followed by two men in suits. Petrino announced, "These are Agents Fields and Smithson from FDLE."

"Can I see her? The scene?" Amanda inquired quickly.

"No is the short answer," Petrino was curt, his face a mask. "These guys are going to need some samples from Ralph and David, and in view of the circumstances, from Jon too."

"What kind of samples?" Amanda demanded.

"Well, they already got swabs from David's hands, because they were covered in blood. We'll want hair and fibers, fingernail scrapings, saliva, to begin with. We're going to want the clothes they are wearing."

Amanda started to speak, but Petrino cut her off, his manner brusque, business-like. "Amanda, you know we can get this, either with or without a warrant. You can advise them to cooperate, or I can act to preserve any possible evidence."

"Are you arresting us?" Ralph spoke up.

"The night is still young," the officer named Smithson replied tartly.

Amanda ignored him and turned to Petrino. "What can you tell me so far?"

Charlie looked at her gravely. "Amanda, you know better. I can't tell you anything about a pending investigation."

"But this isn't your case," Amanda began, but he held up his hand, silencing her.

"It is now. I just got the call—I've been appointed Acting Sheriff, and for the moment the sheriff's department is lead agency on this homicide."

He looked at her face, flushed with surprise. "Don't add to my problems. Now is not the moment to call in any friendship markers," he warned, his voice low.

Amanda replied hotly, "Well, for now at least I'm representing both Ralph and David."

"You sure you want to do that?" Petrino's eyebrows shot up. "There's a potential conflict of interest there."

"They both apparently need an attorney right now, so there's not any other option. Furthermore," she continued, "I've advised them not to say anything to you. I'm notifying you that I'm to be present at any attempts to interview them, and want to be informed of their status. Inasmuch as you can't interrogate them and don't have the probable cause to arrest them, what do you intend to do?"

"We can hold them as murder suspects for as long as we damn well please," Smithson spurted angrily.

Petrino held up his hand again. "Silence, both of you. Let's use some common sense. Amanda, we'll work as fast as we can, faster if you and your clients cooperate. Agent Smithson, don't pick a fight with Mrs. Connor; she and Mr. Carmichael are two of the best criminal defense lawyers in this area, and you are already sadly outnumbered. Just let's get through this one step at a time, please."

He stared at Amanda. "Will you agree regarding the samples and clothes, or do I have to wake a judge?"

Amanda, stony-faced, nodded.

"Smithson, go to the closet with Ralph and pick out something for Ralph to change into, jeans and shirt, underwear. Then I'm going to have to remove the two detainees to the police station for now."

"I'll stay here to make sure the place is secured," Jon offered. "Amanda, you take my vehicle and follow David and Ralph to the station."

"I'm not going to allow him to interfere with the investigation," Smithson objected.

"He's not going to interfere. He's going to sit in a corner and make quiet," Petrino interjected quietly but authoritatively, his eyes on Jon. "Or he'll end up at the station behind some bars. Don't get in the way, Jon."

He paused. "On second thought, you could be of some use to us. Does Ralph have any clothes anywhere else?"

"I keep an extra suit and some jeans at the office," Ralph spoke up. "Why?"

"The office—yes. And that's where you were this afternoon?"

Amanda looked at Ralph warningly, but he replied, "Yes."

"OK, how about we send Jon over to the office with a unit to do a sweep for any evidence?"

Jon looked at Amanda, whose eyes flashed ominously. Petrino added, "Yes, Amanda, I know, you may object, and I could obtain a warrant. But then I could secure the place and keep you out until the judge signs it. You don't want to piss off FDLE. They could take their sweet time, and that would interfere with your business, I suspect. I suspect your clients won't like the police crawling all over their confidential papers. It's your call."

"Go ahead and search it," Ralph interrupted before Amanda could answer. "Hell, it's my office too, so I give you permission."

"And I will want to search both Ralph's and David's cars. You can confer with your clients, and tell me whether consents or warrants are in order. David, where have you been staying?"

"I just flew in last Tuesday, and have been at the condo in Panama City. I was going to spend tonight at Jon's and Amanda's," David offered hesitantly.

"OK, so now we are getting somewhere," Petrino said with satisfaction. "I will need that address, Jon, if you are so inclined, so that the condo can be secured and a warrant obtained. Fields, Carl," he motioned to the other FDLE agent and a uniformed deputy, "I'm putting you on Mr. Connor here. Firstly, I want you to accompany him to his home, let him change clothes and take those into custody, get his samples."

"Jon too?" Amanda hissed.

"Don't, Mandy. You know exactly why," Charles growled under his breath to her. "Jon, get an extra set of your duds for David here. Fields, do a walk-through of the house and see if there's anything there to concern us. That is," he paused, turning to Amanda, "if Mr. or Mrs. Connor so extends the courtesy."

Amanda looked at Jon. "OK," she conceded.

He turned to Jon. "Car keys?" he held out his hand.

Jon shrugged and handed them over. Petrino turned to Ralph and David, his hand out. Both complied. Petrino gestured to an investigator. "Go secure them. Jon, I guess you will need to bring back Amanda's vehicle from the farm."

An officer handed Petrino some papers and a pen. He in turn proffered them to Amanda. "Sign," he ordered. "I'm not having you change your mind on the consents if we do find something."

Amanda signed the forms. Petrino sighed. "Let's get cracking. I'm already tired. And Jon," he added grimly, "we'll need to question you as well."

Jon looked questioningly at him. "To find out your whereabouts this afternoon and evening. You know why." Petrino stared at him.

Amanda heard Petrino's words. "I represent him as well," she remonstrated. "And he is making no statement," she stated flatly, looking past Petrino directly at Jon.

"Yes, Mandy, I guessed that. I'll put you down as attorney of record for the entire town, OK?" Petrino retorted sharply.

Jon walked up to her and kissed her. She whispered, "Not a word to anyone, Jon. Trust me on this."

She took Jon's arm and walked a couple steps away from everyone. "And Jon? Ralph got served with a paternity complaint too."

Jon blanched. "Lauren?" he croaked. "How does he know her?"

"He says he doesn't." Amanda's eyes searched Jon's face, her voice low as she squeezed Jon's arm. "It will be a matter of public record soon enough. The papers are on Ralph's desk. Don't let the cops see them." She looked over at Charlie. "We'll make Charlie earn his pay there. And keep the deputies out of my clients' files. If they don't comply, all bets are off, and they are out until a warrant is obtained."

Jon nodded and kissed her cheek.

Her back to Petrino, she stated flatly, her voice carrying, "Unless David and Ralph are in custody, they will be traveling to the station with me."

"No, ma'am," Petrino contended testily. "Y'all will be traveling with me. Jon's vehicle will be searched as well."

There was a pause while he waited for her reply. "OK," she assented, her anger thinly veiled.

She started to leave, then turned back to Petrino, her voice low. "I want a DNA sample of the victim preserved," she announced. As Petrino's jaw clenched, she added, "You're going to do it anyway. I can't demand it civilly at this point if she's dead. It's a double-edged sword, but we're going to have to establish or eliminate paternity of that little girl at some point."

"You know that may provide motive?" Petrino searched her face.

"I don't have a choice, do I?" Amanda glowered.

Jon left with the two officers. Ralph was escorted to another room by Smithson. Amanda started to follow, but was detained by Petrino.

"You don't have to watch Ralph undress," he admonished.

"I want to see exactly what they take from him," Amanda asserted. "And there's little of Ralph I haven't seen before," she added with a slight smile.

Smithson sneered, "Oh, really?"

Petrino snapped, "Just let her watch, damn it. I don't have time to deal with running interference between you two."

Petrino stalked back into the hallway, giving orders to crime scene operatives and looking on. Amanda watched as Smithson had Ralph empty his pockets and noted change, a cell phone, and his wallet. She stepped up and retrieved the cell phone. Smithson started to prevent her, but she noted, "That will take a warrant, Officer."

She watched as Smithson cursorily examined the contents of Ralph's wallet, then she took the wallet from Smithson. This time the latter did not object. Smithson handed Ralph some briefs, shirt and jeans. Ralph looked questioningly at Amanda, who rolled her eyes and turned her back for him to change. Lastly, Smithson took his socks and dress shoes and Ralph changed into socks and loafers.

"Happy?" Smithson leered at her.

"Better than watching you undress any day," Amanda retorted, as she followed them back out into the living room.

"We're done here," Petrino spoke behind her. "Keep me apprised," he demanded of the chief investigator Bruce Williams, who nodded. "Let's go." Petrino jerked his head toward the front door.

Amanda followed him, Ralph and David trailing behind her, to Petrino's unmarked unit. As they drew abreast of the car, someone called, "Chief Petrino."

He scowled. "I'll be right back. Get in."

Amanda detained the two men, her voice quiet. "Just a minute. Ground rule number one: There will be no statements, nada, tonight," she announced tersely.

They both gaped at her. Ralph protested, "I intend to cooperate fully. I have nothing to hide."

Amanda hissed, "Shut up, damn it, and listen to me, both of you!"

They were both shaken at her response. She took a deep breath and continued, her voice uneven. "It's been a bad day. I don't want to argue with you. Ralph, you've always wanted to be a good old boy, and you are in denial, just as many of our clients are. You think this can't possibly be happening to you, that you know the police, and that everything will come out all right if you just cooperate. You've always represented the well-to-do, and have never had to learn street-lawyer smarts. But I've been a public defender and down this road before. This ain't a tea party tonight. Deep down you know I'm right.

"David, you've probably never been in this kind of trouble before, and you really need to listen to me. I don't intend to let anything happen to you."

They both started to interrupt, but she held up her hand. "I don't want to hear it right now." She took a deep breath as she watched Petrino deep in conversation with Bruce Williams. "They are looking for a defendant," she explained soberly. "Anything you say, no matter how innocent, is going into their equation for a possible murder indictment. Ralph, the victim was found in your house, and David, she's someone you knew intimately. So take some of your own advice. Ralph, keep your damned mouth shut. That goes for you too, David—do no harm."

Ralph found his voice. "But we know Charlie. We can't keep him out in the cold. We have to let him know what is happening. You know otherwise he'll play hard ball, and David and I will end up locked up."

Amanda smiled grimly. "Charlie already knows more about what is going on than we do at the moment. We have to barter to find out what that is. All information needs to travel through me. I am your conduit. What I tell him does not carry the same damning effect as when it comes from you. That's the way it's got to be," she added, reaching and squeezing David's arm reassuringly, noting his anxiety.

Amanda took a deep breath. "Ralph," she continued, more calmly, "Charlie just got appointed to this position. He's always wanted it badly. He is immediately handed a homicide, and is under a microscope. He's going

185

to do everything by the book. For all his homespun facade, he's always been by-the-book. And this mess landed right in his lap just as he's gotten the call from the governor. And you are his friends but suspects. Do you realize what a nightmare this is?"

Ralph, frowning, nodded unhappily. "I know."

"He's doing this because he has to. You were both at the scene. He has to if nothing else eliminate you as suspects. You know and I know that nothing is likely to happen tonight." Amanda was reassuring. "It's going to be a long night, and we just have to get through it. Please, Ralph," she pleaded.

"OK," he smiled grimly, squeezing her arm.

She saw Petrino nodding in their direction and moving toward them. She quickly turned to David. "What personal effects do you have on you?" she demanded.

"My cell phone and my wallet," he replied dazedly.

"Give them here," she ordered.

He complied, and she took them, along with Ralph's wallet and phone, and put them in her purse. "I feel better now," she quipped.

They got in the car, Amanda in the front seat. Petrino let himself in, glancing around at his somber passengers. They were silent on the short drive to the station.

When they arrived at the sheriff's department, Petrino was out first. Amanda climbed out before he could get her car door. He held the front door for her and she breezed past him into the large anteroom, where officers were busy coming and going, interviewing witnesses, processing arrestees, and typing reports.

Petrino led them into an interview room. "Please have a seat," he invited them. Amanda looked at her two charges and nodded, as they all sat down.

"Excuse me," Petrino said as he caught the eye of an officer outside and left. Amanda watched as he was deep in conversation with the officer, nodding toward them, then reviewing some papers.

They sat tensely at the table. Ralph was uncharacteristically quiet, and David seemed withdrawn, morose. Amanda studied them. How could they and Jon have all gotten entangled in a mess with Lauren Mallory? It was just too fantastic.

Amanda didn't know how many minutes had elapsed before Petrino returned with Smithson in tow. Petrino stared at her, his face a mask.

Amanda began, "I've already advised my clients that they will be making no statements this evening."

Petrino bristled. "And you know I can lock them up as my chief suspects, and make their short-term lives a living hell."

The Connors' Crisis

David blanched. Amanda spat, "And I can wake up a judge just as easily as you can. Furthermore, I'll be slapping enough civil rights suits and habeas corpus writs on you to make you weep every time you see a tree. Your career as sheriff will start out with your name in the headlines, but it won't be pretty. I still know a few honest Supreme Court justices. Shall we dance?"

Smithson started to interrupt, but Petrino cut him off. "You stay out of this," he warned menacingly. "If your mouth is moving, you are stirring shit, so just can it. You," he motioned to Amanda, "come with me. Smithson, get these men a cup of coffee while they cool their heels. And please don't engage them in conversation. In fact," his voice rose, "I don't want you in the same room with them. I do not want the collecting of evidence screwed up on a technicality."

As she rose, Amanda warned the two men, "Say nothing. The room has ears. Remember what I said."

Charlie stopped by the coffee pot in the hallway and poured himself a cup. He looked questioningly at Amanda, who shook her head. "Let's take a walk, shall we?"

"Chief—I mean Sheriff, Bruce is on line 1," a deputy called.

Petrino walked into the first office and picked up a phone, hitting a button. "Petrino." He listened a minute. "Good. Let me know. Tell the medical examiner to keep a lid on it. I don't give a damn if he sings in Amanda's choir. I'll cut his balls off if Gerald talks to her before he does me."

Hanging up, he motioned for Amanda to follow him. As someone else called to him, he held up his hand. "Give us a minute," he called as he led her outside.

They stepped out on the sidewalk next to the parking lot. The air was sultry. She could look through a window and glimpse Ralph and David sitting quietly in the conference room. David was sipping coffee, but Ralph was staring at the cup, drumming his fingers on the table.

"Medical examiner is at the scene. Don't be calling him for information," Petrino warned. "I will hurt you both."

Amanda's jaw tightened.

"Turn your back to the parking lot, and speak softly," he whispered warningly.

Amanda complied. "Why?" she asked, her voice low.

"Good show in there, Amanda," Charlie spoke softly.

"Thanks," Amanda replied, the hint of a smile on her face. "I knew what you were doing."

"What are we going to do?" Petrino was careful not to look at her. "I could not have been handed a bigger mess than what we have tonight. And I am now under scrutiny." He ran his hand through his hair distractedly.

Amanda nodded wearily. "You know I can't cooperate if the information incriminates one of them. I have to protect them." She nodded toward the room with the two men. "And this is a homicide."

"Agreed. You know I have to preserve the crime scene and gather all the evidence I can, and at least eliminate them as suspects. And I can't hand out any favors either, not with Esme Townsend looking on, ready to pounce at any time."

"Do you think she has it in for you?" Amanda's brows knitted questioningly.

"I don't think there's any question," Petrino smiled thinly.

"Do you think she could be behind this?" Amanda asked eagerly.

Petrino drily rejoined, "No, I can't picture even Esme setting up a murder." Sipping his coffee, he added, "But now this paternity scandal smells like her." He paused. "Where is Claire?"

"She left for Ohio earlier yesterday for a family reunion," Amanda replied, her eyes watching the two men through the window.

He stared at her. "What can you tell me? And make it look like you're arguing."

Amanda gazed at him skeptically, but Petrino added, "There's a guy in the black Crown Vic in the back of the parking lot watching us. I am not sure, but I think he has a bionic listening device. Turn your back to him, and whisper," he echoed, his voice so low she could barely hear. He casually took her arm and led her to another spot, where several cars obstructed the view.

Amanda complied. "Ralph says he had just gotten home, and David was getting out of his car. They say they got there the same time. The front door was ajar. Ralph called 9-1-1, but then busted on in. They found her. She was already dead."

"Why was David at Ralph's home?" Petrino wanted to know.

"He said he got a call to meet Lauren at that address. He didn't know it was Ralph's house."

"Why would he be getting a call from Lauren Mallory?"

"Sorry, Charlie, let's go back," Amanda interrupted, as she saw Ralph stand, saying something. "Ralph is about to make a scene. I'll give you what I can."

"Amanda, be careful," Petrino offered. "You're being watched, too."

"Me?" Amanda laughed shortly. "I don't have anything she wants."

"Don't be too sure."

They walked back in to the department as Ralph came storming out. "I'm not staying here," he snorted angrily.

"Where are you going?" Petrino quipped. "Your home is a crime scene."

"He can stay with us," Amanda announced quickly. She put her hand on Ralph's arm. "Just chill."

"Are you going to give us a statement tonight or not?" Petrino was gruff.

Ralph gazed at Amanda, then shook his head. "I'm taking the lady's advice," he remarked.

"I need to check on David." Amanda excused herself and moved back to the conference room. There she found David, his head on the table. He looked up at her, his eyes bleary with tears.

"David, it's going to be OK," she soothed him, hugging him.

A deputy came in and placed some clothes on the table. "Just brought in by an officer," he explained. "I need for Dr. Connor to change clothes."

"You wanna watch?" David asked, the first smile on his face since he showed up at the farm earlier that evening.

"Honey, I've seen you naked before," Amanda laughed softly, as the deputy looked from one to the other in consternation.

Amanda stood outside the door of the restroom while an investigator retrieved David's clothes and David changed. They returned to the conference room where the investigator placed some papers and a pen before them. "Consents, property releases," he announced curtly.

"Sign them," Amanda instructed. Ralph came in behind her, and was also told to sign.

Petrino strode into the room. He informed her, "Jon has left your car outside." He held out the keys to her.

"Can we go?" she requested of Petrino, her voice carrying.

"For the moment, as long as I know where you are," he replied, his face again a mask. "I guess I don't have to tell you to stay put."

"They'll be at my place tonight, then we'll make arrangements tomorrow."

They walked out of the interview room to the front lobby.

"What about Jon?" Petrino queried. "He is still at your office. I have collected his clothing. Are you going to let him make a statement?"

Amanda slammed her hand on the front counter, her voice raised in anger. "Do you even have to ask that question? Keep pushing me, Petrino, and I'll be roasting marshmallows on—"

"I get the picture," Petrino interrupted her icily. "Let's not paint it for the entire staff to see."

"I want to go by the office," Ralph insisted suddenly.

"Not tonight," Petrino stated flatly. "If you cooperate, I'll have them out of there with a minimum of fuss. Jon is there to make sure we don't overstep any bounds."

"It's OK, Ralph," Amanda looked at him and nodded knowingly. She turned toward the door. "We're out of here," she told her charges. "Don't bother seeing us out," she said to Charlie over her shoulder as she led the way.

CHAPTER 17

WEDNESDAY

Jon arrived home some time later. Walking in, he found Amanda asleep sitting on the couch, dressed in a long pajama t-shirt and robe. He bent down to kiss her, and she stirred.

"Oh, hi," she mumbled and stretched. He plopped down beside her. "What time is it?"

"Almost three," he informed her and put his arm around her. "Why are you still up?"

"I was waiting for you to find out if you knew anything new." She snuggled to him.

"No other information yet."

"Did they trash my office?"

"Actually, no. They took the garbage and Ralph's clothes. They looked through drawers, but I didn't allow them to open any client files." He stroked her hair. "I took care of the matter as you requested. Everything is pretty much still in place. And just in time, because Bruce Williams made an appearance and did a walk-through behind his men."

"Good," she murmured drowsily, pulling him closer. "We have guests—Ralph in the guest room, David in the dressing room. They wanted to stay up and wait for you, but I made them turn in, told them getting some rest was more important now, because we don't know what we'll be facing tomorrow."

"How long have you been home?" he asked, nuzzling her earlobe and pulling her robe open.

"We didn't give the new sheriff the time of day, so I guess around midnight." She turned to meet his mouth with hers.

"Hmm, I like that," he whispered as he reciprocated.

"Please tell me you did as I told you and gave no statement to Petrino tonight," she murmured as she unbuttoned his shirt and ran her fingers down his chest, down to the fly of his pants.

"Actually, I did give a statement." His lips left hers and traveled down her neck, his hand stroking her thigh.

She froze, suddenly wide awake. "You did what?" she demanded, pushing away from him. "Damn it, what did you say? Don't you have any sense?" she cried, shaking free of him and standing up.

"Shh," he warned. "You want to wake everyone up?"

"I can't believe you," she responded icily, turning away and pacing.

He watched her through hooded eyes. "What is wrong with that?" he rejoined.

"Jon, if I recall correctly, you went somewhere to law school and took a degree?"

"To Duke, as a matter of fact," he responded, his eyes narrowing in irritation. "Why?"

"And you gave a voluntary statement to law enforcement when you are a suspect in a murder?" she hissed.

"OK, Amanda, what did I have to hide?" Jon stood and took her arm, shaking her gently.

"Must I give you the same speech I gave Ralph?" she whispered angrily. "That they are looking for a defendant, and that everything you say goes into the mix for an indictment? What part of that do you, a lawyer, not understand? How can I protect you, when you blithely spill your guts?"

"What, do you think I murdered Lauren?" he laughed hoarsely.

"You think your being named in a paternity action and being unaccounted for during the general time of the murder don't make you a suspect?" Her voice involuntarily rose, as she jerked away from him. "Just where were you earlier tonight?"

"OK, Amanda, you're upset. I get it. You have every right to be." Jon turned her back around to face him. "The paternity suit, all that's happened tonight. But let's just calm down."

"You apparently have no clue," she continued, moving away. "At this point defense counsel is not entitled to any discovery, no information; it is a strictly *quid pro quo* situation. Charlie can exclude us from all information right now. I assume you've heard of *Miranda*? It's not just some pretty words for crime drama television shows. We have to bargain to find out what is going on and plan accordingly."

"I don't agree with your strategy," he argued, his voice soft. "You are talking about Charlie here."

"You were law enforcement, Jon. You know this. Charlie is under tight scrutiny, and is going to tread very cautiously right now and hold his cards close to his vest," Amanda explained, her voice strained, even though her jaw was clenched and her eyes were flashing.

"Even for you?" Jon demanded.

"Especially for me," Amanda insisted. "He has just been appointed sheriff, and this investigation involves his close friends, represented by someone he used to date."

Jon flushed. "I thought you said that was short-lived, and that no one knew," he contended, his eyes glinting with jealousy.

Amanda laughed quietly, trying to cover her embarrassment. "That's right, it was," she quipped. "But others, including Esme Townsend, might not view it that way if they find out." Esme's insinuations the day they had lunch together flashed in her mind momentarily.

He stared at her, barely concealing his anger. "There's been a lot more than a weekend between you two, hasn't there?" Jon's tone was accusing. "Maybe more than just a mistake?" he inquired pointedly.

"No," Amanda lashed out defensively. "I told you. My past is irrelevant to the murder investigation, unlike yours with Lauren Mallory."

His eyes narrowed. "That's unjust," his tone was icy. He took a step toward her.

"I'm sorry. I'm tired. We'll talk about this later." Amanda, suddenly exhausted, held both hands up in surrender. "I'm going to bed."

She moved quickly to the stairs, bounding up them. He followed close behind her, grabbing her arm as she reached the bedroom.

"No, you're not sorry." He pulled her to him insistently. "You're spoiling for a fight. And I'm going to give it to you."

His mouth covered hers, angrily, commandingly, hotly, as he snatched her robe off, crushed her to him and backed her to the door, pinning her there with his body. She could feel his sudden savage hunger, and she was helpless as he pulled her shirt off over her head in one fell swoop.

"No," she protested weakly as he imprisoned her and his hands stroked her. She whimpered, wanting him, but trying to maintain her train of thought.

"I really don't want to fight." Feeling herself losing control, she jerked away desperately.

Pushing him and walking away shakily, she rubbed her temple with her hand wearily. "I'm tired and confused, Jon. There's so much we don't know about each other. And with all these accusations flying, it is a bad time to be finding that out."

He stood behind her, his eyes on her. "Amanda, you have to trust me. I know you have every reason to doubt and question. And the situation you went through with Bill Barnes has left you with ample ammunition to distrust the whole world."

"Just don't let me find out about you from someone else," Amanda pleaded, her back to him, her hand rubbing her temple.

He turned her to face him. "That's a tall order, Amanda. I don't know what you need to know, and in what order. But I will always tell you the truth. All you have to do is ask."

Amanda pulled away, yawning. "I just wish you would have taken my advice and not talked to Charlie. I need all the leverage I can get. I have to get up early and call Alex. I don't have the energy to deal with this right now."

He turned his back, undressing. "Why are you calling Alex?" he inquired, as she walked over to the closet.

"With Ralph, David and you being involved, I'm going to need Alex's help to sort through all this," Amanda mumbled, "particularly if you continue to kiss and tell all to law enforcement."

"Don't you want to know what I told him?" he demanded, his eyes following her.

"I'll probably find out anyway when they hand down the indictment against you." Amanda was sarcastic, as she yawned again and reached for a nightgown.

"Don't do that," Jon interrupted her.

"Do what?" she mumbled sleepily.

"The nightgown." Jon was suddenly behind her, taking her nightgown out of her hands and throwing it into the nearby chair.

"Jon, I'm exhausted and mad at you," Amanda began, but Jon silenced her with a kiss, his hands on her breasts.

"I know. It makes you irresistible," he murmured against her ear.

"I want to hurt you," she muttered, her eyes closed, as she leaned against him.

"Then we need to finish that fight, because you're succeeding. I'm in pain just looking at you."

He picked her up and ungently deposited her on the bed, crawling on top of her.

She looked at him crossly, but he lost no time. He teased her unmercifully as she writhed with sensation, her body suddenly alive. He bent over her to claim her mouth with his, smothering her with his kiss. "Do you forgive me?" he whispered urgently. "Please don't remain angry. The Good Book says not to let the sun go down on your anger."

"The sun was already down when you made me angry," she argued weakly.

"But you love me? Say it, Amanda," Jon begged.

"Yes, Jon, I love you," she admitted, biting back a cry. "Please take me now."

"Not yet," Jon whispered. "I love it when you beg."

But Amanda had ideas of her own. She wrapped her legs around him and tightened her muscles, making him moan in turn. "Do you love me?" she asked. "Say it."

"I love you, Amanda Connor," he gasped. Blind with passion, he thrust until they both shuddered, their desire slaked. He held her as she quivered, until she lay spent in his arms.

"Now I'm wide awake," Amanda grumbled good-naturedly, as Jon snuggled to her back, kissing her shoulder.

"You'll be asleep in minutes," Jon kissed her ear, as she melted to him and sighed.

CHAPTER 18

When Jon made it downstairs a little before seven the next morning, the smell of frying bacon was in the air. Surprised, he walked into the kitchen, where Fred Vaughan was serving up omelets, bacon, grits, toast, coffee and orange juice to a somber Ralph and David.

Jon looked at the three men a moment, started to ask a question, then thought better of it. He shrugged and walked to the counter to pour himself a cup of coffee.

"That was some fight last night," Ralph greeted him. "Do you two go at it like that all the time, or was that just for our benefit?"

"I'll bet the makeup sex was fabulous," David offered, not looking at Jon.

"Both before and after what little sleep they got," suggested Ralph. "I'll bet she won. She usually does."

"I thought I heard her scream once, but then I thought maybe I should keep out of it," David added, the hint of a smile playing around his lips. "And I didn't hear the shower going but once upstairs this morning," David continued.

"They're conserving energy," Ralph provided.

"Enough." Jon's voice was low, but his shoulders tensed, as he sat down at the table.

"We have to do something to take our minds off the nightmare last night," Ralph was defensive.

"Just don't do it once she gets down here, or she will mop the floor with both of you."

Ralph nodded solemnly. "Why are you so tense? It's my house where they found her, my ass on the line as the most probable suspect, and my marriage that's going south when Claire hears about this."

"But you didn't know her, did you?" Jon looked up and stared at Ralph. David's eyes also rested on Ralph.

196

The Connors' Crisis

"I have never seen that woman before Sunday's party," Ralph averred emphatically.

"But you were served with a paternity suit too?" Jon persisted.

"You know?" Ralph's head whipped around. "Too? Who else?" As understanding dawned, his eyes met Jon's disbelievingly. "You too? Why?"

David turned to Ralph, stunned. "You were named in a paternity suit by Lauren?"

Jon was contrite. "I'm sorry, Ralph. But Amanda asked me last night to make sure the police didn't see the complaint you left on your desk."

Ralph noted that David had turned white. "I guess it will be public knowledge soon enough," he replied glumly. "But I swear I've not seen her before, much less have sex with her."

"There's obviously another motive for the suit," Jon mused, his eyes on his coffee cup.

"Well, if it is to discredit me in my bid for county judge, that should do the trick," Ralph rubbed his forehead agitatedly, his tone bitter.

"But why would she do that?" David questioned confusedly.

Fred interrupted, looking at Jon, then the doorway. "Your omelet will be ready in a moment. Is Amanda coming?"

"She's powdering her nose or something," Jon remarked noncommittally.

"Where's the good butcher knife?" Fred demanded.

"I don't know. Amanda accused me of losing it. It will turn up," Jon replied, a hint of irritation in his voice. "It always does."

"We need to get out of your hair," Ralph commented, "you being a newlywed couple and all that. I don't want to be the reason you two tie up and fight."

"Me neither," David chimed in.

"Petrino said for you to stay put," Jon retorted, his voice commanding. "We will figure out the next step." He took a sip of his coffee. "Besides, the 'discussion' last night," he emphasized the word, "had nothing to do with you, and was all my fault."

"It most certainly was," Amanda asserted, walking into the room, dressed in a suit. She tried to smile cheerfully at the men, but she was also tense. Jon glanced up at her. "But it takes a big man to admit when he's wrong," she turned and kissed him on the cheek.

Ralph remarked, "I hope they left my spare suit at the office."

"You won't be going in today, "Amanda remarked, as Fred placed a plate before Jon.

"Sit," Fred commanded her, pulling out the empty chair and handing her a plate of food as well.

197

"I have arraignments, Mandy. And I can't just sit around here doing nothing, hiding out from the inevitable," Ralph remonstrated.

"You are not," Amanda smiled at Fred and thanked him as he placed a cup of coffee and a glass of orange juice in front of her. "Alex is coming here today."

They all stared at her in surprise. She continued unperturbedly, "This is a nasty piece of business, guys. None of it is an accident. I don't know where it is heading. But we can't just wait around and see what happens next. We've got to have a contingency plan, in case one of you gets charged with something." She munched her bacon and buttered her toast.

"Aren't you being premature?" Jon interposed. "I mean, we don't know that anyone at this table is Charlie's prime suspect. He knows us, so I would tend to think we aren't. And there's the conflict of interest angle. I mean, we have no idea if one of us might be charged, which one might get charged, or whether more than one may be charged." His look included Ralph and David. "The possibility of multiple defendants, plus the possibility of in a crunch one's defense pointing the finger to the other to avoid conviction . . . ."

"Exactly," Amanda nodded, sipping her coffee. "Without compromising anyone, we have to come up with a strategy for dealing with those questions. We have got to stay one step ahead of Charlie. We need to discuss everyone's rights so that you can be prepared to make some informed decisions before we have to face Charlie and his deputies again. And we need to do it as soon as possible. So I've made the executive decision. It's today." She bit into her toast.

"But I don't need an attorney," Ralph broke in excitedly. "I am an attorney."

"Yeah, and the man who represents himself has a fool for a lawyer," Jon reminded Ralph.

Amanda gazed at Jon. "You really need to be in on this," she beseeched him quietly. "You are in as much potential danger as Ralph or David."

She stood, picking up the orange juice glass and downing the contents. "I'm off," she announced. "I'm handling Ralph's court and getting a couple of motions filed. Then I'll be back. I'll bring Ralph some more clothes. David can wear some of Jon's."

David stood and stared at her wide-eyed. "Do I need to hire an attorney?" His anxiety was apparent.

"That's one of the things we'll discuss." Amanda reached over and patted his arm. "After that, if you want to hire an attorney, by all means I will encourage it." She smiled at him. "David, it will all work out, dear."

She turned and looked at Jon. "Well, what about it?" She was brisk, business-like.

"No 'dear' for me?" Jon's eyebrows shot up, and she could tell he was biting back jealousy.

She bent down and covered his mouth with hers. "Will that make it up to you, dear?" she whispered against his lips.

His hand caressed her cheek as he kissed her back. "I think so, for the moment," he murmured. "I'll call the office and let them know I need to be out today."

Fred suddenly demanded, "Aren't you going to eat my breakfast?"

"Sorry, gotta run," Amanda replied, as she picked up another piece of bacon and chewed it on her way out. "Great dead pig, Fred, just the way I like it."

She headed out the door, and ran into Alex on the porch. He steadied her. "Hey, girl," he greeted her, grinning. "Where's the fire?"

"There are a couple of matters at the office and courthouse that won't wait, then I'll be back," Amanda smiled at her colleague. "Thanks so much, Alex, for doing this."

She took his arm and returned to the porch, sitting on the swing with him and filling him in. Jon, looking through the window, could just make out the two of them talking earnestly.

David followed his gaze. "Was Alex a former boyfriend of Amanda's?" he asked, suddenly interested.

Ralph's voice cut in. "They were attorneys at the public defender's office together when Amanda first came back home."

"They worked closely together," Jon remarked, his eyes not leaving the view.

"Yeah, they did. They second chaired each other's murder cases, troubleshot cases together, visited crime scenes and did a lot of their own investigation together." Ralph noted the glint in Jon's eye. "They even went to public defender conferences together," Ralph added mischievously. "And those can get pretty wild. The rule of invisibility applied: what went on there stayed there."

David interjected, "Jon, didn't you and Alex go to college together? I seem to remember he was quite a ladies' man, wasn't he?"

Jon stood up and strode out of the room without a word.

Fred looked at the two men remaining. "Shame on both of you," he censured them sternly. "Here you are, both in a heap of trouble, and all you've done this morning is stir up crap."

Ralph looked at him glumly. "Yeah, you're right. Even if I'm not charged, I have to face Claire with all this."

David looked down at his plate. "It's just always so easy to push Jon's buttons. And it keeps me from thinking—" he broke off.

Ralph looked over at him and put his hand on his shoulder. "You knew this Lauren, didn't you?"

David nodded, his eyes closed, fighting tears.

Ralph was sympathetic. "I'm sorry, man. She was someone special to you?"

"I once thought it might turn out that way. I just don't understand what's going on, why all this is happening." David's voice was low, hoarse.

Meanwhile Jon let himself out of the house and walked up to the two sitting on the porch swing. "Hi, Alex. Long time no see," he smiled broadly, as Alex stood and they shook hands and clapped each other on the back.

"I see you didn't waste any time catching and marrying the prettiest girl in the county," Alex laughed pleasantly. "That happened so fast I don't recall getting an invitation to the wedding." He grinned. "How the hell are you?"

"Good, except for this trouble right now." Jon sobered.

Amanda also stood. "I don't think I'll be too long. Alex, these three guys are special to me. We cannot let anything happen to them. And Charlie isn't going to cut us any slack, with his just being appointed acting sheriff."

"Petrino?" Alex's eyes shot around and met Amanda's. "Surely you can wangle some information out of him, Mandy. I mean, Charlie has always been a sucker for a good-looking female, particularly when it's you, so use some of those feminine wiles on him. He'll tell you anything, and certainly before he does any of us."

Amanda flushed as she saw Jon's eyes upon her. "We have to tread carefully, Alex. But we need to get on top of this situation and quickly."

Alex put his hand on her shoulder. "I'm your man. I'll get started while you are gone."

Amanda took Jon's hand in hers and led him down the steps to her car.

"You know I am jealous of all these men in your past," Jon whispered to her, as he took her face in his hands and kissed her.

"Alex?" She was surprised.

"I know Alex. Remember we were college roommates. Yes, even Alex," Jon laughed.

"I am flattered, but there's no reason for you to feel that way," Amanda assured him, kissing him back. "And, Jon, none of them is you."

"Hurry back," he smiled as he opened the car door for her. "And don't be flirting with Charlie, no matter what Alex says."

He watched her drive away.

Amanda made her way to the office. Sheila met her at the door.

"What happened yesterday and last night?" Sheila demanded anxiously.

"There was an—incident last night. The sheriff's department perused our office for possible evidence," Amanda remarked, glancing around the room.

"Does this have to do with the homicide on this morning's news?"

Amanda looked at her sharply. "Yes. What are they saying?"

"That there was a murder investigation, a body of an unknown woman found in the bathtub of a local attorney's house last night." Sheila's eyes searched Amanda's face. Sheila whispered, "Claire?"

"No, no," Amanda assured her. "Claire is still in Ohio. But it was at their house. Everything is fine. What's the damage here?"

"All the trash cans were stripped of bags, it looked like they rifled through the drawers of the desks, and Ralph's spare clothes are gone." Sheila's voice dropped to a whisper. "And Amanda, there was something in the Stephenson file this morning."

"A pleading?" Amanda responded with a question.

Sheila nodded. "What does that mean?"

"We don't know yet, but none of it is true. I had Jon place it away from prying eyes last night."

"Where is Ralph?" Sheila persisted.

"At my place. He won't be in this morning."

"Is he OK?"

"He's OK. I told him to stay there, and I'd take care of this morning's docket, then I'm going back myself to deal with some matters." Amanda was already running through the phone messages as she started toward Ralph's office.

She stopped in the doorway and took everything in. The usually immaculate, sleek masculine office looked a bit mussed. Amanda was glad she had not allowed Ralph, always so meticulous, to come in and see it in his current state of mind.

"One of the investigators was here when I arrived this morning," Sheila supplied. "He said he was there as a courtesy, and that the place had been cleared, whatever that means."

Amanda nodded and moved to the desk, surveying it, and opening the middle drawer, her mind processing.

"Is anything else major out of place? Missing?" she asked.

"His letter opener is missing," Sheila replied. "And yours. And mine. And the butcher knife from the kitchen."

Amanda's eyes narrowed at that information. She shook her head, irritated.

"Did you hear from Dinah?" She tried to dispel the mood of anxiety.

"Yes, last night. She arrived safely in Miami, was on the cruise ship about to pull up anchor and leave, and said the weather is very nice."

"I'm happy for her," Amanda responded absently, her mind whirring. She sat down at Ralph's desk, resting her elbows and arms on it crossed in front of her. Sheila knew that look.

"Sheila, we have business to attend to. We have to get this place back to normal quickly, before Ralph comes back. I'm going to keep him otherwise occupied for most of today. Put things to rights as best you can and get the cleaning crew in here this morning. Pick us up some letter openers, whatever. We have to keep him from going off like firecrackers."

Sheila turned to leave, but Amanda stopped her. "And, Sheila, for your information, Chief Petrino is now Acting Sheriff Petrino."

"I also heard that on the news this morning," Sheila nodded.

"I'm going to need the files for this morning's court."

Sheila was back momentarily with the files. Amanda thanked her and scanned them quickly. Satisfying herself, she rose and crossed over, out the hallway to the main work area and to the back door.

"Sheila, cancel all Ralph's and my appointments for today. Just say he is out sick, and I'm covering his court. We'll deal with the rest when I get back."

Amanda opened the door and let herself out. As she walked toward her car, an older model Ford pickup stopped beside her.

"Hello, Amanda," a male voice spoke from the open window.

"Morning, Titus," Amanda replied, looking up and recognizing Titus Campbell, the editor of the local paper.

"Are you or Ralph going to give me a statement for the paper this morning?" the white-haired gentleman inquired.

"Titus, you know you're going to have to get any information from the sheriff's department," Amanda sighed tiredly. "I can't tell you what I don't know myself."

"The story is this woman was in town filing certain civil actions against some people you know, and making some mighty serious allegations," Titus offered meaningfully. "And she apparently was all over Ralph at an engagement party on Sunday."

"Perhaps Esme Townsend will have you a press release ready if you check with her," Amanda muttered.

"You know I don't play Esme's games either," Titus reproved her. "But this story could explode quickly."

Amanda mumbled, "I'm doing what I can, and if I can give you anything later, I will."

"Amanda, be careful," Titus spoke quietly.

The Connors' Crisis

"Me?" Amanda looked at him sharply.

"I'm just looking at the birdshot patterns," Titus gazed at her shrewdly. "You are right in the center of whatever is going on."

Amanda laughed shortly. "I fail to see why." She met his gaze. "I honestly don't know what is going on."

"Just watch your back," Titus warned as he pulled off.

———————

Amanda completed the arraignments quickly and returned to the office. She did some dictation and signed documents for Sheila. She picked up the telephone and called the sheriff's department, and was soon put through to the administration office.

A female voice answered the phone.

"Is that you, Trudy?" Amanda asked.

"Amanda? How are you?" the voice replied.

"OK. So I see Charlie wasted no time in drafting you to make the move over to the S.O.," Amanda laughed.

"Yeah, he called me at 6:00 this morning and told me just to head over here. Charlie said he couldn't do without me and all that B.S. men say to talk us women into doing what they want." Trudy laughed with her. "It is my guess you are wanting to speak to him."

"If I can. I know he's suddenly a busy guy," Amanda countered.

After a few minutes, she heard the familiar voice. "Petrino here," he said curtly.

"Sheriff, this is Amanda Connor." She decided to err on the side of formality. "I really hate to bother you this morning, but I need to obtain some clothes for Ralph. Looks like your men took his spare suit from the office. Is it possible for me to get into his house long enough for you to release some to me?"

There was a pause. "Just a minute." She heard him call to Bruce, then cover the mouthpiece. She waited patiently while a muffled conversation ensued. He returned. "Can you meet me there in about twenty? Bruce is not quite finished, but I'll escort you in for that purpose, and that purpose only." His voice brooked no discussion.

"Sure," she replied. "I really appreciate this. I'll see you there."

She hung up. So the new sheriff, as busy as he suddenly found himself, was agreeing to personally walk her through, was he? She wasn't sure what to make of that, but intended to get as much mileage out of the opportunity as she could.

203

She suddenly thought, Charlie is taking a personal interest in this case because his new status as sheriff hangs on this investigation. He wants statements from Ralph and David. He has several pieces of the puzzle, but needs to fill in some blanks. So he's going to accommodate me so that I will consider returning the favor.

She reviewed the calendar for the rest of the week, scanned and gave instructions on cancelling appointments and dealing with the phone messages for herself and Ralph, and discussed with Sheila what information to give out, deciding that the matter was too fresh to say much.

She pulled a pen out of the holder on Sheila's desk to scribble a note. "Damned thing doesn't write," she muttered crossly, noting it was one of the pens she had remarked about to Ralph. "Get rid of them and bar that salesman from getting his foot in the office again."

She rearranged some more of her appointments for the rest of the week, and left some last-minute instructions. Then she walked out, crawling into the Mercedes and heading for Ralph's house.

When she arrived, there were an FDLE crime scene van and three unmarked units, two sheriff's department, the other police. Charlie and Bruce Williams stood outside waiting for her.

Amanda stepped out of the car, masking with brisk confidence her uncertainty about what to expect. Charlie nodded to her, and she spoke. "Good morning, Sheriff, Undersheriff."

Bruce smiled slightly. "So you're already aware of my promotion?"

"I guessed," she quipped, looking from him to Charlie, who glared toward the front door of the house.

"Come with me." Charlie wasted no time, and led the way into the house. Amanda followed him, with Bruce following behind them.

They stopped in the living area, and Charlie frowned at her. "I don't guess you are going to be satisfied with one of my men's just providing you some clothes?"

"Charlie—I mean, Sheriff, you know how particular Ralph is about his clothing," Amanda countered carefully. "If you want to take that chance, fine. But I can't guarantee he won't show up and storm the place. I'm only acting as his attorney and liaison, so that you can get your work done quickly and without interference."

"That's what I thought you'd say," Petrino's frown deepened. "Follow me."

He led the way down the hallway to the master bedroom. Amanda immediately noted the absence of the carpet in the hallway, and could see ahead of her that some carpet was missing from the bedroom as well. Amanda stopped in the hallway in front of the bathroom door, her gaze arrested by the blood in the large sunken bathtub and on the wall and window sill.

Bruce, behind her, whispered, "The Man's in a foul mood. Don't push him right now."

But Amanda was frozen on the spot, taking in the scene, trying to memorize details, questions whirring in her head.

Charlie was already at the doorway to the master bedroom, and turned back, scowling. He walked up to her, taking her arm and pulling her after him. "Damn it, Mandy," he muttered under his breath, irritated.

He dragged her into the bedroom, where an FDLE operative and sheriff's investigator were still inventorying items. She noticed placards on the bed and floor and the bedspread, sheets and pillows missing. She posited, "Can you tell me anything?"

Petrino ignored her as he addressed the man. "Are you finished with the closets and clothing?"

He nodded.

Petrino turned back to Amanda and gestured. "OK, tell me what you will need. Bruce, take this down."

Amanda dragged her gaze from the bed and the dresser where the crime scene officer was still working. She moved to the walk-in closet. She quickly identified a couple of suits, some shirts and sets of business and casual clothing, then moved to the drawers, selecting ties, underwear, socks and shoes, and placing those items in a piece of carryon luggage.

"This much?" Charlie was not pleased.

"We're talking about Ralph, Mr. GQ himself," Amanda retorted.

"OK, OK," Charlie mumbled.

"And this will only hold him a day or two," Amanda added. She turned to Charlie. "You know Ralph will need a set or two of cufflinks. He's old school."

Charlie's jaw was set ominously as he looked at her suspiciously. "And they just happen to be over at the dresser. As you can see, we're not finished there."

OK, her antennae picked up, there's something to do with the dresser. They're looking for something. But what?

Charlie continued. "If I'm not mistaken, Jon has quite a collection himself, and can loan Ralph a pair. And I seem to recall that neither of you are indigent, so you can obtain him some toiletries to tide him over."

Amanda held up her hands defensively. "All right," she replied.

Charlie noted her examination of the room. He took the clothes and the carryon and nodded toward the door. "After you," he spoke shortly.

Amanda reluctantly exited with Charlie close at her heels and Bruce following in their wake.

Once they made it back outside, Charlie looked pointedly at Bruce.

"I'm on my way there now," Bruce acquiesced enigmatically, walking to his car and leaving.

Charlie walked over to Amanda's car and placed the items in the back seat, hanging the suits up. As he shut the door, he remarked, "Jon's alibi checked out. His whereabouts are accounted for yesterday."

"So he is off the hook?" Amanda countered quickly.

"Not entirely," Charlie replied.

Amanda contended, "What do you mean? His alibi being—?"

"The last time I checked you're married to the man; therefore, he can tell you that himself." Petrino didn't look at her.

"And the rest of his statement to you, the one I specifically vetoed your getting?" Amanda insisted sharply. "The one given without his attorney present?"

"Same answer—ask him. You'll get it from me when I'm good and damn ready," he retorted icily.

Amanda gazed at him as he studiously refused to return her stare. "And my other two clients?"

"They are not so lucky as of this moment," he answered. "They both need to stay put. Thanks to you, I have no alibis for them. Are they still refusing to give me statements?"

Amanda bit back a knowing smile. "At the moment, yes. That could change after today, but I'm making no promises. Alex and I are dealing with that as we speak."

"Alex?" Charlie echoed, frowning. "Any reason for you to already be assembling the dream team?"

"You know me, always prepared," Amanda quipped. She paused. "Charlie?"

He looked directly at her upon her use of his name. She swallowed as she recognized the turmoil in his features, before the mask quickly settled again. This situation is difficult for him, too, she realized, to suddenly attain his dream of being sheriff, only to be immediately embroiled in a homicide investigation involving his best friends. He shook his head almost imperceptibly, warning her, his face expressionless.

"I assume you won't have any objection if I house Ralph and David at the cottage, if Ralph's house and the condo are not released today or tomorrow?"

"No. Why? Getting too crowded for the newlyweds?" For a moment, he was the old Charlie, teasing her, gauging her reaction.

She smiled, her heart going out to him, suddenly wanting to reassure him in some way, to hang on to the sliver of camaraderie. "You know when Ralph gets his vehicle back he isn't going to want to drive it over the dirt trail several times a day. I sense David is rather anal about his Jag as well." She bit back a grin. "And I overheard them this morning with Jon at the breakfast table; they were rather merciless over a 'discussion' he and I had last night."

"Over his giving me a statement, I presume?" Petrino prompted.

"Exactly," Amanda nodded.

"I told him you would hurt him over that," Charlie murmured, his voice low. "But I also assume you two kissed and made up?"

She blushed.

"The vehicles will be released a little later today, if you want to call Sam or Bruce after noon and make arrangements for pickup."

He opened her car door for her. Their eyes met briefly, and he glanced to the side deliberately. She understood.

"Thanks, Sheriff," she spoke carefully. "Please have the department inform me when Ralph can regain access to his home."

He nodded, closing the door for her. As she pulled away, she noted the black sedan parked across the road. The driver's face she could not see, for a newspaper he was ostensibly reviewing was obscuring his features.

Amanda drove back to the farm, mulling over matters in her mind.

So this Lauren Mallory had a brief affair with Jon over eight years ago, and had a child. But why would she name Jon if, as Jon said, they had used contraception? Why after all this time? What was she hoping to gain?

Why would she name Ralph in a separate paternity suit, if she and Ralph had never met before last Sunday? Amanda could think of only one reason: to discredit Ralph in some way, but why? It would have to be in his home life with Claire, or his work. Or his bid for county judge. Her eyes narrowed thoughtfully.

She thought back to seeing Lauren in the room with the legislators and Esme Townsend at Tallulah's on Monday. Could Esme be involved in some way? Was she trying to thwart Ralph's chances at judgeship by hiring Lauren to file the suit? That seemed far-fetched, but she realized that stranger things had happened in politics. And Amanda was aware that a breath of scandal, even if the allegations were patently untrue, could easily ruin an otherwise good man's chances at attaining political office, particularly a judgeship. She also knew that Claire was a jealous woman, and she understood Ralph's fears that his marriage could be in jeopardy.

Her thoughts turned to David. David apparently at least thought himself in love with Lauren Mallory at one time, and had acknowledged to Amanda that he could be the child's father. If so, why wasn't he named? Why did

Lauren cut off all contact with him until recently? Why did she suddenly show back up? Why did she call him yesterday evening?

Amanda was convinced that none of the three men could be guilty of murder. Someone had gone to some length to murder Lauren in Ralph's house, and there were the paternity complaints against Ralph and Jon. Why? Why was the woman in Ralph's home? Ralph had no enemies to her knowledge. She could think of no one who would do such a thing.

Who was spying on Charlie? Who was so interested in the details of the investigation? Esme Townsend would be, Amanda thought to herself.

She suddenly wondered at the statement Jon gave Petrino. Where was Jon yesterday? Why was he late getting home? Why wouldn't Charlie divulge the information? Amanda was suddenly sorry she had cut Jon off the previous night, and wondered about his alibi.

She was no closer to an answer when she pulled up to the house. She let herself out of the car, pulled the clothes and bag out of the car and started toward the door, deep in thought. When she looked up, Jon was standing on the porch waiting for her.

He reached for the items and leaned over to kiss her. "I missed you," he said simply.

"I missed you too," she smiled. "What's been going on?"

"We had a large pow-wow, and all decided none of us believed the other could be guilty. We decided to pool all our information, but Alex is taking individual statements first, so that our memories don't get all mixed together. I went first."

He opened the door for her and followed her in. She looked around. "Where is everyone?" she asked.

"Alex is in the den interviewing Ralph, and David is on the back porch. I think he is fast asleep on the swing. I don't think he got much sleep last night."

"I don't think any of us did," Amanda shook her head ruefully, walking through the living room to the guest room, placing the bag at the foot of the bed. Jon walked past her and hung the clothes in the closet. When he turned around, she was looking pensively around the room.

"I don't come in here much," she murmured. "This was Andy's and my room. It's very different from those days, everything rearranged, even the wall color different."

Jon drew her to him. "Maybe you need a new memory to go with the change in décor."

He kissed her, insistently, hard, and she responded, molding herself to him, her breathing quickened. "We shouldn't be making out in the guest room when we have guests using the room," she whispered.

"But you are so seductive, Mrs. Connor," he said against her ear.

"I need to be helping Alex," she protested softly as he trailed kisses down her throat.

"You're absolutely right," he agreed as his fingers unbuttoned the top buttons of her blouse and slipped inside. She closed her eyes.

The thought flashed in her head. "Where were you last night? Why were you late getting home?" she queried.

"Charlie didn't tell you?" he pulled away and looked into her eyes.

She gazed back. "No. He told me to ask you." She bit her lip.

"You don't trust me?" His face became serious.

"Jon, this has nothing to do with trust, and everything with planning a defense in case the unthinkable happens."

"You didn't want to know last night," he remarked enigmatically.

"I was mad last night. I want to know now," she looked at him anxiously, pulling away slightly.

"I had an appointment at another office on the way home." He regarded her solemnly, dropping his hands and stepping away.

"What office? Where?" She stilled him, her hand on his arm.

"I've already told Alex," he remarked, not looking at her.

"Tell me, Jon," she flung, agitated. "Please."

Ralph walked into the bedroom. "Oh, excuse me." He stopped in the doorway, chagrined.

"Jon was just helping me bring in some of your clothes from home." Embarrassed, Amanda turned from Jon and smiled tightly.

"I must have been interrupting something." Ralph pointed to her blouse.

She looked down. "Oh, shit," she muttered, flushing and pulling her blouse together and buttoning it. "Excuse me," she blustered, striding past him and to the den, opening the door and letting herself in.

"Well?" she remarked to Alex, who was sitting at her desk and taking notes.

"I've taken statements from Jon and Ralph." Alex halted and turned around to face her. "David said he preferred that you be present when I talked to him. What have you discovered?"

She described to him the home condition as she saw it, and the statements by Charlie. "Charlie was short and sweet, not giving anything away. But Charlie is definitely under scrutiny. There was someone watching us at the sheriff's department last night, and again today in front of Ralph's house. He did say that Jon's alibi checked out, but wouldn't say he was no longer a suspect."

"What do you think is going on? Why is Charlie being watched?"

"I think someone, probably Esme Townsend, isn't happy about his appointment, and is looking for some reason to either have him under her thumb or to have him drummed out." She described her efforts on behalf of Charlie with the chief of staff, and of the cryptic conversation she and Charlie had.

"Why Esme?"

"She likes to think she is the one making and breaking the deals of who gets what political appointment in this area." She described what she saw at the restaurant on Monday, and named the persons she recognized in the room. She filled him in on Ralph's announcement to her of his plans to seek the judicial appointment, and Esme's conversation with her over lunch.

Alex nodded, deep in thought.

Amanda questioned, "What was Jon's alibi, Alex?"

Alex looked at her, his face impassive. "I think Jon should be the one to tell you that."

"Please, will someone tell me? God, what is so bad that no one can tell me?" she became agitated, her voice raised.

"It is supposed to be a surprise for you," Jon's voice answered her from the doorway. She turned at the sound. "I was hoping it might stay a surprise." He stared at her. "I have been trying to decide where I want to take you on our honeymoon. I was meeting with a travel agent."

CHAPTER 19

Amanda regarded Jon speechlessly. Alex noted it and stood. "Do I need to give you two some time alone?"

Amanda held up her hand. "No," she croaked, taking a deep breath. She gazed at Jon, her eyes bright with unshed tears. "That's why I don't like surprises and guessing games," she said hoarsely. "I've had enough lately to last me three lifetimes."

Jon took a step toward her and started to reply, but she shook her head. "We'll talk about this later, alone," she dismissed him brusquely, her voice low, turning away. "Why don't you ask David if he would like to come in?"

Jon frowned. He turned to Alex. "Give us a minute, will you?"

Alex nodded and left quickly, shutting the door behind him.

Jon walked up to her and turned her to face him. "Mandy, I—"

She lashed out, "Do you have any idea the hell I went through just now? Not knowing what was going on, and no one telling me? You not telling me? So much bad has happened to me in the last year, and the thought of something so secret and so bad coming between us, and perhaps taking you away from me . . ." she covered her face with her hands, overcome.

Jon was stunned. "Oh, love, I'm so sorry." He enfolded her to him. He could feel her trembling, and pressed her tightly to him. "I never thought that you would take it that way. I wanted to surprise you, see your face light up."

She mumbled against his shirt, "I can't handle surprises from you, Jon. I have to know that what we have is something secure and solid. I don't want to be second-guessing it. This Lauren Mallory business, this murder, the paternity suit, your being involved, have all hit awfully close to home, to our sanctuary. I have trouble thinking logically when it's about you."

Jon released her and took her face in his hands, forcing her to look at him. "Mandy, I'm sorry for scaring you."

She smiled at him tremulously. He kissed her, his kiss long and lingering. He whispered against her lips, "And I promise I will even warn you in advance about your Christmas and birthday presents. You can keep mine a surprise if you like."

His remark had the intended effect, and she laughed. He chuckled with her. "Now finish up this business, so that we can have some meatloaf for supper."

"Sorry, no can do," she demurred. "Fred is making my favorite tonight. Meatloaf is another thing we should avoid with company in the house."

He laughed out loud then. "Don't expect me to forego dessert too." He caught up her hand and kissed it.

He strode out of the room and into the living room, to an anxious Alex and David. "Sorry for the interruption," he quipped. Looking at Ralph, just walking into the room from the guestroom, he added, "I've got to get out a bit, do something. Let's go pick up whatever extra items you need from town and some lunch for everyone, while these guys do their thing." He looked over at David. "Anything in particular that you need while we are in town?"

"Yeah, if you find another girl like Amanda, buy her at any price for me," David retorted shortly as he walked out of the room.

Jon looked after his brother a moment, biting back his sudden irritation, then picked up the car keys from the console table and headed out the door.

Ralph followed him to the Mercedes. As they were buckling their seat belts and Jon started the engine, he fumed, "Why is David like that? He just has to needle me."

Ralph looked over at Jon. "Isn't it obvious? David is jealous. He wants a relationship like what you have with Amanda. He apparently hoped for something like that with this Lauren Mallory."

"I can't believe that. I don't understand what he saw in her," Jon muttered through clenched teeth.

Ralph snorted. "You slept with her, but you don't understand what David saw in her? Come on, Jon, you can do better than that."

"But Lauren was never the type one falls in love with," Jon protested. "There's nothing wifely or maternal about her. In fact, I find it hard to believe she carried a child, much less raised one."

"Well, that's what the paternity complaint states," Ralph replied, his jaw set, his voice tinged in anger. "But if David had a relationship with Lauren about the time of conception, why didn't she name him?"

Jon just shook his head with frustration.

Meanwhile, David and Amanda were in conference with Alex. David and Amanda sat on the love seat while Alex remained at the desk. Amanda looked over at David and read the tension in his face. She took his hand and squeezed it comfortingly.

"You're among friends, David," she smiled, trying to put him at ease. "I mean that. Alex and I will do everything we can to protect you, to preserve your rights. Having said that, you are entitled to consult with an attorney of your choice, and don't have to talk to us or anyone else at all, particularly the police. I doubt it will happen, but there is a possibility one of you may be charged, and that's why what we do here is important. Because of that, there is a possibility of a conflict of interest, because if one if charged, his defense counsel could easily argue, or evidence could end up pointing, that one of the others is guilty. And what you say in front of Ralph or Jon could be used later. What you say to us would not be; however, it might cause us to not be able to represent any of you if the worst happens. I'm willing to take that chance in order to make sure you are all informed and protected right now."

"I'm sure that none of us are guilty of Lauren's murder," David stated emphatically. "And while I want to see the murderer brought to justice, I am equally committed to preventing any of us being charged. Jon is my only brother, and Ralph is my friend. I know they are as incapable of murder as I am. So I am putting myself in your hands."

Amanda squeezed his hand. "But I want to make sure you realize the gravity of that decision."

He turned to her and smiled pensively. "I do."

She looked at Alex, who nodded. "Let's start at the beginning. How long have you known Lauren Mallory?"

"About nine years," David replied. "She showed up at my parents' Arlington townhouse one day looking for Jon. I had dropped in for a few days. I knew right then that if she had something going with Jon, it wasn't serious, because he had his own place and was seldom at my folks'. She would have checked there first. In fact, he shared his place with your husband when Andrew was up there."

"Did you know Andy?" Amanda leaned forward, interested.

"I met him several times," David nodded.

Amanda wanted to ask more about Andrew, but knew they needed to stay on-topic. "What happened between you and Lauren?"

He looked at his hands. "Well, I invited her in and flirted outrageously with her." He looked sheepish. "I always had this mean streak, and was always messing with Jon's dates. Anyway, I asked her out and she declined. That piqued my interest.

"During our conversation she mentioned some hot club that she liked to frequent. So I wangled my way in that weekend, and there she was, dressed to kill, short skirt, long legs. She was looking bored with the guy who brought

her, and I struck up a conversation with her. We ended up leaving together."
He swallowed. "I took her to my parents' place because she didn't want to
go to a hotel."

Alex looked up from his notes. "I assume you slept together?"

"Yes," David acknowledged. "She stayed over several nights, in fact, then
invited me to her place when my parents announced they were coming into
town.

"We were just having fun, but then something happened after several
weeks, and I kind of got used to having her around. I was jealous of her
other men friends, and she laughed at me. One day I mentioned to her the
possibility of my getting a place and settling down in the area, and asked if
she was interested in our moving in together.

"The next day she was up and gone, and it was like she dropped off the
face of the earth. She didn't show back at her apartment, she didn't return
calls, her landlord and work place didn't give out any information."

"Why did you think her child could be yours?" Amanda urged softly.

He looked studiously past her at the bookcase. "Well, there were a few
times . . . . I really thought maybe I—I loved her, Amanda." He fidgeted
uncomfortably. "I guess she sensed that and got the hell out of Dodge," he
finished unhappily.

"Did you see her again?" Alex pressed.

"Not until a couple of weeks ago," David answered, looking up. "I was up
in D.C., had come up to do a couple of surgeries by referral from a colleague,
and to assist in some reconstructive procedures. All of a sudden, I ran into
her, and she called me, just out of the blue, wanted to know if I wanted to
get together."

He swallowed. "I wasn't expecting it. Damn, she looked just the same,
acted as if nothing had happened. I was so flabbergasted. When I finished
my surgeries, I asked her if she wanted to come down to Panama City Beach
with me, told her about George's engagement party."

He paused. "She asked if Jon was going to be there. I didn't think anything
of it. I told her yes, that Jon had just gotten married and was living in the
area. We flew down together, and she stayed with me a couple of days at the
beach, then disappeared, leaving a note that she had some business to take
care of.

"She was gone for a couple of days, then showed up the day of George's
party and asked to go with me. I said sure, why not? But at the party, she
kept making a play for Jon, and told me she was not going back to the condo
with me that night. We had words."

"What words?" Alex inquired.

David paused, looking at Amanda sadly. "I told her that if all she wanted was an invitation to the party, she could have just asked instead of leading me on. And I told her she needed to keep her hands off my brother, that he was happily married to a wonderful woman. She just laughed at me, shook me off, and that was that."

David rubbed his forehead tiredly. Amanda stroked his arm. "I'm sorry, David," she said softly.

"Did you see her any more after that?"

David just shook his head negatively.

"When did you find out about the child?"

"When I saw the papers at the house here last night." David's eyes met Amanda's. "I had no clue that there was a child, or that she was claiming Jon was the father. She said nothing to me about this. I knew from looking at the dates that the little girl could be mine, and I was angrier than hell. She used me yet again." He fell silent.

"Did you hear any more from her?" Alex persisted.

David rubbed his hands on the legs of his denims. "Yes, last night. I stormed out of here when I saw those papers. I was going to drive around, cool off. But I noticed a voice mail, and it was from her. She said to meet her at 4276 Meadow Lane. I have no idea why, didn't know where that was. I tried calling her back, and there was no answer."

He shook his head, tears in his eyes. "I found the place with my GPS and pulled up in the driveway. Just as I was getting out of the car, Ralph pulled up beside me. He asked why I was there. I told him I was told to meet someone there, and asked why he was there. He laughed and said it was his house. He asked who told me to show up there. I told him an old girlfriend.

"He looked at me funny and said something like Claire never mentioned knowing me. I didn't know what he was talking about. He said Claire was his wife, and she was out of town. I told him Lauren Mallory gave me this address. He was surprised, said he couldn't understand why she would give his place, and that he wasn't aware she even knew where he lived.

"We were walking up to the front door together, and I noticed that it was cracked open. I pointed it out to Ralph. He started to charge in, but I convinced him to call 911. He did, but then said he wasn't waiting, that he had to pee, and it was his house.

"I tried to stop him, because I could hear the sirens headed our way. It was dim. He cut on lights as he headed down the hall. There was blood all down the carpet from the bedroom to the bathroom. He got as far as the bathroom and turned on the light, and I thought he was going to faint.

"There was—Lauren lying in the bathtub, covered in blood. She was naked. I ran over to her and checked for a pulse. There was none. A lot of the blood had congealed. Oh, God." He buried his head in his hands. Amanda put her hand on his shoulder comfortingly.

"The place was suddenly crawling with medics and cops. They grabbed us and pulled us out of there. Chief Petrino was suddenly there and dragged us into the den." He paused, shaking. "I had her blood all over my hands."

"What can you tell me about what you saw in the bathroom? The body?" Alex asked gently.

David was silent, sniffling. After a moment he responded. "I don't remember any clothes in the bathroom. The blood pattern looked like she had been dragged from the bedroom to the bathroom. She was draped in the tub like someone had placed her there." He paused. "Whoever did it had to have been covered in blood. I had blood on my hands from trying to see if she was still alive. The cut was sharp and deep, sliced through the carotid and jugular. She didn't stand a chance."

"Did you see any sign of a weapon?" Alex asked.

"No."

"Did you or Ralph ever go into the bedroom?"

"No, we were yanked out of there pretty quickly."

"Where were you from the time you left the farm until you got to Ralph's?" Amanda urged gently.

"I drove to town and was riding around the lake with the top down, when my phone buzzed. It was Jon, wanting to know why I ran out. I don't even remember what I told him. It was after I talked to him that I noticed there was a message on my voice mail."

"Had you gotten out of the car before Ralph got there?"

"No."

"And Ralph wasn't already there when you arrived?"

"No." David was emphatic.

"You were not in the neighborhood, didn't drive by the house, before Ralph got there and saw you there?"

"No," David shook his head. "I had to look for the place."

"You saw nothing, no one unusual on your way there, or when you got there?"

David shook his head.

"How long from the time you left the farm until you made it to Ralph's house?"

"I made it here about 7:00, and left around 7:35. I guess I got to Ralph's about 8:30."

"And the time of her call?"

Amanda walked over to the desk, unlocked the desk drawer and pulled out David's wallet and phone. "May I?" she requested.

"Of course," he nodded.

She sat down beside David, flipped open the phone and checked phone calls received. "Do you know which one is hers?"

David pointed it out. "7:10, about the time you and I were in the kitchen together." David frowned. "We were carrying on, and I must not have noticed it."

"So the murder occurred sometime between 7:10 and 8:30 p.m.," Amanda said aloud. "We suddenly know more than Charlie." She looked at David. "May we play the message?"

"Sure, if it's still on there. I generally delete them after listening, but I honestly cannot remember in this case."

He took the phone and hit the button, then hit the speaker phone function and his speed dial. After a moment, he punched in a code, and the message came on.

"David, it's Lauren." Amanda recognized the throaty sound of Lauren's voice, the little breathless quality. "I need to see you. Right away. I'm at 4276 Meadow Lane, Mainville." A small laugh. "My ride left me here to deliver a message, but the recipient didn't show. I'm aware you had plans to be in this godforsaken town all day today. Come pick me up, darling."

Amanda was chilled. Lauren was supposedly at Ralph's house at the time she called David. She was alive at 7:10. "What was she doing there? What message?"

"How did she get there?" Alex questioned aloud.

"Should I erase this?" David asked.

"No," Amanda and Alex said together. Alex explained, "This shows that you weren't with her when she first got there, because she is giving you the address and telling you to pick her up there."

Amanda pushed the button to view calls made. "You got the call from Jon at 7:51, and called voice mail at 7:56, and this number at 7:59, per the call counter. This is something we, or you, may consider sharing with Sheriff Petrino," Amanda placed the phone back in David's hand.

"No," he countered quickly, handing the phone back to her. "I'm leaving that to your discretion. Use it how you think best."

"But David—" she began, but he put his hand on her shoulder.

"Please, Amanda. I trust you to do what needs to be done. If it somehow helps one or more of us, use it. Keep the phone. I'll get another."

Amanda's phone started ringing. She stood. "Excuse me a minute."

She walked into the living room and picked up the receiver. "Hello?"

"Mrs. Connor?" a male voice asked.

"Yes," she replied.

"This is Sergeant Thompson at the Sheriff's Department. The undersheriff asked that I inform you that your husband's and Mr. Carmichael's vehicles have been processed and are ready for release back to you."

"And Dr. Connor's? The Jaguar?" she pressed.

"No, ma'am, they are not finished with it yet. The undersheriff said he would notify you as soon as they are done."

"I'll make arrangements to pick them up this afternoon," Amanda promised, hanging up, deep in thought.

OK, so either they are taking their sweet time on the Jag, Petrino's men have found something in David's car, or he is hoping to find something, she guessed.

She walked back into the room. "Tell me, David," she interrupted the small talk of the two men, "is there any reason you can think of why the Sheriff's Department would be taking longer than normal to process your car? Anything suspicious in there they might find?"

David and Alex both stared at her. "No," David responded slowly. "However, Lauren and I were both in the car on several occasions while she was—was—down here," he finished lamely.

"So her prints are going to be found in your car?" Amanda gazed at him.

He nodded, then snapped his fingers. "And she cut her finger on something she bought at the store earlier in the week. Some nail polish she bought and was trying to open the bottle. When she did, the top was chipped, and she cut herself. Dripped some polish on her jeans and broke a nail. She was pissed."

He was thoughtful. "But I had the car detailed Monday at this little place on the beach. Nice place—used them before."

"Any blood on the carpet, upholstery?" Amanda asked excitedly.

"I don't remember any," David shook his head. "Is this bad?"

"Not necessarily. Law enforcement could have always saved your car for last to process." But Amanda knew that if Petrino had anything to do with it, David's Jaguar, the car belonging to who in Petrino's mind was the most probable prime suspect of the three men, would be first on the list. She kept that surmise to herself.

Amanda turned to Alex, who was regarding her intently. She knew Alex's thoughts had mirrored her own. "One more thing. How did Lauren know you were going to be in town Tuesday?"

David shook his head. "I have no idea. I hadn't talked to her since Sunday." He snapped his fingers. "But she was in the car with me on the way to the party when the realtor called and I made the appointment."

Amanda nodded. "Can you think of anything else?"

David shook his head. "Not right now."

Alex stood. "I think Amanda and I need to go through everything together. But I have to check in at the office by phone and get a few items out, if you don't mind."

Amanda came up and put her hand on his arm. "I am so grateful you made this time."

"You pay well," Alex laughed. He handed her his legal pad. "I made notes of the interviews, and want you to have a chance to run through them. I really need to go in to the office for a while sometime today. So how do you want to handle this?"

"What if you stay for lunch with us and we discuss it? That way we can decide what else we need to do, then you can be free to go handle your other business."

Alex nodded and turned to David. "I would like to say you, Ralph and Jon have nothing to worry about, but we just don't know. Honestly, Charlie is a man of common sense, and would probably reject out of hand any of you three as a suspect. However, there is no local official more steeped in political scrutiny than the sheriff's position. You have the right to consult with an attorney.

"But, David, as things stand right now and in the foreseeable future, Amanda and I are in your court. We will not be divulging what you have told us without your permission. And you can feel good that we're a pretty mean team. I will be the first to tell you if I feel you need to hire outside counsel. If you have any doubts whatsoever, I encourage you to go ahead."

David nodded, shaking Alex's hand. "I trust both of you to steer me right."

They all exited. Fred was standing in the doorway to the kitchen. "I'm going to need a couple of things from the store for supper tonight, so was heading to town."

Amanda gazed at him. "Number one, you don't have to cook and clean for this crew, Fred, but I do appreciate you. Number two, David and I could use a lift after lunch to pick up a couple of the vehicles being released from the crime lab, so if you don't mind . . . ."

Fred looked at her critically. "Number one, I don't mind, and number two, I don't mind."

Their eyes locked, and Amanda smiled. She walked up to him and kissed him on the cheek. "I love you, Fred," she whispered.

He winked at her and squeezed her arm. "I gotta finish making a list, then we'll head out."

Amanda turned to David. "I want to change." He looked ruefully at his rumpled khakis.

She pointed toward the door of the bedroom turned dressing room. "There's a bathroom. Jon's closet is in there. Help yourself, dear."

She and Alex walked together out the front door to the porch. Alex turned to her, leaning against the rail. "Amanda, depending on the physical evidence Charlie has, we have at least two potential defendants here. If Jon's alibi panned out, his whereabouts can be accounted for to the extent it would be extremely difficult for them to finger him for the murder.

"Ralph's case is a bit more problematic. He is served with the complaint, and no one yet can verify his whereabouts from then on. David gives him an out by stating that he was at the house when Ralph pulled up. But it doesn't rule out the police claiming that Ralph could have done the deed, left and came back, although that would be implausible."

Alex paused. Amanda prompted, with heavy heart, "And David?"

Alex hesitated. "That's the most dangerous of all. Petrino knows Ralph and Jon. He doesn't know David as well, so that will make David the more likely to be suspected. Lauren calls David with her whereabouts as of 7:10 at least, and his whereabouts are unverifiable for approximately the hour before she is found. If he found the complaint and was angry that his brother was named in a paternity complaint, the prosecution can say he had motive. He was with her a few days prior to the murder. They could have had a lover's quarrel. And law enforcement can claim he could have been leaving the scene when Ralph pulled up, and had to make it look good."

"But Ralph and David each say there was no blood on the other at the time they ended up at the house together."

"You know and I know how Petrino's men construct the time line will be critical there," Alex reminded her.

"But it still doesn't make sense to show back up at the scene if you are the culprit," Amanda argued.

Amanda fell silent. Alex pressed, "Just how well do you know David?"

Amanda gazed at Alex. "Not long, but I feel I've known him forever. Alex, he's my husband's brother, and he saved my life. He was broken up about her murder. I just don't believe him capable." She reached out and took Alex's hand. "He didn't do it. I saw his face last night. He was devastated. I have to believe that. And I have to protect him."

Alex nodded and squeezed her hand, as the Mercedes pulled up to the house, and Jon and Ralph alighted. Jon stared at them piercingly as he and Ralph gathered several bags out of the back and started up the steps. Alex dropped Amanda's hand.

"Lunch is about to be served," Jon remarked, his eyes roving from Alex to Amanda.

"I need to make a few calls. I will be there in a minute," Alex smiled, looking at his watch.

Amanda asked Jon, "Need any help?"

"No, I've got it," Jon was short as he turned for the door.

Amanda held the door open for the two men as they trudged into the house. She followed Jon to the kitchen as Ralph peeled off to the guestroom.

He set his bags on the counter and handed her a slip of paper. "Ralph insisted on stopping by the office," Jon informed her, his voice clipped. "The cleaning crew was there. I thought he was going to blow, but he just looked at the calendar and phone messages, shrugged and was ready to leave. He recognized one of the girls, said she was at the office last night from close of business until he left. I asked her, and she confirmed that he was at the office until almost eight. I asked her if she would mind giving a statement to law enforcement, and she appeared nervous but agreed. This is her name and contact number. She is apparently a cousin of Joanna's, and has been working for her."

Amanda looked relieved. "Good, that's two down," she murmured.

"Two? Who's left? David?" Jon's brow furrowed.

"We'll discuss it with everyone when Alex gets back." Amanda turned toward the cabinet.

Jon's demeanor changed. He took her arm and turned her to face him, full of concern. "What is it, Amanda?"

"Nothing," she tried to smile. "After we eat, David and I are going with Fred to pick up your and Ralph's vehicles."

Jon stared at her. "What about David's Jag?"

"They're not through with it yet." She forced herself to sound light.

Just then David walked in, freshly showered and wearing a medium blue checked button-down shirt and khakis. Jon stared at him. "That's my favorite shirt," he muttered.

"I know. I picked it out for him to wear," Amanda interjected mischievously. "Don't you think it looks good on him?"

David looked at the shirt, then at Jon, chagrined. "Honest, I didn't know. I can go change."

"No, it's perfectly all right," Amanda purred as Jon turned his back, taking containers out of the bag, his face flushing.

"Excuse me," David spoke, walking back out of the room.

Amanda set the table as Jon emptied food into serving bowls. "Chinese and salad—I hope that's OK," he spoke, his voice tight.

"Where did Ralph go?" Amanda tried to keep the conversation flowing, although she could feel the tension.

"I think he is putting his purchases up and is trying to get Claire on the phone again." Jon did not look up. "He's tried all morning. He doesn't want her to read something in the news or the internet, or hear about it before he can talk to her."

Ralph walked in. Amanda turned to him. "Any luck?" She was direct.

"No," he shook his head sadly. "The longer I go without hearing from her, the more worried I get," he admitted.

They soon had the food laid out on the table. David walked back into the kitchen, this time with a yellow pullover on.

Jon's jaw set angrily. "That's my other favorite shirt," he spat angrily.

David exploded. "Just how many damned favorite shirts do you have?" He looked at Amanda, his hands clenched. "I can't do this."

"Stop it, both of you," Amanda spoke sharply as Fred walked into the kitchen. "We are tired, we're all stretched thin, and we're beginning to poke holes in each other. None of us caused this situation, but we're all in it together and have to make the best of it." She held up her hands. "Please."

Jon relented. "You're absolutely right." He crossed over to David and put his hand on David's arm. "You're my brother. Wear all my damned shirts. They are only shirts, after all." He attempted a grin. "Everything I have is yours, except my wife."

Everyone joined in half-hearted smiles. They sat down at the table. Amanda patted the chair beside her. "Come on, Fred, join us. You're family, too."

Fred sat down as Alex strode into the room. Soon they were passing food, all making a lackluster effort at small talk.

The conversation lulled, and Jon looked at Alex. "OK, spill it. What do you know?"

Amanda spoke up. "Alex, Jon just told me that one of the cleaning ladies can put Ralph at the office working until approximately eight o'clock."

"I got her name and phone number for Amanda to give to Petrino," Jon supplied. "That is," he looked at Amanda sharply, "if she wants to share the information."

Amanda looked down at her plate, saying nothing.

Alex smiled. "Good. I just called someone at the medical examiner's office, my former secretary who works there now. She said Gerald has threatened that heads will roll if anything is leaked before he has finished his testing. She said Bruce Williams was personally present at the autopsy, and actually has an investigator camped out at the medical examiner's office. So no go there for now."

"Well, Jon's alibi checked out. Charlie said, though, he is not off the hook. I don't know what that means," Amanda offered. "Charlie escorted me through Ralph's house himself to get the clothes, but he is wanting to interview Ralph and David badly."

"Did he say that?" Jon inquired.

Amanda didn't look at Jon. "He asked if I was going to relent and allow them to make statements. I told him I'd let him know. I also asked him to let me know the minute Ralph's house and the condo are released." She allowed a smile. "It is my opinion that the whole reason for Charlie's personal appearance to release Ralph's clothing was to get me to agree to allow interviews.

"And David's phone sets the time of Lauren's call at 7:10 last night, while he was here. He left around 7:30, got Jon's call at 7:51, checked voice mail at 7:56 and tried to call her back at 7:59."

"It was a little before 8:30 when I pulled up to the house," Ralph offered. "And David was getting out of his car then. He would have had blood on him if he had killed her, but he didn't."

"The same thing goes for Ralph," David submitted.

Amanda nodded. "She was apparently killed in the bedroom. The sheets and bedspread were gone, and the carpet was taken up. But per David and Ralph there was a bloody trail down to the bathroom where someone either carried or dragged her, looked like the latter. And there was blood on the window sill." She paused. "The FDLE operative was processing the dresser, and I was not allowed to get cufflinks for Ralph. I'm not sure how to read that. They could have been looking for something in particular. Charlie was not forthcoming with any information, and didn't let me tarry." She glanced at Ralph, but he shrugged helplessly.

"It sounds as if I'm in the most danger of being charged with this," David vouched quietly. "They still have my car, I was there with blood on my hands when the police got there, she had called me, and I don't have an alibi or anyone to vouch for my whereabouts."

"Don't go there," Jon growled, but Amanda put a warning hand on his arm.

"I know it may seem that way, but it is much too early to tell, and we don't know what evidence Charlie has," Amanda spoke soothingly. "We are trying to gather information, and the rest is speculation. Charlie knows in his heart none of you did this. But he cannot just dismiss the evidence before him. And as badly as Charlie is going to want to solve this case, he is going to be extremely cautious before charging anyone with this crime."

"Why?" David stared at her anxiously.

"Because he knows that Amanda and I are already on the case, and if one of you is charged, he had better be loaded for bear," Alex spoke up, his voice ominous. He glanced at Ralph. "Amanda and I have cross-examined

Charlie before. I witnessed at least one trial when Amanda made him wish he hadn't been the case officer, and another when he probably wished he hadn't chosen law enforcement as a career. It wasn't pretty.

"Charlie is an extremely thorough investigator, and he is as aware of the holes in his case as we are. No matter how good friends they are, he knows Amanda won't stand on ceremony when it comes to embarrassing him in court if he missteps. And he cannot afford to be embarrassed right now, on the heels of this appointment to the position."

David managed a smile. Ralph placed his hand on David's shoulder. "Alex is right. I just negotiated a truce between Amanda and the chief prosecutor. She was making his life hell because he had just a couple of months ago arrested one of our childhood friends." Ralph winked at David. "Charlie was at the first appearance when she won, and he told me he had to pull her off the prosecutor—said he thought she was going to strangle the guy with his own tie right in front of the judge, even after winning."

Jon started laughing, and the others did too. Amanda smiled, coloring with embarrassment. "It wasn't quite that bad," she murmured.

"I'm sold," David nodded.

"But I want to bring something up," Ralph interjected. "David and I can't continue to stay here indefinitely. Jon and Amanda are newlyweds and deserve a bit of privacy. I thought I would just get us a room at the hotel for a night or two."

"I agree," David breathed.

"No need," Amanda interposed. "I told Charlie that if your house and the condo weren't released come tomorrow, I might set you two up at my cottage. I didn't seriously think I'd have to do that, but with everyone so stressed right now," she glanced at Jon, "I think I may get it readied, just in case."

She stood. "But for tonight at least we're all staying put. David, you and I have a date, if Fred will be so kind."

"I can go with you," Jon spoke up.

"No," Amanda was firm. "We'll get the cars, and I will check out the cottage to see what needs to be done to make it occupant-ready. I want to run by the office just a minute, and David may need to pick up a few items in town, including some favorite shirts," she smiled slyly at Jon, "then we'll be back."

Fred also stood. Amanda turned to him. "If you need dinner preparations done, such as dicing onions and peppers for the steak, peeling potatoes, and the like, these two," she pointed at Ralph and Jon, "had their jolly-ride already and are available for the job while we are gone."

Fred nodded and gave instructions, then the three left together, saying good-bye to Alex who followed them in his car out to the road.

CHAPTER 20

Amanda sat between Fred and David in Fred's large older-model pickup truck. David regarded her anxiously. "Is this shirt really one of his favorites?"

Amanda grinned. "I bought those two shirts not long after the wedding. He does like the blue button-down, but I'm not even sure he's worn the shirt you have on, dear." She laughed, then suddenly sobered. "What is it between you two? Is the sibling rivalry that strong?"

David grimaced. "It's my fault. I always suffered from 'middle child syndrome'. Mom doted on Jon, and Kelly was Dad's baby. Jon could do no wrong, and I was always picking a fight with him. Of course, I seldom won.

"We always got along well, hung together, were pretty close growing up, despite all that. Then when we were in college I visited him for a weekend during football season. I stole his girl—he walked in on us making out. That's when he stopped liking me. And I—I guess I just kept pushing his buttons, making a play for anyone he dated, flirting with his first wife."

David colored. "Actually, she came on to me, but I knew Jon would never believe that. I didn't do more than flirt. But now he doesn't have a very high opinion of me. And frankly I guess I am jealous that he found you first."

"So Lauren was one of those times?" Amanda questioned.

David's face turned somber. "It started out that way. But I guess I was hoping that I'd find someone. Lauren was beautiful, sexy, sophisticated, but sometimes she would shed all that and be just a—a nice person, likeable, down to earth, someone I wanted to spend time with. We enjoyed each other, or so I thought. That I pinned my hopes on Lauren . . . that was foolish, I guess."

"I'm sorry, David," Amanda murmured feelingly.

"And now she's dead, and there are all these questions. Why did she run away? What was she doing here? Why paternity suits against two guys? Why not me? Why was she at Ralph's that night? Who killed her and why? My head is spinning, and now I'm a suspect."

"I've been there," Amanda whispered. "I know it can be overwhelming."

"That's right, you have," David smiled sadly. "I hope I come out of this in one piece."

"That is what I intend," Amanda responded fervently.

They were silent a moment, Fred saying nothing.

Amanda cleared her throat. "Did you—did you know Andy?"

David reached over and squeezed her hand briefly. "Yes, I had seen and talked with him several times. I think he was the only reason Jon didn't thrash me and throw me out when I visited. He was a great guy. I could never get him to go out bar-hopping or clubbing, and he never seemed to have any interest in the females that would give him the eye. He told me he had 'the real thing' waiting at home."

Amanda nodded sadly. David continued softly. "I knew then that it wasn't Jon I should be jealous of, but Andy." He looked at her and smiled. "But now Jon has found and married you. I should be so lucky."

"It will happen for you, David." Amanda patted his knee.

Embarrassed, he cleared his throat. "I'm hoping it might happen for Kelly and Joey. My parents are the obstacle there."

"How so?" Amanda was surprised.

"Well, Mom put in sabotaging that relationship, pushing Kelly toward other 'more eligible' guys and trying to micro-manage her life. And Kelly feels this overwhelming loyalty to Dad, that he somehow needs protection from our Mom's ways. I personally believe Dad made his bed with Mom, and he can sleep in it. I guess Joey got tired of toeing the line and hoping it would all work out. He says he is taking the position Silas is offering down here. I'm at the point I think I'd like to settle down here too."

"How does Kelly feel about all this?"

"Well, it is a double-edged sword. She has always been crazy about Joey. He proposed once, but Mom talked Kelly out of it. Kelly is tied to Dad, and she is also a driving force behind the company right now. But as long as she stays in Colorado, I don't think she will ever make the break from the parents and allow herself to find love. I've tried to talk to both Joey and Kelly, but they are both stubborn, and I don't know whether they can find a compromise. Dad is really worried about her too."

"Maybe your mom's not liking me will take the heat off Kelly and Joey long enough for them to work it out," Amanda suggested softly.

"Gloria? Don't let her scare you. She is secretly intimidated that Jon is head over heels for you, and that she can't control the situation. Don't back down when she comes charging at you. If you push back, she can't handle that, and suddenly she crumples. She's used to being the family tyrant, and Kelly and Jon allow her. Joey and I don't. And I'm getting the feeling that Dad is beginning to swat back."

David smiled. "Mom wasn't always this bad. I think we helped make her the monster she is."

Amanda shook her head. "David! What an awful thing to say about your mother."

"But true," David persisted. "Amanda, by now Mom has had your past thoroughly investigated, and she thinks there's little about you she doesn't know."

Amanda looked shocked. But David patted her arm. "But she doesn't know the important stuff. And Jon fed her some of that the other night at dinner when you were off with the senator. He told her to lay off. You needn't fear Jon's loyalty to you."

"Really? I don't want to be the cause of friction between him and his family," Amanda murmured, her face creased into a frown.

"It seems to me that Jon has made his choice and is happy with it," Fred, silent until this point, interjected. "And he brought his mother out to the farm while you were in the hospital sick. I think she came away with a taste of Jon's happiness."

"She did," David confirmed. "Now if she can just turn loose and allow him to be happy with you . . . ."

"I just want you all to like me," Amanda countered, blinking.

"Dad and Kelly do, and Mom does too, if she would just admit it," David grinned. "And, Sis, I adore you. You're my favorite sister-in-law."

Amanda laughed. "I'm your only sister-in-law."

"That's irrelevant," David retorted, laughing too.

Amanda turned to Fred. "Could we stop at the cottage?"

Fred nodded, turning a corner.

Soon they pulled into the driveway of the small neat residence that Amanda used to call home for a couple of years. She remembered how Marjorie had talked her into buying it at a foreclosure sale. It had belonged to a family she knew. When the parents died, the offspring had by that time moved away and had no interest in redeeming the property, which was by that time sadly in need of repair.

The property had become a small source of contention between her and Marjorie. Marjorie had lost the battle of trying to get Amanda to move in with her after Andy's death. Even though Amanda could not bring herself to stay at the farm, where everything reminded her of Andrew, Amanda still had periods where she withdrew into herself and craved solitude, shutting herself away from the world where she had to pretend that everything was all right. After Amanda's breakdown Marjorie had become a mother hen, always close at hand and checking on Amanda.

Amanda had demurred about buying the property, saying she didn't need it and was perfectly content to stay at the apartment above the law office. But Marjorie had insisted that she needed to get away from living at the office, that the house was a good investment, that the house did not need to sit empty and was too nice to become just another rental property. So Marjorie had involved Amanda in a project of renovating the small house, and the next thing Amanda knew she was living there, as a compromise to Marjy.

She gazed at the house. There was a realtor's sign outside.

Fred noted sourly, "Whoever is supposed to be doing this landscaping needs to be fired. I can get out here in the morning and whip it into some shape. It looks sad."

Amanda nodded. "You're right. Pedro has had his hands full with his new business, and he has been sick lately. I told him not to worry about landscaping until he got better."

They got out, and David glanced around admiringly. "This is yours?" he asked.

"Yes," Amanda replied. "I lived here for a time before I ended back at the farm."

"It's nice," David remarked.

Amanda went to the door, disengaging the alarm. They walked in.

"It's a bit dusty. I had some of Marjy's things stored here, but we set it up so that the place could be shown." She looked around ruefully. "It otherwise looks just like I left it."

"I like it," David enthused. "It's for sale?"

"Yes. I really don't need it any more, and it's a shame to leave it unoccupied. There has been some interest, but mostly by people wanting to use it as a rental property. It needs an owner that will love it and make it a home, like it used to be before I owned it."

Fred smiled, and David laughed. "I didn't know you were such a romantic," he teased.

"I'll get the cleaning crew in here in the morning." Amanda's mind was making a list, as she walked quickly through checking the rooms. Then she led the way out and reset the alarm.

They were soon back in the truck and on their way. They pulled up to the sheriff's office administration building and noted the two vehicles sitting in the parking lot.

"Well, we are here," Amanda quipped. "Fred, I don't think we'll be long. We'll see you back at the farm."

The Connors' Crisis

David and she climbed out, and Fred waved as he pulled away. Amanda walked in, David following her. The woman at the front desk looked up and recognized her.

"Hi, Trudy," Amanda greeted the woman. "This is my brother-in-law, Dr. David Connor. David, this is Trudy Shapiro, the Chief's—I mean Sheriff's—right hand person."

"Nice to meet you," David nodded politely.

"We came to pick up the keys and the vehicles," Amanda explained. She could see Petrino and Williams animatedly discussing something through the glass windows of an office.

"Just a minute, and I'll let Bruce know you're here," Trudy offered, picking up the phone receiver and buzzing the office.

Williams picked up the phone and looked out, spying Amanda. He said something to Petrino, who nodded, then beckoned Amanda to come in.

"Wait right here," Amanda told David. Trudy buzzed her in, and she followed the hall and let herself into the office.

"Hello," she started. "I don't mean to bother you. David and I came to pick up the vehicles, and I was told you have the keys."

She idly picked up a pen from the pen holder. "The S.O. must have the same office supply salesman," she quipped.

"What do you mean?" Bruce's attention was drawn to the pen, and he held out his hand. She placed it in his palm and he looked at it curiously. "You have pens like this at the office?"

She nodded. "Yes, some guy left them there with Dinah as samples. Why?"

Bruce was still studying the pen intently. "Can I send someone over to collect them? Might be important." Bruce stared at her, Petrino staring in turn at Bruce, his curiosity piqued.

Amanda was confused. She fought a sudden lethargy. "Yes. Why?"

"Just humor me," Bruce smiled enigmatically, his gaze meeting Petrino's. He quickly scoured the room, then turned on a clock radio blaring music and excused himself. "Hang on just a minute," he walked out and waved one of the investigators to him, handing him the item and gesticulating around the room.

Her temples pounding with a sudden headache, Amanda allowed her eyes to roam over the desk, where an object was lying encased in a clear plastic evidence bag. Suddenly alarmed, her eyes grew wide.

"Where did you find this?" she demanded, startled.

"Speak softly," Petrino warned, alerted to Bruce's actions. "Do you recognize it?" Petrino watched her face closely.

229

"Yes, it's mine, my butcher knife from home," she stammered involuntarily. She noted that there was dried blood on the handle and blade.

Bruce returned, taking in Amanda's interest in the knife. "It was found by a jogger about a block from Ralph Carmichael's house alongside the road," Bruce volunteered, his voice low. He bent over and whispered in Petrino's ear. Charlie nodded.

Amanda turned white. Petrino noticed it, stepped up and gently pushed her into a chair in front of the desk.

"Have you been missing it?" Petrino interrogated her.

"Y-yes," she stuttered, her hand going to her throat. "I just thought perhaps one of us mislaid it somewhere, because we use it for everything." Her thoughts were whirring. She fought down a sudden bout of panic. Why? How? she asked herself.

"When did you last see it?" Bruce urged excitedly.

"I—I don't know." She tried to recall. "Maybe Sunday. We have several, but this—" she stared at the object, "this is my favorite, because it was Mom's."

She trembled. "Was it—?"

"We don't know yet," Petrino maintained softly. "We just retrieved it, and it's going to the lab." Charlie leaned back against the desk in front of her.

"Who has been in your home since you last saw it?" Bruce wanted to know, his voice a whisper over the blaring of the radio.

"No one," she muttered. "Jon, me. Charlie came to dinner Monday, David was there a little while Tuesday evening. Fred maybe. Joanna generally comes on Monday mornings to clean, but Jon was off Monday, so she came Tuesday instead."

"What about the security system—have you had it on while gone from home?" Bruce inquired quietly.

"Not always," Amanda said slowly. "We had gotten lax since Jon—since he moved in. And I leave it off if I know Joanna is coming."

She suddenly stared at Bruce. "So it was your men who took the letter openers and the knife from the law office?"

Bruce's head jerked involuntarily. "There were none there. I wondered about that."

Petrino looked grave. "So someone has been in your home and office as well, and before we got there."

"Speaking of which," Amanda fished in her pocket, "Ralph saw one of the cleaning crew today at our office that can put him there Tuesday night until after 8:00. This is her contact information." She handed the slip of paper over.

Petrino looked out the window and saw David standing in the lobby. His eyes narrowed speculatively. "Can we get a statement from Dr. Connor?" he wanted to know.

Amanda stood shakily. "No," she insisted agitatedly. "Not right now. I'll see about tomorrow. Can I have the keys, please?"

Petrino stared at her a moment, then shrugged. Bruce walked to the desk and pulled out the center drawer, producing the car keys and handing them to her.

"Thanks," she managed as she turned to walk out.

"Are you OK?" Petrino's voice was gentle. He took her arm. "Are you sure?" She saw him glance out suspiciously at David standing in the lobby.

"I'm just fine," she quavered, shaking him off.

"Amanda, don't share this with anyone just yet," Charlie stopped her, his voice almost inaudible.

She gazed at him, wide-eyed. "Why? I'm supposed to keep this secret? You don't seriously think—?"

"Just promise to give me some time to do what I need to do with this," Charlie whispered, his voice almost pleading. "Otherwise, I will have to haul them all in again for questioning today, now."

"Why? I just volunteered this information to you, identified the knife, and you are now asking me to keep it from the ones I love and am trying to protect?" Amanda's voice rose angrily.

Charlie glanced quickly around, his jaw jutting ominously. He shook his head warningly. "Don't say it," he growled, his volume rising as well, ignoring Bruce's silent admonition. "I see the words forming on your lips: 'Do your worst'. But you know and I know that I will if pushed. Do we need to run last night's play again? You may think it an exercise in futility, but I think I'll get something out of them this time, perhaps even a waiver of counsel and a statement in lieu of another public invitation to stay in our fine facility."

Amanda paused, her hand reaching out and grabbing the back of the chair by the door, her fingers curling into a fist. She knew Charlie was trying to warn her, but she also knew he was not bluffing. The tension at the farm was already palpable, and she knew that nerves were frayed to the breaking point.

She was suddenly afraid at what might occur if Charlie made good his threat. She also knew how relentless Charlie was during interrogation, and how an innocent reply could turn into something else entirely. And Bruce, always been Charlie's protégé, had honed the same techniques. They made a formidable and sometimes ruthless team, and had broken many a case with their tactics. Jon had already provided a statement, but luckily had an alibi. She knew it wouldn't take much to have Ralph and David cave in as well, and they were not as fortunate. Ralph was already wanting to cooperate, and might have a witness putting him elsewhere. However, David did not, David was frightened, and Charlie was primed and angry.

"You wouldn't?" she whispered. She was suddenly frightened too. She thought of the butcher knife. What if—? No, don't be foolish, she told herself. She had a duty to protect them, even if she was suddenly filled with doubts about what was going on.

She noted that Charlie was regarding her, his eyes suddenly questioning. I mustn't let him see my uncertainty, she thought as she pulled herself more erect, her chin defiant.

Charlie also hesitated. Amanda gazed at him, suddenly alert. "What is it?" she countered, her voice suddenly soft.

"Someone is watching this very carefully, planting things for us to find," Charlie said very quietly. "There is a lot at stake here, and I'm not just talking about my future as sheriff."

"What are you saying?"

"Just to watch your step, and make it look good," he whispered, his lips barely moving. "We're being watched."

He looked around and saw several sets of eyes curiously regarding them through the windows. He went over and shut off the radio. "Damned nuisance," he snapped. "So, Amanda," his voice rose, and he turned cold, "looks like you have a decision to make. To borrow your words from last night, shall we dance?" He slammed his fist against the desk for emphasis.

Her jaw set angrily to mask her fear, she remonstrated, "I'll hold off for now. But I'm warning you, Petrino, this isn't over. Stay away from my clients."

"Or what?" he sneered, his eyes not leaving her face. "I will not allow you to interfere with our investigation, Mrs. Connor," he said derisively. "If I have questions, I will ask. If your clients want to exercise their rights, they can tell me so, and I will honor their request."

"Didn't you tell one of your cronies just last night you didn't want your evidence tainted?" she bristled. "They have already exercised their rights last night. You mess with my clients, and I promise you it won't be good for you too."

"Oh, I think it will," Charlie almost smiled, his voice suddenly lethally calm.

"You step over the line, Sheriff, and your ass is mine," she spat.

"Is that a promise? Sounds like fun," he retorted, his eyes flashing. Wouldn't be the first time, he thought ruefully.

The Connors' Crisis

She turned on her heel and stormed out, slamming the door behind her. The confrontation had drained her. She marched to the lobby, feeling the eyes of others on her.

David saw her ashen face. "What is it?" His face showed concern.

"Nothing. Let's go," she said shortly.

They walked out together, and she handed him the Land Rover keys. "I'll take Ralph's car. If you will follow me, we'll stop at a men's clothing store down the block here. I'll introduce you to Jerri, and she will help you." Amanda spoke rapidly, her eyes not meeting David's. "We'll just say you made an unexpected stop to visit, and your luggage got lost. I have accounts at the stores, so pick up what you want. There's a salon and pharmacy on the block as well, everything you might need. Jerri knows everyone, and there's no denying from your looks that you're related to Jon. Then I need to stop by the office, and will meet you back home."

"What's wrong?" he insisted. "Something just happened in there. What did I do?"

"Nothing," she smiled distractedly. "We've got a lot to do, so let's get started."

"Amanda?" His voice was a question, a plea, his eyes wide, staring at her.

"David, it will all be OK," she smiled with more confidence than she felt.

David nodded mutely, his eyes still on her anxiously.

They walked out. She climbed into Ralph's Escalade and adjusted the seats and mirrors. Soon they arrived at the men's store and she introduced David to Jerri, who was unfailingly solicitous, her eyes lively with curiosity and interest over the good-looking man. Jerri promised to show David around, and Amanda smiled her thanks.

Amanda left the store, the questions churning in her head. She knew Jon and Ralph could not be guilty. Or could they? What about David? She realized she knew far less about David than she realized. If he was in love with Lauren, and she showed back up in his life, just to turn around and accuse two other men of fathering her child while she had been with him, would he be angry enough to—?

For that matter, there were large unknowns between her and Jon. I'm not going there, she told herself stoically. He's been with me. Enough said.

And although she had known Ralph practically all their lives, this sudden paternity suit threatened not only his political aspirations, but his marriage to Claire. She knew how devoted Ralph had become to Claire, and how much his life now revolved around her.

Any man could be pushed to the point of losing control. Could one of them have snapped and—? No, that's plain silly, she told herself. None of them would resort to violence, to murder.

Amanda was soon striding into the law office.

Sheila looked up, relief in her face. "I've been worried," she confessed.

"Everything OK?" Amanda was preoccupied, her mind on Charlie's words.

"Yes. The cleaning crew is finished. Ralph came by earlier, but didn't make a fuss and left. There have been several phone calls for you. Bruce Williams just called and said he was sending a man over."

"These pens," Amanda picked up the one in the holder. "He wants all of them." She stared at the pen.

"Why?" Sheila was startled. "I was going to gather them all up to trash before I left today, per your orders."

"Have no idea." Amanda was studying the pen carefully.

"Anyone in particular call?" Amanda tried to focus, but the sight of her blood-stained butcher knife on Bruce's desk was unnerving, and she was still wondering about the pens' significance.

"Some man keeps calling, asking for you. He has called twice today. He won't leave his name or number, and says he will try again tomorrow, that you will want to speak to him."

Amanda sat down at Dinah's desk. "Let me sign whatever you need."

Sheila quickly brought her documents, which Amanda reviewed cursorily and signed. She glanced through the phone messages and dictated instructions.

"And, Sheila? Please call Joanna and ask her to spiff up the cottage first thing tomorrow morning, in case Ralph and David need to stay there a few days," Amanda stated absently. "The security system is on, so Ralph or I will need to let her in." Amanda looked up. "And, Sheila, tell Joanna that I need her to do it personally, and alone. If she can't, call me. I'll make other arrangements."

"What's going on?" Sheila was alerted to Amanda's mood.

"I don't really know," Amanda admitted ruefully. "And I frankly don't know who to trust, so I don't want just anyone having access to anything of mine right now." She rubbed her forehead wearily.

"Go home, Amanda," Sheila suggested. "This will all be here in the morning. You need some rest."

Amanda nodded. "I'll check in, and you can reach me if there's any emergency."

Amanda made it to the Escalade and headed toward home, her mind playing over the questions over and over. Someone had taken her butcher knife from home, and it ended up near the murder scene. Who and why?

Her cell phone rang. She looked at the number, but it was apparently blocked. She answered. "Hello?"

"Mrs. Connor? We have some business to discuss," a male voice spoke.

"How did you get this number? You can call the—"

"You will want this call to remain private. It involves your husband, your law partner, and even your brother-in-law."

"What do you mean?" Amanda was impertinent, her mind racing.

"You recognized the knife found today?"

"Who are you?" Amanda whispered, suddenly tense.

"You're missing some other items. Maybe you have realized that, and maybe not."

"I'm hanging up." Amanda was short.

"I wouldn't do that if I were you. I have some evidence you might be interested in seeing."

"Evidence? Shouldn't you be talking to law enforcement?" Amanda tried to quell the shaking of her voice.

"I happen to know you have no early morning appointments tomorrow."

"How did you know that?" Amanda interrupted hotly.

The voice went on unperturbedly. "I will be waiting for you in room 426 at the Carlyle Hotel. Eight o'clock sharp tomorrow morning. Come alone and tell no one. No one. Remember I'm watching. Otherwise things could happen that you'd rather not see happen."

The phone clicked dead.

Amanda stared at her phone, fascinated. A car horn blew, and she was brought back to the present, jerking the steering wheel as she noted she had strayed across the line.

Charlie was right. But who was this? Why was this happening? Amanda felt her chest constrict with sudden tension, smothering her. She forced herself to take a deep breath.

She called Sheila quickly, her hand shaking. When Sheila answered, Amanda spoke rapidly, not bothering to identify herself. "Sheila, have you shared my schedule with anyone? Told anyone what I have on the calendar tomorrow? Has anyone wanted an appointment tomorrow?"

"Of course not. I'd have told you. Ralph looked at the calendar on my computer when he came by. Why?"

"No one came in? There was no chance for someone to perhaps glance at the calendar?"

Amanda knew she was alarming Sheila. "Amanda, I am very cognizant of client confidentiality," Sheila's tone was suddenly brisk, defensive. "No, I've let no one see the calendar other than you and Ralph."

"I'm not accusing you of anything," Amanda spoke rapidly, soothingly. "I trust you completely. It's just that some weird things are happening."

"You can say that again," Sheila muttered.

"I'm sorry for scaring you, Sheila." Amanda slowed her breathing down. "It will all be OK." She realized she had said that to David earlier today. "I'll be in a little late in the morning. I have—have to take care of something."

"Put the alarm on when you leave," she ordered. "Change the code." I'm just getting paranoid, but I'm not taking any more chances, she thought.

"Amanda, what is happening?" She could hear the concern in Sheila's voice.

"Just humor me." Another phrase heard today, from Bruce Williams. "It's probably nothing. I will talk to you later."

When she pulled up to the farmhouse, Amanda noted that Fred's truck was parked outside, but David and the Land Rover had not returned.

She made her way into the house. She could hear voices in the kitchen, but went straight upstairs. She stripped off and stepped in the shower, lathering up with scented body wash, hoping to wash away her turmoil. Now I have to keep this information to myself, she concluded angrily as she let the hot water wash over her, rinsing the soap off and needling her aching neck.

She finally cut off the shower and dried herself off, throwing a terry robe around her. The doubts lingered. Could one of them actually—? David? Ralph? Jon?

"No," she irritably answered her image in the mirror.

"No what?" Jon's voice interrupted her thoughts.

She turned, and Jon was framed in the doorway, lazily leaning against the doorpost, regarding her.

"Nothing," she tried to smile, turning away.

Jon took her hand and drew her into the bedroom. "I'm not convinced," he spoke softly as he pulled her over to the bed.

"I'm so hot," she complained as he drew her down with him, caressing her chin, his arm around her.

"Normally I would ignore that statement and make you hotter," he murmured. "But instead I shall be merciful and allow you to cool off first." He ran his fingers down her side, and she closed her eyes.

"Now tell me what is bothering you, love," he whispered.

"Nothing," she insisted.

"I can see it in the set of your shoulders," he murmured, pulling the robe loose and kissing and kneading them.

"I guess I'm just stressed," she replied, her eyes closed. "So tired."

"Where's David?" he asked.

"I gave him the Land Rover and left him in Jerri's hands. He's getting what he needs in town." She glanced up at him.

"Did Charlie give you any more information about the investigation?"

"No," she lied quickly, her eyes flickering away from his.

"You would tell me if he had, wouldn't you?" Jon asked suddenly.

"Of course I would." Amanda was still.

Jon stopped, his eyes searching her face. He sat up. "I know you. Something is up."

"It's nothing." She closed her eyes. "Please, Jon, believe me," she added desperately.

He stood abruptly. "Fred is preparing dinner, and it should be ready around six. I'll go back and see if there's anything I can do."

He left quickly, Amanda looking bleakly at his retreating form.

Jon made it downstairs to the kitchen, where Ralph was setting the table and David had returned and was folding napkins. Fred was presiding over the stove.

Jon without preamble launched into David, his voice cold. "What the hell happened while you and Amanda were gone?"

David, surprised at Jon's angry tone, turned defensive. "I have no idea," he answered sullenly. "Why do you ask?"

"Something isn't right." Jon was agitated as he grasped the back of the dining chair, his knuckles white.

"She got into it with Petrino at the sheriff's department."

"What about?" Ralph intervened, putting his hand on Jon's shoulder warningly.

"I don't know. Amanda had me wait in the lobby, but I could see them in the office there. They were practically shouting at each other. I thought they might even come to blows. Then she stormed out. She wouldn't say what happened. She just clammed up."

Jon turned, white-hot with anger. "OK, that's it. Charlie is not going to badger my wife. Petrino's going to tell me what's going on, or—"

"Stop it," Fred growled, his voice low. "There's something bigger going on, and Amanda and Charlie know it. Don't you see? They don't ever fight in public, unless it is in court. They are both unfailingly polite to a fault. That's their parents' upbringing. So this is unlike both of them."

"Fred's got a point," Ralph agreed. "They don't fuss and fight and carry on with each other like Amanda and I do. I mean, even this murder investigation wouldn't cause them to turn on each other like this, would it?"

"You think they are posturing?" Jon asked as the thought hit him. "That means they know they are playing to an audience."

"What audience?" David rubbed his head confusedly.

"Did you see anyone there who seemed inordinately interested in what was going on?" Ralph was specific.

David frowned. "No, but at one point almost all the staff was watching the fireworks, even Trudy and I." He chuckled. "Amanda's kind of sexy when she's angry."

He realized what he had said, and looked quickly, apprehensively at his brother. But Jon smiled. "Yes, she is," he conceded. They all laughed.

Amanda walked in, casually dressed in slacks and white button-down long shirt, her hair pulled back, without makeup, appearing pale. "What is so funny?" she asked stiffly.

"Oh, nothing," Jon remarked, as the others grinned.

"Some humor at my expense?" she bit her lip, still tense.

Fred had disappeared, but he walked back into the room, a Waterford tumbler with some liquid in his hand. "You look like you could use this." He handed it to her. Jon pulled out a chair and indicated for her to sit.

"I want you to enjoy this meal. I think you once said it was your favorite," Fred supplied.

"It is," Amanda smiled then.

They all pitched in and served up the food onto dishes and soon had everything on the table. Jon brought in a couple bottles of Bordeaux and expertly opened them, as David set wine glasses on the table.

Jon poured wine in the glasses and they sat down. He lifted his glass and said, "This too shall pass, to be replaced by something equally tedious."

They smiled and drank.

As the dishes were being passed, David spoke up. "I think perhaps Ralph and I should get out of your hair tomorrow. Amanda's cottage looks quite nice, and I think we can hole up there for a day or two."

Amanda suddenly spoke up. "No, I think we all need to stay put for right now."

Jon looked at her, surprised. Ralph chimed in, "No, David is right. There's work, and we can't remain cloistered out here while speculation grows. We need to act as normally as possible."

"But—" Amanda faltered.

Jon covered her hand with his, his gaze penetrating. "What is it, Amanda? Tell us."

She saw that all eyes were upon her. "Nothing. I just think—but you're right, of course. With all of us under one roof and this cloud of tension, we are at the point of snapping each other's heads off," she capitulated reluctantly. "Joanna will clean up the place first thing in the morning."

"Then it's settled," Ralph remarked. "David and I will pull out for our temporary quarters tomorrow."

Amanda was silent. Jon watched her surreptitiously.

Ralph continued, "Besides, I get jealous of all this nightly activity going on while Claire is so far from home. Could you kids hold down the noise tonight? Geez."

"Yeah, or else I'm going to need a bigger pillow," David complained good-naturedly.

Jon picked up Amanda's hand and brought it to his lips. "That's a tall order," he murmured, and Amanda smiled tightly, squeezing his hand.

Later that night, after they retired to bed, Jon snuggled up to Amanda's back. "What's going on with Petrino?" he asked gently, nuzzling her neck.

"What do you mean?" He felt her body stiffen.

"David said you two had an almost knock-down brawl at the sheriff's department today." Jon kissed her ear and ran his hand around to cup her breast, nibbling her shoulder.

"He was just demanding statements, and I was giving him as good as he sent," Amanda yawned.

"Amanda, you are coiled up as tight as a spring. Please talk to me," Jon whispered, drawing her closer.

"I'm just so exhausted," she whispered, her voice tremulous.

Jon pulled her around to face him. "Too tired for me to make love to you?"

Amanda swallowed, then reached to entwine her fingers in his hair and bring his mouth to hers. "No, never that."

Sometime after midnight later that evening, there was a knock on the front door of Charlie Petrino's house.

Charlie opened the door, still bleary from sleep.

"Sheriff, I'm sorry to bother you." Toby Townsend stood on the porch, his face grave. Another man, whom Charlie immediately recognized, was with him. "But could we have a few minutes of your time? I need your help. It's urgent."

CHAPTER 21

THURSDAY

Amanda hesitated before the hotel room door, then opened it, stepping inside. The room was dim, light emanating from a lamp beside the door. She stood there uncertainly.

A lamp was on in the corner of the suite. Illuminated was a man, dressed all in black, sitting in a chair at the desk there. His features were in shadow, but his dark face was thin, his hair close cropped. His build was deceptively slim, but his shoulders and arms appeared sinewy under his jacket. He smiled slightly as he stood.

"Mrs. Connor, please sit." He indicated the other chair at the table.

"I'd rather stand," Amanda blinked, speaking more confidently than she felt.

"I insist. We have business to discuss." The man waited for her patiently.

"I am unaware of any business I should have with you," Amanda insisted, her eyes steely.

The man's eyes bored into hers. "It won't take long. You are a busy woman. But it is in your best interests to hear me out."

She approached the desk and seated herself stiffly in a chair drawn in front of it. The man reseated himself.

"Do you know who I am?" he inquired, watching her closely.

"No," she denied, "but I've seen your face before. You were at the restaurant the other day with Esme and the legislative delegation. Shouldn't we be introduced?" Her jaw had a determined set.

"No need," he smiled again, his face looking sinister against the harsh shadows cast by the lamp. "I believe you know who I'm representing."

Amanda was brisk. "I'm not into clandestine meetings. I told Esme if she wanted to talk to me to contact me herself."

"We have rather delicate matters to discuss, so I am here instead." The man gazed at her intently. "I am certain you would not want anyone to overhear."

"You are mistaken about me," Amanda tensed. "I have no secrets that require me to skulk around. Tell me, is Esme behind all this?"

"It is not necessary to use her name in this discussion," he smiled thinly, but his eyes glinted with annoyance. "I have personally taken on this project. This meeting is to make sure you and I understand each other. You have vital interests at stake. Now what do you mean by 'all this'?" The man's eyes bored through her.

"The paternity suits, the casting of suspicion, the murder, the planting of evidence?"

"That's quite a mouthful of accusation, Mrs. Connor," he laughed humorlessly. "All baseless speculation on your part. You know better than to ask. She is simply a law-abiding citizen of great influence, just doing her civic duty and informing the officials of her informed opinions, trying to guide them to make decisions in the best interest of the public."

"Like hell," Amanda countered, her eyes flashing angrily. "She's a power monger. Answer me—was she happy with the appointment of the acting sheriff? Charlie wasn't her first choice."

"It's not all bad." The man's voice was calm, as if he was explaining to a child. "And it can always change at any time. He may become a hero, or he may become dispensable." He smiled, his face leering. "Esme adds a touch of class to her little intrigues. I, on the other hand, am not so solicitous. My plans do not come in pretty packages, and are solely outcome-based."

A touch of fear flitted across her mind, but Amanda was determined not to show it. "Why is all this happening? What does she, you have in mind?"

"Just a periodic political restructuring of the governmental elite." He was chillingly polite. "It happens all the time."

"It's apparent that Ralph is being discredited, but the methods seem extreme to me. Why? Why would you ruthlessly destroy his life? He is a fine man, an excellent lawyer. This is a dream of his. Just who does she have in mind for judge, if not Ralph Carmichael?"

He leaned forward, his amber eyes intent upon her. "You," he said simply.

Amanda choked, then laughed mirthlessly. "Oh, that's a good one. But I am not amused. I wouldn't be on her list if I was the last attorney in the circuit."

"Oh, don't be so sure of that," the man continued staring at her. "You are the candidate that we want."

"Why?" Amanda's jaw jutted out stubbornly. "I've told her I'm not interested. I'm not minion material. What do you want from me?"

"Nothing—yet. Don't you think it's time the county had a woman judge?"

Amanda was emphatic, her anger rising. "I've already given my answer."

"You would not reconsider, even for the sake of your law partner and friend? For your husband? And there is his brother as well, of whom you seem quite fond. All of them mired in this mess. It is frightening, the possibility of being charged with murder at any time," he queried, his voice almost gentle.

"What do you mean?" She fought a surge of rage. Was she being blackmailed?

"Isn't it obvious? You must think of the well-being of others," he replied, his voice low. "So many lives and reputations are at stake these days. Police suddenly stumble upon damning evidence. It is so easy to lose one's good name and never recover. There's a real need for honest, trustworthy, loyal public officials these days."

He picked up and tossed a manila envelope in front of her on the desk. "I believe these will help influence your decision. They are quite good, if I must say so myself."

Amanda stared at the envelope. "Please," the man urged, smiling cat-like. "I would like your opinion on my handiwork."

She opened the clasp. Inside were various 8" X 10" glossy photographs. She swallowed convulsively. There were two of Lauren Mallory, in a state of near nudity, kissing Jon, Jon's arms wrapped around her. There was one photo of Ralph in nothing but a pair of boxers, dancing arm-in-arm with Lauren, who was naked, his face laughingly looking at hers. Amanda noted that the backgrounds were indistinguishable. There was a photo of David and Lauren, also dancing, but both fully dressed. She remembered seeing them thusly at the party.

Amanda caught her breath sharply. But she was unprepared for the last photo, which was of her and Charlie, in swimwear, entwined on a bed in an intimate position.

"You son of a bitch," she managed when she found her voice. "You're just some two-bit chiseler. How did you do this? They are all lies," she choked, standing.

"Are they?" he replied calmly. "Are they real, or masterful artistic creations? I don't think an expert could really tell what is real and what is cut and pasted."

He smiled malevolently. "Don't you think these should be shared with the sheriff as part of his homicide investigation? Or perhaps not all of them? The media might be interested."

He also stood, facing her across the desk. "I would really prefer to keep them between us for now." His voice was low. "Sit down, Mrs. Connor."

"So you would so callously destroy reputations with this—these lies?" Amanda spat, still standing. "Just to get me to apply for judge? I'm not for sale, not for Esme, not for you."

"Let's just say that I'm sure you have vested interests you will protect, and that you're perfect for the job and will do the right thing." He pulled out a silver cigarette case. "Care for one?"

She shook her head, seething, trying to calm herself and determine what he was not saying. The blood was hammering in her head, and she fought the urge to reach out and throttle him. "Who else is on her payroll? Who is breaking and entering my premises, stealing items? You? If you can manufacture these, you must be multi-talented," Amanda offered coldly.

The man was unperturbed as he lit the cigarette carefully. "Mrs. Connor, you sound quite paranoid to me. Why anyone would go to such lengths is beyond me. You are grasping. You must ask yourself why these things are happening. I think the old expression, and one followed by the simple folks of this town, is that if it walks and quacks like a duck, it must be a duck. A corollary of Occam's Razor, I believe. The simplest explanation must be the best one. Don't you think so?"

"So if evidence points to someone, he is automatically guilty? Even if someone is manipulating the entire scene?" she stared at him icily. "Even if you are creating a fiction and hustling me to do your will?" She sank back into her chair, her hand over her mouth, suddenly nauseous. Damn, she thought, I don't need to be sick right now. I can't show any weakness with this man.

"Are you all right? Have I frightened you?"

"I'm so angry I could hurt you without thinking twice," Amanda muttered.

The man laughed benignly. "They have medications nowadays for that."

Amanda swallowed, the memory of Bill's plying her with drugs without her knowledge suddenly flashing through her mind. She suppressed a shiver.

He continued, his voice almost kind. "You realize that you have taken on probably the most complex and multi-faceted case of your career. You have many warring allegiances involved. So much could go wrong, evidence popping up pointing to those you care for. These photos—they are not all contrived, I assure you. You must wonder which are not. And you have doubts. I can see it in your face."

"I have none now," she snapped.

"Oh, but you should. For instance, I'm wondering if perhaps you aren't being willfully blind about your husband's past."

"I don't think so," Amanda's eyes flashed. She stood shakily and turned to leave.

"I mean, there's so much about him you don't really know," the man went on, his eyes watching her as he waved the cigarette smoke away, his fingers graceful like a pianist's. "He was a highly decorated FBI agent. But are you so sure of Jon Connor's virtue?"

She stopped. He paused dramatically. "For instance, did you know that Ms. Mallory was pregnant at the time of her murder? That she had named Jon Connor as the father of this child as well?"

Amanda was startled. "No," she rejoined forcefully, turning back to face the man. "You are one incredible liar. I don't believe you. No such information has been provided to me."

"Well," he smiled benignly, "the investigation is still young. DNA testing will produce much useful information for the prosecution. Are you so certain now that your husband has had no contact with Ms. Mallory prior to her demise?"

"He's been with me. I believe him," Amanda insisted. "Why are you so interested, and why are you doing this, blackmailing me?"

"I'm surprised at your accusation," he responded in mock derision. "No blackmail is involved. I'm merely freely imparting some information, something I'm sure that would be critical for the defense team to consider. I assume from your reaction that the Sheriff and his men have not shared this?"

Amanda was silent, her mind whirring.

The man looked at his watch and stood, approaching her. "Consider carefully what I've imparted. But I would advise that you not share this conversation with anyone else. My network is rather widespread, as I'm sure you must surmise by now." His voice dropped to a whisper. "Perhaps even what goes on in the privacy of your home."

"My home?" Amanda was stunned, and her hands clenched into fists. "Whoever you are, you are going to wish you never met me," Amanda flung out coldly.

"I think otherwise. Brave words, but I can see you are worried. And your disclosure of this conversation I fear would likely result in unintended consequences."

"Unintended consequences for whom?" Amanda demanded.

"For you, for others, those you are so anxious to defend," his voice raised slightly, as if he was aggravated by her question. "Don't forget your copies. I think they are of a quality for framing." He stood too, placing the photos back in the envelope. "And it might be advisable for you to check your own mail for a while, in case some additional 'evidence' should make its way to you."

Amanda froze. The man held the envelope out to her. She hesitated, then took it. They faced each other, only a couple of feet between them.

Amanda's anger overcame her. "Do you understand the judicial selection process?" she asked coldly. "This is not some simple appointment process. There are applications, and interviews by the judicial nominating committee, who send up names of the top picks to the governor for consideration." She stared at him, her lawyer's skills at argument awakened. "I'm not in the running, even if I apply. I have no political bent, and have participated in none of the activities that the committee generally regards as marks of a good judge.

"So what do you plan to do about that? Bully the committee? Bribe, threaten, blackmail them? Surely you're not going to kill them off? I'm not going to help you commit whatever crimes you have planned. I don't intend to be part of this."

The man moved quickly, silently toward her. Amanda, suddenly apprehensive, backed away, but the chair prevented her escape. He grasped her wrist with his hand, pulling her closer to him. She gasped as his hand cupped her chin.

"Your husband hasn't tamed you, I can see," he smiled, his face so close she could feel his breath on her cheek. "I have learned my lessons well at the side of Esme Townsend, and I have the matter well in hand. And Mrs. Connor, I generally get my way, and I don't much mind how I go about it. So if I were you, I would take this matter very seriously," he said, his voice lethal, his mouth only inches from hers.

"Let go of me," she hissed, trying to snatch away. Panic suddenly seized her as he released her chin and reached in his pocket.

"Perhaps you require a bit more incentive to accede to my wishes?" he snarled.

There was a loud knocking at the door of the adjoining room.

"Come in," the man ordered expectantly, his grip on her tightening as she desperately tried to jerk free.

The door opened, and a young man dressed in a tailored tan suit strode in, followed by a bellman. The first, Toby Townsend, was obviously enraged, his lips bloodless. The latter looked familiar, but she didn't have time to figure it out. Her assailant, surprised, stepped back and released Amanda.

"Keep your hands off her, you bastard." Toby moved quickly toward the man.

"What are you doing here?" he demanded angrily, drawing himself up arrogantly but stepping back.

"Was I not who you were expecting?" Toby Townsend's eyes were cold, his movements quick. For a moment Amanda thought he might strike the man. But Toby stopped at Amanda, taking her arm. "Are you OK?" his voice softened, his brow creased with concern.

Amanda breathed a sigh of relief. "Yes, Toby." He could feel her trembling.

"What are you doing here?" Toby asked, his eyes glittering on the man before them.

"She was here at my invitation, discussing some mutual business," the man replied smoothly, trying to mask his irritation.

"Our business, as you call it, is finished," Amanda managed, turning and looking at him coldly, still grasping the envelope.

The other man smiled thinly. "We'll be in touch again soon. I shall eagerly await your decision."

"Leave her alone, or you'll answer to me." Toby was brisk.

Without another word Toby squeezed Amanda's arm gently as he urged her out of the room with him. He dismissed the bellman, led her to the elevator, punched a button, and pulled her in after him.

"That man is dangerous," he spoke tersely. "You have no idea how much."

Amanda nodded, feeling faint. "Who exactly is he? How did you know I was here?"

Toby looked straight ahead. "Let's just say I stumbled upon some intelligence that led me here."

Amanda started to speak, but he put his finger to his lips, shaking his head. She nodded. He put his arm around her comfortingly. He felt her shivering. "It's OK, Amanda," he whispered. "It's time Mom and I had a talk. I'm not going to let this—whatever he is to her—terrorize the community and those I care about. He won't hurt you."

"It may be too late," her voice was almost inaudible. She blinked back tears.

"No," he squeezed her shoulders quickly, then reached over and slipped something surreptitiously into her pocket. Surprised, she looked at him. He smiled tightly.

The elevator doors opened and they stepped out. "Please excuse me, Amanda. I must find Mom." Toby's jaw had a determined set. "I have some urgent business to discuss with her. It won't wait. I will see you later? We need to talk." He looked at her inquiringly.

She nodded mutely. He reached over and pecked a kiss on her cheek. "Take care of yourself. Stay away from him," he whispered. "I'll be in touch later today."

Toby walked determinedly away. Still inwardly shaking, Amanda hastily made her way through the hotel foyer to the front.

I've just been made a pawn in this man's game, she seethed. No, Esme Townsend's game. Why? Why go to such elaborate lengths? Why discredit Ralph? Why frame others for murder? Why the photos? Just to coerce Amanda into applying for a judgeship? It made no sense. And why her? For what reason?

How did Toby know? Why did he show up? Surely he is not part of this?

Her mind went to the photos in her hand. They're all elaborate cut and pasted pictures for the express purpose of discrediting one or more of the people depicted therein, she determined. But, she argued with herself, are they? The one of me with Charlie is, so it follows that the others are too.

However, she knew the photo of David and Lauren was not a retouch. So, she concluded, what about the ones with Ralph? With Jon?

Amanda wanted to find and confront Jon about the mysterious man's accusations, but doubts assailed her. What if it was all true? What if Jon has not been truthful? What if he's been unfaithful? What if Lauren was pregnant by him? No, she rejected the possibility, that cannot be true, but the thought persisted. Her gut was churning, and a tremor shot through her.

"OK, Amanda, get a grip," she whispered to herself. You're just upset because of your encounter with this man.

She walked briskly out the hotel entrance and summoned the valet for her car. As soon as it arrived, the young man sprang out. "Mrs. Connor, are you well? You look like you're about to faint," he spoke deferentially.

"I'm fine, Jake." She forced herself to be pleasant. "And you?"

"Oh, just another day." He held her door open. She tipped him and dropped into the seat. As she adjusted the seat, he shut the door and she smiled at him.

She laid the envelope in the seat beside her, pulled out the scrap of paper from her pocket and glanced at it. "Fred's—midnight. Alone. We're being watched. Pete."

Chapter 22

The day was grueling, despite Amanda's attempts to lighten the schedule. Ralph was morose and moped around the office dispiritedly. Amanda repented that she had cancelled his appointments.

She finally sent him to the cottage, giving him a key and the new alarm codes for the house and office. "I went by and let Joanna in to clean the place early this morning. Make a list of what you're going to need the next couple days," she ordered.

"Why did you change the office code?" he demanded.

"Because I am frankly nervous after all this business. I just think our security everywhere needs to be tighter." Amanda was wary. "Just humor me, OK?"

After Ralph had gone, Amanda gazed unseeingly over her desk, her thoughts jumbled. She thought about the photos, still in the envelope buried in her attaché case under the desk. She fought the urge to pull them out and review them again. Her gut was still churning in rage.

I need to just give them to Charlie, she told herself. But she knew she couldn't. At that point they became evidence, whether they were authentic or not. And they would damn Charlie as well as the others. She felt the panic rush over her again, and willed herself against its overwhelming her.

I need to confide in Jon, she thought. It's all a pack of lies. But tears filled her eyes. He wouldn't; he loves me. And Ralph wouldn't do anything to jeopardize his marriage to Claire. I know this. Why can't I just accept that? This man is out to ruin us all if I don't dance his tune. But the doubts lingered.

Her eyes alighted on the pen in the pen cup.

"Sheila," she called peremptorily, her face livid.

Sheila walked into the room. Amanda was holding the pen in her hand. "I thought I told you to get rid of these. Didn't Bruce send someone yesterday to collect them all?"

248

"Yes, Amanda." Sheila was perturbed. "I swear I rid this office of them, and even told Joanna if she found any to throw them out."

"Sheila, I depend on you to do what I ask." Amanda was impulsive, angry, her voice strident, her temper frayed.

"Amanda, I have never ignored any request or command of yours," Sheila's jaw set defensively. "I don't understand, but I swear to you they were gone yesterday."

A look of sudden terror crossed Amanda's face. Sheila noted it. "What is it?" she demanded.

"Nothing," Amanda replied, biting her lip, looking away. "I believe you, Sheila. I'm sorry for snapping at you."

Sheila turned to leave, but Amanda stopped her. "Sheila, do you think I'm acting paranoid?" Her voice was soft.

"Amanda, I'm feeling like I'm going mad right now." Sheila gawked at her, shaking her head with frustration. "I'm telling the truth about these pens."

"I know," Amanda whispered. "Let's search the office for them and bundle them up. Call the investigator and tell him we found some more." She tried to joke. "We'll keep the S.O. supplied in magic pens."

Amanda stayed at the office to handle a large multi-party real estate closing, thankful for anything to keep her mind off the events of last two days. She resolutely shut out the memory of the disturbing conversation with the man at the hotel that morning. The pictures haunted her, but she drove the memory out of her mind.

After the closing she summoned the IT man she used for the office systems.

"Tim, I really need for you to make sure no one is hacking into our computers here," she informed him when he arrived.

"Why?" Tim smiled winningly.

"Let's just say I have reason to believe that someone has accessed certain programs, like perhaps the calendar. Maybe I'm just overreacting, but I want to preserve my clients' confidences," Amanda smiled brightly.

Sheila, on the phone, glanced over at her, alarmed.

"OK," Tim replied doubtfully. "But I will probably need some time, perhaps the whole weekend."

"Are there any checks you can do this afternoon?" Amanda demanded anxiously.

Tim looked at her amazedly. "You really are worried," he whispered. "What is happening?"

"I can't say," Amanda admitted miserably.

"OK, OK," Tim said comfortingly, sitting down at Dinah's computer. "I can do some things with the firewall and change some internal codes today.

But the rest is really going to require that your system be down. So you're going to have to close shop or wait for the weekend. And it's Thursday now."

"OK," Amanda agreed reluctantly.

Sheila hung up and walked up to the desk where Amanda was standing looking over Tim's shoulder. "Amanda, Titus Campbell has called twice wanting to talk to you. And some reporter from the Daily News, and yet someone from something called National People Watch Magazine. They asked for Ralph, then you. I told them I'd give you the message."

Amanda turned away. "I don't have the time to deal with the press right now. If they call back, tell them we'll issue a statement very soon. Maybe that will get them off our backs."

She went back into her office, did some dictation, and called Ralph. She avoided meeting Sheila's worried gaze as she left the office for the grocery store to pick up some essential items to stock the cottage pantry. Then she met Ralph and David at the cottage, putting away the items and chatting with them, trying to cheer them up.

Walking out from the kitchen, she found Ralph sitting on the sofa, his head in his hands. Amanda walked up to him. "We're going to make it through this, Ralph," she said softly.

"The press is calling the office, wanting to know what was Lauren Mallory doing in my house, had I slept with her, do I think I'm qualified to be judge inasmuch as I'm under suspicion for murder," he moaned. He looked up, and Amanda saw despair in his eyes. "My whole life, my marriage and career are flashing before my eyes, and I'm innocent. I haven't done anything, Mandy. I'm helpless to stop it."

Amanda believed him. So why can't I believe Jon? she argued with herself. "Ralph, I'll figure out something," she promised, her hand on his shoulder. "It's going to work out, if I have to sue every newspaper in the Southeast."

The corners of his mouth lifted in a small smile. She hugged him. "And I'll do it, too."

"I know it," he murmured. He grasped her hand. "You look tired, Mandy. Are you well?"

"Yes," she assured him, smiling more brightly than she felt.

David stood in the kitchen and looked out across the island at them, saying nothing, his face creased with anxiety.

She dropped by Alex's office just as he was seeing out his last client for the day. He waved her into his office, and she sat down in one of the leather seats.

"Drink?" he offered, pouring himself one from a bottle into a glass, both of which he had pulled out of his lower desk drawer. She shook her head no.

She relayed the information regarding the undisclosed news of the victim's pregnancy, but had on reflection left out her source and the theory that the child was Jon's. She omitted reference to the photos. She debated with herself whether to tell him about the knife. He looked at her shrewdly.

"I know there's something you're wanting to say," he frowned. "What is it?"

"Alex, the police found a knife on the roadside about a block from Ralph's house."

He stared at her. "There's more, isn't there?"

"I promised not to tell so that Charlie wouldn't haul the boys into the station and attempt another interview," she stammered cautiously. "I'm worried."

Alex stood up and moved over to the chair beside her. "Amanda?"

"It was a butcher knife. From the farm, Alex. And it was covered in blood. It's my knife, was my Mom's."

"Does Petrino suspect you now?" Alex was alarmed.

Amanda shook her head. "I don't think so. On Tuesday I was at the courthouse until late, then went directly home. Only minutes later the deputy delivered the paternity papers, and Charlie himself showed up right after that."

"Charlie?" Alex stared at her. "What—?"

"He apparently heard about the paternity complaint, and came out to the house to—to check on me, I guess," she faltered. "He was there when Jon arrived home, and left right after that."

"Did Petrino share any other information with you?" Alex wanted to know, his eyes studying her.

She shook her head. "I did discover that certain items that were missing from the office were not taken by the police." She informed him about the disappearance of the knife and letter openers from the office.

"Amanda, this is dangerous. Can't you get Petrino to divulge what is happening?" Alex probed anxiously.

"We—got into a bit of a public lather at the office," Amanda stammered. "But Charlie thinks, and I know, that someone is manipulating us behind the scenes."

"How do you know?" Alex insisted gently. "Where did you get this information?"

She shook her head. "I can't tell you that just yet. There's so much pointing at Ralph, at David, at—even at Jon. There's a—a lot at stake." She fell silent.

Alex looked at her hard, then downed the whiskey in his glass. "Amanda, is someone threatening you?"

Amanda hesitated. I need to tell someone, she thought. But she swallowed and was reticent, looking down at her hands. Alex reached over and touched her arm. "This isn't like you. What is it? Does Jon know?"

She didn't look at him. "I will get to the bottom of this. But you need to focus on the possible defense we may have to mount. I don't need you involved with this other, and—" she paused, "I don't want you compromised."

Alex's eyes widened. "You are being threatened, aren't you?"

"Just don't say anything." Amanda's eyes suddenly flashed, meeting his, her voice cold. "To anyone, not even Jon."

"Amanda, there has to be something we can do about this." His eyes bored through her as he leaned forward.

"I will take care of the source," she said evenly.

He paused, then nodded reluctantly, his face etched with anxiety. "Is there anything else I can do?"

"You're doing more than enough. I'll let you know if I come up with any other information." Amanda tried to smile.

Alex's secretary Marian knocked and stuck her head in the door. "I'm out of here, but Sheila is on the phone for you, Amanda. Says it's something she thinks you and Alex would want to know. She said she had called you on the cell phone but didn't get you."

"Here." Alex pushed his desk phone over to Amanda.

Amanda picked up the receiver and pushed the blinking button. "Yes, Sheila." She listened for a moment, her face registering surprise. "Dan Cowan of Rhodes & Peterson? I know the firm, but not him." A pause. "No, it is news to me. No, don't call him back. I have to confirm with David. I advised him he could. Maybe he did, but I just left the cottage—oh, don't worry about it, Sheila. You did right. I'll take care of it in the morning. If someone from there shows up before I get there in the morning, tell them to kiss—well, you know what to say."

She hung up. Alex noted the tension. "What is it?"

"A Dan Cowan of Rhodes & Peterson called this afternoon, saying he had been retained to represent David and Jon Connor. He demanded that I turn over any and all items belonging to them, and all statements obtained as part of this homicide investigation. He said an associate would be there first thing in the morning to collect the items."

"Never heard of him. And Rhodes & Peterson does not do criminal defense work." Alex was as perturbed as Amanda.

"I just left David at the cottage. If he had hired an attorney, I think he'd have told me," Amanda mused.

She picked up her cell phone to call him. "Damn, my phone is dead. I'll try him from home."

The Connors' Crisis

Alex looked at her. "You don't think Jon hired them?"

"Why would he?" Amanda retorted, aggravated. "Surely he trusts us to do the job."

Alex stood. "You need to be home with your husband. He'll be frantic with worry."

Amanda smiled distractedly. "I guess so." She looked at her watch. "Thanks, Alex."

When she arrived home, Jon was waiting at the door. "I was worried. Why didn't you call?" he demanded, as he held the door open for her to enter.

"I stopped by to touch base with Alex."

"Why?" Jon's eyes narrowed.

"I needed to bounce some ideas off him," she replied cautiously.

"Did you see Charlie today too?" Jon demanded.

Amanda was too tired to discern Jon's meaning. "No, not—" she caught herself, suddenly remembering the rendezvous scheduled that night, "not today. I had a—a lot of business to take care of, and made sure David and Ralph were settled at the cottage. Then I stopped by Alex's office. I just lost track of time, and my cell phone is dead," Amanda answered wearily, still unsettled. The picture of Jon with Lauren flashed through her mind. "How was your day?"

"OK," Jon turned away. "We were supposed to have dinner with my parents tonight. I assume you forgot."

Amanda's eyes went wide and she sank to a seat on the couch. "Oh, my God, Jon." Amanda was suddenly apprehensive, attuned to his mood. "I'm really sorry for being late. All this is weighing on my mind. Please forgive me." Tears filled her eyes. "I just can't seem to make it right with your mother," she whispered.

"Don't worry. I made our excuses yet again," Jon remarked, his tone cool.

Something in Amanda snapped. "Jon, I am not avoiding your mother, whatever you may think. Should I just blithely ignore the fact that you, David and Ralph are under suspicion for *murder*?" She almost shouted the last word. "You are absolutely right. Instead of working all day, I should have been shopping for a new dress for dinner tonight, getting my hair and nails done. I really need to get my priorities straight."

"Amanda, I—" Jon began, but she cut him off.

"You know, I keep trying to figure out what to do, how to combat the growing evidence against first one, then the other, of you. I'm at my wits' end, and all you can hit me with is that I've forgotten we were supposed to have dinner with your parents, who don't like me to begin with?"

Her anger boiling over, she plunged heedlessly. "And you and David can't trust Alex and me to protect your interests, so you get some pipsqueak attorney from a big Panama City firm that doesn't even do criminal defense work to represent you?"

He regarded her, dumbfounded. "I have no idea what you are talking about."

"Yeah, right. Maybe you've confided it all to your mother, and she was afraid I'd botch it up. Maybe she talked you into hiring a 'real attorney'," Amanda spat viciously.

She stood and pushed past him to head for the kitchen, but he grabbed her by the arms, pulling her to him.

"Don't," she sobbed angrily, struggling against him desperately.

"Stop it, Mandy," he ordered quietly, his grip tightening, suddenly concerned at her reaction. "I'm sorry, love. It's going to be OK. Take a deep breath."

She tried to push away, but he wouldn't let her go.

"Please, you're hurting me," she cried.

He wrapped his arms around her. He could feel her trembling. "I don't give a rat's ass about whether we have dinner with my parents. And of course I haven't hired anybody else. I was upset that I've been waiting for you, worried, and you didn't call, didn't return my calls. All I care about is that something's going on and you won't tell me. You are beside yourself. This is not like you. If I'm suspected of something, I need to know. Please, Mandy."

Amanda felt hot with shame at her outburst. Jon held her and rocked her, and she made herself go passive in his arms. *He's right. I need to tell him,* she told herself. *But what if the man from the hotel has bugged their home? What if his accusations were true? I can't live without Jon, no matter if—no,* she stopped herself. She knew that she was falling apart, and she had to get a grip, to pretend that all was well.

She willed herself to calm down. Jon finally released her and led her to the couch, pulling her to sit beside him, putting his arm around her. "Talk to me. Any new leads? What evidence is this you are talking about? What's going on?"

"Not much new is happening," Amanda smiled, the smile not reaching her eyes, as she touched his cheek briefly. "I really am sorry, Jon. I just let my nerves get the best of me. I did forget about dinner tonight with your folks. And I had no business going off like that."

"What is this about some firm?" Jon demanded.

"Some attorney called Sheila and demanded that I turn over everything I had on this investigation, and that Rhodes & Peterson had been retained to represent you and David. I had just seen David, and he said nothing. There's no reason he wouldn't have told me, is there?"

Jon's eyes narrowed at the news. "No, dear, I'm sure he would have."

"I need to call and make sure," she rose distractedly.

He was silent as she moved to the phone and called David's number. "No answer," she said aloud. She left a message. "David, it's Amanda. The office got a call that the firm of Rhodes & Peterson was now representing you and Jon. Jon doesn't know anything about it. Did you hire them? I want to confirm before I release anything to them. Please call me."

She turned back to Jon. "I assume then you've not had dinner?"

"No. Are you hungry?" he asked her, walking over, his hand engaging hers.

"Not really," she admitted, still haunted by the revelation earlier that day. "I just want to rest a moment," she added, pulling away, trembling.

Jon demanded, "Something is wrong, Amanda. What is this evidence you are referring to, pointing to first then the other of us? Tell me," he begged softly.

Amanda faced him. "Jon, I must know. Is there anything you haven't told me? Anything at all I should know? No matter how much it might hurt? I just want so badly to help you, but I must know everything."

Jon's eyes dilated in surprise. "What is it, Amanda? I've told you everything."

Amanda, feeling faint, sank down on the couch, but persisted. "Everything? Have you perhaps—I—I .... Any contact with Lauren Mallory over the last few—weeks or months?" she faltered. "Anything that might pin blame on you? On someone else?" She hesitated. "Any detail, no matter how small? You can tell me."

Jon's demeanor became shuttered, and he mumbled sullenly, "I've told you. You don't believe me. There is something new, isn't there?"

Amanda's chest grew tight with fear as she gazed at him, then looked away. "Nothing really. Alex and I are just looking for anything," she answered him. "I—it's just so hard. I'm trying to anticipate Charlie's next move. We keep hitting brick walls," she finished lamely. "I need to know everything Charlie has. I have to figure out some way to get it out of him."

Jon froze. She stood and walked toward the kitchen, unaware of the effect her last words had on him. "Would you like for me to prepare you something to eat?"

"No," he replied shortly, turning and taking the stairs. She heard the bedroom door shutting.

Jon was livid, and angry with himself. He paced back and forth in the bedroom. Amanda was spending a lot of time around Charlie, around his brother David, around Alex, in fact, more than she was with him the last few days. He told himself that she had a legitimate reason, and that he was letting his suspicions get the better of him.

But what was making it worse was Amanda's behavior. He could sense that she was on edge, that something was terribly wrong. He knew that she was keeping something from him. But what? Why? What new evidence? What was out there that was pointing to him, to Ralph, to David? Why would she not share everything with him? She had preached to him that marriage meant no secrets. Had she tired of him so quickly? Why wouldn't she trust him? He thought with horror, Does Amanda suspect me of something?

Amanda's eyes filled with tears as she watched Jon disappear. All this was too good to be true, she thought sadly. Now I am reduced to not trusting the man I love. A wall is going up between us. But I have to protect him, and that means I cannot disclose this—what? Information? Innuendo? Who can I trust? she thought, agitated. This man has isolated me, and any move I make could hurt someone I care for.

She realized that she was exhausted, and couldn't understand why. I cannot allow Esme to divide and conquer. I must tell Jon everything, she thought. I cannot lose him because of my distrust.

Her mind raced, and she started worrying, reconstructing in her mind every time they had been apart in the last few months. This is crazy, she told herself. But the man at the hotel did not seem the type to make empty allegations. She thought of his aborted assault, his face leering at her, and her breath caught in raw fear.

The man is a manipulative bastard, she told herself. He wants to plant these doubts, to control me. But she could not bring herself to totally let go of the thought that Jon could be the father of a little girl out there somewhere, and that Lauren Mallory could have been carrying Jon's child at the time of her death, that Jon and Lauren had perhaps . . . .

And if so, he has lied to me, she thought. Her mind, fatigued and whirring with doubts, continued down its course. If he has lied about that, could he have killed—no, she screamed inside. Never. He has been with me. He would never do that, she argued with herself.

She gave up, and decided to take a shower to ease the throbbing in her neck and head, even if it meant facing Jon. She slowly mounted the stairs and walked through the doorway to the bedroom, where she came face to face with Jon, who was undressing. He was shirtless as he looked at her.

"I—I need a shower," she stammered as she gazed at his torso, suddenly weak with desire.

"Do you want me to join you?" he asked her huskily, swallowing his hurt.

Closing her eyes, she swallowed. "Yes," she admitted. She wanted him, no matter what may have happened between him and Lauren.

"Amanda?" Jon pulled her to him, running his fingers through her hair. "I love you."

She willed herself to believe him. "I love you too, Jon," she answered as she pulled him behind her into the bathroom.

CHAPTER 23

FRIDAY

Later, as Jon slumbered after their lovemaking, Amanda quietly dressed in the dark for her rendezvous, choosing running shorts and dark t-shirt with athletic shoes. The air was oppressive, sultry and still. Another miserable August heat wave is upon us, she thought.

Amanda slipped out of the home noiselessly, and jogged up the trail to Fred Vaughan's home. The night was dark, with only a sliver of moonlight to help her make her way.

It took several minutes for her to reach her destination, but she finally arrived on the front porch, damp with perspiration from the thick humidity hugging the ground, looking around for any sign of activity. She saw none. The house was dark. Opening the front screen door, she only then noticed that the front door was open. Hearing a growl and whine, suddenly she felt a tongue licking her hand.

"Good boy, Bozo," she crooned quietly, as Fred appeared behind the door.

"Evening, Amanda," he motioned for her to come in. "Bozo, out; watch," he commanded quietly to the dog, who padded outside.

As Amanda's eyes adjusted to the dark room, surprisingly cool from the ceiling fans, she saw a figure sitting in the large leather club chair. She immediately knew who it was. "Hi, Charlie," she greeted him.

"Have a seat," Fred invited, as he put a glass of bourbon in her hand. She sank onto the sofa, sipping her drink slowly. Fred sat in the other club chair.

"Where's Jon?" Charlie was wary.

"Asleep," Amanda's response was short.

"So you met with Esme Townsend's head henchman Salvatore Varas this morning?" Petrino asked without preamble.

"So that's his name," Amanda murmured. "Yes."

"And I'm sure he filled your head full with his mind games," Petrino growled.

"Such as the information that Lauren Mallory was pregnant when she was murdered?" Amanda was equally direct. "That bit of information was conspicuously absent from what law enforcement has disclosed." She stared at him accusingly.

"I don't know where he is getting his information," Petrino growled. Then he looked at her and attempted a smile. "There's a good reason for everything I do, Amanda," he drawled. "Did he also try to pin the badge of fatherhood on your husband?"

"How did you know?" Amanda was shocked. "What is going on, Charlie?"

"I'm only guessing. I'm mighty interested in why Esme is interested in you," he leaned forward, his voice low.

Amanda sipped her drink. "She wants me to be the next county judge."

Charlie suddenly moved and sat down beside her, startling her. "I'm serious, Mandy," he spoke, aggravated, grabbing her arm.

"I'm serious, too," Amanda responded, her voice a whisper.

"Shit!" he exclaimed. "Why?" he asked wonderingly.

"I don't know, Charlie, but he threatened me." She quickly relayed the conversation to him, with Fred listening intently. She made a conscious decision to refrain from mentioning the photographs. "And Toby appeared and rescued me from the man."

Petrino's jaw worked angrily. "That son of a bitch." His voice was quiet. "Toby came to see me last night. He said he had gone by his mother's house to talk to her, gave me some information he had overheard from Varas, and learned that Varas had forced a meeting with you. He expressed his concern for you, and was asking for intervention if necessary." He smiled grimly. "I wasn't far away this morning."

"You were?" Amanda breathed.

"Yeah, but not as close as I wanted to be," Petrino remarked enigmatically, suddenly sullen. "Toby insisted he would go in himself, and that I should make an appearance only as a last resort." Charlie frowned. "He says Varas is intimidated by him for some reason, and Toby thought if he busted in there it would be enough. But I sent in one of my men, dressed as a bellboy and wearing a wire, just in case."

His voice lowered. "Toby wanted to impress upon his mother the need for her to re-evaluate her association with Varas without embarrassing her publicly, if possible. But he wanted me in on it in case the plan didn't work."

Amanda swallowed convulsively. "I wondered how he knew, but was sure glad to see him." Amanda bowed her head, rubbing her temples. "But Esme apparently didn't take no for an answer when she asked about my running for judge." She also detailed the luncheon discussion with Esme. "I didn't think she was that serious. Guess I was wrong."

"Have you told Toby all this?" Fred asked gently.

"No, the opportunity didn't present itself today," Amanda admitted. "He obviously didn't want us to discuss it there with the possibility of someone overhearing."

Petrino demanded, "Are you going to do it?"

"I don't intend to, no," she laughed shortly. "But, Charlie, I don't know what to do. People I care for deeply are implicated in this mess, and it seems I cannot make a right move. I cannot prove I'm being blackmailed, and I'm smart enough to know this Varas will make good his threat. He as much as said he could plant evidence to finger any of the guys." She stared at her glass. "He has been busy manufacturing some."

"Such as what?" Petrino asked, his eyes locked on hers.

She was silent, pursing her lips.

"Please tell me, Mandy," he whispered, taking her hand.

"Photographs," she blurted, choking back a sob, turning away.

"Of what?" Fred asked, looking at her sympathetically.

She shook her head. "I can't say," she stuttered hoarsely.

Petrino squeezed her hand, pulling her around to face him. "Baby, I promise I won't reveal what you tell me, but I need to know what's out there."

She sniffed miserably. "Pictures of Jon with Lauren, Ralph with her, and David," she answered haltingly. "And—" she swallowed, "of you and me together. In bed."

Charlie looked at her blankly. "But we—" he started.

"He has been taking surveillance photos of us, and somehow came up with a method of making some realistic looking cut-and-paste photographs," she muttered. "Charlie, he is blackmailing me."

"My God," she heard Fred exclaim.

"Why don't you just apply for the judgeship?" Charlie inquired, looking at her, kneading her hand gently.

She withdrew her hand and grunted as she took another sip. "I don't know what to do. But I have no interest in cow-towing to Esme Townsend or this man, and I don't want to sell my soul."

"They have no promise that you will grant them whatever they are seeking," argued Petrino, surprising Amanda.

"But I don't want that responsibility. And if I am by some miracle appointed judge, shall I spend every day of my life with it hanging over my head, not knowing whether I, or the people I care for, will be subject to chronic blackmail at any time? No." Amanda was emphatic.

Fred interrupted gruffly. "I agree with Amanda here. How would you feel, Charlie, if you were appointed to your current job only by promises of favorable treatment or of taking a particular position? If you had to wake up every morning wondering if the other shoe was about to drop?"

Charlie frowned in the darkness and nodded. "You're right." He gulped down his drink. "But it might not hurt for Amanda to play along and buy some time for us to catch up with Varas, garner some evidence against him."

Fred held out his hand for the glass, and Charlie passed it to him. As Fred refilled it, Petrino laughed shortly. "But I probably wouldn't have gotten my appointment if it hadn't been for Jon's intervention on my behalf."

Amanda turned to him upon hearing his words. "What do you mean?" she demanded, stung.

"I thought you knew. Jon used his influence to have me recognized for my 'contribution' to the Barnes cases, and spoke to the governor personally."

"Influence?" Amanda echoed uncomprehendingly.

Fred looked at her sharply as he returned Petrino's filled glass to him. "Has Jon not told you, Amanda? He and his family have close ties with our governor, and with the President for that matter. He was not merely an FBI 'agent'."

Amanda emptied her glass with one swallow and handed it to Fred. He regarded her questioningly. "Fill it up, please," she said shortly.

Petrino gazed at her, alarmed. "I apologize. Apparently I have stepped in it big time. I was not aware that you didn't know." He took her hand momentarily. "I'm sorry."

She stared back at him, in shock. "N-no, it's all right," she stammered. "Tell me what else you can about the homicide," she managed to change the subject, as Fred handed her a glass. She disentangled her hand from Petrino, took the glass and hurriedly took a big draught.

"Whoa," Fred whispered. "There's nothing but bourbon and ice in there. Slow down, girl."

She gripped the glass tightly. "Tell me," she echoed insistently.

Petrino grimaced. "Victim was slashed across the neck, execution-style, a very smooth cut with a sharp instrument. Her clothes were in a pile on the floor, not scattered around. No evidence that she was attacked and stripped, no blood on them. Best we can determine, she was in the bedroom at the time. Blood spatter seems to indicate she fell backward on the bed. There was evidence of vaginal penetration, some bruising, but no semen. Hard to tell whether there was a struggle, but apparently not much of one. Coroner's best estimated scenario is that she was slashed in the middle of coitus, consensual. She was apparently then dragged down the hall and deposited in the bathtub. No weapon was found."

"Her clothes were in a pile in the bedroom?" Amanda repeated. "And there was no blood on them? No sign of struggle? That means—"

"She removed them herself voluntarily, most probably," Charlie finished for her. "Mandy, it looks like she was lying in wait for Ralph to get home," he added, his voice a whisper. "The bed was mussed, and her hair was found on the pillow."

"But he doesn't know her," Amanda choked, not trusting herself to look at Charlie. "Someone dropped her off there to frame Ralph for adultery, or something else."

"How would you come to the conclusion that she was dropped off?" Charlie's eyes were intent upon her face.

"Because there was no vehicle found, and because of the phone—" she stopped herself, suddenly aware that she was giving information away.

"The phone what?" Charlie grabbed her arm and shook her gently. "Tell me, Mandy."

Amanda hesitated. She knew David had given her permission to divulge the information, but she tried to gauge whether she should, whether the time was right. Her mind seemed to be working in slow motion.

"Mandy?" Charlie's voice held a note of anguish.

Amanda finally replied reluctantly. "She left a voice mail for David that she had been dropped off at that address to leave a message, but the recipient didn't show. She asked him to pick her up," Amanda offered, fingering her glass.

"What else do you know?" Charlie demanded, his voice rising in volume.

"What about my butcher knife?" she stammered, trying to change the subject.

Charlie looked over at her. "OK, we'll come back to that," he responded softly. "I don't think the butcher knife had anything to do with the murder. I feel it is a red herring. I'll know tomorrow. But Gerald at first told me it had to be an execution-style blade."

The Connors' Crisis

Amanda nodded with relief, sipping her drink. "What else?"

"There were bloody footprints all over the place, no real pattern to them." Charlie paused. "Tread was a bit familiar and distinctive. Then I remembered that just a couple of weeks ago Ralph and I stopped in at Jerri's, and he bought a new pair of athletic shoes." He sipped his drink. "Tread is a perfect match. And his pair was not in the closet."

Amanda sucked in her breath.

Charlie added significantly, "Jon has a pair just like them, too, so Ralph said at the time he bought his."

Amanda was silent, but she gulped her drink deeply.

Charlie continued. "There was one other shoe print, a partial next to the bed. Nothing special, perhaps a dress shoe, hard to match even if we had a full print. Not really enough for us to determine a shoe size."

He paused. "We found a cufflink in her hand, only one. A large yellow stone." He paused. "We haven't found a match yet."

Amanda nodded quietly, but her shoulders tensed.

Charlie looked at her knowingly. He demanded, "Doesn't Jon have cufflinks matching that description? Ralph?"

Amanda was wary, careful not to look at him. "I don't know, Charlie," she spoke carefully. "I would have to see the cufflink."

Charlie was gruff. "Funny—I have a pair just like it. Jon bought himself, Ralph and me matching cufflinks to wear for your wedding. Very nice ones, distinctive."

Amanda was silent a minute. "What are you saying, Charlie?" she whispered.

"Well, let me put it this way. The cufflink isn't mine." Charlie continued slowly, "Then we found bloody athletic shoes, as well as a trash bag of bloody clothes, in Lauren's hotel room. The place had been turned upside down."

Amanda stared at him fearfully.

"I recognized the clothes." Charlie examined his glass.

"Whose?" Amanda's mind was working in slow motion. She didn't realize she was holding her breath.

"Ralph's clothes, Amanda," Charlie whispered.

Her breath caught in a sob, she didn't know if in pain or relief. "That doesn't make sense, Charlie," she managed. "Are we to believe Ralph did the deed, went over and trashed her place, left his bloody clothes there to be found, and returned to the scene of the crime? And all this before the cops made it to his house?"

"No, and I'm baffled," Charlie agreed.

"So are you going to make an arrest?" Amanda's voice was hoarse, and she was trembling inside.

"Mandy, I'm trying like hell to find out who really did this before I'm placed in a position of having to make an arrest of an innocent person," his voice was low.

"Wouldn't Varas be the prime suspect?" she quavered.

"Yes, if I could get any evidence linking him to the crime." Charlie pursed his lips.

Amanda took another draught. "What about Varas' news—was she pregnant?"

"I'm waiting confirmation from the medical examiner." Petrino looked away as he downed his drink, then set it down on the table.

"You know the answer, and are just not telling me," Amanda accused quietly, setting her glass down as well and putting her hand on his knee, staring at him.

"Yes, Mandy, she was pregnant." Charlie looked down at her hand, his voice husky. "Coroner says about six to eight weeks' gestation."

Amanda shuddered, closing her eyes. "Jon has been with me all that time," she murmured. "It's not him," she whispered, swallowing convulsively.

Charlie took her by the arms roughly and turned her to face him. "I am sure it is not him," Charlie comforted her. "But you see how delicate the matter is? I've got to do something, and quick. It's all too obvious, and the 'evidence' swings from one of them to the other at will. There's damning evidence on David, then on Jon; now Ralph is the prime suspect. And you're right: none of it makes any sense. We don't know what is real and what is being planted by that bastard. But the prosecutor presenting it to a grand jury will go after his best case, and right now we're dancing someone else's tune."

He paused. "Clarence Banks requested that his boss assign someone else to the case." He smiled grimly. "He didn't want to piss you off and face your wrath again." The smile vanished. "There won't be any friendly face on that side of the table, Mandy."

"How does Varas know this stuff?" Amanda queried, standing and pacing.

"I have not found a leak inside the department, but I have not ruled it out." Charlie was angry. "The information about the pregnancy was known only by Bruce and myself and the medical examiner. I've crawled Gerald's ass again, and we are sweeping his place in the morning for bugs, and before daybreak the sheriff's administration building."

"I think it has something to do with the pens. They keep showing up," Amanda countered wearily. "I don't know how. They must be bugs, Charlie."

The Connors' Crisis

"Then I need to figure out who is planting them." He studied the ice in his glass. "It's someone with access to your office and mine. I hate not knowing who I can trust," he muttered darkly.

"Join the club," Amanda whispered, rubbing her forehead wearily.

Fred divined her tone. "I think you can trust your husband, Amanda," he spoke softly.

"But he had an affair with this Mallory woman years ago, and she filed a paternity suit against him, and against Ralph also," she retorted in momentary rage. As soon as the words left her mouth, she turned to Petrino, her eyes wide with fear as she realized she had just divulged damning information.

Charlie, noting her alarm, shook his head. "Amanda, I already know, remember? I knew about the summons served on Jon *and* Ralph. And Jon admitted as much to me."

"I told him to keep his mouth shut," Amanda muttered.

Petrino, instead of getting angry, smiled. "They're my friends too, Mandy. I don't believe for a minute that they or David are guilty. But you know as well as I do that I've got to walk a chalk line on this." He grew somber. "What is David's connection with this woman?"

Amanda looked away, sipping her drink. Petrino pulled her down to sit by him, and turned her chin to face him. "Mandy?"

She did not meet his eyes. "You know I cannot divulge something to you that could be held against David," she replied evenly. "Even if we're friends, we are on opposite sides, Charlie."

He continued to hold her chin. "What if I guess? Jon once told me that David made a play for every woman he dated. David had an affair with this Lauren too, and he thinks the child named in the complaint is his?"

Amanda looked away, not responding. He stared at her. "I'm right," he affirmed softly, letting her go.

"She was at Ralph's house and still alive at 7:10 that evening," Amanda offered.

Charlie stood suddenly. "How do you know?" He towered over her.

"I have proof from the voice mail message she left David," Amanda volunteered. She colored. "I just broke my own rule by telling you that, but I had permission to use it if I thought it could help."

"So David was still having contact with her?" Petrino demanded.

She was silent.

He laughed a short laugh. "You know I will find out the answer. Jon said in his statement that David was at your house until a little after 7:30, left in a hurry. Jon called him around 8:00. He and Ralph met up at Ralph's house around 8:30. So there's an hour for which his whereabouts are unaccounted."

"She left a voice mail, but it came while he was at my house. He didn't check his messages until 8:09," Amanda whispered. "I checked his phone."

Petrino looked at her impassively. "That's OK. I'll have independent proof of that. Bruce had already ordered her call logs, will probably get them tomorrow. As well as David's, Ralph's and Jon's. And yours."

Amanda stood also. "Am I a suspect?"

Charlie and she faced each other, only inches apart. "No, baby, you are not," Petrino whispered. "But I have to check it out because of the butcher knife business, and to verify the others' activities."

She nodded mutely. They stared at each other.

Fred, silent until this time, noted the exchange. "What a mess," he interjected, his voice low. "I hate to break this up, but Amanda looks all in. Amanda, you need to go home and get some rest."

"No," Amanda protested. "We have to determine what to do next." Her voice was weary. "Pete, I cannot go on keeping all this from Jon, from Ralph. It's killing me."

Petrino nodded. "I know, Mandy, but first we've somehow got to plug the leak so that you can tell them without it getting back to this Varas. Otherwise it snowballs into something we can't stop. You are all in danger."

"And you too," she rejoined, her voice almost inaudible.

"I can take care of myself." He gazed at her concernedly. "You can't let all this wear down your stamina. We've got to stay on our toes. I agree we need to come up with a strategy, and I need you with me on this. I have an idea." He smiled grimly. "As soon as I know for sure, I will keep you in the loop, but you're going to have to help me, too. And we mustn't let anyone know that we're working together, at least until we can flush out who to trust and who cannot be trusted." He jerked his head toward Fred. "Fred will have to be our liaison." He stepped away.

Amanda moved away too. "OK," she conceded. "But I don't think we're any closer to a resolution."

"I'll know quickly whether my plan will come together," Petrino reassured her. "Just hang in there a little longer. If you can see your way clear, I'd sure like statements from Ralph and David. I appreciate you feeding me what you can, but formal statements may help nail down events before more 'evidence' comes to light." His meaning was clear.

"But formal statements can also put them in real danger," Amanda argued. "You nail down their story under oath, and then this Varas can plant evidence against them that discredits them, destroys any defense we could mount." Her eyes flashed. "You can't ask them to play nice when the enemy is using guerilla tactics."

Charlie looked at her a moment, then nodded. "Just remember we're on the same side, baby."

As her eyes met his, he added, "Mandy, I've always wanted to be sheriff, but it isn't worth railroading my friends into a murder rap. If a choice has to be made, rest assured which side I will end up on." He shook his head. "I could always tell the governor I have a conflict. But he told me he needed someone to handle this matter, and wanted my assurance that I could." Charlie smiled bitterly. "You have to admit we're better off with me wearing the white hat for now."

His voice softened. "I want to make sure you make it back home safely."

"Take the back path," Fred suggested. "Less chance of being seen, and quicker. Bozo will go with you."

"I can handle getting home on my own," Amanda murmured.

"I'll be watching," Petrino insisted.

Amanda hugged Fred, then stepped outside. Petrino followed her to the porch. "Be careful, Mandy," he whispered.

She nodded nervously and stepping off the porch. She made her way home gingerly along the path with Bozo as company.

Arriving home, she let herself silently into the house and into the bedroom. Quickly undressing, she lay down beside the still form of Jon, his back to her, his breathing regular.

Just as she thought it safe to exhale, a voice spoke. "Where have you been?"

Jon turned to face her, glowering.

Amanda started. "I couldn't sleep, and I went out on the dock to think a while," she lied, swallowing.

"And drink? I smell the bourbon on your breath." He pulled her to him roughly. She winced, chagrined.

"Yes, I had a drink," she admitted ruefully. "I hoped it would relax me."

"I know you're frightened," Jon whispered.

She pulled away nervously.

"You hide it well, but I feel it in your body, I see it in the way you move. I don't know what's going on. But I love you, Amanda, and somehow we're going to get to the bottom of it. It will all work out."

He held her and kissed her hair. Despite her anxiety, within minutes she was sound asleep.

Jon was up early the next morning, and skipped his morning run. He quietly shaved and changed into his suit. He walked into the closet of the spare room, which Amanda had ordered enlarged to hold their business suits, and where Jon generally dressed. He bent down to pick out a pair of shoes, and spied a small piece of crumpled paper on the closet floor. Retrieving it, he saw that it was a note.

"Fred's—midnight. Alone. We're being watched. Pete."

He just stared at the slip of paper, transfixed. He recognized Petrino's scrawl. So that's where Amanda was last night. She and Petrino were meeting secretly, he thought. And she couldn't tell me? He was troubled.

A more sinister thought insinuated itself. Amanda said she had to figure out a way to get information from Charlie. He suddenly remembered Alex's words to Amanda on the porch. What if—?

No, he argued with himself. But she had been drinking. Would she and Charlie—?

He sat down heavily on the bed. No, he thought, of course not. That's silly. But his mind churned in turmoil, his gut like lead.

He suddenly heard some movement upstairs. Hurriedly he put on his shoes, stuffing the note into his jacket pocket. I can't face her right now, he thought, his heart heavy, as he slipped quietly and quickly out of the house.

Amanda awoke, and Jon was already gone. Surprised and wandering through the house, she crossed into the closet of the spare room. She frowned as she realized that he must have left early without saying good-bye. That's not like him, she thought. Why? Have my actions caused that?

She turned to leave, and her eyes fell upon a post-it note lying on top of his dresser chest. Picking it up, she saw in Jon's handwriting "Lauren cell" and a number.

She gasped, staring dumbfounded at the slip of paper. She heard the sound of his vehicle outside. She hurriedly slipped the note back where she found it, and moved down to the racks holding her clothes. She pulled a grey suit out and pretended to study it as Jon rushed in.

"Good morning, beautiful." He spied her, and moved to her, planting a light kiss on her forehead, his face flushed.

"Where did you go in such a hurry this morning?" she murmured, turning back toward the closet, not trusting herself to look at him.

"I have an early appointment, and I forgot something," he smiled distractedly. Although she appeared engrossed in selecting a blouse, she noticed that he surreptitiously slipped the post-it note into his pocket. Turning back to her, he impulsively took her by the arms and kissed her. Troubled and dazed, she returned his kiss tentatively.

"I'll see you this evening." He released her, walking out rapidly.

Amanda sank to the bed, holding the suit to her, her chest pounding. Why did Jon have Lauren's phone number?

She suddenly remembered a detail of the conversation with Charlie the previous evening. She stood and made her way to a little chest on top of the dresser. Opening it, she gazed at the contents, matching sets of Jon's cufflinks, all in neat rows. She stood there, studying them for several minutes. His topaz cufflinks weren't in the chest.

She felt a chill run through her.

CHAPTER 24

Amanda was troubled and distracted as she made it to work. Although her heart was heavy, she had little time to dwell on Jon's behavior, for she was swamped with work all morning. She found her concentration waning.

Later that day Amanda walked into the courthouse for her late afternoon motion hearing. Stepping off the elevator, she headed toward Judge Latimer's chambers, deep in thought. She was rudely accosted by a stranger at her elbow. "Mrs. Connor, what do you think of your partner's being a suspect in the Mallory murder?"

Her head jerked up, startled. She stared past the man down the hall, where a small mob of reporters had cornered a beleaguered Ralph, who gazed back at her in desperate supplication.

She walked quickly over to the group. "What's going on?" She smiled at him, trying to reassure him.

Before he could answer, a reporter cut in. "Mrs. Connor, is it true that Mr. Carmichael is a prime suspect in the murder of the woman found dead in his house? What was she doing there?"

She spied Titus Campbell standing back, looking on. He caught her eye and shrugged sympathetically.

"You will have to ask the sheriff's department that," she responded carefully. "But Mr. Carmichael is innocent of any wrongdoing, and had never met the victim until this last weekend."

"Isn't it true that he danced and flirted with her at an engagement party? Is that why his wife has left him?"

"Wasn't the victim found naked in his bed?"

"What about the paternity action that has been filed against him?"

"Do you think he is fit to seek judicial office?"

Amanda took a deep breath, and held up her hand to silence the group. "Mr. Carmichael possesses the highest integrity of any attorney and

270

man I've ever known. He has done nothing wrong, and your allegations against him are scurrilous, meant to cast aspersions on his impeccable character. His wife has not left him; she is away on family business, so your comment is libelous. Ralph is an honest, hard-working, intelligent man, the very best attorney I know, extremely qualified. I am convinced that someone is mucking about with his excellent reputation, and I for one intend to find out who is behind it and have that person prosecuted to the fullest extent of the law. And yes, Ralph would make the best kind of judge. I fully support him."

"So you're saying this is one big conspiracy? Who is behind that?" a newsman sneered.

"Oh, so why are you running against him for judge?" another reporter interrupted.

She laughed uneasily. "I have no idea the source of your information. I have not put my name up for consideration."

"But—"the first person started.

"Isn't it true that your own husband has also been accused of fathering a child by the victim? Isn't he also a suspect?" another reporter broke in.

"Listen, all this is the subject of a criminal investigation. That's all that we can say at the moment. If you will please excuse us." Amanda grabbed Ralph by the arm of his jacket and dragged him out of the crowd.

"I wasn't expecting to be mobbed coming out of court," Ralph confessed as she pulled him out of earshot. "I wasn't prepared for that."

"None of us are." Amanda patted his arm. "Are you through here?"

"Yes," he nodded.

"Then get out of here as fast as you can. Go back to the office, and I'll meet you back there as soon as my hearing is over. We'll figure out what we need to say and what to avoid with the press. I guess Alex and I will craft a statement for you all."

"The application deadline for the judgeship vacancy closed yesterday, so a list will be published this afternoon and interviews scheduled." Ralph sighed mournfully. "Mandy, I don't stand a chance."

"Don't say that, Ralph." Amanda was brisk. "The decision hasn't been made yet. We're going to get to the bottom of this. Don't throw in the towel."

She put him on the elevator, then turned back toward the judge's office. Two of the reporters started to approach her, but she gave them a frosty smile as she quickly strode past them.

Ralph wheeled the Escalade into the parking lot at the law office, only to find Jon walking toward his Land Rover. Jon stopped as Ralph climbed out.

"Hi," Jon greeted him tersely.

Ralph, noticing his solemnity, asked, "What's wrong? Any news?"

"No. I came by to check on Amanda."

"She's at the courthouse waiting for her hearing to be called. She just saved me from the voracious press that mobbed me. She looks really tired."

Jon looked down at his shoes. "I called Kimball at the Bureau to see if they knew anything about Lauren Mallory and could share the information. He already knew about the murder. Seems they are doing a little investigating themselves, but told me he couldn't divulge why. He promised to try to get information on her, where and for whom did she work, where did she live, who was she seeing, things like that."

Jon paused a minute. "He offered me my job back."

Ralph whistled. "Do you want it?"

"I don't know," Jon admitted unhappily. "Maybe it was wrong of me to quit."

"Wait a minute," Ralph interrupted, confused. "Where is this coming from?"

Jon sighed. "I have been so happy to be with Amanda. But it's hard being out of the loop, Ralph. It's much more difficult to get information, even though I am not without resources. When incidents happen like what we're in now, I would be all over that. I feel helpless now. But you know Amanda would never go for my returning to the Bureau."

"If that's what you want, why not talk to her?" Ralph suggested.

"Because it's hard enough to get her to talk to me now," he muttered. "And I love her more than the job, Ralph. Look at what she's been through with Andy. Could I consign her to that again?"

Ralph nodded. "Is private practice that unappealing?"

"Actually, no," smiled Jon. "But it is going to take some adjustment on my part. And I think I can be content doing this kind of work. But—"

"I imagine the pace is not what you are used to." Ralph clapped him on the shoulder. "Come on in. We need to talk, and you can wait for Amanda."

Jon didn't move. "Ralph," he offered, his voice low, "something is going on with Amanda. She disappeared yesterday afternoon. I didn't hear from her. She didn't respond to any of my messages. She got home late, and was distant, withdrawn. She said she had stopped by Alex's office.

"I know something's going on, but she will not tell me. She blew up with me, something she has never done before. She demanded to know if I have told her everything about Lauren."

The Connors' Crisis

Ralph nodded sympathetically. Jon continued. "But that isn't all. I woke up later in the night, and she was gone. When she came back, she said she couldn't sleep and was outside on the dock. Ralph, she had been drinking. She admitted she had, said she was trying to relax."

Ralph gazed at his friend. "I think this murder is preying upon her. She's worried. We all are."

Jon declared, "She's pulling away from me; she does not trust me. If she does not confide in me, I'm not going to spy on my wife."

Ralph put his arm around Jon's shoulder. "Jon, you know Amanda has tasted hell. Her life with Andrew was a relentless amount of work, punctuated by a series of little holidays when he was home. Only recently has she relaxed her stranglehold on work and church. It was nothing for her to work late every night, go to the church and practice or rehearse, and return to the office, or take work home with her."

"I know," Jon mumbled.

Ralph moved away. "No, you don't know. Now she beats you home every night. She has changed her priorities. You are first. But trust comes hard for Amanda. Look at the results. Everyone she has loved died. Bill, her childhood best friend, implicated her in criminal investigation, drugged her and almost killed her. Andy was murdered. Marjorie is gone, and she found out that the woman was her mother. Meeting with her long-lost father who almost ruined her life resulted in her facing murder charges. You came out of the blue, investigating her. Now the two of you are married, after an uphill battle, and suddenly you and I are suspects in a murder of one of your ex-girlfriends." He paused. "Give her a break; she's trying."

Jon nodded. "It's just so hard. And we're in a black-out where information is concerned. We're almost better off if one of us was charged. At least the discovery and *Brady* rules would kick in. But," he smiled mirthlessly, "at least that means law enforcement doesn't have enough to make an arrest."

"I wouldn't count on that," Ralph said slowly.

"What do you mean?"

"It's early yet. I believe they're waiting until the grand jury convenes. Or Charlie could be dragging his heels, hoping we'll catch up."

"He's pretty tight-lipped about it," Jon offered, a mask over his features.

"He has to be. But I think he may be sharing information with Amanda on the sly," Ralph countered quietly.

Jon's head jerked around. "Why do you say that?"

"Jon, Charlie and Amanda go way back. And we're his friends. He may do things by the book, but he is going to leave a trail of crumbs for Amanda to follow. But he's got to be mighty careful about it."

Jon hesitated. "They met secretly last night," Jon announced slowly.

"How do you know?" Ralph demanded, staring at Jon.

"I found a note from Charlie to Amanda this morning," Jon almost whispered.

"I wouldn't put it past Petrino," Ralph remarked, not noting Jon's distress. "He's not going to let this go without a fight, and he's going to let her know what's going on."

"But she felt she couldn't tell me?" Jon argued. "What do you know about Charlie and Amanda? They dated, didn't they?" He watched for Ralph's reaction.

Ralph, not catching Jon's meaning, replied, "Charlie was sweet on Amanda in high school, but Bill was determined that nothing would come of that. And Amanda was always a knockout, but had no clue."

"So they were never serious, even after high school?"

Ralph peered at him, the corners of his mouth curving into a smile. "Jealous, are we?" he teased.

Jon flushed, but said nothing. Ralph jerked his head toward the law office. "Come on." He started toward the door, Connor following. "I was gone to Duke by then, Jon, but I'm pretty sure nothing blossomed between them. If so, neither of them has ever alluded to it. And with Bill around, he kept any romance in Amanda's life pulled up by the roots, at least per Charlie, until Andy came along."

Jon nodded. "He told me that too. But he made a comment to me some time ago that he at one time thought he had a chance with her."

Ralph stopped suddenly, his eyes narrowing as he stared at Jon. "Hmm," he said thoughtfully. "When I first came back to Mainville to practice with Amanda, there was some distance between them. I asked about it, but they both said they were just busy. Andy had been dead about a year then."

Jon was silent.

Ralph paused, looking at Jon hard. "You don't seriously think there's something going on between them now, do you? That's crazy. You're crazy."

Jon sighed. "No, I don't want to believe that, but Ralph, something is happening. I know it. I am not imagining the change in Amanda's behavior the last couple of days. Why would she not confide in me?"

Ralph shook his head. "I don't know, but I know how Amanda feels about you, and she has never exhibited those feelings for Charlie Petrino. So something else is going on."

"I just wish I could be sure," Jon muttered.

They walked into the office's back service door, as Sheila was sitting at her desk, letter opener in hand. "Mail come in?" Ralph inquired.

She nodded.

He picked up an envelope addressed to him and opened it. "Judicial nominating committee interviews for the judicial vacancy." He read it, as Sheila went through the remaining documents, sorting them. He noticed an identical envelope and picked it up. "This is addressed to Amanda," he remarked, frowning. "Aren't you going to open it?"

"Amanda told me she wants to open her own mail." Sheila didn't look up.

"What? Since when?" Ralph demanded, surprised.

"Yesterday," Sheila coughed, suddenly uncomfortable.

"Damn, that's not like her." Ralph took the envelope and tore it open. "She has an interview scheduled too? But she didn't apply," he exclaimed incredulously.

On the desk was another large packet. Angrily he grabbed that and opened it too. "Feels like a transcript," he quipped, then stared, transfixed at the contents, a bound copy of an application to the judicial nominating committee. Opening the cover, he exploded. "An application by Amanda? She applied and didn't tell me?"

Jon shook his head in disbelief. "Something's wrong. That can't be."

"You're damn right something's wrong," a voice spoke behind them. Amanda stood there, her eyes flashing, livid. "What are you doing opening my mail?"

"Since when are we keeping secrets from each other?" Ralph's voice rose angrily. "When did you decide to apply for the judgeship behind my back?"

"I don't know what you are talking about." Amanda pushed past Jon, jerking the volume out of Ralph's hands. As she glanced at the cover page, she turned white, fear showing in her eyes. "I didn't do this," she muttered darkly. "She's gone too far."

"And your interview is first on the list," Ralph jeered.

"What interview?" she asked dully, gathering up the mail, and gazing at the opened letter. "Shit!" she exclaimed.

Jon came up to her, having noted her reaction. "Who is doing this, if not you?" he demanded softly.

She did not look at him, blinking back tears of frustration, her back to him.

"Amanda, don't shut me out," he pleaded.

"I can't tell you," she whispered, the mail in her arms, as she fled to her office, shutting the door.

Ralph strode after her. Trying the door, he found it locked. "Amanda, talk to me," he shouted through the door. "I demand an answer, or I'll break this door down," he added, rattling the door knob and beating the door with the flat of his left hand.

Connor came up to Ralph and placed his hand on Ralph's shoulder. "Leave her be," he berated him gently.

"But—" Ralph began.

Jon interrupted. "There's a reason behind everything Amanda does." He pulled Ralph away, dragging him by the arm past Sheila and outside.

They stood out in the parking lot as Ralph paced excitedly, beside himself. Jon spoke. "You know Amanda has never kept secrets from you before."

"Why now?" Ralph demanded.

It suddenly dawned on Connor. "She is trying to protect you and me. She said she didn't do this. I believe her. Why would she? Someone else is pulling the strings." He took Ralph by the arm, stopping him in mid-stride. "That's why she is behaving so strangely. Someone has threatened Amanda."

"With what?" Ralph was frustrated. "And you don't know her very well if you think she can be blackmailed."

"Not even if you or I are in danger? If we are facing a murder charge?"

Ralph sputtered. "I don't know, man." He walked over and sat down on the steps, placing his head in his hands. "Maybe she is protecting David."

Jon hadn't considered that. Hurt showed in his eyes momentarily. "Where is David?" he wondered aloud. "Have you heard from him?"

"No," Ralph sighed. "He left yesterday afternoon, came in late last night, and left the cottage before dawn this morning without a word."

"I'm going to contact Petrino, murder or no murder," Jon whispered. "We have to know what's happening." And I have to assure myself that my wife isn't having an affair with Charlie, he thought but did not say.

"I'm going with you," Ralph rejoined.

"No." Jon was firm. "That's too suspicious. I want you to locate my brother and find out what he's up to. I'm going to try to figure out how to contact Charlie on the sly. And I will also wear Amanda down tonight and see if I can get her to disclose why she is—like she is," he finished lamely.

"Why don't you contact David?" Ralph was curious. "He is, after all, your brother."

"You heard him at your house the night of the murder. He for some reason does not want to confide in me. We have always been somewhat competitive. He has stolen my girlfriends before, and I'm frankly jealous of him around Amanda." Jon paused. "I love him, but ours has not been an easy relationship."

"You're too much alike," Ralph posited.

Jon smiled tightly. "You couldn't be more wrong."

"No," insisted Ralph. "You two are more alike than you realize, and it's more than outward resemblance. I think that's the problem."

"I hope I'm not like my brother," Jon stated emphatically.

"You don't see the good side of David, and don't recognize yourself in his actions and mannerisms." Ralph looked at him soberly. "You need to think about it."

"Well, just get up with him, please," Jon muttered irritably. He looked at his watch. "Damn, it will have to wait." He turned to leave. "Please tell Amanda I have some business to attend to, and will be a little late getting home."

"What business?" Ralph was curious.

"The firm set a late appointment in town for me for some 'local bigwig'. Do you know a Reba Thompson?"

"Never heard of her," Ralph laughed humorlessly. "You sure they know what they are talking about?"

"I don't know, but she apparently asked for me by name, and wanted to meet here in town, not at the office. Let Amanda know for me, please?"

"You don't want to tell Amanda yourself?" Ralph asked hopefully.

"I think I like my body parts in their present order." Connor's face was grim. "And she didn't appear to want me around just now, anyway. Later."

CHAPTER 25

Amanda waited in her office until she heard Jon's car driving away. She was still seething and troubled about the fact that her name had been submitted behind her back for consideration of the judgeship.

Esme, I'm not letting you do this, Amanda thought, clenching her hands in rage. I'm not going to tiptoe around afraid of what this Varas is going to pull next. I need to tell Ralph what is going on. I cannot afford not to be candid with my partner and my husband. This mess is going to hell in a handbasket. Charlie and I must come up with a way to stop this, stop them.

Amanda could not understand why she was so fatigued. She knew that with so much whirling around her, she was quickly losing control herself. She suddenly realized that since her marriage to Jon she was almost never alone. I can't concentrate, she told herself.

She stood, wondering where Ralph was. I need to slip out of here, she thought, holding her head in her hand. I have to go somewhere and be alone, pull myself together, map all this out in my head, figure out a strategy. I need to beat them at their own game somehow.

She unlocked her door and opened it a crack, listening carefully. She could hear no noise from Sheila's central office. She let herself out noiselessly, then turned, running right into Ralph.

He grabbed her by the shoulders. "We need to talk," he announced, his jaw set ominously.

"Not now, Ralph," she warned.

"Now." He was insistent, as he opened her door and pushed her inside, following and closing the door back behind him. "Sit," he ordered, directing her to one of the overstuffed chairs facing her desk. He seated himself on the corner of her desk, towering over her and blocking her escape.

"Tell me what's going on, Amanda," he spoke softly, surprising her with his calmness.

"I don't know," she responded wearily. Suddenly remembering Varas' words about his network, she wondered, has the office been bugged? Could someone be hearing all this? She glanced all around the office anxiously. If so, where are the eyes and ears?

Her eyes lighted on the pen cup. Staring her in the face was one of the offending pens. Where are they coming from? she asked herself, agitated. I know Sheila and I rounded up all the pens yesterday.

It suddenly hit her. She told herself, Varas has hired someone who somehow has access to this office, perhaps even the S.O. It's not one of us, she concluded.

The thought flashed through her mind: Charlie is right. I have to buy time, make Varas think I'm considering the judiciary, at least until I can come up with a plan to combat him and Esme.

"What have you got against my applying for this?" she spat, her demeanor changing like lightning.

"Amanda, you've known all along that I wanted this position," Ralph was shocked. "If you wanted it, why didn't you say so?" he raised his voice exasperatedly. "Since when have we been keeping secrets from each other?"

While he was speaking, Amanda picked up the pen, walked over to the bookshelf, and planted it in the middle of an old volume of the *Florida Cases*, closing the book and replacing it on the shelf. She then returned to the desk, reached over, grabbed a legal pad and scribbled unobtrusively. Ralph peered at her quizzically.

"Maybe I'm tired of your treating me as your doormat. I'm good enough to give you a job here, but not good enough to be a judge," she sneered.

Ralph's eyes grew wide. She allowed the pad to drop to the floor. He picked it up and read silently. "The walls have ears. Keep talking."

He handed the pad back to her. "Damn, Amanda, where did you get that idea? I don't understand why all of a sudden you're hell-bent to piss me off," he responded in kind, as she took the pad and jotted something else.

"Because, Ralph, you piss me off all the time, but I just don't say anything about it. It's time I looked out for myself. I'm going after this."

She quietly and casually turned the pad so that he could glance down and catch her message. "Church—15 min—park in alley, kitchen entrance." She continued loudly, "I'm tired, and I'm not discussing this further with you right now. I'm going home."

Ralph nodded. "I hope your attitude improves by tomorrow. I thought marriage would improve your disposition," he lashed out.

She quietly ripped the page out and stuffed it in her pocket, pushing past Ralph, leaving her office. As she walked past Sheila's desk, Sheila handed her an envelope. "Sheriff Petrino called to inform you a grand jury will be convened next week. He said to expect the subpoenas to be issued tomorrow."

"Thanks, Sheila," Amanda interposed smoothly, even though the news chilled her to the bone. "I'm going home."

She left quickly, driving to St. Catherine's and parking by the side door. She quickly checked to see if someone might be following her, but could see no one. She tore open the envelope; inside was a note reading, "The cavalry is on its way. I'll let you know as soon as I have details. Pete." She stuffed the note in her pocket.

She unlocked the door and let herself in the administration wing, turning on no lights. Amanda made her way through the silent darkened hallway, stopping at the individual mail receptacles by habit, checking the items in her box. Among the various notices and correspondence and invoices, she found an envelope bearing only her name. She tore it open. It was a simple handwritten note.

"Amanda, there are some things I need to tell you in strictest confidence. Let me know a convenient place and time to meet. Toby." He had scrawled his cell phone number under his name.

Oh, Toby, she thought, tears in her eyes. "How can I tell you what awful things your mother is doing or allowing to be done?" she asked aloud despairingly. Maybe Toby could intervene in some way to stop this madness, Amanda thought. But would he if it involved his own mother?

She continued down the hallway toward the alley, waiting for Ralph. She was lost in thought. "I don't know what else to do," she told the large print of the famous William Holman Hunt's *Light of the World* hanging by the back door.

She stood there, mulling over what little she knew, frustrated at the lack of handy solutions. She resolved to send a message to Petrino through Fred that they needed to meet anyway. She realized the risk of squandering a rendezvous with Charlie, but they had to do something before the grand jury convened next week.

She heard no sound, but suddenly Ralph was standing at the door looking at her through the window. Quickly she let him in and locked the door behind him.

"Where's your car?" she asked as she led him through the nearest doorway, which was the entrance to the nursery. She cut on the light and shut the door.

"I parked down the street at the library. Louise is still at work. She let me out the back. I jogged down the alley."

He took her by the arm and turned her to face him. "You didn't mean any of that back there, did you?" He scanned her face concernedly.

"Of course not, Ralph." She was solemn. "But I'm pretty sure our office is bugged." She described the events surrounding the reappearing pens.

"But why? What is going on?" he asked again.

"Ralph, there is someone out there behind the scenes manipulating us," she began. "I am trying to protect you, David, and Jon. I have reason to believe evidence is being planted to frame one or all of you for murder. I was told there would be consequences for divulging this information. So you must not divulge it, or even let on that you know."

He stared at her, dumbfounded. She continued, "Ralph, I didn't prepare or file that application. I swear it. Someone else is doing this."

"Who? Esme Townsend?" he asked softly.

She gasped. "How did—"

"It's not too hard to figure out who in our area would have the influence and motive," he laughed hollowly.

She summarized for him her conversation with Esme and the meeting with Varas.

"That bastard!" he exclaimed hotly. He paused. "Lauren Mallory claimed to be very chummy with Esme."

"Lauren?" Amanda echoed. "But why would Esme offer to back you, then push me forward?"

"Why indeed?" Ralph echoed. "And why was Lauren Mallory killed at my house? Why was I served with a paternity suit? Amanda, Esme Townsend may be powerful, but I have trouble believing even she would go this far."

Amanda shook her head. "I have no clue, Ralph. But this Varas who has been working for her is behind it, I know. We have to figure out something quickly. A grand jury is being convened next week."

Ralph blanched. "We cannot continue sneaking around like this," he argued vehemently. "She cannot control us like chess pieces."

"But at any time, you, Jon or David could be charged with murder one. Apparently there is enough to make out a motive, and your whereabouts are just unverified enough to provide opportunity. And Ralph, this Varas intimated there were more tricks, more 'evidence' to plant, if I didn't go along."

She swallowed, her eyes on Ralph. "Ralph, he has pictures. Some of them are of you with her." She faltered. "You didn't know her? You've never—?"

"Pictures?" Ralph looked as if he would faint. "That cannot be. Geez, Mandy, no," Ralph cried in anguish. "I haven't been with any woman but Claire for the last five years." He choked, "I haven't even looked at anyone else. I didn't know her, I damn sure didn't kill this woman, and I'm pretty sure Jon or David didn't garrot her," Ralph whispered. "Oh, my God," he breathed.

Amanda nodded sympathetically. "I believe you, Ralph. I am sure these are manufactured." She reached up and hugged him. "It's OK. Have you told Claire?"

"No," he confessed, wiping tears from his eyes. "But she told me not to expect to hear from her. She is currently at the family cabin up on a lake somewhere—no phone reception." He looked forlorn. "Amanda, you're going to have to help me there. Claire will never believe any of this. She's always been so jealous."

"It's OK, Ralph." Amanda's eyes had tears too. "I will talk to Claire when the time comes," she promised.

Amanda looked away. "Has Jon discussed Lauren with you?"

"No," Ralph replied. "Amanda, you don't honestly believe any of this about Jon?"

"No, I don't," she confessed. "But there are pictures of him too." Her voice broke. "I have reason to believe he is not being entirely honest with me about recent contact with her." She swallowed convulsively, willing herself not to cry.

"Jon is not going to lie to you."

She shook her head, her face mirroring her doubts. She had a thought. "Ralph, have they let you back into your house yet?"

"Not yet," a flash of anger crossed his features. "Why?"

"I just think we need to get in there as quickly as possible and see if there's anything the police did not think of."

"We can always break in," he smiled.

"We might just have to do that," she smiled back.

"Thanks for putting me up at the cottage," he squeezed her hand gratefully.

"I'm just glad I procrastinated on putting it on the market," she asserted, sniffing.

"I told David he could stay there with me until law enforcement allows him back in the condo. Bruce Williams apparently called and left word that they'd be out of there by tomorrow, maybe even tonight."

Amanda frowned. "How is David? I left a message last night, and he did not call me back."

"I don't know," Ralph admitted. "He was gone early this morning. He is not saying much."

"Has he mentioned anything about hiring an attorney?" Amanda queried.

"No," Ralph replied, looking at her quizzically. "I don't get the impression he wants one right now. Why?"

"Sheila got a call from a hot-shot Panama City firm that they were representing David and Jon."

"No!" Ralph was surprised. "You know neither David nor Jon did that."

"But their mother may have," Amanda proffered, her voice low.

Ralph put his hand on her shoulder. "David trusts you. I just think he is truly worried, and we're both afraid to discuss the matter too much."

"I know," Amanda agreed. "Charlie is working on a plan."

"Charlie?"

"Yes. We are having to sneak around as well."

"Have you told Jon any of this?" Ralph demanded.

"How can I?" Amanda walked to the door, resting her forehead against it. "Lauren was pregnant. Varas intimated that DNA will prove the child to be Jon's. Ralph, I don't believe it, but I'm afraid. Jon had Lauren's cell number, Ralph. Why? Meanwhile I'm being blackmailed into this judgeship application.

"Besides, I don't even know if it's safe to talk to Jon in my own home. And what if it's true about her being pregnant with his child, and he will not admit it to me? What if he's been unfaithful?"

"But it's not true," Ralph turned her to face him. "Jon loves you. He would never look at another woman twice, and certainly not Lauren Mallory. I don't know why he'd have her number, but there is a good reason, I'm sure."

"I want to believe that," Amanda whispered.

"Believe it," he murmured, putting his arms around her and hugging her reassuringly.

She pulled away, tears in her eyes. "I need to go home. I am not getting a lot of sleep lately."

Ralph nodded. "May I share this information with Jon?"

Amanda hesitated, fear in her eyes. "Jon is already suspicious. I can't tell him what's really going on." She sat down in a chair, faint with apprehension.

"Are you OK?" Ralph asked concernedly. "You are white as a sheet."

"I don't know." She took a deep breath, then finally nodded. "You can share this with Jon, but only if you make sure that you don't discuss this anywhere you might be watched or overheard. Varas was quite clear that his network was extensive."

"OK," Ralph assented. "I gotta slip back into the library before it closes. See you tomorrow. Oh, and by the way, Jon said he had a business matter to take care of, some late client appointment, and would be a little late getting home."

Amanda quietly let him out, then retraced her steps, leaving the church. She drove home, her mind running in endless circles.

The more she assessed the situation, the angrier she became. She suddenly found herself on the avenue leading to Esme Townsend's home. I'm not slinking around afraid of this woman, Amanda resolved. I'm not letting her ruin Ralph's life, Charlie's career, and my marriage.

She impulsively pulled up into the driveway of the home. Before she could change her mind, she bounded out of the car and up the large steps to the front door. She pounded on the door, refusing to make use of the doorbell.

After several minutes, a black housekeeper came to the door.

"Lois, I'd like to speak to Mrs. Townsend. I feel pretty sure she will see me," Amanda stated, swallowing her temper.

The maid curtsied. "Miss Amanda, I'm sure she would if she was here. But she has been away all day. No one is home."

"Not even Mr. Varas?" Amanda couldn't help asking.

"No, ma'am. He's not here." The housekeeper bit her lip, looking embarrassed.

"And I guess Toby wouldn't be here, would he?" Amanda inquired despairingly.

"No, ma'am. He came by looking for his mamma about thirty minutes ago. Said he was on his way home to the south end."

"Will you let her know I stopped by?" Amanda was deflated.

"Yes, ma'am, as soon as she makes it home."

CHAPTER 26

As Amanda stopped at the gate by Vaughan's house he flagged her down. "I had to sign for two packages," he explained, handing her two bubble-wrap envelopes, one bulkier than the other.

Thanking Fred, Amanda asked, "Has Jon come by yet?"

"No," he shook his head.

"He left word he would be late," she stated. "I just wondered."

"Is there anything I can do, Amanda?" Fred was curious.

"Could you please get word to Charlie that if possible we need to meet?" she countered anxiously.

"Something new happen?" He was suddenly full of concern.

"I've apparently had an application for the judgeship sent in for me," she laughed mirthlessly. "And I happen to have an interview, the first on the list." She took a deep breath. "I'm running out of time. I have to do something and quickly, if possible, if a grand jury is about to convene," she clarified. She briefly filled him in, and his eyes widened.

"And Fred, you need to give him a message that these pens keep showing up in my office. I feel pretty sure they must be bugs. He needs to check for them at the department."

"I'll see what I can do," he promised, and Amanda smiled her thanks.

She covered the remaining distance quickly, parking in front of her home and letting herself in, packages in hand. The black and white cat ran in under her legs, purring and meowing.

"OK, Cleo, I hear you," she smiled wearily as she walked to the kitchen, dumping her purse and packages on the counter. She quickly prepared the cat's dinner and gently toted her and the bowl outside on the front porch.

Returning to the kitchen, she examined the envelopes, curious as to the contents. The first, smaller envelope was addressed to Jon. She started to lay it aside, then noticed the handwritten return address: "L. Mallory, Panama

City, FL". Staring transfixed at the envelope, she noted the postmark—the date of Lauren's death.

Gazing at it, she felt a momentary fury, and tore open the envelope. Inside were a handwritten note and a single cufflink with a large yellow topaz in the center. The note read, "Love, you dropped this at the condo. I had a good time. When can we do it again? Lauren."

Amanda, hypnotized, stared at the note and the link. She suddenly remembered. Jon wore the links the evening of Bubba's and Della's engagement party. A sense of horror filled her: she thought she remembered his putting them on before work the morning of Lauren's murder.

Recalling Petrino's description of the lone cufflink found in Lauren's hand, she gingerly laid the item on the counter, her heart thudding. But he has been with me, she thought. But not on Tuesday, a voice inside whispered. But he didn't kill her, Amanda argued with herself. But what other explanation is there for this cufflink and the one found in her hand?

Trying to stem the violent shaking, Amanda let her eyes fall on the larger package. Pulling it out of the outer envelope, she looked at the wrapping. The package was addressed to her, with the same return address and in the same handwriting. The postmark was the same day.

Tremblingly she tore open the brown paper wrapping. Inside was a hardcover edition of *A River Runs Through It*, by Norman Maclean. She was stunned. She remembered that Andrew had bought them both matching first-edition copies before their wedding, and she still possessed hers. Opening the leaf, she saw a note.

> I found this in Jon's attic the other day when I was over, and thought you would like to have it. Lauren Mallory.

She let the note flutter to the floor, her mind in shock. Inside the leaf was another note addressed to her, written in what she recognized was Andy's handwriting. It read:

> To Amanda Katharine, my bride—I was sitting here thinking of how much I miss you after our weekend together. I wrote this for you:
>
> There for the briefest of moments, we danced
> Entwined, our heads hung around each other,
> And somewhere the moon and stars nodded.
> The world did not stand still—it never does;

Instead, our minds engaged, gasping and grasping
At the expense of the stolen moment.

Yours eternally, Andy

It was dated only days before his murder.

She felt faint, and her throat convulsed. This was in Jon's attic all this time? Why? Why would he have something of Andrew's and keep it from her? Why would he allow Lauren to handle something so sacred to Amanda? What else were he and Lauren doing together at the condo?

All rational thought fled. Feelings of agony, of loss and betrayal, came rushing over her. She clutched at the book as though she were drowning. She forgot everything. She staggered to the bar and blindly groped for a glass and decanter, pouring a drink. She gulped it, then choked, sputtering as she tasted Glenlivet, Andrew's favorite. A sob escaped her, and the tears stung her eyes. She downed the rest of the contents of her glass, then pushed it back on the counter. Spying a bottle of Absolut, she grasped it.

Turning unseeingly, she stumbled and almost fell, her body slamming against the doorpost, the tears burning, blinding her. "Oh, my God," she gasped, the sobs ending in a small scream, "oh, my God." She felt her way to the back door, heading outside toward the dock, toward the chair, Andy's chair.

David pulled up in front of the farmhouse. The house was dark, with only a few lights peeking through the front windows. He could see that Amanda's car was parked out front.

"Fred said she was home," he mused aloud.

Walking in, he noted that the place looked deserted, but there was a light coming from the kitchen. Sauntering in, he was stopped by a note lying on the floor.

Picking it up and reading it, his eyes narrowed. "Lauren?" he frowned, his heart constricting. He then saw the items on the kitchen counter and reviewed the second note.

Stricken, he called, "Amanda?" Going into the living room, he turned on a nearby lamp. "Amanda?" he called again, worried.

Galvanized into action, he walked through the door to the guest room and to the bathroom. Tapping on the door and calling, he tried the door. The bathroom was empty. Alarmed, he checked the other rooms, and bounded up the stairs. From an upstairs window overlooking the lake he thought he spied a dark form on the dock.

He made his way back downstairs and through the house, outside and to the dock. He hurried down the pier toward the huddled mass in the Adirondack chair. Just as he approached, an empty bottle sailed past him and splashed into the water.

Peering into the dusk, he called softly, "Amanda? Is that you?"

"Get the hell away from me, Jon Connor," he heard an unsteady voice warn.

"What's wrong, Amanda?"

She stood, swaying drunkenly. "If I had my gun, I'd kill you myself." Her eyes were cold, and she had her arms wrapped around herself.

She staggered forward, and David ran forward to catch her. "You son of a bitch," she spat, clawing at him viciously with her free hand.

He quickly grabbed her hand and restrained her, pulling her to him. "Amanda, it's David," he crooned. "Take it easy. I'm your friend."

"David?" she croaked, looking at him dubiously through bleary eyes. "Why are you here?" she muttered, leaning against him.

She swayed again, and he propped her up. "What has happened?" he pressed gently. He then noted that she was clutching something to her. "Let me see," he whispered.

"NO!" she shouted, pushing against him, clasping the tome to her like a talisman. "It's mine—it's all I have left, and he kept it from me," she cried brokenly.

"It's OK," David spoke reassuringly, drawing her to him. "Come on, Sis. I'm not going to take it away."

"I thought I could trust him," she whispered, her voice catching in a sob, as David cradled her head against his shoulder.

"You can," David told her softly. "Believe me, you can. And you can trust me."

She clung to him, crying inconsolably, and his heart went out to her. He held her and shushed her, letting her cry.

David murmured, "Come on, let's get you to the house. You're in no condition to discuss this right now. It will be all right."

Amanda slumped down. He picked her up like she was a rag doll and carried her up the hill to the house. She continued clinging to him, crying, her sobs wild, uncontrolled, wracking her body.

Pushing his way through the door, he ferried her through the living room to the guest bedroom, and deposited her carefully on the bed. He noticed she was as white as a sheet. Bending down, he pulled off her shoes.

"You're not well. Here, Amanda, let's get this jacket off," he crooned soothingly.

She sat there complaisant, still clutching the book, as he helped her shrug off the jacket. As he bent down to pull the covers and urge her to lie down, she grabbed his arm.

"David, do you find me attractive?" her eyes blinked up at his, as she bit her lip, her face tear-streaked, her words slurred.

"That's an unfair question," David laughed and smoothed the hair from her forehead. "When you look at any man that way, he is going to melt."

"But do you?" she insisted with a frown, her eyes large.

"Amanda, I find you irresistible," David stroked her hair.

She wrapped her arms around his neck and pulled him to her, kissing him roughly. "Show me," she murmured.

Without thinking, he crushed her to him, finding her mouth and abandoning himself to the temptation, cupping her head in his hands. He lowered her to the bed and molded himself to her, momentarily reveling in the feel of her as his hands traveled the length of her.

Coming to himself and muttering an oath, he pulled away.

"Jesus, Amanda, what are you doing?" he exclaimed irritably, releasing her and sitting up.

"I want to hurt him as much as he's hurt me." Amanda's face clouded, her eyes closing as she turned away, bursting into tears again, her body curling into a ball.

"Damn it, no, you don't." David pulled her up to him and embraced her again as she wept and held on to him. "You're much too wasted to think rationally right now. And there is a rational explanation for all this.

"Jon adores you, dear. He hasn't been unfaithful. I know it for a fact." He spoke against her ear. "And you need to quit tempting me, you vixen," he laughed softly. "He's my brother, but I'm only human. And as much as I love you, I don't want to steal his wife and the love of his life. I'm trying to mend fences with him."

He held her for a long time, quietly rocking her as she wept. After a while she calmed down. Amanda's grip loosened, and he noted her breathing slowing, becoming more regular.

"Good girl," he whispered. "Go to sleep now."

He carefully disentangled himself, laying her down against the pillows and covering the unconscious Amanda with a blanket. Sitting beside her on the bed, he carefully extricated the book still clutched in her hand. Stroking her hair out of her face, he gazed at her, his features troubled.

He picked up the book and opened it, reading the note stuck inside the cover. It all suddenly made sense. Shit, he thought. No wonder she's drunk.

He heard a noise and turned. Ralph Carmichael stood frozen in the doorway. "What the hell—" he began angrily, but David put his fingers to his lips, getting up and pushing Ralph out of the room, following him and shutting the door behind him.

"She's asleep," David whispered.

"What are you doing here with Amanda?" Ralph's eyes were wide with surprise, his voice raised.

"Keep your voice down," David spoke authoritatively. "I found her on the dock just a little while ago, drunk out of her head, hysterical. She's just fallen asleep."

"Why?" Ralph whispered, shocked. "I just left her an hour or two ago at the church."

David shook his head, frowning. "She hates Jon's guts right now. Leave her be; let her sleep it off."

"But why?" Ralph echoed suspiciously.

"Because of this and the presents in the kitchen, I imagine." David thrust the book in his hand.

"What is this?" Ralph stared confusedly at the volume.

"Look inside the cover," David advised.

Carmichael opened the book and read the note, his face contorting in pain. "Where did this come from?" he demanded, his voice hoarse.

David took his arm and propelled him to the kitchen. "Look," he suggested.

Ralph picked up the note. "Lauren Mallory? But—"

"Yeah, it was postmarked the date of her death," David pointed out to him. "And this," he pointed to the cufflink and note, which Ralph read, his eyes wide, stunned.

"This can't be," he whispered.

There was a knocking on the door.

"What the hell?" David muttered. He left Ralph and went to the door. There stood Charlie Petrino.

"Chief—I mean, Sheriff." David let him in, suddenly apprehensive. With Petrino was another man with some equipment.

"This is Jimmy Faber, Florida Department of Law Enforcement. Jimmy, sweep the entire house."

The man nodded.

"Fred's probably behind me." Petrino was gruff. "Where's Amanda?"

Ralph walked into the room. He stopped short. "Who's he?"

"Not a word. Let's walk outside a minute and let him work."

"But—" David started.

Petrino put his finger to his lips. "Where's Amanda?"

290

"She's passed out in the bedroom," David answered him.

"Is she OK?" Petrino was surprised.

"It's a long story."

"Jimmy, be careful in there. Don't wake her." Petrino pointed to the bedroom. He motioned the other men to follow him out the front door.

David said softly, "Call me if she awakens."

They walked out onto the front porch. David began. "OK, why are you here, Sheriff?"

"I could ask the same about you two." Petrino looked at him suspiciously.

"I actually needed to talk to Jon, but couldn't raise him on his phone," Ralph answered defensively.

Petrino pointed to the rocking chairs. "Why don't you have a seat?"

Ralph complied dazedly, but David remained standing, still gazing through the screen door inside.

"Now what's this about Amanda?" Petrino demanded.

David looked at Ralph. "I came over to see her. I couldn't find her anywhere. I finally located her on the dock. She was stoned drunk. She at first thought I was Jon and said she wanted to kill me. She was clutching the book."

"Why? What book? I don't understand," Petrino frowned.

"I never expected to see Amanda like that." David shook his head. "Has she ever done that before?"

Ralph interjected, "I've never seen Amanda drink more than one at any function. She is very strict, particularly after Bill tried to poison her. She hardly drinks at all."

"Only once before," said Charlie softly. They looked at him.

"Right after Andy died, she disappeared. We didn't want to create a fuss, but we were worried. Mrs. Witherspoon had me come out here with her to the farm after we couldn't raise Mandy by telephone. We found her sloshed, incoherent, sitting on the dock in the driving rain. She caught pneumonia, and was seriously ill for a while."

"That's where I found her this evening," David nodded. "I guess the book brought it all back."

"Book?" Petrino demanded again.

"Why are you here?" David asked Petrino, changing the subject.

He hesitated. "Oh, the hell with it. Amanda got word to me that she needed to see me. A grand jury is being convened next week."

Fred walked up out of the dark. "I saw her this afternoon, and handed her some registered mail packages that came. She asked me to contact Charlie for her, said she needed some answers."

Charlie stopped him. "You had to sign for these packages?"

"Yes," Fred nodded.

"Let me see them," Petrino demanded.

"No," David objected. "Amanda's out of it, and Jon is not here to give you permission."

Petrino said slowly, "I'm not asking as Sheriff, David. You're going to have to trust me."

David hesitated, then strode back into the house. Moments later he returned with the envelopes and items, handing them to Petrino.

Petrino reviewed the envelopes, notes, book and cufflink. His jaw set ominously when he saw the cufflink.

The man named Jimmy walked out. "All clear, Sheriff. And the woman in the bed didn't stir. I located no other devices."

"Thanks, Jimmy," Petrino said, not looking up. "Here," he added, tossing his car keys to the operative, "take my car and go back to the station. Tell your boss I'll brief him shortly. I'll get a ride back. And remember you didn't see me, and you have never been here."

The man nodded and left.

"We can go back in," Petrino nodded. "I had the place swept for bugs."

"Bugs?" David echoed. "Why?"

"Can't be too careful." Petrino was terse. "And we found evidence of them at the law office, along with the recorder pens. There were some strategically located at the sheriff's department as well."

Ralph's eyes grew wide. They all walked back inside, David preceding them and going to the bedroom door to look in on Amanda. Ralph's eyes followed him momentarily while he turned on a couple more lamps.

"I know I should not be asking this. However, we're off the record here. Do either of you have any explanation for any of this?" Petrino inquired. "And where is Jon?"

Ralph answered, "He told me to tell Amanda he would be late tonight—had some business to attend to." He shrugged. "Some bigwig client he had to meet."

"A cufflink matching this one was found in Lauren Mallory's hand at the crime scene," Petrino responded.

Ralph's eyes grew big. "Oh, my God," he muttered, sinking down into a nearby chair.

David was astounded. "I don't believe it. Just a minute." He disappeared a moment, before Charlie could stop him. Ralph looked at Petrino and shrugged.

David returned, his face white. "Jon's cufflinks are missing."

"No, they're not," Petrino replied.

The men looked at him, dumbfounded. "Jon was wearing them Tuesday when I had him turn over the clothes he was wearing." He smiled grimly. "On a hunch I had Bruce check on that today. We have them.

"Ralph, Jon, and I all wore matching links the day Jon and Mandy got married. So the link isn't his. By process of elimination, it's either Ralph's, or someone else has purloined a set just like ours."

Ralph shook his head, stunned. "I lost one of my links at the engagement party," he confessed. "I didn't say anything, because I was upset. They were my favorites."

"We looked for the matching link at your house, and didn't find it," Charlie volunteered. "Where did you keep yours, Ralph?"

"They were generally on top of the dresser. I wore them to the engagement party. When we got home and I noticed the one missing, I left the other out, thinking I might go to Jerri's with it and see if I could get a replacement set. But the next morning I took Claire to the airport really early, and forgot about it until just now."

"When we looked, we didn't find it," Petrino offered. "But what about this book?"

"I'm stumped," David replied.

"We found some of Andrew's personal effects in a box in the attic at the condo," Petrino said flatly. "Do you know anything about that?"

"No way," breathed David. "Why would his stuff be there?"

Petrino looked at him hard. "Could Jon have taken Lauren Mallory to the condo, or met her there?"

"No," replied David slowly. "But I did."

They all looked at him expectantly.

"That's why her prints were all over the condo?" Petrino persisted.

"I ran into Lauren in D.C. early last week." He spoke so quietly they could barely hear him.

"David, please don't say anything they can use against you," Ralph warned him, standing and putting his hand on David's shoulder.

David slumped down onto the sofa. "No, I need to get it out." He took a deep breath. "I wasn't expecting it; we just ran into each other at a restaurant." He briefly outlined their affair.

"When I saw her the other day, Lauren acted as though we had not been apart all this time. Then she called; she picked up where we left off nine years ago. After a couple days together, she flew back down here with me, and we stayed at the condo. She said she had never been there. She wanted to go to the engagement party. I said 'sure'. She disappeared a couple of days before, then showed up for the party. Then she disappeared again after the party. I couldn't get her to return my calls.

"I was out all day Tuesday looking at properties with a realtor. Then I got the call Tuesday evening to meet her at this address, which turned out to be Ralph's house. As I arrived, Ralph pulled up too. That's when—" David choked up.

"So Lauren found the book, and then sent it to Amanda the day she's murdered?" Petrino mused aloud. "Why? What about the cufflink?"

David asserted emphatically, "I can't believe Jon was with Lauren."

"Did Lauren tell you for whom she was working? Did she mention Esme Townsend?" Petrino questioned David.

David replied confusedly, "Who is that?"

Petrino summarized the information he received from Amanda about her meeting with Varas.

Ralph chimed in, "Amanda and I met secretly at the church this afternoon, and she relayed this to me. But she hadn't told Jon."

"Why not?" David shook his head in disbelief.

"Because the information this Salvatore Varas gave was that this Lauren was pregnant, and that the baby was Jon's." Ralph looked down at the floor. "Amanda didn't want to believe it, but had also been warned that Varas would know if she shared this information with anyone, and there would be consequences. She said Jon had Lauren's phone number."

He turned to Charlie. "Meanwhile Jon knew she had met with you last night, and was imagining the worst. I came out tonight to tell Jon this, because I couldn't get up with him after my talk with Amanda. She gave me permission to share it."

"No wonder she is out of her mind," David finished for him.

Petrino's cell phone rang. "Petrino here. Yes?" he responded irritably. As he listened, his face grew grave. "Notify the FDLE boys to get rolling. I'm on my way. Secure the place. What about Varas?"

He listened for a minute, his face hardening. "OK. Get me the whereabouts and contact numbers for Toby; I'll have to notify him."

He hung up. "Fred, I need to borrow your truck," he said tersely.

"What is it?" Ralph asked.

"Esme Townsend has just been shot," he said over his shoulder. "Don't anyone think about leaving. Stay put, and make yourselves comfortable. Take care of her; don't leave her alone."

Charlie and Fred disappeared. Ralph and David were left alone.

"I'm not leaving her," David was emphatic. "If Jon returns, she wakes up and finds him here, she may go for her gun."

Ralph remarked, "I'm afraid to leave you alone with her, what with your history with Jon's girlfriends."

David protested, "I would never do that to Jon and Amanda."

Ralph went to the bar and mixed a couple of drinks. David returned to the bedroom door and opened it, gazing at the sleeping Amanda. Ralph walked up to him and handed him a drink, staring at her too.

David whispered, "Why does life have to be so difficult for the two of them?" He slowly pulled the door closed.

"But that is life," Ralph voiced hoarsely. "One step forward, two steps back. She adores Jon, but I told him that trust comes hard for her. And apparently Varas has been playing both ends against the middle. They're both now afraid to trust each other."

"Hope she gives him a chance to explain." David looked at Ralph. "Are you hungry? I can raid the refrigerator."

"No. I don't have much appetite after today." Ralph was gloomy.

David moved over to one of the sofas and sat, silent, preoccupied. Ralph followed and sat across from him. David remarked, "I never expected to see Amanda wasted like that. It was—frightening, I guess."

"Why don't you and Jon get along?" Ralph stared at his friend.

"There's been a distance now between Jon and me for a while," David remarked. "I know I'm to blame for most of it. Amanda has been trying to heal that breach. And I've been trying, too," he added somberly. "I am sorry that we haven't been closer, and I've been the reason for his distrust. But I would never come between him and Amanda."

Ralph nodded. "And Jon has a definite jealous streak. But he's the one she has eyes for, that she talks of, that she is building her life around. This manipulation of her has chipped away at the faith she built in him. I think once the truth is exposed, she will recognize it for what it is."

"Well, hope springs eternal," David smiled grimly. "I'm going to take her some juice, try to combat the hangover."

David headed to the kitchen. In a moment he returned with a small tray. He let himself in the bedroom and turned on a small lamp beside the door.

He carefully placed the tray on the bedside table, and sat down beside her.

She stirred and opened her eyes, blinking, then placing her hands over her eyes. "Oh," she moaned softly.

"Hi," he spoke. "Sis, will you take a seltzer for me, and a little juice? It will help counteract the living death you will feel tomorrow."

"I want to die now," she whispered hoarsely.

"Humor Brother David on this," he crooned. He helped her sit up and propped some pillows behind her, handing her the small glass of fluid. "Here, all at once."

She obediently gulped the liquid. Taking the empty glass from her, he handed her the glass of vegetable juice. She shook her head, but he insisted.

"A known antidote—restores antioxidants. I know from personal experience," he smiled. "I want you to drink it all."

"Without vodka?" she quipped, a weak attempt at a joke.

"You've had enough of that," he retorted, smiling. "And here is some Gatorade and water for later, to try to restore some electrolytes."

"I'll be floating," she smiled weakly.

David stroked her hair out of her face. "Amanda, there's a good reason for what happened, for the items you got in the mail. You need to give Jon a chance to explain. He loves you." He saw her sudden distress. "Just think about it. He would never hurt you."

"Did I do anything stupid?" she whispered, her face flushed, as she looked away.

He squeezed her hand and laughed lightly. Some matters are better off forgotten, he thought. "No, Sis, but I would like the ammo clips to keep you from mistaking me for Jon and killing me. Promise you'll not murder anyone, OK?"

She closed her eyes. "I don't want to kill him. It's just that—" Tears formed.

"It's OK," David whispered. "Just get some rest. I'll be in the living room if you need anything."

"You won't leave me alone, will you?" she cried softly.

"No, Amanda, I'll be close at hand." He patted her arm reassuringly. "I need your help with something tomorrow. So drink your fluids and sleep."

He sat there until he was satisfied she was succumbing to slumber, then let himself back out.

Ralph was still sitting on the couch. "How is she?" he asked gravely.

"I think she's sobering up. She is already feeling the effects of the hangover. She took some juice and drifted back to sleep." He looked at his watch irritably. "Where the hell is Jon?"

"I thought he'd be here by now," remarked Ralph. "Let me try his phone." Punching buttons on his cell phone, he listened a minute. "Jon, this is Ralph. Where are you? I'm waiting for you at your house. Call me."

"Where did Fred go?" David questioned.

"I think he went with Petrino," Ralph offered wearily.

"Go lie down," David commanded.

"Not until Jon gets here," Ralph insisted.

"OK, then sack out on the couch." David walked over to the guest room and in a moment brought back a pillow and coverlet which he dumped on the couch beside Ralph. "I'll keep vigil."

CHAPTER 27

Jon left Amanda's law office, looking at his watch. He had an appointment at the courthouse with a new client. He didn't know why the client insisted on meeting somewhere other than his office in Destin, but the appointment had been made by one of the senior partners without consultation with Jon, so Jon knew it was someone with connections. Why didn't she meet with the senior partner? Jon wondered again.

When he questioned the man, Bobby had laughed over the phone. "This—Reba Thompson—is a bigwig in the area, and she was quite insistent she was not driving to Pensacola. She asked for you, because you were local. Insisted on you, as a matter of fact. Seems you have fans in high places, Jon. I'm jealous—she never asked for me by name."

Jon, his mind still on Amanda's behavior, pulled into a parking space at the courthouse and debarked, a leather folio in his hand, along with his keys and phone. Just as he locked the car doors, a black limousine sedan pulled up beside him and the passenger window slid down. Expecting someone asking for directions, he was surprised when a well-coiffed woman looked out.

"Mr. Connor?" she smiled sunnily.

"Yes, ma'am," he smiled politely, wondering how she knew his name.

"We've not met. I'm Esme Townsend, your 4:00 appointment. You may have been given the name Reba Thompson, but I assure you it was done out of an abundance of discretion."

"Oh." Jon covered his surprise. "You felt it necessary to use a pseudonym?"

"I have my reasons, and you might not have agreed to meet me otherwise. Please join me," she spoke authoritatively. "I require privacy in discussing my business with you."

As he hesitated, she smiled. "Don't worry. I'll have Tom bring you back here. Although you are mighty good-looking, I would not risk Mrs. Connor's wrath by hog-tying you and running off with you."

297

The chauffeur appeared out of nowhere and opened the passenger door. Jon shrugged and climbed in.

"That's better," she laughed, a silvery sound. "You've obviously heard my name. Do you know who I am, Mr. Connor?"

"You can call me Jon, and I've heard your name," Connor stated smoothly. "I'm not sure why you would be requiring my services, when I'm pretty sure you have several high-dollar firms at your disposal."

"Could I interest you in a drink? Glenlivet, perhaps?" She pointed to the bar beside him, her smile broadening.

"No, thank you." Jon's eyes narrowed.

"I know quite a bit about you, it seems. Former FBI, did some work with the Secret Service, impressive connections, quite a few commendations, from a very influential family. Close friends with the governor, ties to the President. I do my homework."

"I'm afraid I'm not as well versed in your history, Mrs. Townsend." Jon was uneasy. "But I have certainly heard of your influence in political matters."

"Call me Esme. And we have at least one common interest, Jon." She bent forward, her voice low. "Your wife Amanda."

"How?" Jon's throat tightened.

"I've known Amanda all her life," Esme laughed again. "Do you know we are actually friends of sorts? I've contributed to the recital fund, and tried to involve her in several community functions, but she has resisted my efforts to cultivate her for moving up in society. She is a lovely girl. You are very lucky to have her."

"I like to think so, but I still fail to see the connection."

"She's my great white hope for the new county judge of these parts," Esme smiled. "But I'll bet she has not shared that with you?"

Jon's eyes widened. "No, she hasn't. So I guess you had something to do with the application that was sent in for her?"

Esme laughed. "Let's just say I have the means at my disposal. But don't be quick to blame her for not telling you herself. She had declined before, but I wanted to make sure she didn't pass up the opportunity. I believe my associate Salvatore Varas may have frightened her into keeping this information to herself."

"I don't think she would—" Jon started, but Esme laid her hand on his knee.

"Keep it from you? But, my dear, she would if it meant protecting you from harm."

"Mrs. Townsend," Jon's voice was icy, "please state your business. I'm not into games."

"Call me Esme," she gazed at him, suddenly solemn. "And I'm not playing games." She suddenly looked very tired. "I backed Kilmer, and he did a good job, but then entangled himself in a mess. Some men cannot keep their fly zipped, and he certainly picked a career-breaker. That was most unfortunate. And Billy Barnes had come to me wanting a judicial position, but I felt he was too much a maverick, a chip off the old block, with too many potential liabilities to count. That proved a wise decision on my part."

"So you're telling me you are the reason all the politicians rise and fall?" Jon countered dubiously.

"Only the positions in which I'm interested," she smiled. "To be successful at this game is to know when to push, and when to concede and let some other 'unlicensed lobbyist', as I think of myself, win. I pick those battles which are important to me."

"So why are you meeting with me, Mrs. Townsend?" he asked tightly.

"It's Esme," she reminded him. "Jon Connor, I'll come to the point. I have cancer. I am dying. I have kept this information secret so far. I have been fighting in the political arena behind the scenes for years, making and breaking the great and small. Now my minions, all vultures, are sniffing blood, and I have to have henchmen to watch my henchmen.

"Mr. Varas and I have been—associates—for several years now. He hopes to step into my shoes as a wheeler-dealer. He is already a power-monger in his own right. His schemes are a bit more ambitious than I have ever aspired to, and his methods include strong-arm tactics of which I do not approve.

"I have recently discovered that he has branched off on his own, using my name as a stepping-stone. I have become alarmed at some of the reports coming in." She laughed self-deprecatingly. "The manipulator is being manipulated. That's why I am meeting you here, in my car, which has been swept clean of bugs."

She paused. "You know my son Toby?"

"Yes," Jon looked at her sadly. "He sings in the choir at church, and serves on the vestry now. A fine young man."

"A fine young man, who refused to follow in his father's footsteps," the woman continued briskly. "He was not interested in law or politics, but went off and became an architect, living on the beach and generally doing exactly the opposite of what I planned for him. I was upset with him when as a teenager he left the Presbyterians and flocked to St. Catherine's youth and choir groups.

"But he thinks the world of your bride. In fact, he is the one who suggested that I back some honest hard-working capable people for positions of leadership, and thought Amanda would make a great judge. I'm generally my own boss, but I do want to leave this world with my only son thinking highly of me."

"So that's why the 'offer' to Amanda?"

"Partly, yes. But I've always had this hankering to immerse Amanda into politics, wipe away that naïveté of hers. She now has the wealth to go with the smarts, and that talent shouldn't be wasted. I always thought she'd bring a freshness to the bargaining table, and she'd be good at it. But of course I wanted her on my side; she makes a formidable opponent. So when Toby suggested it, I wanted so badly to make him happy and make it so. But when Varas gets involved, he has a way of making even the innocuous seem threatening. And I fear he has gone too far."

"In what way?" Jon pressed

"Let's just say that my suggestion to Amanda about seeking the judiciary has become a much larger project to Salvatore." Her eyes met Jon's. "Varas is a dangerous man, Mr. Connor. And Toby has confronted me and issued an ultimatum. But I worry I might have waited too late to stop him."

"Why wouldn't you just back Ralph Carmichael?" Jon expelled an angry breath.

"I always held a grudge against Ralph, because I asked him to talk Toby into going into law, and Toby did not."

Jon censured her, "Did you not ever give your son credit for making up his own mind? Why would you hold that against an attorney as good as Ralph?"

"Why indeed? Because I can," she sniffed autocratically.

"But Amanda does not want to be judge, and we've already pledged to support Ralph."

She thought a moment. "Why wouldn't Amanda want to be judge? Wouldn't you like to see her become successful, someone to be reckoned with?"

"She is already successful, someone to be reckoned with. And she likes being a lawyer," Jon retorted softly.

"That makes no sense," Esme sneered.

"Maybe not to you, but then again your problem is that Amanda does not fit your mold. She is not interested in political connections, being a player. She likes to fight her battles one on one, in a courtroom, with her adversary out in the open. She likes influencing the decision in that fashion, not making it."

He paused. "You are trying to enmesh her in the very practices she despises. You know, if you really like her, you might consider that she really doesn't want that."

Esme stared at him dubiously. "But Toby—"

"Do you think he would want Amanda pushed against her will into the slot? I think not. Toby does not strike me as one who would be terribly happy if he knew his 'nominee', so to speak, was being forced into a role not of her choosing. And Amanda does not take well to being pushed. Surely you already know that."

"Ah, the honeymoon must be over, if you say things like that," Esme retorted, laughing shortly.

"It's part of her charm, the naked honesty, the fire in the belly, the missionary zeal," Jon observed. "What you so callously refer to as her 'naïveté' is not that at all, but a fervent wish that the world's decisions not be totally made by the power mongers of the world, and that people of merit fulfil their dreams of success."

Esme was silent a minute, as though digesting his words. "I'll think about it. But there's more than me to convince now. I believe Salvatore has a mission of his own to ensnare your pretty little wife." She smiled tightly. "According to Toby, Varas apparently forced a meeting with Amanda. Toby found out and intervened, apparently quite timely. My son was not amused."

Jon swallowed his shock at this news. He leaned forward, anxiety etched on his face. "Mrs. Townsend, I am not amused either. My wife's safety and wellbeing are my top priorities." His jaw clenched. "And if your top henchman has been threatening her, I will protect what's mine. I am not about to let you and your 'associate' destroy Amanda with your influence peddling machinations."

Esme gazed at him, making no reply. He continued, "Why did you hire Lauren Mallory?"

Esme smiled stiffly. "I didn't. Varas did. This Lauren was hired to manipulate the players to make the cards fall as he wanted when my efforts appeared ineffectual. My methods are tried and true, but take time and finessing. Salvatore does not believe in evolution. He is more impatient than I am, so he likes to force and bend things and people to his will."

"You mean blackmail?" Jon raised his eyebrows.

"Among other things," Esme nodded.

"Other things?" Jon echoed, his voice strained.

"Well, let's just say that Salvatore is a master of creativity," Esme spoke, her eyes scanning out the dark tinted windows.

"What are you saying?" Jon demanded.

"He manufactures evidence if he cannot find it. He's quite good at it. He has recently become emboldened by his successes. He sees this murder as an acid test of his skills."

Esme turned and stared at Jon, her face somber. "I never thought Amanda Childs was afraid of anything, but I believe she is now. What I was unable to obtain by persuasion Varas is getting through coercion. She has professed her loyalty to her friends already. She must really love you."

"Just what have you done?" Jon's hands clenched into fists.

"I did nothing but ask Amanda to consider applying for the judgeship. But Varas hired some expert counterfeiter, and has provided her photographs, pretty good ones, that he has threatened to make public."

"Photographs?" Jon echoed.

"Ones that cast her husband, her law partner and her brother-in-law as intimates of Ms. Mallory."

"What?" Jon leaned forward, his eyes wide, his face bloodless.

Esme leaned back as though afraid of his reaction. "Like I said, he is skilled. I think he went so far as to create some of her with our new sheriff as well, as extra incentive for Amanda to do his will. So Lauren Mallory was of far more use than Varas originally thought."

Jon sucked in his breath sharply, stunned.

"Yes, he has found Amanda's weakness," Esme disclosed, suddenly solemn. "He has threatened to destroy those around her, those she holds in high esteem."

"And Lauren Mallory was part of this scheme? You knew about Lauren?" Jon demanded.

"I found out, guessed the truth when I received an invitation to a D.C. soiree from her. I smelled a setup, and my suspicions were confirmed when Varas later prevailed upon me to invite her to a conclave of the area officials. However, I do not know why she was killed or by whom. Would Varas? He's capable, but she was his hired gun. I don't understand it."

"So you didn't?" Jon inserted coldly.

"No, Jon Connor. I have never stooped to murder." Esme's voice was cool.

"But after all this you still can't tell me who killed Lauren? You didn't? You don't think Varas did? I didn't, and I'm pretty sure my brother and friend did not. I hoped you were about to give me the clues to what is going on here. Maybe that was momentary wishful thinking on my part."

"I can answer some of those questions. I'm about to entrust a sacred detail to you," she said confidentially. "Hold out your hand."

He did so, and she placed a thumbdrive in his hand, reaching over and closing his hand over it.

"What is this?"

"This is documentation as to Varas' systematic theft of monies from me, and records showing his nefarious activities. That was Ms. Mallory's primary function—she was part of the plan for Salvatore's latest and greatest scheme

The Connors' Crisis

to relieve me of some of my fortune. I think it might prove enlightening, and might lead law enforcement to other needed evidence."

"But why would you give it to me?"

She sighed, looking tired. "Jon Connor, despite what you think of me, I try to stay on the right side of the law in my dealings. I am sorry to say that Salvatore, as much comfort and help as he's been to me at times," she paused, "is not so circumspect. Lately my good name has been somewhat tainted in the higher circles."

She laughed humorlessly. "Your good buddy our current governor is actually a cousin of mine. He pulled me aside to let me know that Varas has been trading freely upon my name, to my detriment. As fond as I am of Salvatore, that won't do. I'm not leaving this world with the family honor besmirched. I want Toby to be proud of his mother, or at least not ashamed of me. And despite what you may think of me, I really like Amanda, and feel sorry for her distress over those she is so fond of. I would not do anything to harm her. I admire her, after all, but don't want her to know that."

Esme took a tremulous breath. "I've therefore made a deal with the guys in the white hats, your buddies with the FBI. And, to show my good faith, Charlie Petrino needs this, because he should be in on the cleanup detail and resulting glory. Toby has already provided him some vital information. Of course, I am not going to personally deliver it to Petrino. Furthermore, I had to find someone I could trust, someone without prior ties to me. Toby was insistent that it come from me, that I personally provide this to the good guys and restore his faith in me."

"But why me?" Jon was incredulous.

"I know your record," Esme smiled. "Petrino would not trust me anyway, even though Toby talked me into backing him at the last minute. And your Amanda was quite eloquent in her defense of her two friends to me. Of course Charlie would never believe that I supported him. That I had to handle very discreetly, to avoid tipping Varas off."

She looked at Jon's surprised face. "My sources say I'm not the only one peddling influence with the powers that be, Mr. Connor," she added meaningfully.

"One does what one can," he gazed at her dispassionately.

"So why do you look down your nose at me?"

"My providing occasional support to someone can hardly be classed the same as buying and selling positions." Jon was blunt. "And if what you've told me is true, you have been instrumental in creating a monster to carry on your legacy."

"Ooh." Esme stared at him. "You don't pull punches, do you? You think so little of me?"

303

"I don't know you, but I know your type." Jon realized he was treading on thin ice, but his simmering rage drove him on.

"Oh, now I'm really hurt. I hoped I was one of a kind." She smiled saccharinely. "Do you know that your wife has friends in very high places, who also lobbied for Charlie Petrino and Ralph Carmichael?"

"That could very well be." Jon was noncommittal.

"Seems her former father-in-law placed the phone call that finally clinched the deal for Charlie Petrino."

Esme was gratified to see the sudden consternation on Jon's face. "You know, for a newly married couple you keep a lot of secrets from each other."

The car pulled up in front of a spacious imposing white antebellum home with large Ionic columns framing the facade. "I'd like to continue this discussion over tea."

"I'd rather not," Jon countered, his mind whirling. I need to get this information to Charlie, then find Amanda right away, he thought. He was anxious to be by her side after Esme's revelations.

"Oh, but you see, I've retained you for two hours for a reason," she waved away his protest. "It's tea time, and I don't miss tea. The way I see it, we have over an hour left. And I'm very interested in knowing what 'type' I am."

Noting that his jaw was set stubbornly, she took his arm. "You're not expected home yet, and you just might learn some additional information to help you solve your puzzle."

"My puzzle?" he looked at her.

"I know you have questions. I may have answers," she quipped. "You see, we will be joined by Varas. I will tell him that I accosted you as to Amanda's becoming judge, you countered wanting to know why I was not backing Carmichael, and I brought you home to tea to explain it all. That's the truth. What he doesn't know is that we're turning the tables on him, and I've allowed my home to be bugged by the Bureau. What's good for the goose . . ." she smiled urbanely.

"Wouldn't it make more sense to keep our meeting a secret from him?"

"Yes," she replied, "but he has spies, and already probably knows that we've had this little *tete a tete*. We must put our own spin on the situation."

The door opened, and she waved her hand. "After you, dear."

Connor reluctantly slid out, and Esme took his arm as she followed. "Welcome to my humble abode," she smiled as they walked up the steps.

As they reached the front door, it opened and Varas stood there. "Mr. Connor," he smiled sanguinely, almost bowing to him. "How pleasant to finally make your acquaintance. I'm so happy that Esme has brought you home to tea."

The Connors' Crisis

Suddenly several shots rang out.

Jon reflexively hurled himself on top of Townsend. Varas pulled out a semi-automatic and fired back, before collapsing, injured, on the threshold. "After him," he shouted to Tom, who took off after the running figure in the woods.

Jon felt a stinging, and saw blood on the arm of his jacket sleeve. He quickly rolled off Esme Townsend and turned her to face him. "I'm shot," she whispered, before blacking out.

CHAPTER 28

Varas with difficulty pulled himself up. "Stay with her. I'm going after him."

"You're hurt," Jon objected. He pulled out his cell phone and dialed 9-1-1. Requesting an ambulance and sheriff, he stopped. "What is the address?" he asked Varas.

"Tell them Esme Townsend's home. Everyone knows where that is," Varas spoke, holding his side where a bloody spot appeared to be spreading.

Jon gave the information. "And let Charlie Petrino know right away. Tell him Jon Connor made the call."

He rang off without waiting for a reply.

Varas slowly and painfully lowered himself to beside Connor and Esme. "How is she?" he looked at Townsend lying there, his face grave.

"She's unconscious. I think she was hit in the lungs." Jon glared at Varas. "Who was the shooter?"

"I—I don't know," Varas denied.

"You're lying," Jon said bluntly. "You knew him. He was a pretty good shot, hitting all three of us. I think he was aiming to kill her. Was he one of yours?"

"I don't know what you are talking about," Varas stared at him, gasping as he shifted and more blood flowed.

"Lie back and let's put pressure on the site," Jon ordered, as he carefully tried to prop Townsend up against the steps. Pulling off his jacket, he made a pillow and placed it behind Esme's head. Ripping off his tie, he quickly unbuttoned his shirt and wadded it up, using it to apply direct pressure to the site of Varas' wound. Varas shrunk from him, as though expecting a blow.

Within moments the place was swarming with a couple of suited men and servants. Jon took command, telling them to leave the two victims where they were as ambulance sirens were heard, heralding the approach of help.

306

As the EMTs took over, he slowly made it to his feet and moved out of the way, allowing them room to work. He frowned as he realized that the sheriff was still not present. He pulled out his phone.

"Petrino," he heard the familiar voice say.

"Charlie, this is Jon. There's been a shooting at Esme Townsend's house," Jon explained. "Esme is in critical condition. The ambulance has just made it here."

"I'm on my way now. Where are you?" Petrino demanded.

"I'm here at the scene. I'll explain later. You need to get here."

"Where is Varas?"

"He's been shot, too. They're treating both of them."

"Stay there until I get there," Petrino commanded.

Jon hung up. An EMT approached him. "Sir, you've been injured," he exclaimed, as he pointed to Jon's arm, which was oozing blood.

"It's nothing much," Jon assured him. "Just a graze."

"It doesn't matter. At least let me look at it for you."

Jon allowed himself to be led to a rescue vehicle as sheriff's deputies pulled up with sirens and lights blazing.

"How is Ms. Townsend?" he asked, as a paramedic walked by.

"Pretty serious. They're trying to stabilize her before getting her to ER."

"Varas?"

"He's fighting them—doesn't want to go to the hospital. He's bleeding badly."

The EMT treating him spoke up. "You're lucky. It didn't nick too deep, but you could use some stitches. Don't you think you should accompany the others to the hospital?"

Jon glanced quickly at his name tag. "I've had worse, Matt. It'll wait until Sheriff Petrino arrives," Jon replied grimly.

"OK, but I'm going to at least put some antibiotic and cover it with a butterfly and some gauze," Matt countered firmly.

As Matt finished his ministrations, a pickup truck pulled up, and Petrino and Fred Vaughan got out. He spoke briefly to the ambulance personnel, then waved them out. Spying Jon, he walked over to him.

"OK, out with it," he growled. "Tell me what happened, and why the hell you are here in the middle of it."

"First I need to call Amanda and let her know where I am," Jon remarked.

"No need. I just came from there. David and Ralph are there."

"Why? What's wrong?" Jon started. "Why were all of you there?"

"Long story. Everyone's OK. Nothing you can do right now."

"But I need to be with her," protested Jon desperately.

"Not before you fill me in," Charlie responded briskly. "Now tell me what is going on." Charlie gazed critically at Jon, standing there in a t-shirt and trousers. "And where are your clothes?"

Matt the EMT interrupted, "He apparently used them for first aid."

Petrino called over one of his men, and spoke to him, pointing inside the house. The man looked at Petrino dubiously, but nodded and disappeared.

Jon filled Petrino in on his meeting with Esme Townsend, and about the shooting.

"Did you get a look at this shooter?"

"A glimpse. Tall, blonde, good build, and not a bad shot. He disappeared into the bushes there." Jon pointed. "I think the chauffeur took off after him. I stayed with Mrs. Townsend until the ambulance arrived."

"Know him? Ever see him before?" Petrino cut to the chase.

"No, but I'm convinced that Varas fellow knew him," Jon remarked. "He denied it.

"Oh, and by the way, Charlie, Mrs. Townsend gave me a present to deliver to you." He reached in his pants pocket and pulled out the thumb drive.

"What is it?"

"Some evidence she has compiled against Varas. She said it would be very useful to you," Jon shrugged.

"We'll take a look at it." Charlie stuck it in his shirt pocket, as an officer ran up with a folded shirt. Charlie took it.

"Here." He handed it to Jon.

"What's this?"

"A replacement shirt for you. I figured if you helped save Varas' life, he could loan you a shirt."

"But this is a Ferragamo dress shirt, and it looks new," Jon protested.

"He won't miss it," the young officer laughed. "Chief was right. He has drawers full."

Jon shrugged, then unfolded it and slipped it on.

Petrino grinned. "The cuss has been living here. I knew it. I'll bet Toby is fit to be tied, after all the hell his mother has given him about decorum and discretion and keeping up appearances."

"What are you talking about?" Jon demanded.

"Varas not only worked for Esme, he was her—I don't know, live-in boyfriend, giggolo, perhaps?" Petrino's voice lowered until only Jon could hear. "She tried to keep it secret. But you know about small towns and their secrets."

"I'm beginning to find out," Jon retorted.

"Jon!"

The Connors' Crisis

As he turned, he saw a familiar face making his way toward him. "Kimball!" he motioned to the man.

"Why are you here, Jon?" Kimball shook his hand.

Jon winced. "What is it?" Kimball asked.

"Just a graze—it will be OK," Jon rubbed his arm with his left hand. "Maybe Matt's wrap will keep me from bleeding all over Varas' shirt." He looked at Kimball. "What are you doing here?"

"Actually tracking down a rogue CIA agent who has contracted himself out for private killings," Kimball said.

"Here?" Petrino's head jerked up.

"Yep," Kimball nodded. "And you'll never guess the connection we found." He paused, as he gained their full attention. "Lauren Mallory." Jon was stunned, but had no opportunity to ask questions. The chauffeur appeared through the trees, and Jon held up his hand. "Just a minute. I've got to hear this." Jon pushed his way to the man. "Well?"

"He got away." Tom hung his head. "But Varas hit him. He's hurt. He apparently had a motorcycle hidden in the woods just off the road. I saw him take off. A BMW."

"Did you get a look at him?" Petrino came up behind Jon.

"Yes. Blonde, big-shouldered, wearing all camouflage gear. He was fast. But there are drops of blood in places down the trail."

"Look anything like this?" Kimball thrust a photo in front of the chauffeur.

"That's him," the man nodded.

Petrino waved at a plainclothes officer. "Go with him and get samples of the blood, some photos," he ordered.

Turning back to Kimball, Charlie said, "I'm all ears. It took you long enough to get here after you promised some major assistance."

Jon looked quizzically at Petrino. Charlie continued, "Are you FBI bastards finally going to share information or what?"

Kimball shook his head. "He just identified Karl Vause, former CIA, lately selling out to the highest bidder. Actually, he's not an assassin, but plans ops and hires killers. His specialty is actually counterfeiting documents and photographs. If he was a better shot, probably none of you would be alive to tell the tale."

"He was good enough to hit us all with a handgun at long range," Jon muttered. "And Esme Townsend might not survive."

"Well, we've been trying to track him down since an agent of ours was found killed in his own bed a month ago," Kimball asserted. "We had just recently made a connection, and had reason to believe he is in the employ of this Salvatore Varas."

"What's the connection to Lauren?" Jon questioned, as the two ambulances disappeared out of sight.

"Very interesting. She was also in Varas' employ, apparently, as best we can trace the paper trail. Varas owns some corporation, ostensibly contracting to provide security.

"But the Mallory woman and this Vause go way back. Apparently they have had an on-again, off-again relationship spanning over several years, and we have evidence showing they were feeding each other information while in government service.

"But more importantly, they were married about eleven years ago. Apparently Lauren had the records sealed up North. Made it hard for us to track, but Bubba of course is a genius."

Jon was stunned.

"OK, but what has that to do with the current situation?" Petrino wanted to know.

"Sorry I couldn't share this sooner, but we've been listening in on Varas' conversations for a while," Kimball continued. "We've only just been able to put two and two together, because they of course were using code and pseudonyms. Apparently Mallory was hired to run a scam against Esme Townsend, discredit key players and provide Varas ammunition to blackmail certain community persons to do as he directed." Kimball paused, his meaning clear.

"You mean like Amanda?" Jon's eyes were suddenly cold.

"Yes, Jon, Amanda was one," Kimball affirmed.

"And you didn't tell me?" Jon demanded, his eyes wide.

"Jon, you know we couldn't do that," Kimball sighed. "But we came to the conclusion this afternoon that Karl Vause may have been hired by this Varas guy to provide a myriad of services, forging documents, running surveillance, and even effecting the demise of Esme Townsend herself."

"Shit!" Petrino exclaimed. "Why would Varas bite the hand that has fed him?"

"He apparently thinks he can do business without her," Jon answered. "Ms. Townsend made the comment that the 'minions were smelling blood', and she had to 'hire henchmen to watch the henchmen'."

"Yes, and we had finally found a way to contact her in an effort to get her to turn, to tell her what was happening right under her nose, after we determined that she wasn't in the know, at least as to Vause's identity and purpose. She actually contacted us. Tom there is our man sent to infiltrate the network."

Tom, coming out of the woods with the officer, looked over at them and nodded.

The Connors' Crisis

"Tom was the one who managed to suggest that Ms. Townsend approach you, to provide the necessary insider evidence against Varas. But Tom got word to us that he thought Varas was planning something against her imminently, based on something he had overheard. That's why we're here."

"The thumb drive," Jon said slowly, "that I gave to Petrino at her request contains evidence against Varas. She apparently wanted Charlie in on it."

"And Toby as joint owner of this property gave permission for a search of the old stables out back," Petrino offered. "My men were doing that when the call came in here. Apparently Esme allowed Varas to renovate the buildings and make a lab of sorts, with all sorts of sophisticated copying and surveillance equipment. Toby found out by accident when he walked back there, thinking of restoring the stables himself."

"And just when were you going to share that?" Kimball interjected.

"Hey, we just got in there today," Petrino protested. "If you had made it here earlier as you promised, you would have been invited to tag along." Charlie's eyes flashed ominously, as though daring Kimball to cross him. "And I was going to get around to it, just like you were going to get around to telling me about what went down in that hotel room between Varas and Amanda." He stared at Kimball reproachfully. "She was in more danger than you let on."

Jon's eyes widened as he gazed at Petrino. Charlie continued, "But with the murder and Varas' other manipulations that we've been following, my men and I have been stretched thin. We could have used your help."

"Hotel room?" Jon echoed.

"Yeah, your buddies here had Varas under surveillance when he met with Amanda," Petrino's eyes flashed angrily as he looked over at Kimball.

"But Toby Townsend insisted that we notify Petrino, and Charlie sent in his own man with Toby when he broke up Varas' little party," Kimball offered coolly. He looked at Jon and his face softened. "Your Amanda was putting up a helluva fight, refusing to dance his tune. The conversation netted us quite a bit of good hard evidence against Varas."

"But if Toby hadn't walked in when he did, Amanda could have been hurt," Charlie muttered.

Jon paled. He turned to Kimball, who raised his hands. "I'm sorry," he apologized. "But we weren't about to let anything happen to her."

Charlie demanded, "What does Lauren Mallory's murder have to do with all this? Did Varas arrange that?"

Jon offered, "Esme felt sure Varas wouldn't kill Lauren when she was providing him a service."

Kimball looked down. "Jon, that needs attention," he spoke, as he pointed to a small red stain appearing on the new shirt. "I suggest we adjourn to the hospital where you can be treated and we can hopefully interview our victims."

Petrino quickly gave Bruce Williams, who was heading the crime scene, some instructions, and spoke in low tones to Vaughan, who nodded.

Matt ran up with some gauze. "I told you we need to do something with that. You need to go to the ER."

Kimball said tersely. "I'll get him there pronto. Sheriff, you can accompany us, so that I can fill you in, and vice-versa."

Within seconds Kimball had them en route to the hospital, and a few minutes later they had arrived, just as the ambulances had offloaded their human cargo. The emergency room was filled with medical personnel trying to do triage on the newcomers.

Alan Young was walking across the floor toward the cubicle where Esme Townsend lay. He was surprised to see Jon. "What happened?" he pointed to his arm.

Jon waved him off. "I'm fine. They need attention."

Alan nodded and disappeared. Jon could make out Dr. Cardet in the cubicle ministering to Esme, as Alan took charge over Varas.

Jon heard a familiar voice. "Here, son, let's have a look at you."

Turning, he saw Dr. Howells, who gently led him over to a room out of the bustle of activity. Jon shrugged out of his shirt.

"What caused this?" Howells asked as he snipped off the gauze on Jon's arm.

"An ambush at Esme Townsend's house," Jon replied. "It's just a graze." He turned to Charlie. "I need to call Amanda. I'm already late. She'll be worried. There are some things I need to let her know."

"I've already taken care of that," Petrino said, his face a mask. "Fred's on his way back there."

Jon turned to Kimball. "Now answer my question. What's the connection between Lauren Mallory and Varas and Vause?" He winced as Howells applied peroxide to the wound.

"Be still," Howells admonished sternly.

"We have not figured it all out yet. Hopefully, Bubba can review the documents Mrs. Townsend gave you, and we can figure out what is going on."

"What about the paternity actions? Is there any connection there?"

"What are you talking about?" Kimball stared at Jon blankly.

Jon explained about the paternity actions against himself and Ralph, and about David's belief that he was in fact the father.

"Bubba found a birth certificate of a child born to Lauren Mallory. No father was listed. Child is about eight, named Allison."

"That's the child," Jon said excitedly.

"Lauren was married to this guy during that time, and apparently still is," Kimball stated.

"That means—"

"That in most of the fifty states there is a presumption that the child was legitimate, the biological issue of the husband," Kimball finished.

"But David, and I for that matter, was with Lauren during the time period of probable conception," Jon supplied, his voice low.

He heard Howells' sharp intake of breath, and flushed guiltily. "Amanda knows," he assured Howells. "I told her about Lauren the night of Bubba's engagement party when she met Lauren, and again when the paternity complaint was served. David and I knew nothing about a child before then. I feel certain the girl is not mine, Doc. But if so, I'll take responsibility."

"This will need stitches," Howells replied matter-of-factly, not looking at Jon. "I'll be back. Don't move the arm. I need to stop the bleeding."

Jon buried his head in his other hand, embarrassed. "Damn", he whispered. But the information was bound to become public anyway, he knew.

"Doc's heard worse," Charlie murmured comfortingly.

"However, there's been no clue as to this child, whether she has survived, where she is, nothing," Kimball continued. "Bubba has been checking on that, among other things. It has been as though Lauren Mallory wanted her to disappear, never to be found."

"Until now," Jon muttered.

"Apparently," Kimball agreed.

Howells reappeared with a nurse and tray in tow. He expertly threaded a surgical needle then laid it aside on a tray. "You're probably going to feel some of this," he informed Jon.

Jon nodded to him. He continued, "It doesn't make sense that she would have a child, then hide the child away for eight years, then file two paternity actions."

The men were silent, all digesting the information. Jon tried not to wince as Howells pulled a stitch tight. "Did that hurt?" Howells asked solicitously.

"If I say no, are you going to hurt me more?" Jon queried, biting his lip.

Howells smiled slightly. "Depends." He winked at Charlie, and Charlie grinned.

Howells pulled the needle through again, this time more gently. The other men were quiet as he worked. "You are going to be faithful and make my Amanda happy, aren't you?" he demanded wickedly as he knotted the last stitch, and Jon bit his lip again, swallowing a groan.

Charlie looked at his watch, and his face suddenly went somber. Jon noted it. "What is it?" he asked.

"I've got something to tell you," Charlie started.

Alan Young stepped into view. "My patient is demanding to see you, Jon. He's lost a lot of blood, and it's critical. So let's make it quick."

Howells placed a bandage over the stitches. "I'll give you instructions later," he murmured.

"Thanks, Doc," Jon smiled tentatively, as Howells smiled back.

Jon, followed by Charlie and Kimball, hurried across to the cubicle where Varas lay, pain evident in his features.

He looked up at Jon. "I didn't kill Lauren Mallory, and I didn't order it done," he rasped. "But I know who did."

Jon tried not to show his surprise.

"She was doing a job for me. It was obvious that Esme was not getting what she wanted from your wife. So I took matters into my own hands. My methods aren't as gracious." He paused, taking a breath.

Alan stepped forward. "Can't this wait?" he demanded.

Varas held up his hand weakly. "Doctor, I'm sure you're excellent at your job, but I need to let these men have this information in case I don't make it."

Kimball intoned quickly, "You know you are giving information to law enforcement, and anything you say can be used against you. You have a right to remain silent, and to counsel."

"Yes, yes." Varas dismissed the words with a wave. He continued. "I didn't realize until it happened that there was any connection between Vause and Mallory. I had used both of them before to gather intelligence for me, and I generally pay well.

"I broached the hypothetical possibility to Esme of discrediting Mr. Petrino and Mr. Carmichael. She seemed to like my suggestion, but at the last minute she told me to hold off on the Chief. She never explained why.

"I hired Ms. Mallory, knowing she had the skills to do what I wanted. I wanted Mr. Carmichael caught in a compromising position with her. Then Vause showed up out of the blue, said he was between some large jobs and wanted to know if I had anything for him."

Varas paused, grimacing. Dr. Young started forward. "I insist. Just another minute, please," he commanded. Alan hesitated, then nodded reluctantly.

"I put Vause on the detail of tailing Ms. Mallory. I had my doubts about whether she would successfully complete the job. I didn't know he—he knew her, that they had a past.

"My man discovered that she had filed two paternity actions, not one, and that one of them was against Jon Connor. That was not part of the plan, and I was angry at the unwanted—complication, because it was Esme's wish to push Mrs. Connor toward the judgeship, and I didn't want any scandal in that direction.

"Lauren and I had words. I dropped her off and was watching when she gained access to Mr. Carmichael's house that evening to wait for him. Vause was supposed to be watching the law office to tip us off. But I saw Vause enter the house. He had a small duffle with him.

"I didn't see either of them leave. I was anxious at that point, and made my way into the house, where I found her. She was already dead. Vause had apparently left by the window.

"I knew at that point I had a dilemma. I didn't want to waste the opportunity. So I took a great chance. I put on some of Carmichael's clothes over mine and a pair of his shoes from the closet, walking on the carpet and tracking the blood, and repositioned the body, dragging her to the bathroom. I wanted the scene to be as gruesome as possible. I found a cufflink of Mr. Carmichael's on the dresser and pressed it into her hand. I intended for the clothing to be 'found' later discarded nearby."

He took a breath, waving away the doctor. "I made my way to her hotel room, and that's when I discovered the file of information in the safe." He paused. "I had a key to her room, and I generally left her payments in her safe. The room was ransacked when I got there. The safe had been opened. I found the file and discovered about her child, her marriage certificate, and apparently a couple of restraining orders, one in Maryland, and another in Virginia, against Vause."

"And you left the bag of shoes and clothes there," Petrino added grimly. Jon looked at him sharply.

"Yes," Varas confirmed, his voice weak.

"OK, that's enough," Alan said.

"One more question, please," Jon spoke. "Why would Vause have shot at you and Esme?"

"He called, distraught and wanting payment, wanting to leave on an urgent mission, he said. He was my lead surveillance guy, was planting the bugs daily for me. I was not sure whether I wanted to leave the situation as it was pointing at Mr. Carmichael, and stalled." He smiled grimly. "Part of his job was to keep recording devices installed at Mrs. Connor's office and the sheriff's department. I didn't know, nor did I ask, exactly how he accomplished that.

"I didn't really intend for the scheme to go as far as murder, and guess I had a twinge of conscience. And I had led him to believe Esme was behind the entire operation. She really knew nothing more than I had hired someone to plant suspicion on Carmichael, to knock him out of the judge's race."

The man's head dropped back on the pillow. "Out," Alan, alarmed, ordered them.

The man looked at Jon. "Will Esme be OK?"

"We don't know yet," Jon answered grimly.

"She was always a suspicious woman. I might be guilty of relieving her of her money and influence, but never trying to murder her. I knew she would never marry me, but I was fond of her just the same."

Jon nodded soberly, and Alan superintended the staff as they wheeled Varas out of the room into surgery.

As he left the room, Toby Townsend strode into the ER, walking up to Howells. "How is she? Where is she?" he questioned anxiously.

Howells took his arm. "She is in surgery, Toby. It's pretty serious."

Jon and Petrino walked up to him. "I'm sorry, Toby," Jon spoke sympathetically.

"What happened?" he looked anxiously at the two men.

"She was shot," Petrino answered gently.

"By whom? Varas?" he asked angrily.

"No, he was shot too," Jon supplied.

"We're after the perpetrator right now, but both of them are in surgery," Charlie added.

Toby turned to Howells. "Is she going to make it?"

"I don't know, son." Howells put his arm around the man's shoulders.

"What did she do to this guy to make him shoot her?"

Petrino looked at him, surprised. Toby shook his head. "She was always messing with someone, wheeling and dealing. I'm surprised someone hasn't tried something. I just assumed it would be this Varas." Tears shone in his eyes. "I love my mother, but she hasn't made it easy."

"I'm sorry, man," Petrino said feelingly.

Toby turned to him. "I'm just glad you got the appointment. I told her I would never speak to her again if she did something to cut you out of what you've wanted your whole life."

Petrino's eyes opened wide. Toby looked at Jon. "And I told her Amanda would make a great judge, and asked why she didn't help some good honest qualified locals for a change. Then I overheard Varas, and knew he was planning something against Amanda. I heard him set up the meeting, then call someone to meet him there. I was afraid he might actually harm Amanda."

He gazed at Petrino. "Mom had apparently already contacted the FBI, and they had set up surveillance on Varas. I insisted we involve you. That's when I came looking for you."

Petrino nodded. "And there's no telling what Varas might have done to Amanda had you not walked into that hotel room, Toby. We identified an accomplice and detained him." He glanced at Jon. "The man had a high resolution camera and a vial of something. The lab identified it as s type of anesthesia."

Jon's eyes widened, and his jaw worked convulsively.

"Jesus," Toby blinked, his emotions near the surface. "Varas had grabbed Amanda, and I could tell she was frightened. I pulled her out of the room. I was afraid what security cameras and devices might be planted around the hotel by Varas, and told her I would contact her later. I just wanted to get Amanda out of there and to confront Mom first."

"What did Esme say?" Jon wanted to know, his face flushed with anger.

Toby shook his head. "I couldn't find her, and then I got her on her cell. She told me she was working on something to solve 'the Varas problem', as she put it, and that she'd see me this afternoon and explain all." Toby closed his eyes and hung his head. "She wasn't home when I went by the house, and I couldn't reach her by phone."

"She was meeting with me," Jon supplied, his voice low.

Toby looked up. "Really?" he exclaimed, relief in his voice.

Jon nodded as Petrino looked on.

"I'm afraid of what Mom may have done to Ralph." Toby's voice dropped. "I read the papers, and was trying to get up with her, find out if she was behind it. I didn't know he was running for judge. Damn, I never realized she might actually do something to hurt him—" He fell silent.

"It's OK," Jon spoke. "She was trying to turn state's evidence, Toby. I think she was attempting to do the right thing. Let's just worry about getting your mother past all this, OK?"

Toby nodded, looking at Petrino. "Have you found anything at the stables?"

"Yes. I'm inviting the Bureau to help us sift through it all." Petrino put his arm around Toby. "I have to thank you. Things were getting critical when you came forward. Thank God you did, or I don't know what might have happened." He tried to smile. "Just concentrate on your mom for now."

Looking at the distraught young man, Jon thought, It is going to be a long night.

CHAPTER 29

SATURDAY

Ralph stood up, stretching and yawning. He looked around the room, dim with only one lamp burning. It was still dark outside, the sky only beginning to lighten.

He noticed David sitting up, his head resting against the back of the couch, his eyes closed. "Get your beauty sleep?" he heard David ask.

"Guess I did," Ralph acknowledged. "Where's Jon?"

"He is not answering his phone." David did not open his eyes. "But Petrino called and said Jon was at the hospital with him. He didn't answer my question about what Jon was doing there. I asked if he told Jon about Amanda, and he said no, that things were hopping over there, and he'd tell Jon when it calmed down. He asked that we keep an eye on Amanda."

"Did he say anything about Esme Townsend? What was happening?"

"No details—he was short and sweet. He rang off before I could ask anything more."

"It's almost 5:00," Ralph looked at his watch. "I'll stay with her."

David rose slowly. "I don't think she'll feel much like anything, not after downing a bottle of vodka. But one of us needs to stay with her, and the other of us track Jon down." He looked at Ralph penetratingly. "You know you're better able to communicate with Jon than I'm going to be."

"OK." Ralph was clearly reluctant. "I'm going to try to find out what's happening. I need to shower, shave and change. I'll hunt him and Petrino down. Thankfully it's Saturday, or you'd have trouble keeping her from going in. You may still have to hog-tie her. Can I do anything, bring you anything?"

David shook his head. "No, thanks. I'll hold down the fort until Jon gets here."

"You think you can handle Jon when he finds you here?"

"Better that than leaving him to face Amanda alone," David quipped.

Ralph nodded. "You got that right. I'm outta here. I'll call as soon as I get some news."

After he left, David walked into the bedroom. As he approached the bed, he noticed that Amanda was lying there, her eyes open in the dim light, shining with tears.

"How are you feeling?" He sat down on the bed.

"Rough," she replied, turning toward him, wiping her eyes.

"How about we drink a little of this awful Gatorade?" he smiled.

"I'd rather not." Her voice was hoarse.

"Doctor's orders," he laughed quietly. "Come on, you'll thank me for this later."

She slowly sat up as he poured some into a glass for her. "Here," he handed it to her, and she sipped, grimacing.

"Good girl," he whispered. "You're not a half-bad patient, Amanda." He gazed at her.

"Where's Jon?" she whispered.

"He's been detained elsewhere, helping the sheriff do something," David answered her.

"What?" she asked, holding her head and squeezing her eyes shut.

"I don't know any more than that." He took her hand. "You need to rest a while longer, then we'll do breakfast and a shower. Ralph is gone to find out what's going on for us."

"What time is it?" She looked at the clock. "Jon never came home?" Her eyes opened wide, her face creased with concern.

"Something has happened. Some woman named Esme Townsend was shot. Jon was there."

"Esme?" She was obviously surprised. "I don't understand."

"Don't worry, I'm sure we'll find out all about it," David tried to soothe her. "Get a bit more sleep. We have a mission later."

"Mission?" she echoed, confused.

"Yes. I need the pleasure of your company. So you have to feel better fast if you're going to help me. You're not going to let me down, are you?"

"No, David. You're a good friend," Amanda murmured. "Thanks."

"Don't mention it," he answered. "I'll wake you up in a little while, when breakfast is ready."

Her eyes closed.

Later Amanda awakened to find David standing over the bed. She smelled the aroma of the coffee as he teased, "Rise and shine, sleepy head," holding the cup.

She sat up, the sudden movement making her reach for her head.

"How do you feel?" he asked.

She held her hand out as David handed her the cup. "Cream and sugar, just like you like it. And two aspirin."

She drank deeply. "Thanks so much," she murmured. "That's good. Who hit me upside the head with the baseball bat?"

"A bottle of Absolut is the culprit," David remarked. "You were shit-faced last night, Sis."

The memories came flooding back as she swallowed the aspirin. "Oh," she said simply. "The book and cufflink," she whispered.

"Well, the cufflink isn't Jon's," David rejoined.

"No?" she countered hopefully.

"No," he confirmed. "We haven't figured out about the book yet. But I know Jon would never have withheld something so special from you." He sat down by her and ruffled her hair affectionately.

"You need to get prettified while I finish breakfast," he told her. "We have an adventure scheduled for today."

"What?" she wondered aloud.

"You'll have to wait and see," he said mysteriously. "Now up and at 'em."

Jon and Charlie, along with Toby and Kimball, camped out in the surgical waiting room, waiting for some word on the two patients.

"So Lauren Mallory still has a kid out there somewhere?" Jon mused aloud. "That's so hard to believe. And where does one start looking for her?"

"We can try to track down any family," Petrino offered, his voice weary.

"Family?" Jon echoed doubtfully.

"Most people have 'em," Petrino retorted drily. "And I asked Bruce to check on this 'file' Varas said he found. He's checking the papers discovered at the hotel, searching Varas' 'quarters' at Esme's house and getting the hotel to open the hotel room safe to see if we missed anything."

He looked ruefully at Connor and Kimball. "An oversight. I know. My investigators have been spread so thin working this case, we were bound to overlook some detail."

"I would think we need to find the little girl," Jon pointed out. "If the family doesn't know, it may be hard to track her down."

The Connors' Crisis

They were so engrossed in the conversation that they didn't notice a man walking up to them. "Maybe so, but you've got me. And I just found the kid's whereabouts," the man stated.

Jon turned. "Bubba! Trust you to be close at hand if any excitement is happening."

George smiled and clapped Jon on the uninjured arm. "There's a funeral service for Lauren Mallory in Panama City at 10:00 this morning. While you have been busy elsewhere, I determined who claimed the body, and followed the trail to the funeral home. And I was contacted by the sheriff's department down there with some interesting information. I called the investigator back—old hunting buddy of mine. I'll just bet the child and grandmom will be there."

"Grandmom?" Jon echoed.

"Apparently, all that time when we thought Lauren sprang full-size from the head of Zeus, she actually had a living mortal mother, who has been raising this child not that far from us."

Bubba paused. "Lauren Mallory apparently mailed a letter to her father or step-father, giving out all sorts of information about this Vause fellow, her husband, and saying he was in the area and she was afraid something might happen."

Jon suddenly had a thought. "Do you think Vause knows about the child? That he might show up for the service, try to claim the girl?"

Kimball grinned. "Great idea, Jon. Thanks. You really should be back on the team, man."

Jon smiled, saying nothing.

"Speaking of which, would you like to accompany us to the service? Might prove interesting," Bubba grinned.

Petrino held up his hand. "No can do," he announced curtly. "Jon has other obligations. Excuse us a minute."

Pulling Jon away from the others, Petrino walked him out of earshot.

Just as he opened his mouth, Ralph came walking in the door.

Petrino scowled at him. "I thought I told you to stay with her."

"David told me he'd take care of her. She's still asleep. And inasmuch as you weren't giving out any information, he sent me to track you down here. Have you told him yet?"

"David's with Amanda?" Jon echoed, his voice catching. "What haven't you told me?"

Petrino put his hand on Jon's arm. "Jon, you need to know. Amanda was found by David last night. She was stoned."

"What?" Jon's head jerked around. "I don't believe it."

321

"There were two express mail packages waiting for her when she arrived home." Petrino described the events and the contents of the packages. "I didn't tell you at first because she was sleeping it off, I knew there was nothing you could do right then, and I felt it better that she sober up before she saw you. But then so much has happened, and I haven't had the opportunity."

Jon paled. "Oh, my God! A book? Of Andy's? I need to go to her," he exclaimed.

"I'm not sure if that is a good idea or not," Petrino stated. "She told David she wanted to kill you."

"But I don't understand. Why?" Jon paced in front of Petrino.

"Well, we established the cufflink was not yours. However, the book—"

A thought suddenly hit him. "Of course!" he exclaimed. "Oh, dear God." Jon suddenly put his hands on his head. "Amanda has every reason to hate me. Oh, no," Jon moaned. "All these years, and I forgot."

"The boxes in the attic," Petrino supplied, his voice tense. "We found them during the search of the condo."

Jon nodded, too upset to be surprised that Petrino knew. "When Andy was killed, I took off to Mexico trailing Claude Brown. When it looked like I was going to be gone a while, I asked Bubba to box everything up at my apartment, store it in the attic at the condo, and give the keys to my apartment back to the landlord. It was a fully furnished place, because I was always on the move."

Jon's voice was muffled. "I never recalled that Andy had stuff left at my place. I haven't touched any of it. I never even remembered to look once I got back," he groaned.

"But," he added as an afterthought, "how would Lauren have known about the condo? I never took her there, never mentioned it to her. To my knowledge she didn't even know it existed."

"But apparently David had contact with her last week, and they spent the weekend together at the condo. She must have found the boxes."

"David? But why?" cried Jon. "That must have been devastating. Amanda will never forgive me."

"We can try to convince her," Petrino stated, his voice low. "What if I take you home and we talk to her together? I'll be glad to verify what I know so far."

"Thanks, Charlie," Jon whispered gratefully. "Can you drop me by the courthouse so I can pick up my car?"

"We're at someone's mercy for transportation. I sent Fred back to the farm."

"Come on," Ralph said. "I'll drop you off."

"No, I'll do it and come back," Kimball spoke behind them.

"He's right," Jon nodded, turning to Ralph. "You ought to stay with Toby. He doesn't need to be alone right now. His mother's in emergency surgery."

Ralph looked over at the young man sitting with his head in his hands, and nodded. "Go on, but keep me informed."

Amanda sat at the breakfast table across from David, drinking her coffee and munching buttered toast, having inhaled her eggs and bacon. "Very good," she mumbled, as David laughed at her. "I do feel better," she added. "You cook a mean breakfast."

"I'm glad," he smiled. "Actually, what I want you to do is something you're not going to be keen to do. But you promised."

Her smile dried up. "OK. I keep my word. Tell me what this is. Do I have to face Jon this morning?"

"Actually, it's worse than that." He sipped his coffee as she looked questioningly at him.

"I've found Lauren's little girl," he announced gravely. "And there's a funeral service in Panama City this morning. I want you to go with me. I want to see her."

Amanda's eyes grew round. "But David," she began, but he held up his hand to silence her.

"Please, Amanda. I thought at one time I loved this woman, and I think this could be my kid. I can't walk away without finding out. I don't know if I can do this alone. I wouldn't involve you, but it's important, and I don't know who else to ask. I just want to see the child and pay my respects. That's all."

Amanda's heart went out to him, as he looked down at his plate blinking back tears. She stood up and walked over to him, placing her hand over his on the table. "I'll go with you, David," she whispered. "How could I say no, after all you've done for me?"

He looked up at her, gratefulness in his eyes. "You don't know how much this means to me."

"OK," she sighed. "That means you will need to borrow one of Jon's black suits. I need to change." She looked at the clock. "We'd better hurry."

"OK, but one more thing," David spoke, his voice firm. "You need to leave a note so that Jon will know where you are. I insist."

Back behind the wheel of his own vehicle, Jon sped along with Petrino accompanying him. They were silent. He cursed himself for his malfeasance of not providing Andy's personal effects to his widow. Amanda will never forgive me, he thought. God, what she must have thought last night. And I wasn't even there for her, he berated himself.

He was oblivious to the speedometer, intent only on getting home and facing Amanda. Finally, after what seemed like a lifetime, the house came into view. He pulled up, slammed on the parking brake, shut the engine off and stepped out.

He noticed her car out front, along with Fred's truck, and sighed with relief.

Petrino asked angrily, "Where is David? I told them not to leave her alone in her condition."

Jon ran up the steps and inside the house. "Amanda?" he called. Running up the stairs to the bedroom, he found no signs of life. He made his way to the guest room and saw the empty, mussed bed. He stared at it a minute, his mind in turmoil. Walking back into the kitchen, he found a note on the table, sticking inside the book, Andy's book. He stared at it, transfixed, then opened it. Seeing the inscription, he read it. "Jesus," he said aloud.

He picked up the second note and read it: "David and I have gone to Lauren Mallory's funeral. Amanda." He looked at the cold words. No terms of endearment. He swallowed convulsively.

"They left about thirty minutes ago, just as I got back here," Fred said from the back door. "She insisted on going. When I mentioned that you would be home soon and you two needed to talk, that apparently clinched the matter. She dragged David out of the house while I was still arguing with her."

Jon bent his head sorrowfully.

"What were they driving?" Charlie asked excitedly.

"A silver Porsche David rented," Fred replied.

Petrino's phone rang. "Petrino here," he said shortly. He listened a moment. A moment later he returned hoarsely, "Bruce, notify the sheriff's department and the local police down there. Send a BOLO. Good job. Keep it up."

Charlie looked at Jon. "Bruce said one of our guys on patrol spotted a motorcycle with a man matching our description down beachside. He was sitting at a dumpster. The man took off at a high rate of speed, heading east. My man gave chase, but lost him. About thirty minutes ago.

"There was a duffle in the dumpster with a high resolution camera and what looked like some composite photos. And some blood-stained clothes."

The Connors' Crisis

Charlie's face was grim. "Furthermore, Bruce checked all the paperwork found in the mess scattered around Lauren's hotel room. I had them check it all again. But there was a birth certificate in the duffle. The mother was listed as Lauren Mallory."

Jon said slowly, "If Vause thinks it is his child, there's no telling what he might do. And David and Amanda are going—to the service. The child will be there."

"Bingo," agreed Petrino gravely.

"Give me a second." Jon strode out of the room.

Jon returned momentarily buttoning a fresh shirt, with his gun in one hand and a coat and tie draped over his arm. "Let's go. I'm driving. We'll take the Mercedes this time."

As they stepped outside, Vaughan said, "Just a minute."

He reached inside his truck and brought out a small duffle. "If you're packing, then I'm packing," he said shortly.

David flew low in the Porsche, as Amanda sat tense and quiet beside him. "I didn't know how much longer they'd keep my car, so I leased one," he tried to smile. She nodded but said nothing.

Every now and then he furtively looked her way, but did not break the silence.

His phone rang. She reached over and took his hand. "Please don't answer it," she croaked plaintively. "It could be Jon. I just can't deal with him right this moment."

David looked at her sadly, but nodded. He silenced his phone, setting it to vibrate only. They remained silent.

Finally he could take it no more. "Thanks, Amanda. I couldn't do this alone. I know this is hard."

"No harder for me than holding that book yesterday," she remarked, so low he could barely hear her. "I saw that cufflink, and I wanted to die. Then the book . . . . I thought I had put Andy's death behind me and moved on. I was happier than I have been since before his murder. Then the doubts—" she was overcome for a moment, before pulling herself together. "In a moment I was reliving the horror again. It scares me that I could so quickly revert to that cowering female again. When it seems the pain is healing, then something happens to rip the wound open again."

David, his eyes on the road, answered her. "Amanda, there are moments that haunt us, and that is yours. I would give anything if Lauren hadn't done that. And it's my fault."

325

"How is it your fault?" Amanda was dubious.

"Because Lauren was with me last weekend at the condo. I'm sure she snooped and found the book in the attic. I'm equally certain that Jon probably had no idea that book was there, or he would have provided it to you."

"I want to believe you, David," Amanda whispered, looking out the window. "It's so hard. I've been happy with Jon, but it's been too good to be true. I've been on pins and needles, just waiting for something bad to happen."

"I know," David concurred quietly. "I felt the same about Lauren when she showed back up. But Lauren had an ulterior motive for everything. I kept hoping that she showed up to make amends, but I see now that it was to sow more havoc for her own purposes. She used me." There was a catch in his throat.

"David, how can you know that?" Amanda touched his arm. "We may never know why she did what she did. She's gone now. I just hope we can unravel all this before a grand jury pins her murder on one of you."

"I need to see this little girl, to know if she is mine," David spoke grimly.

Amanda squeezed his arm reassuringly. "We're almost there."

Jon sped through the trail, Petrino sitting beside him and Vaughan in the back seat. Charlie tried to summarize their findings thus far.

"So Lauren conceivably got her hands on Andy's book at the condo?" Jon surmised.

"Looks like it," Petrino concurred grimly. "That one will be hard to explain to Amanda."

"Don't I know it?" Jon muttered angrily. "And it is my fault. I just never imagined there were things of Andy's left at my place. He had gone home to be with Amanda just before—" he broke off.

"I'm sorry, Jon," Fred said from the back seat.

Jon was silent a moment, scanning ahead as he entered the road from the trail, his mind racing. He suddenly gritted out, "Petrino, you haven't been messing with my wife, have you?"

Charlie stared at him, stunned. "Where the hell did that come from?" he demanded.

"I know you and Amanda met at Fred's night before last," Jon stared at the road ahead, his jaw hardened. "I found your note to her. When she came back, I could tell she had been drinking. She lied to me." He snarled, "And you knew this about Varas' blackmailing her, but she wouldn't tell me."

Petrino shook his head. "Jon, I know you may not believe me, but I consider you my friend. I would never do that to you. And Amanda loves you too much."

Charlie paused. "Varas threatened all sorts of dire consequences if she revealed to anyone their conversation. She was truly scared, and would not have told me either. But Toby overheard Varas and found out about the meeting with Amanda. Toby informed me, and he insisted on confronting Varas himself. Toby slipped her that note from me just after the meeting. She showed up that night to worm information out of me, and I confronted her about the meeting."

He could see Jon's jaw still jutting in anger. "Jon," pleaded Charlie, "Varas was planting evidence right and left to throw suspicion on you, then David, then Ralph." He detailed the information regarding the clothes, shoes and butcher knife found, as well as the items Sheila discovered missing from the office. "And he was having us watched, recording our conversations, even in Amanda's office. Joanna's cousin, the cleaning lady who confirmed Ralph's whereabouts the night of Lauren's murder, has also confessed that this Vause guy, who she recognized from a photo Bruce showed her, had been paying her extra to plant the pens every morning. He gave her the line that he was an office supply salesman and was trying to introduce these pens.

"Anyway, Amanda had finally figured out a way to let Ralph know, and Ralph went looking for you to tell you. Amanda was afraid that even the farm might be bugged."

Charlie placed his hand on Jon's arm. "Jon, Varas had told her Lauren was pregnant with your child." He saw Jon flinch. "Varas showed her pictures, compromising pictures of you, of Ralph, of even me. I told Mandy about the cufflink in Lauren's hand when she was found."

Petrino shook his head. "Then Amanda got home and found the cufflink and the book, both ostensibly sent by Lauren. She was already frightened out of her mind. At that point it was apparently too much for her. David found her drunk, almost incoherent, presumably convinced you had been with Lauren, that perhaps you even killed her."

Jon blinked back tears. "She didn't trust me," he muttered bitterly.

"Just like you apparently doubted her," Charlie supplied evenly, his return gaze accusing.

They were both silent a moment.

"You're right," Jon nodded morosely. "I knew something was going on, but she wasn't talking. I found out she was with you, and she seemed more solicitous of Ralph and David than of me." He shook his head wearily. "I assumed the worst."

Fred spoke up. "Nobody said marriage was easy. It requires a lot of faith in the midst of circumstances that might indicate that faith is misplaced."

"But I've been down that road before, and the consequences from misplaced trust were pretty horrid," Jon rejoined unhappily.

"But Amanda made a commitment to you," Charlie argued. "She has not been able to do that since Andy's murder. She wants to trust you. Salvatore Varas and Lauren Mallory apparently did everything they could to destroy that trust."

"That's not hard to do, with Amanda and her history," Fred suggested gently. "Her instincts are to withdraw, to run away."

"I know. Ralph has already preached to me. And I know I have some skeletons of my own to bury. I'm just so damned jealous. My track record with women hasn't prepared me for anything else. I guess I fully expected her to lose interest in me and was waiting for the worst to happen, thinking all this was too good to be true."

"She loves you, Jon," Charlie insisted. "She would never have taken the plunge and married you if she wasn't convinced you were the one."

Jon nodded grimly. "I know. She's told me more than once. I guess I just haven't been listening."

He glanced over at Charlie. "Did Lauren's phone number produce anything?"

"Yes, we have been able to trace a lot of the calls. She kept up contact with Varas. Over the last week she apparently called a number in Panama City. We didn't know why, but I'm guessing now it might be her mother, the grandmother. There was the call to your office, of course, and to David, and a couple to Ralph's office as well. There was a flurry of messages to another number we have not been able to trace yet."

"Could be Vause," Jon suggested. "I guess it wasn't such a bad thing after all that she called my office. Otherwise, I would not have the number."

"And you didn't talk to her?" Petrino demanded.

"I swear. The office was closed Monday, and when she called Tuesday, I was swamped, and told the secretary to take a number, because I was on another line. I didn't know it was her until afterward, but I had no desire to talk to her."

"Did you tell Amanda she called?"

"No," Jon muttered. "In all the excitement the last few days it's just never come up.

"Damn," he exclaimed suddenly. "Amanda was in the dressing room when I forgot and went back for the note with the number to give to you. She seemed—strange."

"Do you think she saw it?" Petrino countered.

"With my luck running like it is, she did," Jon rejoined despairingly. "And I had just found your note to her, and I couldn't bring myself to talk to her. She will never speak to me again."

"Well, we may have a bigger problem than that," Petrino reminded him. "If my hunch is correct, Vause is heading down there to collect his kid. If he shows up, that little girl may be in danger. And your wife and brother are heading straight into the tornado."

Chapter 30

David drove into the parking lot of the funeral home and parked. "There are quite a few cars here, but not as many as I might have imagined," he noted to Amanda.

She nodded distractedly. "Was she well known?"

"Yes, I think so. She was always working a crowd when we were out together. But I don't know what sort of notice—" David spoke, his body tensing. "Amanda—" he began.

Amanda smiled, trying to set him at ease. "We're here, so why turn back now?"

He nodded mutely. They both exited the vehicle, and David walked around to her side. She slipped her hand in his and gently pulled him with her toward the door.

They were greeted at the door by a solemn usher, who pushed into their hands a small program. Amanda pointed to an area near the back where they could see well without being observed. David nodded and drew her with him to sit down on a pew in the chapel.

Some soft canned music was playing, and Amanda grimaced to herself. David didn't relinquish her hand as he sat there nervously scanning the crowd of people. She also glanced around, and was surprised to note in a corner across from them and a few pews up a somewhat familiar figure. She thought a moment, then remembered him. It was the blonde-haired man that she had spied outside the restaurant the day before Lauren was killed, she realized. The same man that Lauren had seen and reacted to so negatively. The man had his head down, and she noted he was dressed in army fatigues. She watched him a moment, wondering.

David squeezed her hand and nodded toward a group of people that had just entered the room from a side door and sat in an area to the side but facing toward the closed bier. On the front pew between a solemn-eyed middle-aged couple sat a little girl. She looked anxiously around her, and

330

tugged at the man's sleeve. He put his arm around her and held her hand, as the woman reached out and smoothed the child's hair comfortingly and cried silently.

But it was the child's features that arrested her. The resemblance to Lauren Mallory was so strong that Amanda was certain this must be her child. But the eyes were dark, wide, questioning. Like Jon's and David's eyes, she thought with a start, her heart thudding.

Amanda looked over and saw that the blonde man was also intently gazing at the little girl. What is his connection to all this? Amanda wondered.

The obituary was read, and a father Walton Canton, mother Virginia Canton and sister Allison Canton were named, no offspring. Amanda was startled. Sister? She looked at David, who also appeared surprised. The blonde man looked on impassively.

The service was short, the casket remaining closed. The persons present were informed of a graveside committal and an opportunity to greet the family at their home on Bayshore Drive.

The congregants stood as the family made their way out the door. At that point the blonde man turned and saw Amanda and David, his features surprised then hardening. Amanda noted it. Who was this man?

She caught up to David ahead of her and squeezed David's arm. "Do you know that man over there? The blonde in military outfit?"

He glanced over in the direction she nodded, but the man had already disappeared. "Who?" he asked dazedly, tears in his eyes.

"He's gone now," Amanda replied. "Let's go."

She led David by the arm out to the car. Once in the car, he spoke. "I have to introduce myself to her parents, Amanda."

"David, I—" Amanda began, but he cut her off.

"I don't know what Lauren has done, but I feel I've got to speak to them, let them know that someone regarded her at one time." He looked at Amanda sadly. "I didn't recognize anyone there as someone I had seen her with or that I knew that she knew. They were probably all friends of the parents."

Amanda nodded sympathetically. "For all her alleged influence with powerful people, there was no one here that met that description."

"I'm going to the graveside and to the reception," David stated flatly.

Amanda was silent as he pulled out and they followed the procession behind the hearse.

The graveside service was also short, with a Catholic priest officiating. The little girl and the couple each threw a rose and a handful of dirt over the coffin as it was lowered, then left.

David and she turned to leave too. She looked back, and saw the man in camouflage back at the graveside, also throwing dirt into the hole. She was even more mystified. As she looked on, he straightened, grasping his side in pain. There was a dark stain where his hand was.

David was striding away and she hurried to catch up. "David, there was the man again. I think he's hurt."

David was preoccupied. "What man?"

"The one over—" Amanda pointed back, but the man had again disappeared.

"Maybe you're seeing things," he suggested, although she could tell his mind was elsewhere.

They followed the family's car to a comfortable two-story brick home with a large yard in a quiet neighborhood. Several cars pulled up, and people followed the family into the house. David glanced over to Amanda, his features strained, then shrugged.

"I gotta do it," he whispered.

They both exited the vehicle and followed others into the large comfortable home. A number of people flowed in the well-furnished rooms and milled around speaking in hushed whispers, others going into a large open great room to speak to the family bunched together.

Once in the confines of the home, David seemed to waver. Amanda touched his arm. "You can always walk away. But if you feel you need to do this, now's the time."

He nodded tensely. As a clutch of mourners seemed to ebb away from the family, he grasped Amanda's hand and stepped forward, drawing her along with him. He walked up to the couple with the little girl.

The man gazed at him solemnly. "You must be David," he said simply, blinking.

David stared back in shock. "How—how did you know?" he stammered.

"I've seen some snapshots of you from several years back. I had no way to contact you, but felt somehow, sometime you would find your way here."

He held out his hand stiffly and David shook it. "I'm Walter Canton, and this is Lauren's mother and my wife Virginia. This is Allison."

David took the woman's hand too, her eyes on him almost hostile, then knelt to shake the little girl's hand. "You're very pretty, just like your—" he faltered, "like Lauren."

The little girl smiled tremulously.

The man gazed at Amanda questioningly. Amanda spoke quietly, proffering her hand. "I am Amanda Connor, David's sister-in-law."

The man took her hand and shook it, then the woman shook her hand reluctantly, staring questioningly at her. Amanda also shook the little girl's hand. "Allison, it is nice to meet you." The little girl stared at her soberly.

332

"Come with me, please," Walter stated to David. He turned to his wife, who seemed suddenly overcome. He reached over and kissed her. "I'll be back. Don't worry. It will all turn out OK."

She nodded, but the little girl grasped his arm, tears in her eyes. "No, Daddy, I want to come too."

"Stay with Mommy. She needs you. I won't be but a few minutes." The man bent down and hugged the little girl. "I promise."

"Yes, Daddy," the girl said obediently, as the woman took her hand and gazed tearily, warily at Amanda. Amanda smiled comfortingly and looked at the child, who also stared back unsmilingly, her eyes following Canton out of the room.

"Come this way," the man beckoned. David followed, pulling Amanda with him.

They walked into a study, and the man shut the door firmly. "I knew sooner or later you would show up," the man repeated flatly, but swallowing convulsively. "I guess I just didn't expect it to be today."

"I don't understand." David's eyes met the man's soberly.

"I assume you are here about Allison," the man rejoined, almost angrily.

David appeared shaken, and was rendered speechless.

Amanda stepped in. "Mr. Canton, Lauren had—had intimated that Allison was her child." She took a breath. "She filed paternity complaints against two different men just this week."

"Allison was hers," the man confirmed. "The officer here who helped me claim her—her body also informed us about the circumstances preceding her—her death, or at least what he could find out for me." He swallowed, his eyes full of unshed tears.

Amanda also swallowed convulsively. "Then I must tell you how very sorry I am, and to assure you that the two men named in the complaints and David had nothing to do with the murder."

"I know," the man concurred, surprising them both. "I'm fairly certain that Lauren was murdered by her husband, who has been stalking her on and off for years."

"Husband?" David echoed uncomprehendingly.

The man gazed at David, then waved his hand at a sofa and two chairs. "Please have a seat. I can see we need to start at the beginning."

"Thank you," Amanda murmured, pulling a shaken and mute David with her to the couch. They were seated. The man crossed over to the corner of a room to a little trolley table and poured some bourbon in two glasses.

He proffered the glasses to them. "Looks like you could use this."

David took the glass dazedly, and Amanda smiled her thanks, sipping hers. The man sat down across from them. "I don't know how much you know."

"Very little, I'm afraid," Amanda smiled uncomfortably, setting her glass down. David gripped his glass nervously, staring at it.

The man nodded. "Lauren was born fatherless. Her father was a Marine killed overseas before she was born. I was his CO, had known him and his family for years, and was at his wedding when he married Virginia.

"It was quite a blow to Ginny, who was pregnant when informed of Joe's death, and she was told by the doctors she would probably have no more children. It was a hard pregnancy." He paused. "I fell in love with her later and married her. I adopted Lauren, but Ginny wanted her to keep her father's name, and I agreed.

"Lauren turned out to be quite a spoiled and willful child, and it was probably my fault," Walter smiled sadly. "She had some wish to serve in the military, and did a stint in the Navy while getting her degree. Then she applied to and made it into Quantico. It seemed her career just took off, and she quickly moved from the Bureau to Langley, then to the Secret Service. She appeared to really enjoy it."

Walter's face clouded. "Then she fell in with another young man, a bright, seemingly charming man named Karl Vause, while she was at the CIA. She became infatuated, and the next thing we knew she announced she was married. Just like that, no warning, no engagement, no wedding. She didn't bring him home for us to meet, nothing.

"Well, her mother was understandably shaken, and I too. I had treated Lauren like my own, and thought we had a close relationship. Virginia always dreamed of a big wedding for her only girl. So this news took us by surprise. And we never met this guy, knew nothing about him other than he was CIA. I saw him once when I was in D.C. on business, and Lauren had sent a couple of photographs.

"But what shocked us even more was when she showed up one day to our home in Nebraska not quite a year after that news. She looked terrible, had lost weight. She confided in me that her husband was paranoid and violent, and that he had abused her. Apparently she had tried to get him help but had not been successful, and she ended up miscarrying their child after he had battered her."

Amanda heard David's swift unsteady intake of breath, and touched his knee momentarily to reassure him.

Walter continued, "I was enraged, and convinced her she should divorce him and get a restraining order. I went back to Maryland with her—I still know a lot of people up there with connections, and we got the injunctive relief. I put her in touch with a lawyer for him to initiate the divorce. She appeared to have recovered, and assured me she was OK and ready to go back to work, sending me back home. Her boss was an understanding man, and I met with him, insisted that she tell him what was going on."

He paused. David was watching him, transfixed. Amanda nodded encouragingly. Canton rejoined, "Please stop me if you already know this."

David shook his head. "Sadly, I know very little about Lauren's past. It was something she never wanted to discuss. And," he added, "we weren't together that long before she disappeared."

"There is a reason—I'll get to that," Walter nodded solemnly. "Anyway, this guy showed back up again, found her. He wanted to reconcile, and she let him back in. But he battered her again, just before leaving on an overseas assignment. She ended up, at my urging, with another restraining order. This time she said she made the break and divorced him. I just assumed she did so.

"She was doing so well, moving up the ladder. Ginny and I worried about her a lot, because she appeared rather—I don't know, frivolous about relationships.

"Then one day she called and talked about this guy who was pursuing her. I was afraid that she had a stalker or had fallen in with another Karl. But she said he was a doctor named David. She told me he was not like the government types she was always around; he was a lot of fun, and wanted her to move in with him, was really serious, seemed like a normal, nice guy."

David's face was filled with pain.

"I take it that was you," Walter looked at him penetratingly.

"Yes, sir," he croaked.

"The next week after that call, she disappeared. Her boss said she had taken a leave of absence, but he confided in me that Karl had appeared again, and he had made arrangements for a temporary transfer for Lauren. We didn't know where she was for a couple of months. Then she showed up. She informed us she was pregnant again, but not by Karl. But she admitted that Karl had showed up suddenly. She had gone to the police, but he had disappeared. She was frightened enough to drop out of sight. She didn't want to stay with us. She was afraid he might look for us.

"I sent her up to live with some of my family up in New England until the baby was born. She released the child to us, and we brought Allison home. Lauren was afraid Karl would find out, and wanted to give the child up for adoption. I told her we would adopt Allison and raise her as our child."

"I never knew anything about this," David murmured.

"I asked her who was the father. She said she didn't know, but it wasn't Karl. I felt she was lying. But she convinced me that it would be safer if the child's identity was erased so that Karl never knew about Allison at all. That's when she told me that she had never divorced him. She had not been able to locate him to serve him with papers, and then she had lost her nerve.

"So I pulled a few strings. We completed the adoption process, but I couldn't really do anything about the original birth certificate in Vermont. Thankfully, Lauren didn't reveal she was married, and Karl's name wasn't on the birth certificate.

"Ginny and I have been Allison's parents since then. We retired and moved to Florida. Lauren rarely comes to see us, because she says it is better that way, but she calls in from time to time."

Walter paused. Amanda prompted, "Until last week?"

"Until last week," Walter echoed. "She suddenly appeared out of the blue, said she was here for a couple days, and that she had come down with David. I was surprised, because I think at one point we assumed you," he nodded at David, "had moved on and married some one else."

"No," David just shook his head. "Lauren disappeared, and I couldn't find her, or anyone who knew anything about her. I never saw her again. Then I ran into her last week in D.C., and we—spent some time together, sir," he added, his voice respectful. "She accompanied me down here to Panama City."

"She spent two days and a night with us last week. I asked Lauren if there was a possibility of something serious between you two, but she shook her head, saying she was really here on a job, but you didn't know that, and you probably wouldn't want much to do with her after that job was finished. She told me then that you were Allison's father. I asked if you knew it, and she said she wasn't saddling any man with that, that Allison was being cared for by the best people she knew."

David sucked in air at the words, and Amanda took his hand, squeezing it as tears fell from his eyes. Walter saw David's reaction but rushed on, as if afraid to stop. "She started apologizing to me, saying that there might be some unpleasantness, that Allison's name would be used, but Allison would not be involved other than that, and no one would bother us.

"I was angry then, that somehow she had involved her own child that we had taken such pains to shield and protect. We had words then, and she left." He sighed. "That was the last time we saw her."

Walter closed his eyes, and Amanda could feel his sorrow. "I'm so sorry, Mr. Canton," she said feelingly.

He opened his eyes, and she saw they too were filled with tears. "Then I got this letter Thursday in the mail from Lauren." For a moment he was overcome and couldn't speak. He finally continued. "Postmarked Tuesday, from here in Panama City. She said that Karl had shown up a couple months ago when she was on a private assignment. He forced his way into her hotel room. She said she had sex with him to buy time to get away." He shook his head, overcome. "She told me she was pregnant again, but didn't want her mother to know, that she would 'take care of the situation'. And she went on to say she thought Karl was in this area, that she had thought she had spotted him. Lauren warned me to be very careful and to be on the lookout for him."

Walter paused. "She wanted to let me know, in case something happened, that she was naming an FBI agent she knew as the father of Allison, in hopes that it would draw that agency into the investigation of Karl."

"Jon," Amanda whispered, closing her eyes.

"I don't know his name," Canton said sadly.

"My husband," Amanda replied quietly.

Canton started. "I'm so sorry," he stated feelingly. "That had to be a cruel blow." He paused. "So your husband is David's brother?"

Amanda nodded, biting her lip. "What did you do with the letter?" Amanda asked gently.

"I turned it over to the sheriff's investigator here who had helped me to—to claim her." Walter sobbed. "He said he would contact someone he knew in the local FBI office and get them involved."

The door suddenly opened, and Allison ran into the room to Walter. "Daddy, can I go swing?"

She looked at him and at David, who gazed at her with tears in his eyes. Allison's face clouded. "Why are you crying?"

She crawled into Walter's lap and flung her arms around him.

"Oh, Baby, it's just so sad," Canton murmured, trying to regain control over himself.

"Because of Lauren?" the little girl pressed.

"Yes, dear, because of Lauren," Walter whispered. "Allison, these are some people who knew—Lauren. I need to talk to them just a little bit more, OK?"

"But can I swing?" the little girl whined. Amanda noted that David stared at her, seemingly not able to take his eyes off the child.

"If Jimmy will go with you and you promise to stay in the yard at the swings," Walter ordered firmly.

Virginia appeared in the doorway. "I'm sorry, dear, but—"

"I know." He looked apologetically at Amanda and David. "Allison has a mind of her own, much like her mother." He turned to Virginia, who at his words suddenly appeared fragile. He stood and walked to her, putting his arm around her. "It's OK, darling. It's OK."

Another woman and a boy not much larger than Allison appeared. "I'm sorry," the woman said suddenly, seeing the others in the room.

"No, that's all right," Walter cleared his throat. "I told Allison that it was fine for her and Jimmy to play on the swings as long as they didn't stray from there. Thanks, Janet."

The woman nodded and held out her hand for Allison, who walked to her and took it. "Come on, you two, and let's let the adults finish their talking," the woman crooned to the two children.

Walter shut the door behind them and drew Virginia into the room. "I've just told them most of it."

She burst into tears. "It's just too much. To lose Lauren and Allison at the same time?"

"Honey, we don't know for certain that he is Allison's father, and I'm not letting him snatch her away from us," Walter countered, his voice authoritative. "We will fight to keep her."

David stood. "I'm not here to cause any more pain," he found his voice. "But as soon as I saw the paternity complaints and knew Lauren had—that there was a child, I knew I could be the father." He took a breath. "I was angry too, that if so, she kept it from me, that she disappeared, that she was naming two other men and not me, and that I knew they couldn't be the father." His voice lowered. "One of them is my brother, the other a good friend."

David looked at Virginia, his gaze sympathetic. "I promise I won't snatch Allison away. But I'd like to know for certain, if possible. If so, I'd like to take some responsibility. I don't want to hurt her." He paused. "She knows nothing about Lauren's being her mother?"

Virginia nodded. "We've never said anything. That was how Lauren wanted it." She smiled sadly. "Some of our friends have wondered."

"Then that's the way it should stay for now, until we know more. And I won't do anything that would be against her best interest."

Amanda also stood. "I think that is wise. I think we could do DNA testing very quickly, if law enforcement preserved a sample as I requested. And Allison doesn't need to be informed of anything until we have more information and can all decide together what is best for her. It could be too much for her to discover she has a mother and father she doesn't really know. We should proceed slowly and cautiously."

"I don't intend to do anything to hurt her or you. There's no way she is going to lose either of you," David added. "I would never take her away from the people who raised her, the only parents she has ever known."

Walter and David stared at each other, and Walter nodded, relief in his face.

"Thank you," Virginia whispered tremulously.

"How did you know about Lauren's death? How to claim her?" Amanda asked tentatively.

Walter cleared his throat. "Lauren would contact me or Ginny about once a month or more, calling by pay phone or at a library internet site, and let us know her whereabouts. It was the only way, she said, to make sure he didn't find us, find Allison. I knew she was in Mainville, and when I heard the news—" he faltered, tears filling his eyes. "I feared the worst. She matched the description given. So I called and asked a sheriff's investigator here that I know, who helped me make arrangements. During all that the letter came, and it confirmed my suspicions. I still can't believe . . ." he left the sentence unfinished.

Amanda nodded. "I'm so sorry, Mr. Canton."

They were silent a few minutes while the Cantons composed themselves.

David cleared his throat. "Is there anything she—she needs? Anything I can do for her?" He looked at Walter. "For you?"

Walter smiled. "I am retired Marine, and retired a second time from civil service. I do well. And Ginny retired from civil service after—after Allison was born. So we are comfortable, and Allison lacks for nothing." He looked at David. "We love her. She is our baby."

David nodded, trying to smile too. "I can see that."

They all laughed, breaking the tension.

There was suddenly the sound of a child screaming. Walter relinquished Virginia and disappeared out the door. David was right behind him. They raced through the groups of people to the back French doors. Jimmy was on the deck crying. "A man just grabbed Allison."

"Which way did he go?" Walter asked excitedly.

The boy pointed. Walter plunged out through the yard and the hedges, David at his heels.

Amanda had followed them, but then decided to cut through to the front door. She raced past the people milling around to the door and outside. At first she saw no activity, then heard a child scream again. She saw below the line of parked cars a man cranking a motorcycle with a child struggling against him, and raced pell mell toward him, making it to within three feet of him, reaching out for Allison.

The man pulled a Glock automatic and pointed it at her. "Stop," he commanded. She recognized the man as the blonde-haired man at the funeral, still dressed in camo, Allison clutched tightly in one arm against him. He gasped in pain, but leveled the gun at Amanda's head.

Amanda froze. "Please, you're hurt," she said quickly, trying to assess the situation. "Don't injure the child."

"She's mine," the man sneered, as he gripped Allison tighter under his arm, and the little girl sobbed hysterically.

339

"No, she's not yours," Amanda rejoined gently. "You are not the father."

"How would you know?" The man looked at her disbelievingly, a fanatical gleam in his eye.

"It can be easy to prove. And you really don't want to hurt her." Amanda tried to keep her voice calm. "Allison, don't cry, baby. Please let her go."

"Her mother kept the news from me, kept my child from me all this time, hid her away. Then I tracked Lauren down, found her a couple months ago. She said she loved me, that she'd never leave me again. But she disappeared, and I found her with him." He pointed to David, who with Walter was running toward them.

"Stop right there," he warned loudly. "Any closer and I splatter the woman all over the yard."

They froze. "Please, just let them go, Karl," Canton pleaded.

"How do you know my name?" He became agitated.

"I'm Lauren's father," Canton said soothingly.

"Did she tell you about me?" he shouted.

"Yes, Karl."

"What did she say?" The man was shaking, and Allison started screaming again.

"Please let her go," Amanda begged. "You're hurting her."

"Did you kill her, Karl?" Walter asked quietly, moving closer.

"Don't," Karl warned him. "I followed Lauren and him," he nodded toward David, "down here, and found my child, found the birth certificate. That slut filed two paternity actions on my child. I actually found her naked in another man's bed, waiting for him. She wasn't fit to live, and I took care of that situation," the man spouted.

"Please, Karl," Walter pleaded, "let the baby go. She isn't your child. She's mine and Ginny's."

"You're lying," the man spat, continuing to hold the gun on Amanda.

A contingent of police cars, with sirens and lights flashing, converged on the area from both directions. People were walking out of the house, observing the sight.

The man assessed the situation, then quickly killed the switch on the motorcycle, popping the stand and swinging himself and the child off. He kept the gun trained on Amanda. "You're driving us out of here, or your pretty face will be spattered all over this lawn."

Amanda responded quickly, "Let Allison go. I'll take you wherever you wish."

Petrino and Jon suddenly appeared about twenty feet to his right, Petrino's gun pulled, Jon's firearm in his hand.

The Connors' Crisis

"Stay back, or I will kill them both," the man spoke loudly.

Jon held up his hand, warning the other law enforcement off. "Stand down," he yelled.

"Put it down," Petrino ordered Vause, his gun pointed at Vause's head. "Let the kid go."

Amanda asked quietly, "Did you know Lauren was pregnant when you killed her?"

The man's eyes widened in shock.

"Testing will determine whether it was your child. It was, wasn't it? And you didn't know," Amanda said softly.

"I killed my kid?" he screamed.

Suddenly Allison wiggled out of his arms, but he snatched her and hung on to her arm tightly as she squealed in terror.

"Look around you," Petrino stated. "You're not going anywhere."

"You're wrong there," the man laughed shortly.

David took a step forward. "Please, if you love Allison and think she is yours, don't let her see you like this. Don't let her be a witness to violence."

Vause looked at Jon, then at David quickly. "There's two of you sons of bitches," he choked. "But not for long."

Allison suddenly wrenched free. Amanda reached out for her. Vause shifted and swung his aim from Amanda, pointing at David and firing.

CHAPTER 31

Amanda snatched the little girl to her, flattening to the ground and covering her as gunfire sounded around them. Allison was shrieking into her ear. Amanda prayed.

Vause fired off one shot before being hit by Petrino. He reeled, firing again. Two more shots rang out, and he fell.

Amanda heard a thud beside her. Opening her eyes, she saw a gun, Vause's Glock.

"Shh, Shh," she spoke into the girl's ear. "It's OK, baby," she whispered, as the girl cowered against her sobbing.

It was silent. She looked up. Vause was lying four feet away, face down. Jon ran toward her rapidly, tucking his Beretta into his back waist. Petrino moved around the motorcycle to where Vause lay, Charlie's pistol still aimed on the still form as he kicked the Glock out of the man's reach.

Amanda glanced around her, then made it to her feet, jerking Allison up into her arms. The girl continued to cling and cry. "Baby, it's over," she crooned, rocking Allison and stroking her hair. "You're OK."

Jon enfolded her and the child in his arms. "Are you all right?" he asked anxiously.

She nodded wordlessly as Virginia Canton ran up to her and the child. "Oh, my baby, my baby," Virginia moaned as law enforcement officers swarmed around them.

Amanda gently pried the child's arms from around her neck. "Allison, turn loose. We need to make sure you are OK."

Allison obediently relaxed her grip, grasping Virginia's hand tightly after Amanda set her on the ground. Amanda quickly examined her, noticing only a darkening bruise on the arm where Vause had held her in a vise.

"I need some help here," David's voice piped up.

They turned, and David was on his knees beside Walter Canton, who was lying on the ground. David turned him over.

Allison broke free. "Daddy, Daddy," she screamed, running to Canton.

"Damn, that smarted," the older man gasped quietly, grimacing. Allison threw her arms around him on the ground.

"Baby, give him some room," David pleaded gently with the little girl.

"Don't touch him," Allison sobbed.

"But I'm a doctor," David tried to reassure her.

"Go to Mommy," Walter whispered.

Virginia dragged the child away, as David continued examining the man.

Amanda turned to go too, but was swept into Jon's arms.

"I thought I was going to lose you all over again," Jon remarked as he claimed her lips with his.

She responded, kissing him back and holding him tightly. Then suddenly she pulled away.

"Amanda, I didn't know—" he began, but she held up her hand.

"It can wait," she whispered, moving off to David's side.

Jon bit his lip, turning around as officers were surrounding them.

Petrino turned Vause over and checked for a pulse. "He's dead," Charlie spoke. He looked at Jon. "Thanks," he whispered. "You know you didn't have to shoot him."

"Yes, I did," Jon murmured, his eyes on the dead man.

Charlie looked at him, understanding and nodding. "If it hadn't been for you running fool-headed up to them, we wouldn't have been close enough to take him," he smiled grimly, as another tall muscular man in casual clothes walked up to them.

"Hi, Sheriff," Petrino said, recognizing the man.

"Hi, Sheriff," the man echoed in reply. He turned to Connor and held his hand out. "I'll take the weapon."

"He's OK," Charlie interposed. "He just left the FBI for a desk job. I deputized him on the way down here. That's Jon Connor, Sheriff Dubois," he made introductions.

"Ah, Jon Connor," the man said. "I've certainly heard of you." He still held his hand out. Jon shrugged and reached behind him, but the man responded, "Don't you shake hands with people when they offer it?"

Jon, surprised, reached out and shook his hand. "I just thought—"

"But you are right. There will, as always, be an inquiry, so you and the Sheriff here will have to surrender your firearms," the Sheriff smiled. "But I, for one, am damn sure glad you got here when you did. This could have been much worse."

"Yes, it could," Charlie agreed solemnly.

Another man joined them. "This is my chief investigator Bill Rogers. You will probably need to map out what went down with him."

Jon nodded solemnly.

Meanwhile Amanda had made it to David, who had bent over and was applying pressure to the man's side. She asked David, "Is he going to be OK?"

David frowned, blinking, his breathing labored. An ambulance pulled up, and two EMTs appeared.

"We need to get him to a hospital fast. I think it missed vital organs. The bullet went through him. But he's bleeding—"

"Why do you think it went through him?" Amanda questioned.

"Because it's the same . . ." David gasped before slumping forward.

Amanda looked stricken. "Oh, David," she cried, as she caught him and pulled him away from Canton.

"Help!" she screamed, her voice catching in a sob.

Rogers and an officer were collecting weapons from Jon and Petrino, when Jon turned and saw Amanda on the ground, crying out and cradling David in her arms. "Oh, my God," he swore, dropping his weapon into the man's hand and striding to her.

The officer reached up a hand to stop him, but Petrino forestalled him. "That's his wife and his brother."

Jon quickly made his way across the grass to David and Amanda. Another paramedic appeared. He directed the EMTs to place Canton on a stretcher, then knelt down by David.

Canton objected weakly, "But he's hurt worse."

The paramedic looked at Amanda. "Give me some space," he said gently.

Jon pulled her away. The paramedic waved to an EMT. "I think he's been hit in the lung. Let's immobilize him, get him there stat before we lose him. He's already unconscious."

Within seconds a gurney had appeared, and David was loaded up. The paramedic spoke while he was working, "Hospital isn't far. We'll call ahead. You can follow us." He threw the car keys from David's pocket to Jon.

"I'm going with him," Amanda demanded.

"No room," paramedic replied. They headed to the ambulance with an inert David.

"Let's go," Amanda said to Jon.

Virginia spoke up. "Please let us go with you."

Amanda nodded, tears in her eyes.

The chief investigator shook his head at the investigator who moved to stop them. "We'll catch up with him. We have plenty of witnesses here, and he's not going far. You can accompany Special Agent Cramer to the hospital."

Jon in turn saw Fred standing nearby and handed him the keys to the Porsche. He took Amanda's arm and steered her away from the scene. Virginia took Allison's hand and they hurried off with Amanda and Jon. The woman they had called Janet rushed out and handed Virginia her purse.

As they approached the car, Jon pushed the button unlocking the doors. They rushed to the car. "I know where the hospital is," Jon spoke grimly, as he gunned the engine and put it in gear.

They followed the ambulances out, Amanda biting her lip to keep from crying, and Jon looking grave. They were silent, both of them fearful. The ride seemed interminable. Amanda bowed her head and prayed.

"Where are they taking Daddy?" Allison demanded fearfully, sniffling.

"We're all going to the hospital," Virginia tried to soothe the child, hugging the child to her anxiously, tears running down her own cheeks.

When they arrived, George Cramer had arrived ahead of them, along with the sheriff's investigator.

They all walked in together, and an attending physician was waiting. He examined David and gave immediate instructions. "He looks familiar," he said.

"He's Dr. David Connor," Jon spoke up.

"Ah, yes, he was just here on a special consult last month," the physician nodded as he continued. "We gotta stem this right away," he told the nurse on the other side.

"What blood type? Do you know?" he asked Jon. "You must be kin, because of the resemblance."

"Type O. I'm also O if you need blood," Jon offered quickly.

"We might. But you all are going to have to wait in the lobby so we can work."

An orderly led the way as the group left the room, Virginia and Allison similarly being evicted from Canton's side.

Once in the lobby, Jon and Virginia were handed forms to complete, and the investigator and Bubba took Amanda aside. "Can you fill us in on what happened?"

Amanda nodded and went through the events as Bubba recorded the statement and the investigator took notes. Jon overheard as he completed the hospital forms. So Lauren identified David as Allison's father to her father? Jon knew in his heart that there even though they had used condoms there was still a slight chance that Jon fathered the little girl. He gazed over at the girl, sitting wide-eyed, scared, beside her grandmother, now her mother as

Amanda had just stated to Bubba. He realized that she looked a little like David, or maybe him. The thought sobered him.

Jon closed his eyes a moment, and the scene of Vause's gun going off and his own shots hitting Vause replayed in his mind. It was not the first time Jon had been forced to shoot someone, but it had been some time since he had found himself in that position, other than the evening Amanda was almost killed by Barnes. He found he never got over that feeling.

He remembered having a beer with Andy and Charlie Petrino not long after Andy first introduced him to Petrino. There, sitting at a bar, the discussion turned to the hazards of their job, and of the horror of having to kill another human being. He remembered that Andy became suddenly quiet, and he knew that it had not been that long since Andy had faced that situation, and that it had been hard for Andy. Jon had asked Charlie if he had ever had to shoot someone.

Charlie had nodded solemnly. "That first time is an excruciating experience, and any time afterward isn't much better, because you relive it all over again."

"How do you deal with it and keep on in the job?" Andy asked quietly, his face exhibiting anguish.

Charlie, his eyes flickering to Jon knowingly, replied. "Andy, I asked my dad that a long time ago. He and I had a long talk once while sitting in a boat all night gigging for flounder. I was about to go off to college and major in criminal justice. He told me that if I went into law enforcement, the time would come when I would have to face that prospect."

Andy had regarded his friend earnestly. Charlie continued. "He told me that was one of the hardest things he had ever done. But he also told me that the first time, he hesitated just a fraction of a second too long, and a good friend and partner was killed. He told me that was the worst experience of his life, because he always felt that if he had not felt that indecision his friend would still be alive."

Charlie leaned forward. "Dad said that he always chose deputies who weren't gun-happy, that felt deeply about not using the weapon unless it was absolutely necessary. But he told me then and there that if I had any qualms about doing it when the time came, I needed to choose another field. We are there to protect and serve, just like the army guy out in battle."

Andy had nodded solemnly, and Jon thanked Charlie afterward for the words, knowing that it had helped Andy through his experience. Now Jon pondered the words. Sure, Charlie most likely could have dispatched the shooter by himself, but what if, Jon kept asking himself. What if Charlie missed? Petrino's first shot had not stopped Vause. What if the guy had turned his gun on Amanda and the child? As it was, Canton and David were seriously wounded.

Amanda had just finished telling Bubba about Vause's confession that he killed Lauren. Amanda glanced over at Jon and saw him scowling, deep in thought. Despite her hurt and anger at him, she felt sorrow and empathy for him.

Bubba's words broke into her thoughts. "I'm really sorry about David," he said. "But you all might have been dead had not Jon taken this guy out."

Amanda only half-comprehended what he was saying. She stared at George as the words registered. "Jon?" she echoed. "I thought it was Char—I mean Sheriff Petrino who was pointing the gun."

"Charlie shot first, but Vause kept firing. It was Jon who burned a hole through him," Bubba spoke, then colored as he realized what he said. "I'm sorry, Amanda. I didn't mean—"

"It's OK," Amanda tried to assure him, but shuddered just the same.

"And you took a grave risk by running out there to catch the guy, and by protecting the little girl. You were in the line of fire with her."

Amanda gazed over at Allison, who was looking curiously back at them. "I didn't know to whom she belonged, but she was just a baby who needed protecting, and it was up to me to do it right then."

As the words left her lips she thought of little Donna Barnes, and of Jon's words to her about the need for someone to help the child.

Bubba and the investigator thanked Amanda and moved over and began asking questions of Virginia Canton. Amanda watched as Allison stood up, left her grandmother's side and walked over to Jon.

"Who are you?" she asked curiously.

Jon put the clipboard holding the form and the pen down in his lap. "My name's Jon. What's yours?" he smiled tentatively.

"I'm Allison," she said, crawling up in the chair beside him. "That guy that was at my house looks a lot like you."

"Yes, he does," Jon replied. "He's my brother."

"Brother," the little girl repeated. "I have a sister," she continued, "but she's dead."

Jon looked at her, confusion on his face. "I'm sorry," he murmured.

The little girl shrugged. "It's OK. I didn't know her, but she sent presents, and it hurt Mommy and Daddy when she died. We put her in a hole today."

Jon blinked. "You mean Lauren?" he inquired gently.

The little girl nodded. "She was really big for a sister. Are you a big brother?"

Jon caught his breath and blinked. "Yes," he nodded quietly.

347

"Who was that man today?"

"Which man?" Jon asked, gazing at her.

"The one that grabbed me?" she looked back, her eyes round.

Virginia overheard and looked up suddenly, her face etched with anxiety. She interrupted the investigator questioning her. "He was a sick man, Allison," she answered the child, walking up and taking her hand. "He needed help."

"Is he going to get help?" the little girl persisted.

The room went silent. Jon looked up, and his eyes met Amanda's, his face gray.

Amanda stood and walked over to him. "Please excuse us. We'll be outside just a minute," she said, taking his hand and walking out the automatic sliding doors.

They walked together slowly, silently, fingers entwined, along the sidewalk winding around the hospital's exterior. Amanda sensed Jon's struggle and remained silent.

Amanda finally broke the silence. "You had to do it, Jon," she whispered, squeezing his hand comfortingly.

He bit his lip, and his shoulders drooped. They were silent again.

"You know I love David," he blurted.

"I know you do," Amanda murmured. "He loves you too. He said he was trying to make up with you for his past indiscretions. He knew he pushed your buttons. There's some jealousy there. He said you two were close until he stole your girlfriend in college."

Jon stopped and looked at her. "He told you all that? You two have talked a lot."

"He told me all this when the two of us went to pick up the vehicles at the sheriff's office," Amanda replied. "I asked him about the rivalry between you two."

"Rivalry?" Jon echoed.

"Yes, dear," Amanda nodded. "You two are so much alike in many ways. I'm amazed that you don't see that. That's part of the problem."

Jon blinked. "Do you love him?" Jon asked suddenly, stopping, pulling her to face him.

"Of course I do. He's your brother," Amanda retorted. She picked up the note of jealousy in Jon's question. "He's a lot of fun, makes a good brother. But he's not you, Jon."

They stared at each other. Jon then spoke. "Amanda, I'm so sorry. Charlie told me about the book. I never even realized that Andy had left stuff behind at my apartment. When I was gone to Mexico after Claude I had Bubba box up my belongings and store them at the condo." His eyes pleaded with her. "It never even crossed my mind that something so precious was in the attic all this time."

"I know," she whispered.

He looked at her, surprised.

"But—"

"Jon, I figured it out just now watching you while you talked to Allison. I realize that when I saw that—" she faltered, "that book and the cufflink I went utterly crazy. I was crushed. I could not even rationalize, could not think it out. I'm sorry I didn't trust you."

He enfolded her to him. "Love, I'm sorry you couldn't tell me what was going on, all the hell you were going through alone while trying to protect us. I admit I doubted you too. I saw the note from Charlie, and I knew there was something you were not telling me."

"I was threatened not to tell anyone." Amanda's eyes filled with tears. "I wanted to confide in you, but I was afraid. Then Varas started planting doubts in my mind. I was so scared I was going to lose you, that maybe I had lost you."

She looked at the ground. "There were pictures. I knew they couldn't be real, but . . . . God, Jon, it hurt so badly. The thought of you and Lauren—" She sniffed, her eyes luminous with tears. "I guess I'm still rather insecure about us."

"I am as well. I am insanely jealous when I think of you with anyone else," Jon admitted. "But, unlike you, I've never felt this way about someone, and it's a new experience for me to be so much in love that I lose my perspective."

"Why did you have Lauren's phone number?" Amanda asked suddenly.

"Ah, that," Jon nodded. "She apparently called my office Tuesday. I was busy, and had Susan take a number. I didn't want to talk to her." He looked sharply at Amanda. "I didn't talk to her. I had no contact with her. When I gave my statement to Petrino Tuesday night I told him about the call, and he asked for me to provide him the number. That's why the post-it note you saw."

She looked chagrined.

"And the cufflink?" Jon reached up and tucked a stray strand of her hair into place. "Ralph lost one of his at the party Sunday. All we can figure is that Lauren found it and thought it was mine, and decided to wreak a little havoc between you and me. According to Varas, that's what he hired her to do, except that she was to discredit Ralph, not me."

He smiled at her slightly. "Yes, I guessed that you saw it and believed the worst. And I should have told you about the post-it, but then we had the argument about my giving Charlie the statement in the first place, and in the heat of battle I forgot."

He gripped her arms and gazed at her. "Love, I swear to you I have had no contact with her, other than what you saw at the party, since the weekend I spent with her nine years ago. Those pictures could not be real."

He took her face in his hands and kissed her, slowly and sweetly. "We are going to have to take some advanced lessons on trust and complete truthfulness," he smiled.

She froze. He noted it. "What is it?" he whispered.

She pulled away. "I guess while we are on that topic, I am going to have to confess something painful."

She didn't look at him as she stepped away, her back to him. "What is it?" he asked, suddenly apprehensive.

"I wasn't entirely honest about my feelings for Charlie," she said slowly.

He was still, silent, waiting for her to continue. "Jon," she swallowed, "I did love Charlie. He was always there for me. I needed to forget Andy, and I did for those few hours with Charlie. I lost myself, and it felt good. I wanted to make a life with Charlie. But when I walked back—back in my office that night, there was Andy's badge and commendation still on my desk. I knew as I touched that badge I couldn't—I just couldn't—" she stopped, overcome.

"I know," Jon whispered.

"You do?" she was surprised.

"I guessed. I knew how Andy felt about you. And I knew you had to be special for him to feel that way. I've heard about your devotion to him, even after his death. I've seen it for myself." He paused. "But I always knew that you felt more for Charlie than you confessed. I also knew how he felt about you. It's OK, Amanda. I understand." He looked away. "But I too was afraid I was losing you the last few days. It scared the hell out of me."

He took a breath, then continued, staring at her back. "The question, I guess, is whether you can make it, with me, for the rest of your life."

He walked up to her, placing his hand on her shoulder. "I told you once that I can't be Andy. I've known for years I can't be David. I can't be Charlie either. I'm who I am, love. I want you, only you, but all of you. Forever. Can we do that? I want to try if you do."

She slowly turned. "I told you once that you have no competition," she smiled. "Jon, I will always love Andy, and probably Charlie as well. But you are the one I've chosen to spend the rest of my life with, the one who makes me complete."

He caught her in his arms, kissing her hair. She teased, "You're going to ᴖ that jealousy thing."

ɪe mumbled against her mouth.

"I love you more than anyone, Jon," she contended, pulling away and gazing at him. "And I can even face your going back to work for the Bureau if that makes you happy, because I love you."

He stared at her. "Where did that come from?"

"I know," she said, a sly look on her face. "And I love having you with me every night, knowing I don't have to worry if you're coming home to me safe. But I want you to be happy."

"I'm happy," Jon whispered.

Amanda reached up and kissed him.

"I guess we're making a spectacle of ourselves. We need to get back and see how our patients are."

A cloud passed over his face. "You're right." He took her hand and they walked back to the emergency room together.

On the way back, he squeezed her hand. "I don't think I can handle it if I lose David. Despite our bad times, I love him."

She nodded, and he could read the worry on her face.

CHAPTER 32

Amanda looked questioningly at Mrs. Canton as they reentered the surgical waiting room, but the woman shook her head. Allison walked up to Amanda and took her hand.

Amanda gazed back at the girl. "Mommy says I need to thank you for saving my life."

"You're welcome. I'd do it all over again." Amanda squeezed her hand comfortingly. "I am hoping that Daddy is going to be all right."

"Me too," Allison breathed as the door opened.

Janet raced in. "Any word?" she asked anxiously.

Virginia shook her head.

Just then a female doctor walked into the lobby. "Mrs. Canton?"

Virginia stood anxiously and approached.

The doctor smiled and took her hand. "Your husband is going to be all right. He lost some blood, and we had a little repair work to do. But he is in recovery." The doctor put her arm around Mrs. Canton and spoke quietly to her, and Virginia nodded, tears of relief flowing down her cheeks.

"Can I see him?" Virginia asked anxiously.

"He is still under sedation, but you may come in for a moment. But only you."

Virginia turned to Allison. "Please stay with Miss Janet, and I'll be right back."

The girl cried, "I want to see him."

"No, not this time," Virginia was firm. "I'll try to get you in later."

Bubba turned to Jon. "Kimball asked if I'd go ahead and take your statement here. If you don't mind, we'll step outside."

Jon nodded and went with Bubba and the officer. Amanda watched them quietly and worked in a puzzle book Janet had brought. That David's, or Jon's, she thought, her eyes resting on the child.

352

But it doesn't matter. All that matters is that Walter Canton and David make it. We can live with the rest.

Virginia came out a few minutes later, drying her eyes with a tissue. Amanda stood.

"He's awake and knew me. He's a little out of it," Virginia was teary. "But he's is going to be OK."

Amanda breathed, "That is wonderful." She walked up and put an arm around Virginia.

Virginia nodded. "If something had happened to Allison . . . . Oh, Mrs. Connor, I'll always be grateful that you saved her."

"It wasn't me." Amanda released the woman and squeezed her hand quickly.

"No, even with all that happened, little Allison could have been—" Virginia shuddered.

"I was glad that she wasn't hit. She is a precious bundle," Amanda said quietly.

"Yes," sniffed Virginia. "Have you heard anything yet?"

Amanda shook her head.

"I can ask Janet to take Allison home and sit with you," Virginia offered.

"No, let Janet take you home and get some rest. Allison needs you right now. Today has been very traumatic for her, too. And you need your strength to help take care of your husband when he is released to come home," Amanda smiled sadly. "I'll see you again."

Janet came up and took Virginia's arm. Amanda said goodbye to Allison and watched them out the door. She saw Allison wave shyly to Jon, who tried to smile and respond. She could see from his expression that serious matters were being discussed.

Her cell phone vibrated. Pulling it out of her purse, she was surprised to see that there were a lot of calls. Among them she noted several calls from Ralph, a couple from Kelly, and some from Joseph Rand. She answered.

"What is going on?" Ralph demanded. "Where are you?"

She filled Ralph in as best she could.

"So Jon and Petrino and Fred are all there?"

Fred walked in the door and spied her. "Yes," she replied. "They are all outside. Fred has just walked in."

"What can I do?" Ralph asked her.

"What is the latest there?" she answered with a question.

"Esme Townsend is in guarded condition. They're not sure Varas will make it."

"What?" Amanda exclaimed.

353

Ralph then brought her up to date on the latest events.

"Is Toby there?" she wanted to know.

"He is in with her right now. How about David?"

"We don't know yet," she rasped, suddenly overcome.

"It'll be OK," Ralph tried to assure her.

"Have you heard from Claire?"

"She called this afternoon while we were waiting word about Esme. I told her there was a lot going on here, but I couldn't disclose it over the phone. She was mad that I wouldn't tell her. She has a flight home Tuesday." She heard his voice catch. "Amanda—"

"I'll go with you to pick her up from the airport," she promised. "But I think, as bad as today has been, we got the break that will solve Lauren Mallory's murder, and maybe we will be able to tell Claire so by then."

"I hope so." She could sense relief in his voice. "Do you need anything from me?"

"No, just keep me updated."

"Ditto," he said. "Love you, girl."

"Ditto," she replied, hanging up.

Fred sat down by her and handed her a cell phone. "It's David's. He left it in the car. Some guy has called several times, and the phone kept vibrating, so I finally answered. It is Dr. Rand. He demanded to know who I was, and wanted to talk to David. I told him you would call him back and fill him in on what's going on."

She nodded and took the phone. A moment later she was talking to Joey, bringing him up to date.

"Who is the doctor?" Joey demanded.

"I think his name tag said Caputo, but I don't know for sure," Amanda replied.

"I'll get in touch with him. Don't worry, Amanda," she heard Joey say.

"Joey, so much has happened that we haven't let any of the family know about David yet. Jon is being interviewed by law enforcement right now. I don't have any news yet, and I'm frankly scared to call his mother with this. Kelly will be frightened out of her mind."

"I'll take care of the family, as long as you have Jon talk to his mother as soon as he can," Joey promised.

Amanda hung up, realizing how drained she was. Suddenly in the momentary lull the moment flashed back in her mind. "Fred," she groaned, "I think I'm at the end of my endurance. If something happens to David . . . ."

Fred put his arm around her and awkwardly hugged her. "We'll make it somehow, girl," he mumbled.

The door to the room opened, and the doctor came out, still in scrubs. Amanda stood, and Fred with her. "Are you Mrs. Connor?" the doctor queried.

"Get Jon," Amanda told Fred, who nodded and hurried off. "I'm David's sister-in-law. His brother is just outside."

Jon came hurrying up. The doctor intoned, "His condition is still grave, but we've stopped the bleeding and inflated the lung. He's in recovery. The next twenty-four hours are critical." He looked at Amanda's wan face. "I wish I could set your mind at ease, but I can't. We just watch and wait now."

"A Dr. Joseph Rand will be calling to check on his condition," Amanda informed him.

His eyebrows shot up. "*The* Dr. Rand? Wow."

"David and he are best friends," Jon explained.

"We will see that Dr. Connor gets the very best care," the doctor assured them. "Leave your emergency numbers at the desk here, and I will personally call if anything changes. Go home and get some rest yourselves, and check back in with me this evening about eight for an update. I'm not letting you see him today, but I'll see about letting you in first thing in the morning."

"We'll be staying in town, and can be here at a moment's notice," Jon informed the doctor.

Amanda wrote out the cell numbers for the staff. Then Jon took her arm and led her out.

Charlie was outside the lobby deep in discussion with Kimball and the sheriff, but stopped when he saw the expression on her face. "What's the news?"

Jon relayed the doctor's statements.

Amanda stared at Charlie. "I told Bubba this, but you need to know. Vause admitted to me that he killed Lauren. Mr. Canton and David were there and heard it." She took a breath. "He had Allison, but she was hysterical at the time."

Petrino nodded. She continued. "And the doctor just told Virginia that Mr. Canton will pull through."

The sheriff's investigator piped up, "I believe her."

Jon felt Amanda shiver. "If you don't mind, we're going to be at the condo. You know how to reach us. Keep the Porsche." He pressed a piece of paper and a key into Charlie's hand. "If you need to stay in town, here's the address and a key where we are. You and Fred can make yourselves at home."

Amanda took Charlie's hand. "Thanks, Sheriff," she said simply.

Jon led her to the car and opened her door. They were silent during the drive, both of them exhausted. Soon they arrived at the condominium. Jon helped her out of the car and took her hand.

355

When they made it inside, she asked, "Do you want anything? Something to eat or drink?"

"No. Just bring the phone in case the hospital calls." He drew her down the foyer and up the stairs to a bedroom. "I'm all in, and I can look at you and tell you are, too. I want to hold you and sleep with you."

They both silently stripped to their underwear. Amanda for the first time saw the bandage on his arm.

"What happened to you?" she cried, stunned.

He looked at his arm. "Oh, I'd forgotten about it. Just a graze. Dr. Howells stitched it up."

"But what—" Amanda started.

But Jon dragged her to him and kissed her, silencing her. He pulled her into bed with him and into his arms. "I'll tell you all about it later," he whispered.

Amanda snuggled to him.

"I missed you, Mrs. Connor," he mumbled, throwing his arm over her.

Within minutes Jon was asleep, and Amanda soon followed.

A couple of hours later, Amanda awoke with a start. It was dark, and she sat up. Jon was asleep beside her, but she was disoriented. Then she recalled where they were, what had happened.

She thought she heard sounds of someone moving downstairs. She quietly rose and pulled her dress back on, then padded down the stairs cautiously.

As she reached the landing, she came face to face with Joey Rand.

She gave a little startled cry. "Oh, you scared me," she croaked weakly, sinking to a sitting position on the stairs, suddenly trembling.

"Are you OK?" he peered at her concernedly. "Where's Jon?"

"He's upstairs asleep. He has been up since night before last. Did you get up with the family?"

From out of the living room walked Kelly.

"Kelly." She stood and warmly embraced her sister-in-law. "How did you get here so quickly?"

Kelly blushed deeply. Joey and Kelly looked at each other sheepishly. Amanda stared at them uncomprehendingly. "What is it?" she asked dully.

"Are you going to tell her, or shall I?" Joey gazed at Kelly.

"Tell me what?" Amanda was confused.

"I was here already," Kelly answered. "Joey and I have eloped. We're married. We had just made it here from Vegas this morning. We've been trying to reach David, Jon and you all morning."

"Oh," breathed Amanda. Shakily she sat down on the stairs again.

"Are you OK?" Kelly asked, alarmed.

"This is wonderful news," Amanda smiled wanly.

"Except that we couldn't raise any of you, and didn't know any of this was happening with David." Kelly's face clouded. Joey put his arm around her.

"Oh, sweetie, I'm so sorry." Amanda went up and flung her arms around them both.

"We just decided to do it, and didn't want to wait," Joey explained. "We took the company jet to Vegas. Then we tried to call you all, but couldn't get any of you. We thought that odd, so we came back to Florida right away to find you all and tell you."

"So your parents don't know yet?" Amanda asked anxiously.

Kelly looked down. "I told my dad, because he let us use the jet, and Joey insisted. But no, we haven't told Gloria yet."

"Ooh," Amanda swallowed. "Does she know about—about David?"

"I called and told James as soon as I hung up from talking to you." Joey was somber. "Only that David is in the hospital. I said it was an accident, didn't want to get into a lengthy explanation over the phone. I'm sure they are on their way down here by now."

Amanda nodded soberly. Kelly took her hand. "After your call, Joey and I got dressed and went to the hospital. He wormed his way in, saw David and talked to the attending physician." Kelly's voice broke, and she flung her arms around Amanda's neck. "I'm scared."

Amanda hugged her back. "All we can do is hope and pray right now."

Joey drew Kelly to him. "He's in good hands."

Kelly looked at Amanda, tears in her eyes. "We must have just missed you two. You were gone from the hospital by the time we got there. We saw Sheriff Petrino and invited him and your neighbor back here for dinner. He said Jon had given him a key."

Amanda was rueful. "It won't be much of a honeymoon for you two, here at a condo full of people."

Joey smiled sadly. "We can't enjoy ourselves unless and until we know David is OK. I am just sorry we have to face Gloria so soon after the news breaks."

"It will be a long night," Amanda agreed.

"Where's Jon?" Kelly asked.

"I'm here," Jon appeared at the top of the stairs, dressed in a robe. He made his way down, yawning. "Who can sleep with all this commotion going on? I woke up and missed my wife."

He put his arm around Amanda. "Kelly, how did you get here so quickly?" he asked.

Joey, Amanda, and Kelly all burst out laughing. He looked at them in consternation.

"You're going to have to replay the whole story for him now," Amanda smiled.

The doorbell rang. Kelly ran to open the door, and Petrino and Fred walked in.

"We're on our way back to Mainville," Petrino informed Jon and Amanda, "and wanted to stop in. There will be a big meeting tomorrow with a special prosecutor and all the agencies involved. All the information will be laid out regarding the murder, the shooting at the Townsend home and today's events." He looked grim. "I hope we can dispose of it all, but tomorrow will tell."

He turned to Joey and Kelly. "Congratulations on your news, and I wish you every happiness. I'm just sorry about David. We will check in tomorrow."

Fred turned and kissed Amanda on the cheek. "Call me if you need anything." He gave one of his quick smiles.

She nodded, squeezing his hand as they took their leave.

Jon stared at Kelly and Joey as they turned back from seeing the men off. "Congratulations?" he asked, an edge to his voice. "Just what sort of congratulations?"

Joey looked at him nervously. "Kelly—Kelly and I—we—we're—"

"Married," Kelly finished for him, staring at her brother apprehensively.

Jon blinked. "Ooh," he muttered, sitting down on the stairs heavily.

Joey and Kelly started laughing again. "That's just how Amanda reacted," Kelly hooted.

"Does Mom know?" Jon asked.

"This is déjà vu." Joey scratched his head.

Amanda intervened. "Your parents are probably on the way down here now. Joey told them only that David was in an accident."

"They're coming here?" Jon echoed disbelievingly, looking around at the place. "Oh, shit."

Kelly's face fell. "Oh, shit," she repeated.

Joey and Amanda looked at each other. "Welcome to the family," Amanda whispered.

"Ditto." Joey hid a grin. "Been here, done it, got the t-shirt. But we're married, and there's not a damn thing Momma Connor can do about it."

"Momma Connor?" Jon repeated. "Is that how you're going to greet her?" he bit back a grin.

"The fireworks are going to be so big I don't think it will matter what I call her," Joey rejoined.

Jon started laughing, and after a moment, they all started.

The Connors' Crisis

"I'm so happy for the two of you. I just wish David was here to take some of the heat too when the news breaks," Jon remarked.

"We all do," Amanda replied. "But he has to make it."

The thought sobered them all.

Kelly said, "OK, we have to do something. Jon, you call and see when the folks are arriving. Amanda and I are going to leaf through the yellow pages and pick out a Chinese delivery restaurant and order food to get here when they arrive."

Jon grinned. "Mom hates Oriental food."

Kelly grinned back. "I know, but everyone else likes it. Then while we are waiting you and Amanda are going to catch us up on everything that is happening." She looked pensive. "I wish the Sheriff and Mr. Vaughan had stayed. Mother would make less of a scene if there was company present."

Joey linked arms with Amanda. "It sounds like the inmates are planning a revolt," he said quietly, winking.

CHAPTER 33

Joseph Rand was helping Amanda set the table. "They never ate off just paper plates? Not even stoneware?" Amanda asked wonderingly as she looked at the huge breakfront with several patterns of costly china.

"Gloria Connor only has the best of everything at all times," Joey remarked. "Hell, when we were growing up David had to come over to my house to wear jeans, and I had to lend them to him. His first hamburger, hotdog and taco were at my place.

"One day Gloria showed up at my house to pick up David unannounced. David and I were dirty, because we had been building a treehouse in the back yard all day. She took one look at David in shorts and tennis shoes without socks, his knee skinned, and gave my mom heck, snatched David and left." He shook his head. "James had to smooth that over and calm Gloria down before David could ever come to my house again."

"Sounds rather stilted," Amanda murmured.

"But Gloria could let her hair down at times," Joey countered. "There were days when she'd play games with us, come up with a story about knights for us to act out, read us one of her children's books. The older we got, though, the more involved she got into politics and society, and she became one of them."

He mused, "David and I were six and in first grade when Kelly was born. Gloria had just been accepted into the Denver Junior League and the Republican Club. We noticed she had less time for us. And as we got older, those fun times were less. Kelly was a tomboy, and tried her mother's patience, because of course Gloria wanted her dolled up in frills and prim and proper. We'd let her play with us. We made her play Guinevere, but she wanted to be a knight too." Joey grinned. "James doted on his baby girl, spent a lot of his free time with her. She learned computer languages at the same time she was learning to read and write."

"What about you? Brothers and sisters?" Amanda was curious.

Joey shrugged. "All I have are a couple of older brothers. I was an accident. My older brother has ten years on me, and the other thirteen, and my Mom thought she was past the diaper-changing. So David and I became more than just neighbors; we were buddies. We both liked Jon and always had a ball when he would hang out with us. He did quite a lot, but then he had friends of his own, and he liked to be alone, read, go with his dad to the gun club, run track, play football and basketball, flirt with the girls."

"Oh, he was a flirt?" Amanda smirked.

"He was one of those quiet understatedly cool dudes that girls like," Joey smirked.

They could hear Jon and Kelly in the foyer. Kelly called, "Have you picked up in the living room and den?"

"Yes. Have you made sure there are fresh sheets on Mother's bed?" he countered.

"Yes," Kelly said. "Jacquie is trying to clean everything up as best she can, but she was the only one I could reach on short notice. She'll just have to do without fresh flowers tonight." Suddenly the sound of a vacuum cleaner could be heard.

Joey laughed quietly. "Preparing for Gloria's arrival is like going down the checklist before takeoff on a 747. And the staff aren't here because no one was expected this week." He looked sheepish. "That's one reason why Kelly and I decided to come here. I was insistent that we let you all know before we disappeared somewhere. And we figured it would be quiet for a day or two, and we could just hide out. Silas was the only one I told beforehand, so that he'd know where I was. But when we got here this morning, the place was a mess."

"Yes, the police were here searching for evidence," Amanda spoke quietly. "All of a sudden David, Ralph and Jon were suspects. The place apparently just got released last night, and there was no time to call someone in to clean. David—David was with me." She fell silent, embarrassed.

Joey looked at her sharply, but decided not to probe.

"Amanda, I'll let you in on a secret," he tried to steer the topic away from troubled waters. "Jon, Kelly and David have a code of sorts. You'll learn it after a while. But for one thing, when they're 'in' with Gloria, it's just the family around and things are going well, they call her 'Mom'. When she is being a bitch, they revert to 'Mother'. When others are around, it's 'Mother'. Sometimes when there is company present and they want to antagonize her, they will call her 'Mom'. She hates that, and they know it. It's their passive-aggressive way of getting her attention."

He smiled. "Gloria got in my face about something earlier this year, just before I made the break and came down to Florida to visit with Silas. I had taken all I could. I called her 'Momma Connor' once and 'Mommy Dearest' in front of the rest, and you could have heard a pin drop. Then I told her that none of her children would ever be able to find true happiness as long as she remained the Wicked Witch of the West in their lives. I stalked out, and haven't been back to a family event. And I haven't been invited, at least by her."

Amanda bit back laughter. "I'm so sorry," she said somberly, but she started laughing in spite of herself. Joey grinned too. "I can't help it. You really said that?"

"Yep," Joey laughed too. "One of my finer moments, if I do say so myself."

"And I loved him even more after that," Kelly piped up, coming up to him and reaching up to kiss him. "When Joey walked out, I knew I had some serious decisions to make. But I couldn't just leave cold-turkey; Dad depended on me, both personally and professionally. That frustrated Joey."

"So what are you going to do now?" Amanda looked at them.

Joey put his arm around Kelly. "I have agreed that she needs to stay with the company. She lives and breathes it; it is part of her, and she enjoys it. And there's always business for me as an orthopaedist and trauma specialist. I have enough to get my sports medicine certification too. I have friends out there at the university that have invited me to join the staff. I can teach and consult with the sports teams."

"So you're going back to Colorado?" Jon had walked into the room.

"Yes," Joey nodded. "But Kelly and I agreed, and James has insisted, that we make our own home. So we will avoid Cherry Creek, where they live. Kelly has suggested we even check out Boulder or Colorado Springs."

Jon gazed at his sister and asked Joey, "Are you sure you can handle being in the same state as Mom and married to my sister?"

Joey looked down at Kelly as she wrapped her arms around his waist. "We talked about this many times lately. We think if we have each other and keep a united front, this will work. James has given his blessing. And David pledged his support."

"You got mine," Amanda said quietly.

Jon smiled. "And mine. But it means we all have to do battle with Mom. I rattled a saber the other night at dinner when I found out she had an investigator probing into Amanda's past."

Amanda's eyes grew wide. "She did?"

"Yes, and I told her that whatever she wanted to know, she could ask outright, and keep her goddamned investigators away from us."

Kelly hooted with laughter. "That he did. Another pin-drop moment at the Connor household. Daddy was bursting at the seams with pride, and David cheered."

Amanda looked up at Jon, trepidation in her eyes. But he hugged her close and kissed her forehead, smiling broadly. "It was so much fun I want to do it again. Maybe tonight," he contended wickedly.

"You know I'm going to be blamed for all this," Amanda smiled nervously. "For Jon's outburst, for Kelly's elopement, for David's injury."

Jon noticed her discomfort. "David dragged you into that situation, not the other way around," he replied, his voice low but stern. "And the reason for Kelly's and my rebellion is that we have both finally discovered what we want, and that it is worth fighting tooth and nail to keep it. And I intend that Gloria be apprised of that," he finished with quiet resolve.

"I'm just not used to all this family tension." Amanda looked at them pensively. "My life was outwardly normal, without conflict. It wasn't until recently that I was faced with the fact that I was surrounded by secrets, that nothing was as it seemed."

Kelly took her hand. "It's not that much different, except that we haven't been in the dark about it. Outwardly we have tried to put our best face forward, to appear the happy loving family. And we are loving, but not happy." She smiled at Amanda. "I guess Jon and I have just staked a claim, set a new goal," she squeezed Amanda's hand affectionately.

"But this ain't getting the place ready for the royals," she said suddenly. She threw up her hands. "To hell with it," she announced. "I think the setting is perfect to interject some chaos into Gloria's ordered little world."

"I just hope we don't give her a heart attack," Amanda rejoined.

"If so, we now have another doctor in the family," Jon smirked.

He noted a buzzing, and looked at the cell phone clipped to his belt. At the same time, Joey's cell went off.

"It's the hospital," Jon said, taking the call.

"It's James," Joey announced. He listened intently. "I don't think that's a good idea. They are not—OK, OK, we'll be there."

He turned to the others. "They've landed. Gloria is insisting that they go directly to the hospital, and that we meet them there," he informed the group.

"David is awake, and is asking for Amanda," Jon smiled.

"That's wonderful," Kelly breathed. "Let's go."

They all looked at each other, at their casual and bedraggled dress, and laughed.

"She'll have a coronary," Amanda spoke first.

"The hospital is the best place for one," Joey grinned.

Within minutes they were all in Joey's SUV heading toward the hospital, where they flung themselves breathlessly into the ER waiting room. Dr. Caputo appeared after they announced themselves.

"You work some long hours," Amanda remarked.

"I took a colleague's on-call. I wanted to keep an eye on Dr. Connor," the doctor replied. "He's really weak, and not out of the woods. He woke up asking for Amanda." He looked at her. "Is that you?"

Amanda nodded.

"Only two at a time, and only for a moment. Who goes first?"

"Amanda," Jon and Kelly said in unison.

Amanda demurred. "It should be Jon and Kelly."

"He asked for you." Kelly looked at her brother. "You go with her," she said softly.

So Amanda and Jon followed the doctor into the intensive care unit. "How is Mr. Canton?" Amanda asked.

"He is stable, and we'll move him to a room in the morning. I will probably release him the next day, if all continues to be well," the doctor replied.

The doctor stopped outside a small room and gestured for them to enter. Amanda took a deep breath and stepped inside, gazing at her brother-in-law.

He heard their approach and opened his eyes. His face was pale. Amanda took his hand.

"You scared me," she whispered.

"I'm sorry I dragged you into that," he asserted weakly, ending in a small cough.

"Don't try to talk. I'm glad I was there," she murmured, tears in her eyes.

"Me too," Jon joined in, gazing down at his brother. "If not for Amanda's being there, there's no telling what might have happened to you and little Allison."

David winced as he took a breath, looking up at Amanda tiredly. "I dreamed I was in your arms, that you kissed me."

Jon's eyes flashed and he bit back a retort. David looked over at him. "Gotcha," he said with an attempt at a smile.

They all smiled. "You need to get well quickly so that I can beat your butt," Jon informed him, his voice hoarse.

Amanda squeezed his hand. "Kelly and Joey are outside and want to see you. They won't let us stay but a minute. We love you, David."

She started to release his hand, but he grabbed it. "Doesn't she look a little like me?"

Sudden hot tears fell down Amanda's cheek. "Yes, dear, she does," she whispered.

"Don't tell Mom. I want to tell her," he gasped, his strength spent.

"But—" Jon started, but Amanda interrupted.

"David's right. It's his story." She bent over him and kissed his cheek. "You get well."

The doctor intervened. "That's enough for now. The others can see him in the morning."

"But Mom will storm the doors," Jon warned.

"And I don't mind calling the police if necessary," the doctor countered firmly.

He accompanied them back. Jon murmured to Amanda, "You know, when Gloria asks what he was doing there and we don't tell her, she will blame you."

"I won't lie to her, but I'll take the blame if need be." Amanda smiled grimly. "I'm a lawyer, Jon. I can handle it."

As they walked through the door, there were Gloria and James waiting with Kelly and Joey. Gloria, dressed immaculately, stood up stiffly as the three entered the lobby.

"Dr. Caputo, this is our mother Gloria Connor." Jon made the introduction.

Gloria's gaze was piercing. "I'm here to see my son and get a report." Her voice was supercilious.

"Your son is in critical condition. He will have no other visitors until morning," the doctor interrupted her icily. He stared at her, and she stared back icily. "He is not up to it," Caputo's voice softened, "and I'm sure you don't want to be the cause of any setback."

Ruffled by the doctor's insistence, Gloria glared at him. The doctor continued. "I have your numbers to call if there's any change in his condition. He needs to rest. You all need to do the same. He'll need you come morning."

The doctor turned on his heel and re-entered through the double doors. Gloria looked at his retreating form.

James took her arm and tried to draw her away. "Come on, dear," he whispered.

But she stood stock still. James moved to face her. She bit her lip, tears coursing down her face. "Is he going to die, James?" she asked piteously.

James enfolded her, stiff and crying. "There's hope." He looked at Jon pleadingly.

Jon took a breath. "He was awake just now and asked for Amanda. He spoke a few words, even cracked a joke. Yes, there's hope."

Amanda stepped forward and put her hand on Mrs. Connor's shoulder.

But the woman stiffened and backed up, pulling away from her husband.

"It's all your fault," she spat at Amanda. "If he hadn't been on some escapade with you, he wouldn't be at death's door."

Jon started to respond, but Amanda held her hand up, silencing him. "He asked me to accompany him to a funeral," she responded quietly.

"If it hadn't been for Amanda's intervention," Jon interjected, ignoring Amanda, "he and a little girl would probably be dead right now."

Gloria's face exhibited shock. "Whose funeral?" she demanded.

"Someone he loved," Amanda expressed quietly.

"Who? What little girl?" James was confused.

"I'm not at liberty to tell you that," Amanda stated. "It was David's expressed wish that he tell you about it himself. And I intend that it be so."

Gloria sputtered, "And if he dies? Are you going to keep it from me then?"

"I guess we'll cross that bridge when we get there. For now, I for one am counting on David to pull through," Amanda retorted briskly. "Now we can all sit here and be miserable in public, or we can go back to the condo, be miserable in private, eat a bite and get some rest. I vote for the latter."

Kelly rejoined, "And we all know how you feel about airing the family's laundry in public, Mother."

Gloria whipped around to face her daughter. "Kelly!" she choked.

James also looked at his daughter, stunned.

Jon and Joey looked at each other, Joey biting back a grin and Jon shrugging. Let the women battle it out, his eyes telegraphed.

But Gloria had recovered. "Yes, we do need to adjourn to the condo. Jon, why don't you ride with us?" she insisted, sniffling.

"Sorry," Jon started, but Amanda placed her hand on his arm.

"Your mother needs an ally right this minute," she said, her voice low. "And James looks a little lost. Why don't you accompany them back?"

"I don't want to be counted among the enemy," Jon whispered.

"I promise we'll call a truce until we get to the condo," Amanda smiled encouragingly.

Gloria looked at them suspiciously. "Are you coming or not?"

"Please go with Gloria, my dear," Amanda smiled her sweetest. "I'll see you at the condo."

Jon gave her a grin as Gloria swallowed her fury.

They all walked out to their cars. As Amanda climbed in the back, Kelly asked, "What was that all about?"

The Connors' Crisis

"David was insistent that he be the one to tell his mother about Allison. I told Jon we are going to honor David's wishes on the matter, even if I have to take the brunt of Gloria's wrath," Amanda explained.

"We can't keep the whole story from her," Joey said quietly.

"No, and I plan on telling her as much as we can without revealing about David's liaison with Lauren Mallory, and about Allison. However, I'm hoping you're going to help me out there."

"How?" Joey glanced at her through the rearview mirror.

"If I'm not mistaken, you also have some news to impart, which is going to deflect her attention away from David for a bit."

Kelly whispered, "Oh, that. Yes, we need to go ahead and drop the bomb, get it over with. Besides, I'm not sleeping without you tonight," she told Joey.

"No, you're not," he agreed, his jaw set in a stubborn line. "But I have a feeling there won't be much sleep going on at the condo tonight."

"Order the food," Amanda instructed Kelly. "We're going to need something to do with our hands. And chopsticks may be safer than forks."

When they arrived home, Kelly was tense. "Jacquie was working hard to restore the place, and I told her to do what she could."

"It will be fine," Amanda reassured her.

"I told her not to worry with our rooms for tonight, so they will still be a little disheveled," Kelly apologized.

"No problem."

They were home before the others, and Kelly ran to the door and inside, Joey and Amanda following. The place looked tidied. "It will have to do," Kelly cried despairingly.

"It will do," Amanda said firmly.

"I think we're all going to need a drink." Joey disappeared into the library. Kelly and Amanda trailed after his wake.

Kelly slipped her arm in Amanda's elbow. "Sit across from me on the other sofa," she whispered. "Avoid the hot seat and Mother's chair," she laughed softly.

As Amanda seated herself, Joey handed her a drink. "Whiskey, right?" he grinned.

She smiled her thanks, as Jon and the elder Connors walked into the room. Jon moved over and took a seat beside Amanda as Gloria glided to her chair, her eagle eyes missing nothing.

"Why is this place such a mess?" she complained.

"Because the police just released it last night," Jon replied.

"The police?" Gloria was shocked. "Whatever for?"

"They were looking for evidence," Jon replied unperturbedly as Joey handed him a drink.

"Evidence?" James echoed, stunned.

"A murder case." Jon was purposefully vague, as Kelly shot a look at him and Amanda sipped her drink.

"Here?" Gloria turned white.

"No, the murder didn't occur here, but they had reason to believe there might be evidence here," Jon smiled, putting his arm around Amanda.

James crossed over and sat down beside his daughter, taking her hand, a question in his eyes. Kelly nodded. "Yes, Daddy."

"Yes, what?" Gloria asked sharply.

Joey handed her and James each a drink. "You're going to need this. We have an announcement."

Without preamble he plunged in. "Kelly and I borrowed the company jet and flew to Vegas last night." He paused a moment to let the information sink in. Gloria looked at him, stunned and uncomprehending. "We are married."

Gloria sucked in a sharp breath. "You're not pregnant, are you?" She turned to her daughter.

"Mother!" Kelly exclaimed.

"Gloria!" James shouted.

Gloria held up her hand. "I just wanted to know. I'm very happy to hear it, if you didn't do it because you had to."

It was the others' turn to look shocked.

Gloria gazed at her daughter, as Joey downed his whiskey in one gulp and poured another. "Your father has prevailed upon me to realize what a witch I've been to Joey, and how unhappy you've been without him. I did not have a clue how out of touch I have been with you. And I'm sorry I made you think you had to sneak off to do this instead of having a big wedding." Her eyes misted. "But if this is what you really want . . ." her voice trailed off.

Kelly moved over to her and knelt beside her chair. "This is what I really want, Mom," she said, taking her hand.

Gloria reached over and stroked her hair. "Then this is also what I want."

Kelly stood and hugged her. Gloria responded, but then pushed her away and stood, moving over to Joey.

Joey stepped back as though he feared his mother-in-law might strike him. But she smiled at him. "I'm sorry, Joey. You are already family, but I've not made you feel so in a while. I'm glad you are now my son-in-law."

Joey and she hugged, and James stood and hugged his daughter, then walked over and pumped Joey's hand vigorously.

The Connors' Crisis

"We need champagne, but there is none chilled," Gloria complained softly.

"I took care of that." Jon stood and walked out of the room. They looked after him curiously. They heard the sound of a cork popping. He returned with a tray, champagne in a bucket with ice and glasses at the ready.

"I hoped we would reach the point of celebrating this news tonight," he explained wryly, setting the tray down on the console and pouring champagne.

Glasses were distributed and everyone stood. Jon regained his place at Amanda's side. "To the happy couple. A lifetime of love and happiness. And may our David return in one piece to harass us and keep us honest."

They all drank. Then James walked over and picked up the bottle, refilling the glasses. "We have another occasion to toast," he spoke. "To our Jon and Amanda, who have braved trials and tribulations to find happiness together. May their happiness fill all our lifetimes."

"Yes," Gloria murmured. Amanda and Jon exchanged surprised glances as they drank.

The doorbell rang. Kelly announced, "That will be our dinner."

She left quickly. Amanda said quietly, "I'll go help her. Dinner will be ready shortly."

She quickly repaired to the kitchen. "Your mother is taking all this pretty well," she whispered to Kelly as the latter brought a couple of sacks into the kitchen. "I'm not sure springing Oriental food is a good idea."

"Don't worry," Kelly smiled. "I also got her favorite caviar and cream cheese on a pizza."

Amanda almost choked. "Pizza?"

Kelly and she pealed with laughter, as they hurriedly emptied food into serving dishes and placed them on the table.

"Dinner is served," Kelly called loudly, then giggled at Amanda. "That has never been done in the Connor household before."

Gloria stood. "Who is serving us tonight?" she wondered aloud.

She walked into the dining room and saw the food set out on the table. Jon walked by and kissed her on the cheek. "I believe it is called 'family style'," he teased her.

They took their seats, and Gloria looked at Amanda expectantly. "I think we should pray. Amanda, will you?"

Amanda nodded as Jon looked sharply at his mother, who smiled. They bowed their heads, and Amanda thanked God for the food and made request for David's speedy recovery.

As they started passing the food, Gloria looked at the pizza, trying to stifle a grimace. "What is this?" she asked tightly.

369

Kelly spoke up. "It is pizza with beluga on top. You eat it with your fingers."

At that point Jon guffawed, and the room erupted, Joey and Amanda joining him, and soon everyone else was howling with laughter. "David will never believe this," Jon commented, tears streaming down his cheeks.

They passed bowls and served themselves, Gloria taking some of what was offered. As they began eating, she turned to Amanda. "Please tell me what is going on. Of course, don't divulge anything that David has forbidden," she smiled. "I guess I will wait for that news. I assume my son is or was suspected of murder?" Her face was suddenly filled with concern.

"Both of them," Jon replied, his mouth full.

"Jon, we're not throwing out everything you were taught about manners," Gloria said severely.

"Didn't you get the details from the attorney you hired for David and me?" he pressed.

Gloria flushed. "I didn't want you to be without representation," she retorted.

"We weren't," Jon's eyes bored through her. "Alex and Amanda are renowned for their prowess in the courtroom, and they actually practice criminal law, unlike the—" he paused, looking at Amanda," what did you call him? Pipsqueak attorney? Yes, I think that was the term."

"Jon," Amanda whispered, embarrassed.

"No, again Gloria has stepped in it, and needs to apologize for butting in where angels fear to tread," Jon insisted. "If it hadn't been for Amanda and Alex, David, Ralph and I would all be sweating bullets at a grand jury inquisition next week."

Gloria stared at him, surprised. "Well, then, perhaps I do need to apologize." She looked at Amanda. "Jon is right. I am sorry. Please tell us what has been happening, dear."

Amanda began summarizing the events, as Gloria and James listened intently and Jon added details. Amanda avoided imparting about the paternity actions or anything relating to Allison.

Gloria was impassive as Amanda finished. "I have lots of questions, but I am assuming that I have to wait for the rest of the story," she concluded. "So I guess my two sons were suspects for reasons other than a past relationship with this woman some time back?"

Jon and his mother locked eyes. "Yes," he said simply.

"Amanda, if you are involved and might be a witness, can you represent them, or both of them?" Gloria was direct but nonaccusatory.

"My friend Alex is one of the finest defense attorneys in the state, other than Ralph himself. I am hoping against hope that the matter has been resolved as of today, but we will not know until after the interagency meeting with the special prosecutor tomorrow," Amanda replied gravely.

"I trust your judgment. If you need help, you know all you have to do is ask," Gloria countered, looking at James, who nodded.

"Thanks. It could come to that, but maybe not," Amanda smiled tentatively.

Gloria looked at her watch. "My, it's after midnight," she exclaimed. "I guess we need to get a little rest sometime. What time do you think we will be allowed to see David?"

Joey responded, "After eight o'clock in the morning. I will go early to be there for the doctor's rounds. There will be testing done, I'm sure."

"Thank you, Joey."

"Mother, Jacquie has thoroughly cleaned the master bedroom, and straightened up the rest of the rooms in the house. So everything should be close to normal," Kelly offered anxiously.

"I'm sure we shall make do," Gloria smiled at her daughter. "Shall I help clear the table?"

James sat back. "This I gotta see," he said, a twinkle in his eye.

They all started laughing again.

"No, please, Mrs. Connor," Amanda intervened. "Kelly and I will take care of it until the rest of the staff arrive here first thing in the morning. Everything will be fine." She tried to sound convincing.

"Then I think I shall retire." Gloria rose.

James did too. "I shall join you."

Jon turned to Kelly. "If I'm not mistaken, you are a newlywed. I think Amanda and I can handle the kitchen duty tonight."

Soon Amanda and Jon were left alone, Amanda quickly disposing of leftover food. She walked into the kitchen looking for dishwashing liquid to wash dishes.

"What are you doing?" Jon asked her. "We'll just put it all in the dishwasher."

"No, darling, your mother's stuff is valuable, and it isn't dishwasher safe," she said softly. "We are placing it in the dishwasher only to be out of sight for your mother's sake until the staff come tomorrow. I really don't want the dishes to stand dirty all night, as lovely as her items are."

"And I don't want you washing my mother's china and silver when you can be in my bed," Jon pulled her next to him and nuzzled her ear. "In fact, I'm wondering what it would be like right here." He picked her up and sat her on the huge wooden island, claiming her mouth as she ran her fingers through his hair. As he started undressing her, she stopped him.

"Not here," she interjected softly. "Not in your mother's kitchen."

"Why not?" he implored her smilingly.

"Because we have tested the limits of her endurance tonight." Amanda grasped his hands in hers and kissed his cheek.

"Damn it, woman," he complained good-naturedly. "But neither are we washing her dishes tonight. I'll wash all the dishes you want tomorrow if the staff don't make it here."

"Go get the glasses out of the library and let me finish up, and I'll reward you richly upstairs," she teased him.

He was soon back with the tray. "Now you go upstairs and get ready for me, and I'll be right there," she smiled slyly.

He kissed her then left. She heard him bounding up the stairs. She looked at the dining room, satisfied, and cut out the lights, checking the doors. She finished rinsing and putting away the glasses in the dishwasher, and made her way upstairs to their room.

Jon was already fast asleep. She stared at his sleeping form. Yes, Jon Connor, I love you more than I have ever loved anyone, she thought.

She undressed and lay down beside him, saying a prayer for David. Jon pulled her to him sleepily.

CHAPTER 34

SUNDAY

Amanda lay in bed, her mind racing. Jon had teased her awake at 3:30 and they had made love, languorously, tenderly. Jon told her, "I don't intend to ever leave you alone again, love."

"You know we can't promise that," she had murmured as he hauled her to him. "I love you, Jon Connor," she whispered.

"Don't ever stop," he replied huskily against her skin.

Afterward he had fallen asleep again. She knew he was still exhausted. She was tired, too, but still worried. Would David be all right? Would he recover fully? Was the case solved? Was Allison the daughter of David? Of Jon?

Although exhausted, she finally gave up on sleep at 5:00 and gently disentangled herself from a somnolent Jon. She looked in the closet and found a bathrobe, wrapping it around her.

She looked at her cell phone, but saw that the battery was almost dead again. She padded silently downstairs to the library. She thought, I need to call Charlie, to see if there's anything I can do, any information I can provide to resolve this case at the meeting.

She saw a phone at the desk. She started toward it, but then felt the presence of someone in the room. She reached over and cut on the lamp at the edge of the desk and turned. There was Gloria Connor in a large wing chair, her feet curled under her, looking forlorn.

"Mrs. Connor? What is wrong?" She approached the woman.

"It's Gloria, remember?" the woman sniffled.

Amanda walked up to her, as the woman sat there silently crying. "What can I do, Gloria? What is it?"

373

"I've made such a mess of things," she whispered brokenly. "My own family is afraid of me, then laughs at me behind my back." She looked up at Amanda, her eyes pleading. "And now I may lose one."

Amanda pulled up the ottoman and sat by her, taking her hand. "I have to keep hoping that David will be fine. Seeing him last night made me feel better about his chances." She smiled. "And he certainly didn't let the opportunity go by without teasing his brother."

"He did?" Gloria sniffed into her tissue. "I keep berating myself over David. I didn't spend as much time with him as the others, and when he was little he was the one who tried to confide in me, sought me out. But he became so independent—that was my fault. I was too busy for him. He developed a sharp wit, with some comeback always on his lips, almost like he gave up on me and didn't want me or anyone else to get too close.

"When Jon was born, he was my first, and I wanted to do everything just right. I obsessed so much, and James was working hard to make his business successful. I used to tell Jon he was my little 'man of the house'. I guess that's why he is so serious and responsible.

"But then David came. It was a hard pregnancy, and I was tired all the time. I felt like I should know how it's done by then, so ought to figure out how to do it all more efficiently. And by then, James had won some big contracts, and he hired me a nanny to help.

"I was trying to be the proper wife and do all the right things to further James' career and contacts. He didn't ask me to, but I thought being successful required constantly cultivating the right contacts, entertaining the right friends. I had secretly started playing with the idea of writing children's books, and was up late at nights writing out ideas and fleshing out plots."

Amanda shook her head. "You know, I think the boys turned out pretty well."

Gloria smiled sadly. "But David always had that rebellious streak. He enjoyed being at Joey's house more than he did at home. I guess I was too afraid they might make the wrong impression, and I never really allowed them to be just boys. And Kelly, well, she always thought she could do anything her brothers could do, and wasn't interested in pretty dresses and ballet lessons."

"She is beautiful, and one of the smartest women I've ever met," Amanda murmured.

"She is, isn't she?" Gloria agreed. "And tonight, well, she stood up to me in public. I thought at first maybe you were a bad influence, but I guess maybe she's just in love."

Amanda grinned. "Maybe it's both. But did you notice how she glowed tonight? And Joey really adores her. He has agonized over the decision whether to move here, because he loves her so much."

"I've said some pretty cutting things to him," Gloria admitted, "and at the last family gathering he attended he paid me back, then walked out. I saw Kelly's face when he left. She hated me."

"I don't think so," Amanda countered gently. "If she didn't love and respect you, she would have left with Joey."

"No, she felt she needed to protect her father from me. Can you believe that?" the woman laughed mirthlessly. "And James hasn't looked at me the same since then. I know it's my fault, but I was just hell-bound and determined to make my family respectable and proper and like it, even if it killed them."

"And now?" Amanda asked softly.

"Now I've lost them all," Gloria sobbed sadly. "Jon is always coolly polite and will never tell me what he truly feels, at least until the other night at dinner when he confronted me in front of the others. Kelly is the same, and makes sure she's not alone in the same room with me. James and I—well, I don't think he's loved me in some time. David has been such a rake and troublemaker, always worrying me, saying witty things with barbs that hurt me, and now—" the woman sobbed.

Amanda pressed the woman's hand and let her cry.

"What can I do, Amanda? How can I bring them all back together, make them love me again?" Gloria looked at her beseechingly through her tears.

Amanda was sympathetic. "Gloria, they still love you. There are apparently some fences that must be mended. I've never been a mother, so I'm not qualified to give you advice. But I do want to make an observation."

Gloria gazed at her expectantly.

"I think that even with the sorrow and worry hanging over us about David's condition, your children and husband enjoyed last night's dinner with you more than any of the others I have witnessed. There is a lot of love and respect there. Your children are actually very close to each other, and you had to have instilled those family ties. And David told me just yesterday morning about how much fun his childhood was, and the great memories he had of you. Joey spoke fondly of those times as well.

"Do you realize that last night we had no servants, no seven-course dinner, no important guests, and the house was not immaculate? We weren't dressed in our finery and trying to impress anyone. And we made it through just fine, and probably enjoyed it more. Tell me you did not enjoy it."

Gloria shook her head. "I did."

"I'll tell you what Jon told me when I worried so much about meeting you, making you like me. He told me to quit trying so hard. And he is right. And I'll just bet you will have just as many friends, influence as many people, score as many political and business deals as before, and suffer not nearly the stress, if you loosen that ironclad grip and have a little fun with it."

Unbeknownst to them, James had silently come downstairs. Overhearing the conversation, he had been sitting in a chair in the foyer and eavesdropping, biting back a chuckle or two.

Jon had started downstairs looking for Amanda, and spied his father, who put his finger to his lips warningly. Jon slipped down and stood listening with James.

"Why would you be so worried about my liking you?" Gloria asked pointedly.

"You ask that?" Amanda laughed. "Tell the truth—at first you didn't think I was good enough for Jon, did you?"

The woman shook her head in the negative, a flush on her cheeks. "But why did you care what I thought? You're rich, you're successful, you're well respected in the community. You certainly didn't need my approval."

Amanda blushed. "Gloria, I grew up a simple girl with wonderful parents. Then I lost them. That was hard. Then I had Andy and Marjorie, who had always been a best friend and another mother to me. She took me under her wing. I would not have made it through losing Andy without her. I didn't know then she was my real mother. Then she died too.

"When I was in the hospital after my accident, David mentioned his childhood memories of you. I had such a warm image of you from David's descriptions and little things Jon said about you." Amanda squeezed her hand. "I miss my mothers, Gloria. I guess I was greedy, hoping that I would gain a third mother in my lifetime."

She smiled pensively. "Besides, you've already seen that I'm quite a handful. I've forgotten a lot about marriage. I'm sure I could use some pointers in what I'm doing wrong with Jon."

"You're not doing anything wrong, if the way my son looks at you is any indication," Gloria laughed softly. "He is somewhat obsessive, as I'm sure you have realized."

"I am too, but coming so close to death has made me relax that grip somewhat. Jon and I realize now that trust comes hard for both of us. But I love him so much, Gloria. I want to do everything I can to make it work, to make him happy." Amanda looked down at their hands. "He adores you and wants us to get along. I want that too."

"Amanda, you amaze me. I can understand why Jon finds you spellbinding." She reached over and drew the woman into her arms. "I'm happy you've become my daughter."

"I'm glad, too," Amanda murmured.

"And I'm sorry if Jon is prissy," Gloria stated.

Jon almost choked.

Amanda heard the noise, and made a gesture to Gloria, mouthing, "I think he's eavesdropping."

Gloria nodded, whispering, "I heard him come down the stairs." She continued, speaking louder. "I was so meticulous in making sure my children were well-dressed, always neat. I guess Jon picked that up and retained that nattiness. He was always so particular, and wouldn't go out of his room until he felt everything was just right with his hair and dress."

Amanda replied, her voice carrying. "ZZ Top wrote a song about a sharp-dressed man. That was one of the first things I noticed about Jon, after I got past his compelling eyes."

"Yes. Many times I had to wait on him to get ready, rather than the other way around," Gloria laughed.

Amanda's eyes twinkled mischievously. "My partner Ralph is anal about matching everything and having his cufflinks and tie and shoes just so. He and Jon are like peas in a pod. I think they secretly call each other and consult about what they are wearing every day. They are much worse than Claire and me about it, and compare notes like two girls going to a dance." She winked at Gloria. "You should hear them."

"We do not," Jon objected, walking in the doorway.

The women started laughing. "That's what you get for eavesdropping," Gloria rejoined.

Jon flushed, realizing he had been had. He feigned anger. "Hey, I'm not the only one." He pointed, and James peeked in the doorway.

"How long have you been there?" Gloria demanded, releasing Amanda and standing, her face flushed with embarrassment.

"Long enough to fall in love with you all over again," James murmured, holding his hand out to her. "Come on, Gloria, and tell me some of these secrets you are sharing with Amanda."

As they disappeared Amanda turned to Jon. "I need to call Charlie. I know he's probably already at work. I have to find out if there's anything we need to do to help that inquiry this morning." She looked at Jon, suddenly tense. "I'm anxious that my boys not be under suspicion any longer."

Jon nodded. "Do you need some privacy?"

"No," Amanda smiled, taking his hand. "I need to preserve the attorney-client privilege from Charlie, in case the prosecutor should not be convinced."

"I hear the help stirring. I'll get us a cup of coffee and be back," Jon nodded.

Amanda smiled and nodded her thanks, picking up the phone. She dialed Charlie's cell phone.

"Petrino. May I ask who's calling?" He was curt.

"Charlie, it's Amanda. My cell phone is dead, I'm without a charger at the moment, and I'm calling from the condo," Amanda explained.

"Are you OK?" his tone warmed.

"We are all fine, but are going back this morning to check on David. Gloria and James made it here late last night. David awakened and talked a moment or two. We've not heard anything in the night, but were told no news was good news."

"I'm glad to hear it. Ralph is here. He just dropped by to see if you had called. He was worried, and said you hadn't answered your phone."

"Tell him I'm sorry for not calling sooner." She took a breath. "Charlie, just what is going on today?"

"We're actually comparing notes and trying to tie up the loose ends, figure out what we don't know." He paused. "Investigator Maynard down there is going to try to get a statement from Mr. Canton about the episode with Vause." He paused. "You're not worried, are you?"

"Yes," she said, as Jon returned with two cups of coffee. "When it comes to Jon and David and you and Ralph, I am always worried. Is there anything I can do?"

"If Mr. Canton is able to provide a statement today, that might give us what we need to bring matters to a close," Charlie replied. "I think there is going to be sufficient evidence, just judging by what we have gathered. I'll know more by noon."

He paused. "Amanda, let me know if Canton and David are OK. I want to know. And don't worry about this. I haven't been able to share all that's been happening since we talked the other night. Varas gave us some vital information in the hospital, and confirming Vause's statements may be the icing on the cake. Vause's saddlebags contained some high-resolution cameras and other evidence. He was surreptitiously taking photos of everyone while tailing us, and creating composites which he manipulated into photos. Toby gave permission to search the stables where Varas had set up shop, and we found the equipment and some of the photos. The FBI actually had wiretap warrants on Varas, and somehow managed to tape the conversation between you and Varas, so have the evidence of his attempted blackmail. The investigator down there provided the letter from Lauren along with what Canton told him." He chuckled. "Most of the pieces have fallen into place. Throwing one's weight around is not always a bad thing, and I'm going to try my hand at it this morning."

Amanda laughed.

"I thought that might get a response from you," he laughed too. "Take care of Jon, and yourself most of all."

"I will." She hung up.

"Well?" Jon asked her.

"He thinks it will all be well. He wants to take Mr. Canton's statement if possible, and he'll let us know." She sipped her coffee.

Jon looked at his watch. "Time we had a shower and got ready."

"Together?" she murmured softly.

"How else?" he laughed.

She stood, and he took her hand. "That was a nice thing you did for my mother this morning," he whispered.

"Your mom is not the tough guy you think her. She has her own vulnerabilities, and she worries about you."

"I know," he nodded. "I just don't think David and Kelly have figured that out yet. Maybe that's one good thing that may come out of all this."

The phone on the desk rang. Jon picked it up. "Hello?"

"Hi. It's Joey," the voice spoke. "Kelly and I are already at the hospital. We came on over early because we couldn't sleep."

"How is David?"

"His vitals have improved. He's still pretty weak."

"Is he going to be all right?" Jon's face was creased with concern. Amanda saw it and wrapped her arms around his waist. He placed his arm around her and drew her to him.

"Too early to tell, but he looks much better today. He asked for Gloria, said he has something to tell them. You might let her know. I can get her in around eight this morning. His doctor really didn't want to allow anyone in before then, but did allow Kelly to see him a moment."

"I'll tell them," Jon promised. "Is Kelly OK?"

"She's holding up, but I think it was hard for her to see David helpless like that. She's always thought of you and David as invincible. Now I can't talk her into going back to the condo, so she is going to stay here with me a while."

"Anything we can do?" Jon's voice was strained.

"Not right now. I'll let you know."

"Joey, I'm really happy to have you as officially one of the family," Jon said huskily. "We'll be there in a little while."

He hung up and kissed Amanda.

"We're both going to need some clothes," she murmured.

"Not for what we're about to do," he countered wickedly. "But don't worry about it. For once enjoy being rich. Jacquie will take care of us. I will put in a request."

He disappeared for a moment, then returned, grabbed Amanda's hand and dragged her up the stairs. As they started toward the room, Gloria's head popped out from another room. "Was that the hospital?" she asked anxiously.

"Joey and Kelly are there," Jon informed her. "David told the doctor he wants to see you, and it's agreed you can go in around eight."

The door opened, and they saw she was in a bathrobe, and James appeared behind her, also in a robe. James placed his arm around her. Jon looked taken aback.

"Is he OK?" James queried concernedly. He kissed Gloria on the hair and she gripped his hand around her waist.

"Joey said he's holding his own," Amanda spoke for Jon, who was suddenly struck dumb. "We're going to go get a shower and get ready."

"Do you think Jacquie could find me some—denim?" Gloria asked timidly.

Jon's consternation grew. Behind them a voice replied, "Yes, ma'am."

Jon fled to his room with Amanda's hand gripped firmly in his. He shut the door behind them and pulled her onto the bed with him, clutching her tightly. She could feel his body convulsing.

"What's wrong, Jon?" she whispered, frightened. "Is there something you haven't told me about David?"

He pulled away, and he was laughing silently, tears in his eyes, his body still shaking. "Damn, Amanda, you've turned my whole family upside down," he blurted out, trying to keep his voice low.

"What did I do?" Amanda was upset.

"Honey, I don't think my parents have had sex in several years," Jon choked out. "And Gloria is asking Jacquie to get her some jeans? It is too much." He finally couldn't contain it, and laughter pealed from his lips.

Amanda colored. "I'm sorry," she stammered, but he silenced her by kissing her, drawing her to him.

"Don't apologize. My whole family has become infected with something quite wonderful, and I think I'm to blame, for introducing you into the clan." He was still laughing. "I just hope David doesn't go into shock when he sees and hears this," he murmured against her lips.

She melted against him. "Now for that shower. But first . . . ."

CHAPTER 35

Amanda and Jon arrived at the hospital with Gloria and James. Joey and Kelly met them in the lobby.

"How is he?" Gloria placed her hand on Joey's arm.

"He is weak, lost a lot of blood," Joey replied. "You mustn't overtax him; don't upset him."

Gloria, instead of bristling, just nodded mutely. She grasped James' hand as Joey led the two of them through the doors.

Jon walked over and sat down beside Kelly, taking her hand. Amanda turned and walked to the receptionist. "Was Mr. Canton moved to a room?"

"Yes," the reception checked her roster. "Room 134," the receptionist smiled.

Amanda thanked her and turned back to Jon. "I'm going to check on him," she informed him.

Jon nodded.

Amanda pushed through the double doors into the hallway and followed it until she came to the room. Hesitating, she knocked.

She heard a voice. "Come in."

She stepped inside. There in the bed lay Walter Canton. He spied her and smiled. "Mrs. Connor, please come in."

"Please call me Amanda," Amanda came up to the bed and took his hand briefly. "How are you feeling?"

"Actually, a little sore, but not too bad," he smiled wanly. "And David?"

"He is still in intensive care," Amanda replied. "What does the doctor say?"

"They are keeping me for observation today, and if all is well, I can go home tomorrow."

"That's great news." She looked at Canton intently. "May I ask you a question, Mr. Canton?"

"It's Walter, and yes," he responded, blinking.

"You stepped in front of David yesterday, didn't you?"

He hesitated, then nodded.

"You didn't even know him. Why?"

He was silent a moment. He took a deep breath. "It's hard to explain. I love Ginny and Lauren dearly, and Allison as well, and I would have taken a bullet for Lauren's father if I could have saved him. There are times when I wonder if Joe's being here and raising his girl would have made a profound difference in her life, would have changed the outcome.

"Yesterday I was suddenly in a situation where Allison's possible father was in danger. I was reliving that moment. I knew I couldn't let it happen without trying to intervene."

They were both silent a moment, Amanda biting her lip. "You both could have died. Thank you for doing what you did," she whispered, her eyes moist with tears. "It probably saved David's life."

He frowned. "Amanda, I have to thank you. If you and David had not shown up, Vause would have gotten away with Allison, or we would have been facing him down by ourselves, without law enforcement or other help. And if you had not chased him down, he might have made off with Allison . . ." Canton choked, then swallowed. "You will never know how grateful I am to both of you."

"I'm so sorry for all that has happened," Amanda said feelingly.

"I don't understand why Lauren felt she had to involve Allison in her plan. I don't even know what her plan was. We may never know."

"We may never know," Amanda echoed. "But I'm happy that Allison still has a father and mother to care for her the way you do," Amanda squeezed his hand. She paused. "Mr. Canton, would you mind giving a statement to the police? It will go a long way toward solving the case of Lauren's death."

"I'm assuming I will need to, and of course I want to as soon as possible, if it will finally yield some answers," Canton replied fervently.

The door opened and Virginia and Allison walked in. Allison ran to the bed. "Daddy," she cried excitedly.

"Yes, my little one," Walter smiled, placing his hand on her head fondly.

"I brought you a picture," she said, thrusting a paper into his hand.

"That is so pretty," Amanda murmured as she stepped back.

Allison turned to her. "I made one for the David guy too," she said, handing Amanda another crayon drawing. "I hope he gets well."

Amanda gazed at the little girl, again struck by her eyes and their resemblance to David's and Jon's.

"It was all her idea," Virginia smiled at Amanda.

The Connors' Crisis

"I'm sure he will treasure this." Amanda's eyes were shining.

"Any news?" Virginia's voice was low.

"He's stronger. His parents are in with him," Amanda countered.

"We're praying for him," Virginia informed her.

"Thanks. I will leave you alone now, and check in later to see if there's anything I can do," Amanda promised.

"You know if DNA testing is scheduled we will cooperate," Walter said. "And tell the police that I'm ready when they are."

Amanda smiled tremulously, tears in her eyes. "Thanks. I am going to see what I can do about both today. I'll let you know. You just concentrate on getting well. And Allison, thank you again."

Amanda made her way back to the waiting area with Jon and Kelly. Kelly's head was buried in Jon's shoulder as he held her and comforted her.

"Has something happened?" Amanda whispered, alarmed.

Jon shook his head. "He's going to be OK," he said soothingly to Kelly.

"How do you know?" she mumbled against his shirt.

"Because he's David, the life of the party, the one who keeps this family bound together. He has to get well." Jon rocked her gently.

Kelly, her face tear-streaked, pulled away and turned to Amanda. "Was the little girl who walked through here a moment ago—was that her?"

Amanda nodded, taking a seat beside Kelly and squeezing her hand.

"She's beautiful," Kelly whispered. "She has David's eyes."

Amanda nodded again wordlessly.

"What do you have there?" Jon asked curiously.

"She drew David a picture." Amanda almost choked with emotion, showing the drawing to them. Jon took it almost reverently.

"Oh, my God," Kelly cried, flinging her arms around Amanda.

Jon stood and turned his back to them, his eyes still on the picture.

"She asked me if I was a big brother." Jon's voice was strained.

"I have been too wrapped in myself to pay much attention to David," Kelly blubbered.

"OK, stop it, you two," Amanda stood suddenly. "You know, families are never as close as they think they ought to be, particularly when a crisis occurs. But you have one of the most loving families I know. You siblings certainly share a closer relationship with each other than most families." Amanda bit her lip, thinking of her own relationship with her brother Jeffrey. "So don't beat yourselves up. It doesn't do David any good. And do you think he'd want to hear you carrying on this way?"

Kelly laughed through her tears. "You're right, Drill Sergeant Amanda," she wiped her eyes. "He'd be pissed and walk out on us. He told me the other day when I was crying over Joey that he had only one strategy to use on crying women, and it wasn't something he could do with his baby sister."

They all started laughing, then Amanda suddenly sobered, an unfathomable look on her face.

"So what was his reaction when he heard you two are married?" Jon gazed at Kelly, not noting Amanda's features.

"We haven't told him yet," Kelly said.

"You know that news might improve his spirits." Jon kissed her forehead.

Kelly nodded. She looked at Amanda. "What's up with Gloria in jeans? Where did that come from?"

They started laughing again, Amanda smiling pensively.

"You don't know the half of it," Jon added, his voice low. "This morning Mom and Dad were, well, you know . . . ."

Kelly stared at him, bewildered. Just then the doors opened, and Gloria and James walked out with Joey. Gloria turned to James and threw her arms around him and they kissed as she cried.

Kelly's eyes grew wide, and she turned to Jon, stunned. Jon nodded his head.

Joey moved past them to Kelly, putting his arm around her and drawing her closer. "Well?" Jon asked.

"He's pretty spent. He just finished telling the folks about Lauren and the little girl. I told him it could wait, but he insisted it could not."

"We don't know for sure, and before this goes any further, we need to find out," Amanda responded quietly. "Joey, can you find out if there's a local certified lab that conducts DNA testing? We can obtain swabs from David and Allison."

Jon looked at her questioningly. "Allison's grandparents gave their consent just now," she answered. "And I had asked Charlie to preserve a sample for Lauren. I'll see what can be done. But I need the contact information for the administrator of the lab. It's Sunday, so we won't get any satisfaction unless I go straight to the top." Amanda smiled wanly. "I'm about to try my hand at the influence game."

Amanda held out her hand to Jon. "Can I borrow your phone?"

Jon handed it to her, and she walked outside and punched Charlie's number.

"What's the latest?" Charlie greeted her. "Are you and Amanda OK? How's David?"

She realized Charlie recognized Jon's phone number. "Charlie, it is Amanda," she identified herself. "David is about the same right now. Mr.

Canton is doing pretty well, and is in a room. He said he was ready and willing to give a statement."

"I'll get someone on it right away," Charlie responded. "Are you all right?"

She paused. "You remember that request for a DNA sample I made to you the night of the murder? It's time, and I really need for you to come through. David needs to know. And if possible, it would be nice to send a sample from Vause as well, to eliminate the possibilities."

"The crime lab can do this, but they are slow. Do you have a lab?"

"I will hopefully fairly quickly," she replied as Joey walked outside and toward her.

"Gerald and I can make arrangements once we know where to send it, and I'll talk to the guys down there about Vause," Charlie promised. "Baby, I hope he's going to be OK."

"Me too, Pete," Amanda countered softly. "I'll call you back with the info."

She hung up and turned to Joey. "How is he?"

"He is weak, but as long as he keeps progressing and we don't have any setbacks, I think his prognosis is good. I didn't agree that he should expend his energy telling his mom about Lauren, particularly with the damage to his lung, but then David has that stubborn streak that seems to run in the family. He seemed to be relieved afterward."

Joey paused. "A lab has been recommended." He handed her a slip of paper. "That's the name, address and phone number. The doctor in there is friends with the administrator, called the man and came up with his private line for us to contact him with details. A tech can come out to do the swabs. I was told that with the right incentive, we might even get it done today."

"Let's make it so," Amanda was brisk. "I'll foot the bill for it, whatever it costs."

She quickly called the number, and asked to talk to the administrator. She identified herself.

"I've heard of you," the man said. "What might I do for you, Mrs. Connor?"

"I'd like to make an appointment to see you. I'd like to retain the lab for something very important. If it is convenient, I can be there today." She briefly explained the situation.

"So as you see, this needs to be done quickly, and discreetly. I'm most interested in preserving this little girl and her family from any damaging disclosure and the pain it might cause. She doesn't know. And I'd like my brother-in-law to know, in case he doesn't . . ." she paused, her breath catching in a sob.

"I understand," the man stated comfortingly.

"And there will be samples from the two subjects who are deceased as well, and—and one from my husband," Amanda faltered. "With your permission I will have the sheriff personally contact you and make arrangements for delivery of samples."

They quickly negotiated the terms. She hung up and turned to Joey. "Is it possible that you could accompany me to the lab, so I can sign the documents and make arrangements for payment?"

"If you want," he smiled. "Anything for David. So you still think Jon could be the father?"

Amanda gazed off across the parking lot. "We need to eliminate that possibility."

Joey stared at her and nodded.

She felt her legs trembling. "Joey, I need to sit down," she whispered.

Joey quickly took her arm and steered her toward a bench close by, sitting down with her. "Are you OK?"

"I haven't been sleeping well lately, with all this going on," she admitted. "I have been so worried about charges being brought against Jon, David or Ralph. I guess the advent of Jon's perhaps having a child scares me a little. And David has been beside himself, even before the shooting. He really loved Lauren Mallory, or at least really thinks he did."

"Yes, I know," Joey nodded, almost impatient. "But are you sure that's all it is?"

She stared at him uncomprehendingly. "All this caused a strain between Jon and me, but I think, I hope we're working past that." She bit her lip nervously.

He looked at her penetratingly. "Amanda, could you be pregnant?"

Her eyes went wide. "No, I mean—I can't, I mean—no, I shouldn't," she stammered, suddenly panic-stricken as the thought crossed her mind. "It's not possible," she quavered.

"You mean you and Jon haven't been having sex?" There was the hint of a smile playing around the corners of Joey's mouth. "When one does the deed, it is always possible. I think we might need to draw a little blood and see."

"No, Joey," Amanda breathed. "I mean, it's not—I mean, it's the wrong time, with David and all."

Joey grinned at her. "Do you think babies wait around for the right time? You sure stutter a lot for a lawyer." He bent closer. "Why are you so frightened? Jon would be thrilled."

Jon walked out the door, looking for them. Spying them, he moved toward them.

The Connors' Crisis

"Please, Joey," Amanda begged softly. "Say nothing. I am pretty sure I'm not, and I don't want to introduce that subject unless I'm sure. There is so much else going on right now."

Joey looked at her quizzically, but nodded. Jon walked up to them. "Is everything OK?" he stared at them.

"Yes, Amanda was feeling a bit faint, and so I had her sit down," Joey smiled, his eyes dancing merrily as Amanda gave him a warning look.

"Do you think she might be pregnant?" Jon asked, his eyes wide.

Amanda, her mouth open in surprise, stood. "OK, that's enough," she spoke curtly, drawing herself up stiffly. "I'm not pregnant. So you two can quit fooling. Joey, I'll tell Kelly where we are going. On our way, I'll call Charlie back with the information on the lab. Let's get this show on the road."

"I'll go," Jon offered.

"No, you need to stay here with your mother and Kelly." Amanda was short as she turned and stalked off back into the hospital.

Jon looked after her. "What did I say?" he asked dazedly.

"Is that a sore subject for some reason?" Joey gazed at Jon concernedly.

"I didn't think so." Jon mused. "Why doesn't she want me to go with her?"

"I think she's right," Joey replied thoughtfully. "The family needs to stay here in case something should happen. And she feels it is important for David to know if he is the father as soon as possible. So the two of us in-laws will take care of the lab. And you will be tested too, so it's better if you're not part of the negotiations."

Jon looked at him sharply but said nothing.

Amanda came back, her purse in hand. Jon took her by the arm and swung her around to face him. "I love you," he whispered.

"I love you, too, Jon," she reached up and kissed him, touching his face. He could see that she was troubled.

"What is it, Mandy?" he asked softly. "No secrets, remember?"

"I just want to get this behind us," she smiled uncertainly.

Joey and she walked out to the vehicle. She directed him, punching Charlie's number and rapidly giving him the information regarding the lab.

Soon they had met with the administrator and completed the arrangements at the lab, and were back in the car. Amanda pointed out a large chain drugstore. "Do you mind pulling in here? I need a phone charger," she announced, biting her lip nervously.

Surprised, he did as she asked. "I'll be right back." She was terse.

A few minutes later she returned, a small plastic shopping bag in her hand. "Could we stop by the condo a minute?" she asked. "I'm sorry to ask you to do all this," she added. "I need to charge my phone." She knew she was repeating herself.

"No, it's fine." Joey looked at her questioningly.

They pulled up, and walked up to the condo. As she started up the stairs, he suddenly spoke up. "Why don't you use Kelly's room? That way the pregnancy test won't be found in your room."

She froze on the stairs. She turned and looked at Joey, swallowing. "How did you know?"

"Just do it," he ordered, turning away.

He remained in a chair in the foyer until she returned. She sat down on the stairs. Joey was silent, looking at her expectantly.

"I have my reasons, Joey."

"You don't have to explain," Joey murmured.

Amanda gazed at him, tears in her eyes. "It's not what you think." She swallowed convulsively. "The thought of being a mother frightens the living daylights out of me." Amanda looked down at her hands. "It's hard work to be a good mother," she stammered. "And I'm scared—I just don't know if I . . ." she fell silent.

Joey was burning to ask, but restrained himself. Amanda looked over at him. "I'm so sorry for involving you." She was shamefaced.

"Think nothing of it," he said, standing and holding out his hand. "You ready to get back?"

She nodded and stood, allowing him to lead her back out.

They made it back to the hospital in a short time, and walked quickly back into the lobby. Jon saw them and came forward, smiling. "David apparently is doing better. Kelly and I went in to see him, and he asked for a steak." He kissed her forehead. "He wants to see you, tried to make me jealous again."

Amanda smiled. "I'm so glad he's improving."

Joey held the door for her. "Let's go see," he beckoned.

Joey and Amanda walked down the hall, made their way into ICU and into the room where David lay. He opened his eyes and smiled tiredly. "Hi, Sis, Joey," he croaked.

Amanda bent to kiss his cheek. "Hi, Bro," she said softly. She noted Allison's picture on the bed and picked it up. "Did you see this?" She held it up.

"Yes," he nodded. "I'm touched that she thought of me."

"Joey and I have made arrangements for the DNA to be collected today and for testing to be done quickly," Amanda informed him.

"Thanks, Amanda," he smiled.

Joey spoke up, "I want to talk to your attending physician and check the chart. I'll be right back."

The Connors' Crisis

Amanda and David were left alone. Amanda was suddenly restless.

"What is it?" David asked, watching her.

"Nothing," she responded, squeezing his hand, looking down nervously.

"There's something on your mind," he said quietly, as he shifted slightly and his breath caught.

"Are you OK?" Amanda asked quickly.

"Yes. Now out with it." He looked at her intently.

"David, the other night, when—when I was drunk," she faltered, her face burning, "I don't remember much. Did," she gulped, "did we—I mean, did I—" she broke off, unable to complete her question.

"No, Amanda," David replied. "We did not." He laughed weakly. "Are you disappointed? I sure am."

"Oh, David." Amanda's eyes were brimming with tears as she squeezed his hand. "I'm so sorry. I didn't mean—"

"You really love my brother, don't you? That was weighing heavily on your mind. I'd hoped you had forgotten about it. When did you remember?" David asked softly.

"Something Kelly said today about a remark you made. I suddenly recalled throwing myself—"

He stopped her. "Amanda, you were not yourself. You were frightened and just lashing out at Jon. And it didn't go anywhere. For the first time in my life I was a perfect gentleman. Although I might not be able to say that the next time," he smiled, a vestige of his devilish grin appearing.

"You are incorrigible," she told him, biting her lip.

"I just wish I had met you first," he whispered, his eyes closing.

"Are you OK?" Amanda cried softly.

"Just tired. Why don't you return the favor and hold my hand until I go to sleep?"

Amanda stood there by him, her hand in his. Jon walked in and put his arm around her, gazing down at his brother.

David spoke, his eyes still closed. "Damn, she kisses really good, Bro."

"David!" Amanda protested.

Jon watched as his brother's mouth curved into a smile. "You are definitely going to get your ass kicked when you get out of here," Jon said softly.

CHAPTER 36

That afternoon Charlie, Jill and Ralph showed up at the hospital. Charlie smiled as Amanda and Jon hugged Jill and greeted the guys. "I thought I'd take the opportunity to bring down the sample myself and deliver it to the lab. It was a chance to get away from the office. And Jill wanted to check on you all."

"So the job is hard?" Jon clapped him on the back.

"Grueling," Charlie sighed. "This murder made me wonder if I really want to be sheriff."

"I know the answer to that one," Amanda murmured. "How are you feeling?" she asked Jill warmly.

"Actually quite good." Jill looked at her concernedly. "And you two? David?"

"We are fine, and David is better," Amanda informed her. "He is still weak, but has been able to converse with us."

Jon put his arm around his wife. "I think Joey and Kelly are in there telling him their news now."

"News?" Jill echoed curiously.

"Kelly and Joey eloped," Jon replied, still smiling.

"Oh, how wonderful," Jill breathed. "They are such a nice couple."

Gloria stood with James and came forward. Amanda introduced everyone.

"I'm so glad to meet you all. I've heard a lot about you." Gloria was gracious. She turned to Ralph. "You are Amanda's law partner?"

"Yes, ma'am," Ralph assented. Amanda shot Jon a look, and he hid a grin at Ralph's address.

"And your wife?" Gloria continued without missing a beat.

"She returns home from Ohio on Tuesday," Ralph replied somberly. "It's been the longest week of my life," he admitted, "what with all this trouble and my wife's not being here."

390

"I hear you are considering a run for county judge," James stated.

"I have a feeling my chance at attaining that position has dried up, what with the adverse publicity from having a dead woman found in my bathtub and a paternity complaint filed against me." Ralph's features were grave. "It's quite a blow. I just hope that my wife will believe me and not leave me when she hears all this."

"All is not lost," Gloria spoke up. "Come over here and let's talk."

Jon looked at his mother in amazement as she took Ralph's arm and stepped away from the group, talking to him earnestly.

Charlie turned to Amanda. "The sheriff's department here also sent samples to the lab at my request," he stated quietly.

"Thank you, Charlie," Amanda smiled gratefully. "How long will it take?"

"The administrator said it doesn't take long to exclude paternity, but it takes a little longer to match up the DNA. So it will be a few days. Thanks for authorizing them to send a copy of the results to me."

"I hesitated on releasing that, but knew you'd be able to get the same results from FDLE, so it seemed silly to withhold the information." She paused. "How did the meeting go?"

"Bubba provided the letter that Lauren had sent her father, which provided valuable information pointing to Vause. Salvatore Varas gave us an oral statement before going into surgery, and admitted he hired both Vause and Mallory. He also confessed that he saw Vause go in, he went in and found Lauren dead, and he planted evidence to point to Ralph."

Charlie shrugged. "Varas is still in critical condition, lost a lot of blood. Alan says there was a lot of internal damage. Varas could always be trying to pin the murder on Vause instead of himself, but the evidence we're obtaining now is bearing his story out.

"Esme Townsend gave Jon a thumbdrive, which he handed over and I have shared with the FBI. It's some pretty damning stuff."

"Jon?" Amanda looked at Jon sharply.

"Yes," Jon returned her gaze. "About the time you were opening those packages, the firm had summoned me to meet with Esme Townsend, at her request. I didn't know the meeting was with her until she showed up. She had suspected Varas of systematically stealing from her and implicating her in several schemes, and she provided me the evidence. She divulged about Varas' attempts to blackmail you. Then she and Varas were both shot by Karl Vause."

"And you as well? The injury to your arm?" Amanda asked, her face apprehensive.

"It was just a graze," Jon smiled, his hand on her shoulder. "But Esme was in serious condition."

"How is she? How is Toby?" Amanda turned her eyes to Charlie.

Ralph overheard and spoke up. "She came through surgery, but is in guarded condition. Toby is there with her. He was a basket case. I stayed with him most of last night until I was able to convince him he needed to get some sleep. I stopped by the hospital before coming here. Father Anselm came this afternoon after church to sit with him and to see Esme."

Ralph paused. "Toby said he had confronted his mother, told her he'd never speak to her again if she screwed up Charlie's chance at becoming sheriff."

"He told us the same thing," Jon confirmed somberly.

"He was horrified about the blackmail scheme trying to force Amanda into applying for judge. He had harangued his mother about supporting some honest locals for office. But he never meant—" Ralph looked at Amanda sadly.

Jon piped up. "She said she didn't support Ralph because she was mad at Ralph for not talking Toby into law school. But I pointed out to her that perhaps Toby had a will of his own and made his own decisions."

"What an utterly silly reason to wreak so much havoc," muttered Amanda angrily. "Power for power's sake."

"But to her credit, Mrs. Townsend didn't apparently authorize all this," Jon pointed out. "Varas decided to take over and try his own methods, which included hiring Lauren Mallory to sow the scandal against Ralph, and bullying you to apply for the judgeship. Per Kimball, extortion seems to be a particular skill of Varas'. Knowing Lauren, I can understand her sending the items to Amanda, but why Lauren included me in the actual paternity scandal I don't know."

"Because she apparently thought you still worked for the FBI," Charlie countered. "Lauren's letter to her father said she was naming an FBI agent she knew as the father, to draw the Bureau into investigating Vause if something should happen to her. She also intimated that she hoped Vause would be sidetracked into going after Jon rather than looking for Allison."

"Mr. Canton told us that. That also seems quite asinine, as well as just plain evil," Amanda commented. She took a small unsteady step backward and gripped Jon's arm. Jon looked at her quizzically, putting an arm around her, but she continued, undeterred. "Why the cufflink and book?"

Charlie shook his head. Jon replied, his voice low, "Because Lauren couldn't stand the thought of someone finding happiness without her. She was the center of her own existence, and thought the rest of the world should have eyes only for her."

Everyone turned and stared at Jon. "It took only one weekend with her for me to find that out. We were at a restaurant, and ran into some old boyfriend of hers who had gotten married. She was incensed, and spent the rest of the evening hanging on to him, planting lipstick all over him and in his jacket pocket, just whatever she could think of to hurt him with his wife. We went back to her apartment, and she was scheming to call his wife the next day and insinuate that he had just left her place. I knew immediately that she had to be sick or something. I broke off with her then and there, and that was the last contact I had with her for several years. She showed up at some conference a few years ago and started coming on to me, and I let her know I was not interested."

"She did the same thing to David," a voice said behind Jon. Turning, he saw it was Joseph Rand. Joey continued, "David told me that she spent the time with him last week asking about Jon, what was he doing, would he be at the party. At the engagement party, they had an argument."

Amanda nodded. "David told me that he confronted her at the party and told her to keep away from Jon, that he was happily married. Right after that, she staged the scene with me and Claire in the restroom."

"And she hung on to Jon at the restaurant at lunch the next day," Ralph offered.

"See, I knew coming here would be much more productive than any stuffy meeting with a bunch of law enforcement," another voice stated.

"Bubba!" Jon turned and smiled at his friend.

Charlie grinned at him. "This group is a virtual think tank. They can brainstorm and fill in all the blanks for you," he laughed, shaking Bubba's hand.

"The Bureau is going to issue a press release, but the only matter we obviously can't clear up is the paternity mess, at least until the DNA testing is completed," Bubba added.

"And I stopped in at the lab with Charlie to give a sample, so that my name can be cleared," Ralph supplied.

"What do you know about Vause?" Jon asked Bubba.

"Well, he had been let go by the CIA for undisclosed reasons, and was apparently for hire. The Bureau actually got involved when a hit was made on one of our men last month. Vause was suspected, and we started sniffing for his trail. How he and Varas met up we don't know.

"But Vause apparently perennially stalked his wife Lauren Mallory. The restraining orders paint a pretty nasty scene, but her boss said she never had any marks on her. After a while he wondered if she might not be using the allegations of abuse as a way to fend off Vause until she had use for him again. However, abusers can be pretty savvy about not leaving bruises where they would be easily visible. And many abused women will reconcile with the abuser. So we just don't know at this point, and may not ever know for sure."

"From what we've been able to piece together, Vause and she hooked up a couple months ago. Then she disappeared again. Vause apparently caught up with her just as she had run into David, and she accompanied David to Panama City to get away from Vause. Vause stalked her, went to Varas, for whom he had done work before, and asked if he had anything for Vause to do. Varas swore he didn't know about the connection between Vause and Mallory, and set him to watch her, to make sure she 'delivered the goods'.

"We think Vause broke into her hotel room and found the information about Allison, then caught up with her at Ralph's house, while she was waiting for Ralph in order to set up a scene and frame him for adultery. Vause went in and killed her, then slipped out the bathroom window. We found his bloody clothes and the knife in the duffle bag he left in the dumpster down at the beach.

"Varas was waiting for Lauren; Ralph didn't show and she didn't reappear. So he went in, found her dead, put on some of Ralph's clothes to reposition the body, planted the cufflink and the shoeprints. He admitted planting the clothes and shoes at Mallory's hotel room, but claims the place was already ransacked when he got there."

"Damn," Ralph swore angrily under his breath.

"Varas had hired her to discredit Ralph, but was angry to find out she had filed a paternity action against Jon, too. Part of Lauren's job was also to schmooze Esme into going along with a scheme aimed at using her influence and parting her from a huge chunk of her money in the process."

Petrino smiled. "The best news is that Jon, Ralph and David are cleared of any wrongdoing. So that cloud of suspicion has lifted."

Jon slapped Ralph on the back happily. "That is wonderful," he laughed with relief.

In the meantime Amanda had quietly disentangled herself from Jon, drifted away from the group, and sat down in the corner, suddenly light-headed. Kelly, who had come out from sitting with David, saw her and went to sit beside her.

"Are you OK?" she asked Amanda. "You're awfully pale."

"Yes, just drained," Amanda smiled wanly. "How did David take the news?"

"He was happy, ecstatic," Kelly glowed. "He asked how Mom took the news, and I told him about dinner last night. I was really afraid for him, because he started laughing and couldn't catch his breath. So I didn't point out Gloria's jeans or tell him our suspicions about Mom and Dad getting it on."

Amanda couldn't keep her attention on Kelly's words. The room seemed to be whirling, and she closed her eyes to shut it out.

Kelly saw Amanda slump forward, and caught her. "Joey!" she screamed as she cradled Amanda in her arms.

Joey sprinted over. "I got her," he told Kelly, as he took Amanda in his arms.

Jon was there immediately, his face gray. "Amanda, Amanda, can you hear me?" he called worriedly.

"Clear a path," Joey ordered, as he picked up Amanda and carried her inert form, striding through the double doors held open by Jon and straight down to the emergency room.

"Where's a vacant bed?" he asked authoritatively. A nurse scurried from behind the desk and pointed ahead of her. Jon followed on his heels as Joey laid her gently down on the bed.

He did a quick examination. "Pulse is slow." He held up his hand. "Your stethoscope, please."

The nurse handed it over. He adjusted it and listened. "Lungs are clear."

He lifted her eyelids. She stirred and moaned.

"Amanda?" he prodded her. "Can you talk? Tell me—how do you feel?"

She opened her eyes and looked at him, her eyes unfocused. "I'm just so tired," she whispered. "I'll be OK in a minute," she protested weakly.

"Call Dr. Caputo if he's on duty," Joey ordered the nurse. "And get a tech here to draw blood for a full CBC and diagnostic. I want to check for pregnancy as well."

Amanda's eyes had closed again. "I've already told you I'm not pregnant," she replied, her hand over her eyes, her voice sounding far away. Joey examined her. She closed her eyes.

Some time later she came to herself. Jon was sitting beside the bed, and heard her stir. He stood over her, grasping her hand. "Amanda?" he called softly.

"Where am I?" She tried to sit up.

Jon gently pushed her back. "Lie down. It's OK. You're in the ER."

Joey strode into the cubicle. "She's not pregnant," he announced, looking down at the patient and frowning. "But she has an inner ear infection, and she's very anemic. Iron deficiency. And apparently her blood sugar bottomed out." He smiled at Amanda. "You've been living off straight adrenalin for the last few weeks, I take it."

Amanda mumbled, "I need a divorce."

Joey, alarmed, blurted, "Why?"

"Because since I've met Jon I've seen the inside of four hospitals," she tried to smile.

Jon touched her cheek. "But she doesn't have to stay, does she?" he asked anxiously.

"No," Joey grinned. "We'll get you set up with some antibiotics and iron supplement, and you can be released. You need to see Dr. Howells right away so that he can rule out other causes for the anemia. I don't see anything right now. But you need to go home and rest. No more murder investigation, no more rescuing people, no more worrying about the rest of us."

He turned away. "I'll let the others know you're going to be OK."

Jon stared at her. "You don't mean it, do you? You don't really want a divorce?"

Amanda squeezed his hand. "You're going to have to work harder than that to get rid of me," she whispered. She gazed at him and added anxiously, "You're not disappointed that I'm not pregnant, are you?"

Jon bent down and kissed her. "I admit that the mental image of you carrying my child was a powerful aphrodisiac," he teased her.

"So you have a thing for pregnant women?" she shot back.

"Only one potential candidate," he retorted gently. He sat down beside her. "Amanda, I was honest with you that I don't think it possible that I had a child with Lauren. But if the DNA results should show that I'm Allison's father, are you going to be OK with that?" His eyes were penetrating, pleading.

"Yes, Jon, I will be OK with that," Amanda said softly.

"I hate the thought that I might have unknowingly conceived a child when I didn't love her mother, and I have really nothing good to say about Lauren to her daughter," Jon murmured.

"We'll cross that bridge when the time comes." Amanda's eyes met his.

Jon squeezed her hand. "Love, Esme told me that Varas had manufactured certain photos which he showed you." He reached over and touched her cheek. "I promise that any of me with Lauren are not true. I have had no dealings with her since that weekend long ago."

She nodded, her eyes solemn. "I knew the ones of Charlie and me were not—not real," she stammered, blushing. "And I didn't think the others were. But I knew the photos of David dancing with Lauren were authentic—that was the night of the party. Then I—I allowed myself to doubt."

"Don't, dearest," Jon whispered, kissing her hand. "That's behind us. We have got to trust each other, Mandy. Now we know just how fragile that trust can be. As long as we are open and honest with each other, I think we can prevent this happening again."

The Connors' Crisis

She nodded as Dr. Caputo walked into the cubicle. He smiled at the couple. "Your family seems to get into a lot of trouble," he quipped. "Of course, I guess it's good for the hospital business." He handed Jon some prescriptions. "Here's what she needs. The nurse is going to give her a shot. Think of it as a magical elixir pep shot. Follow up with your physician within forty-eight hours," he added sternly.

He turned to Jon. "Take her home, make sure she eats well, and make her rest a day or so. No passing 'Go', no collecting $200."

"I want to see David," Amanda protested.

The nurse appeared with a shot, and an orderly with a wheelchair. "I'm not going in to see David in a wheelchair," Amanda's eyes flashed. "Let's not add any stress to him."

"You will use the wheelchair," the doctor ordered. "You can get up and walk into his room to speak to him, as long as you sit in a chair while in there. You will then get back into the wheelchair and stay there until you leave this hospital. Doctor's orders."

So Amanda was able to visit with David, and then was wheeled out to the lobby, where the group was waiting.

"I am fine," she announced before anyone could ask her.

"The doctor has ordered her to rest," Jon added.

"So I guess going out to dinner with all of us is out of the question?" Ralph peered at her concernedly.

Amanda said slyly, "I'm supposed to eat."

They all laughed.

CHAPTER 37

MONDAY

"Amanda?"

"Yes, Ken. How are you?" Amanda could hear the anxiety in his voice.

"I'm fine. Is everything OK there? Father Anselm and I were worried, and we didn't know what to tell the congregation yesterday when they asked if you were OK. Then I couldn't get you on your cell phone."

"I'm so sorry for the short notice. My brother-in-law is—is in the hospital seriously—ill. My phone has been dead, so I was dependent upon Ralph to get word to you that I would be out. I just managed to pick up a charger for it yesterday. Did everything go OK? Did you have enough notice?"

"Yes, yes, everything is fine. Is he going to be all right?" Ken asked concernedly.

"We think so. Ken, what's wrong? I can hear it in your voice," Amanda asked anxiously.

"Well, I got a call from Fred Swann today," he said uncertainly. "I told him you were out, but he said he was calling for me."

"And?" Amanda smiled.

"He wanted to know my ideas on the plans Stephen Audsley sent," Ken blurted nervously.

"And did you tell him?" Amanda prodded.

"I was afraid to say too much," he admitted. "I mean, it's not like I am—an expert or important in the scheme of this new organ," he mumbled.

"Of course your input is important. That's why I asked Fred to call you."

"You did?" Ken was stunned.

"Ken, why do you think no advertisement for applications has been sent out for the new organist/choirmaster position?" Amanda asked gently.

398

"Because—because you've had so much else going on," he answered miserably.

"No, Ken." Amanda was firm. "You are my right hand. I could not have made it in the last year without your help. You've played more than I have, and you have done a stellar job. I'm very proud of you."

"I want to, I mean—I'm interested in possibly remaining a part of St. Catherine's," Ken stammered. "That is, if—" his voice trailed away.

"I'm glad to hear that," Amanda laughed. "Because that's my intent."

"What—what do you mean?" Ken was breathless.

"I want you to be that person," Amanda smiled. "However, Marjy was pretty adamant that if someone took the permanent position, that person needed the necessary degree plus the qualifications. So I'm between a rock and a hard place. I think you're plenty qualified now, but per the terms of the trust, you gotta get that degree. If Marjorie were alive, she'd agree, but she's not here, and I'm bound by the document."

"I intend to," he spoke up. He paused. "You mean you would wait for me to finish my degree?"

"Why do you think I'm dragging my heels?" Amanda cajoled him. "But I told you not to rush, and to enjoy your time at college and make an informed decision whether you want to come back to Mainville. I know that hasn't been the case lately, with you covering so much for me this summer. But the fall term is coming up."

"I could transfer closer to home," he suggested.

"I want you to have the best education money can buy," Amanda told him. "You worked hard for that scholarship. However, I've thought of that option and a few others, like frequent flyer miles, or maybe just buying a plane and having you take flying lessons. I even thought about an organ scholar position to help you out."

"I've always wanted to fly a plane," he breathed.

"We would have to sell your parents on that idea," Amanda chuckled. "I tell you what: you and I need to sit down before you go back for fall term and discuss the options, pick the best ones and present them to your folks. In the meantime, you need to write down your thoughts about the proposed organ so that Steve, Fred and I can look at them."

"You mean it?" he asked incredulously.

"Hell, yes, I mean it," Amanda giggled. "But don't get crazy on me, OK? I want to nail down the requirements so that we can submit it for bid immediately, start getting down to hammer and nails."

"I'll do it," Ken promised happily.

"And Ken?" Amanda added. "Thank you. I don't say it enough."

"But the checks do," he giggled.

"You earn them," she retorted amicably.

She hung up. She called Father Anselm to inform him what was happening, and to find out Esme Townsend's status.

Jon walked in as she hung up. "Is everything OK?" he asked her, sitting on the bed beside her.

"Yes, just a bit of confusion at church. We were apparently missed yesterday."

She paused. "I talked to Toby this morning. Salvatore Varas died this morning. Esme is still in guarded condition. Toby hasn't told her about Varas yet."

Jon nodded solemnly.

"Toby said she had been diagnosed with cancer, and kept it from him. The doctors have not held out any long-term hope. He's angry at her for what she's done, for what she allowed Varas to do, and for not telling him she was dying." Amanda's eyes shone with unshed tears. "I told him she's the only mother he has, and he must let it go and love her as long as he has her."

Jon cradled her head against his shoulder. "Will charges be filed against her?"

"Charlie said the prosecutor is holding off until all the evidence comes in. Clarence said if Ralph wanted, he would go forward. But I don't think Ralph has the stomach to subject Toby to any more right now. And frankly I'm not sure what would stick, how much was Varas' doing on her behalf and how much was him acting alone."

She drew back and took his hand. "I've got to accompany Ralph to the airport tomorrow to meet Claire. He is really nervous."

"The doctor said for you to rest," Jon was stern.

"I promised, Jon," she squeezed his hand. "I don't know but what Claire may take all this badly. Ralph is going to need the support."

"Would you like me to go with you?" Jon asked her. "I really want you to take it easy."

"That might be nice," Amanda smiled warmly. "There's safety in numbers. Then I have to get back to work. Sheila says the clients are restless, even though Ralph did go in today and dealt with matters."

Jon kissed her fingers. "As long as you promise not to overexert," he murmured. "By the way, my mother has decided that she wants to champion Ralph's cause. I think he feels better about it all after talking to Mom. Mom has called the president of the local bar association to enlist his support in helping her. But right now Ralph's main concern is Claire. What about their house?"

"It was released by law enforcement, but it's a mess," Amanda frowned. "I sent a cleaning crew over there. New carpet will have to be laid. I have a feeling Claire is not going to want to live there anymore. Even Ralph says it no longer feels like his home, and the vision of Lauren's body in his bathtub keeps flashing back in his head.

"I've offered Ralph the cottage until they decide what to do next. I made arrangements, if Claire agrees, for some of their stuff to be moved over so that it will be comfortable short-term."

"You're a good friend." Jon kissed her on the forehead. He took her hand. "You didn't eat much tonight."

"I ate all my dead cow," she protested softly.

"Only because I cut it and fed it to you bite by bite." He put an arm around her, pulling her closer.

"I like it that way," she smiled slyly. "Did you get to talk to Joey alone about David's prognosis?"

"Yes." Jon stroked her hair. "The major danger right now is infection. He thinks David will be moved to the main nursing floor tomorrow." Jon cupped her chin in his hand. "You know David is really anxious about this DNA business. He wants Allison to be his child."

"She has his eyes," Amanda concurred, her eyes meeting his. "She's a beautiful child. The Cantons have raised her well. The lab promised us something by the end of the week at the latest."

"I never thought I'd see David like that," Jon smiled. "He's always been such a playboy. All this business with Lauren has been a wake-up call for him."

"It was a test by fire for us as well," she smiled pensively. "What is your family's plan for when David is released?"

"Mom is staying here to care for him until he's back on his feet. Kelly and Dad are going to have to fly back tomorrow if David is OK. Joey is torn: he wants to be with Kelly, but he has promised to help out Silas until he can get a position in Colorado and Silas can find a replacement, and he wants to be available for David. And Dad wants to be by Mom's side now." Jon grinned. He reached over and nibbled her ear. "So there will be some heavy jet-setting done by the Connor family."

"And you?" Amanda placed her hand against his chest.

"What about me?" he questioned, pulling back and looking at her.

"Are you considering going back to the Bureau?" she asked timidly.

"I have several job offers right now. Charlie even offered me a job at the sheriff's department, or to put in a good word for me to be appointed Chief of Police. But I'm actually waiting for a sweeter deal," he whispered as he bent down and kissed her.

She tangled her fingers in the hair on the nape of his neck as she responded. "Such as?" she mumbled, the other hand unbuttoning his shirt.

"A good friend of mine has offered me a position in his law firm. Trouble is that he has an interview this week for the county judge nomination," Jon murmured as he drew her beside him on the bed and unbuttoned her blouse in turn. "If he happens to make judge, he says his law partner is going to need some help, or else be in a world of hurt."

"Who says?" Her hand traveled down to his fly as his lips moved down her throat.

"My friend says he is the brains and brawn of that operation, and someone has got to keep the partner in hand, or she will go belly up within a month," Jon replied before claiming her mouth again.

"Ah, the partner is a woman?" Amanda murmured when he released her mouth, as she slid her leg up his. "That explains his success. A woman can run circles around any man. She is in no trouble. She will probably have more business than she can handle, though. She might need to hire an associate or two."

"You think?" Jon shrugged out of his shirt, then unfastened the catch on her bra and slid her blouse off her shoulder. "I might make a good minion."

"You have potential. I think I happen to know this partner, and could put in a good word with her. Now she might consider another partner, but he'd have to be awfully good." Amanda's hands skimmed along his back and his hips molded to hers.

"At what?" his mouth found her breast, and she arched against him. "I'm really interested in seeing the list of qualifications sought."

"I'll bet she is working on those criteria as we speak," Amanda whispered as she pressed closer to him, sighing as Jon groaned against her skin.

OTHER BOOKS BY
G. K. SUTTON:

The Kreiser Affair

The Amanda Childs series:

The Witherspoon Legacy

The Childs Conundrum

Made in the USA
Lexington, KY
26 May 2010